SINFUL VOWS

Book 3 Sinful C.O.R.E.

KRISTINE MASON

ISBN-13: 978-0-9977831-8-6

ISBN-10: 0-9977831-8-4

Edited by Tessa Shapcott

Cover design by Elle J Rossi of EJR Digital Arts

Connect with Kristine:

Twitter

Facebook

Sign up for Kristine's newsletter

www.kristinemason.net

Also by Kristine Mason

Dedication

Since this story is set in suburbia, a place I know very well, I think it's fitting that I dedicate this book to my neighbors—from the cul-de-sac I'd grown up on, to the people I live near now. That being said, if any of my neighbors, from my past or present, are reading this, none of you have been depicted in this book. Well, maybe Joe. I'm still bitter that you called the police on us twice for using our generator when we were without power for days.

Acknowledgments

I love my review team and want to thank them for their continued support. You ladies are awesome! Thank you, Danielle Murray, who entered my 'get your name in a book' contest, for inspiring Blair. She added a bit of flavor to my book. As always, Jamie Denton, you're a fantastic critique partner and friend. Judie Bouldry, you are fabulous. I'm starting to wonder what I did without you! I'd also like to thank my editor, Tessa Shapcott, my proofreader, Sherry Fundin, and my talented cover artist, Elle J Rossi of EJR Digital Arts. Elle, I love this cover!

Chapter One

Unexpressed emotions will never die.
They are buried alive and will come forth later in uglier ways.
—Sigmund Freud

Ten years ago…

Foxy's Bar, North Royalhurst, Ohio
Thursday, July 20th, 11:43 p.m. Daylight Saving Time

THICK, HUMID AIR clung to his lungs and skin, along with the acrid odor of tar. He released the bar's glass door and stepped onto the recently paved parking lot. As he walked to his truck, he glanced to the street, lit up by the cracked neon sign shaped like a drunken fox, and checked the traffic. Not seeing any cars on the road, he relaxed and fished his keys from his pocket. He'd had seven beers and a shot of Fireball. Or had it been nine beers and two shots? Didn't matter. Four was his usual limit and he rarely drank shots, but with the wife and kids gone for the weekend, he hadn't wanted to go back to the quiet house. He preferred his wife's endless chatter, their toddler son's babbling, or the cries of their three-month-old over the silence. The quiet ate at him. Took him deep into his head. Revealed his demons.

"Hey, wait up," a man shouted as loud music momentarily filled the night.

He turned just as his drinking buddy, Jim, exited the bar. The man staggered, righted himself, then continued toward him. He'd met Jim about six months ago, and would have a few beers with him if they ran into each other at Foxy's. Which was a couple times a week. He wouldn't exactly say he knew the man well—they usually bullshitted about their jobs, sports or talked with the other regulars—but Jim was an okay guy for a bar friend.

"No more booze for me," he said, grinning and half stumbling against his truck. "I reached my limit two hours ago."

Jim chuckled and used the back of his hand to wipe his mouth. "I hear ya, man. My wife is gonna be so pissed at me." Light from the lamppost standing in front of the truck touched along his glassy eyes and crooked smile. "Nothin' new there, right?"

From what he gathered, Jim's wife—he couldn't remember her name, but it was something with a Y at the end...Britney, Tiffany—was the breadwinner. If he recalled correctly, Jim had moved to the Cleveland area because of his wife's job. All he did remember about her was Jim bitching that she blew him shit for not living up to his potential, not pulling his weight around the house, and not bringing in enough cash.

Not knowing what to say, and eager to head home and crawl into bed, he shrugged. "We misbehaved, didn't we?" He smothered a yawn, then used the key fob to unlock the truck. "Honestly, my wife would probably blow me shit, too, if she saw the shape I'm in tonight."

Jim also leaned against the truck. "You okay to drive?"

"I'm five miles from my neighborhood. I should be good. You?"

"No." He shook his head. "Not willing to risk it. You mind givin' me a ride? You're over in that new development, Pine-something, right?"

Damn it. He did not want to detour. He wanted sleep. "Yeah, it's Whispering Pines."

"Well, I'm right on your way. I'm gonna pay hell for leaving the car here, but it beats getting a DUI. Tiffany threatens to make me sleep in the shed for lesser things," Jim said with another chuckle.

Since he liked Jim, and didn't want his wife giving him hell, and because the guy's house was on the way, he agreed. Once they were in his truck, and buckled up, he exited Foxy's parking lot. They drove in silence for a few minutes, then Jim let out a sigh when they stopped at a red light.

"I'm drunk," Jim began. "Drunk as a skunk."

He grinned. "Tonight was fun. My head probably won't say as much in the morning."

"No lie there." Jim glanced at him. "I know you."

Though buzzed, he picked up on...something. He couldn't put his finger on why, but unease weaved its way through him. "What's that mean?"

"It means I *know* you. I know who you are." Jim sighed and turned in his seat to face him. "I remember you."

Apparently, his drinking buddy was more wasted than he'd thought. "Of course you know me." He chuckled. "We've been drinking together off and on for six months."

"No. I mean I *know* you." Jim repeated. "I...I've been trying to work up the courage to say something, but until tonight, I didn't have it." With a shrug, he grinned. "I guess those shots of Fireball did it for me."

The light turned green, and he began driving again. "I think I'll be swearing off shots for a while."

"Same. But for me...look, when I said I know you, I'm talking about way back. Nine years ago. I wasn't sure it was you at first. After a few months, I was positive."

Growing irritated, he glanced at Jim. "Positive about what? We didn't meet until six months ago."

"Positive that you were at Camp Hope. You know, the place we went for *conversion* therapy."

He gripped the steering wheel. Fought the rage. Fought the humiliation. *Camp Hope.* His personal Hell. The place that invaded his dreams to create nightmares. "I don't know what you're talking about."

"It's okay," Jim said, softening his voice. "My wife has no idea, either. I've been pretending to be straight since I was seventeen just to get my parents to leave me the fuck alone."

In an effort to control his anger, to keep his cool, to keep from hitting Jim, he wiped a hand along his worn jeans. "I don't know what you're talking about," he repeated, even though he did. He'd suffered at Camp Hope for an entire summer. Shortly after his sixteenth birthday, his mom had found a box loaded with gay porn—magazines and DVDs—and a number of dildos in the attic. She and his minister father had immediately confronted him, accused him of carrying the Devil inside and tried to beat it out of him. Several months later, when he'd still refused to admit the magazines and devices were his, they had swept him off to Camp Hope after school had ended for the year. The problem was, that box hadn't belonged to him.

It had belonged to his father.

"C'mon," Jim said with exasperation, then hiccupped. "Your daddy was the preacher who used to come by a few times a week to help us pray the gay away." He laughed, but it was false laughter. There was nothing funny about what had gone on at Camp Hope. "Yeah, you kept to yourself, didn't hang out with the rest of us, but I remember you and your daddy."

His mind blurred with images of the boys at the camp, until one stood out from the rest. Jim. "Your memory is warped by booze. Wasn't me," he said, gripping the steering wheel with both hands, and praying for sobriety. Fuck. This couldn't be happening. What were the odds? He'd been born and raised in a small Georgia town, and was now living in North Royalhurst, a nice suburb just outside of Cleveland. Yeah, he'd picked up on Jim's southern accent—one he himself had been sure to lose years ago—but again, what were the odds? And what if Jim told? His wife hadn't a clue what he'd gone through, and never—ever—needed to know. That year had been the darkest time of his life. He didn't want to relive it, didn't want his wife thinking he was secretly gay. He couldn't care less if a man wanted another man, but *he* wasn't *that* kind of man.

"I've kept in touch with a couple guys from camp. I don't

know if you remember Steve, Todd and Greg, but they're all openly gay. Steve's living in Columbus," Jim said, his tone sad, forlorn.

Panic moved through his chest like heartburn. He still talked to those guys? Had Jim told them about him? Jim knew his last name, the name of his business, wife and kids. He also knew where he lived and had his phone number. What if he passed that information to one of their campmates? What if they also tried to contact him?

His stomach soured as he pictured the shock and betrayal on his wife's face. If Jim claimed he'd been to a conversion camp, chances were, she wouldn't believe the man. But if two or more made the same claims… The panic worked through his chest to lodge in his throat. His mouth dry, he had a difficult time gathering spit to swallow.

Jim released a deep breath. "It's hard to live a lie. When we were at the bar, and Chuck and Troy were talking about the size of the bartender's breasts, I was more interested in the butt on the guy playing pool." He shook his head. "How do you do it? How do you keep it secret?"

He finally swallowed, only to have acid from his churning stomach rise up and burn the back of his throat. "For the millionth time, I don't know what you're talking about."

"Do you have an online *friend*?" Jim continued as if he hadn't spoken. "Or do you go to a gay bar in another city?"

"Look, man," he began, keeping his voice neutral and desperately trying to hold his shit together, "I am not gay. You don't know me, and I was never at a camp with you. You're drunk and need to let it go. And if I hear you telling anyone that I'm gay, I'll make your life hell. Understand?"

"Whatever," Jim mumbled, then laughed and shook his head.

How could he laugh about any of this? There was nothing funny about the situation, and nothing amusing about what had been done to them. It sickened him. Enraged him that he was once again being accused of something he wasn't.

"Stay in denial. Me? I'm sick of it. I'm sick of my wife. I hate pretending I want to climb on top of her. I hate that I have to pretend I'm having sex with a man instead of a woman just to get it up." Jim ran a shaky hand along his forehead. "I might be drunk, but I think I'm also drunk enough to work up the courage and tell her the truth."

His heart raced with worry as he stopped at another traffic light. If Jim told his wife, and he came out of the closet, would he try to get him to do the same? What if Jim had pictures from camp? He'd kept in touch with three of their campmates, did that mean he had a camp roster? What if Jim tied one on at the bar and started blabbing to the regulars?

"If you tell your wife, she might kick you out of the house," he said, hoping to reason with the drunk bastard. "She's the one with the money, right?"

"Don't care. I was thinking about moving to Columbus. I've got a secret stash squirrelled away. It's only three grand, but that's enough to get me started, and Steve said he could help me find a job."

Shit. He has a plan. "I think you're making a mistake." The light turned green and he began driving. "Wait until you're sober before you decide to do anything."

Jim slapped the dashboard. "The first mistake I made was claiming I was straight," he said, his voice rising. "The second was marrying Tiffany."

He stiffened and quickly looked to the dash. "Don't take it out on the truck," he warned the other man as his patience quickly faded. He needed to hold onto it, though. Jim was losing it. His tone had been almost manic. He needed to talk Jim into keeping his cool and his mouth shut. Loose lips didn't just sink ships, they sank a man's marriage and career.

When Jim hit the dash again, he fought to control his hands. He wanted them around the man's throat. He wanted the man silent.

"I'm twenty-six and miserable." Jim slammed his fist into his palm. "Damn it, I don't want to spend the rest of my life this way," he shouted. "I want to be accepted for who I am."

He looked to Jim, to where the glow from the dash touched along the tears streaming down his cheeks, and wondered what the hell to do. He had two small kids. His landscaping business had finally taken off and was doing well. He and his wife had also recently moved into a brand-new house. Life was good. And the man next to him could destroy it.

"If you want to live a lie, that's your business." Spittle flew from Jim's mouth as he continued his drunken tirade. "But I won't do it anymore. I won't! I won't!"

As Jim kept shouting the same two words over and over, his head buzzed and his ears rang. Memories surfaced…his hands bound sometimes with ice, other times with copper heating coils, the needles jabbed into his fingers, shock therapy…the cleansing in the lake, the whistle of his father's belt just before it connected with his bare ass. The dark closet. His preacher daddy's version of a hot box…

Jim's shouts penetrated the memories, broke through the muffled haze in his head and unleashed the rage that had been festering inside him for nine long years. He swung his fist sideways and connected against the center of Jim's throat. The man wheezed and clutched his neck. After checking the rearview and seeing no other cars, he slowed the truck, reached over and smashed Jim's forehead along the dashboard. Gripped the back of Jim's thick hair, and did it again and again until the man no longer made a sound.

Sweat trickled down his cheek. Breathing hard, his heart pounding, he swiped it away, then brought the vehicle to the proper speed limit. "Why couldn't you keep your mouth shut?" When he punched Jim in the arm, the man slumped against the door. The interior of the truck was too dark to tell if Jim's chest rose and fell, but his eyes were closed, his mouth hung open and he no longer wheezed. "Oh, no," he muttered as dread gripped him by the balls. "No! No!"

He hit the steering wheel with his palm, then ran his hand through his hair. Jim couldn't be dead, could he? He'd only bashed his head against the dash three, maybe four times. Was that enough to kill a man? He'd go to prison. He'd lose everything.

"Fuck!" He shouldn't have gone out tonight. Shouldn't have

had so damned much to drink. His head swam with alcohol and fear. After dragging in a few deep breaths, he refocused, considered his options. "Okay, you've got this." Foxy's only had one security camera and that was aimed at the register. Jim had left the bar several minutes after he had, so no one could say for sure he'd given the man a ride. They could think Jim had decided he was too drunk to drive and walked home.

He shook his head as he drove past Jim's street and toward his own home in Whispering Pines. Though he'd had his share of fights, he'd never initiated them. He didn't have a quick temper, and considered himself a negotiator, not a fighter. And, yet, he had a dead man, who *he* had beaten, slumped next to him. He hadn't wanted to hurt Jim. If the man had never said a word or accepted his lie about the camp, Jim could be stumbling his drunk ass into his house rather than facing...what? What was he supposed to do with Jim's body?

The truck tires drove over a pothole. The equipment in the back clanked and gave him his answer. Taking a risk, he turned into his development and drove to Shady Circle, where eleven homes—his included—surrounded the cul-de-sac. After reaching his house, he backed the truck into the driveway, then exited. As he waited for the garage door to rise, he glanced around at the other houses. With the exception of lampposts or porch sconces, most of the homes were dark. Good. He needed to make this quick.

Once he hitched the trailer carrying the small skid steer loader he and his employees used for digging holes and trenches, he climbed back into the truck and left Whispering Pines. A half mile later, he turned and took the dirt access road the utility companies used. He drove until the road dead-ended, then parked and killed the ignition.

Acres of undeveloped land stretched into the darkness. He couldn't see what was before him, but rode past the property daily and knew the land was covered in trees, bushes and patches of tall grass and wild flowers. With the area a short distance from his home, it was the perfect place to hide a body. He could keep an eye on the property, and would know if the police were searching the area.

After taking a flashlight from the glove box, he got out of the truck, then went to the passenger door. Grabbing Jim under the armpits, he hauled him from the vehicle and dropped him on the ground. He gripped Jim by the ankles and decided to drag him to his final destination first, then go back for the digger. Crickets and katydids chirped, and a few fireflies signaled their existence, while the hot breeze caused the trees to creek and sway. Jim's head thudded against the fallen tree he'd just tripped over, marring the insects' soothing symphony. After he'd walked forty paces, he stopped, let go of Jim, then carefully jogged back to the truck.

Once he dropped the trailer down and was seated on the digger, he touched the key, but hesitated. Even buzzed, he knew this had to be one of his stupider ideas. Though this digger wasn't as loud as the bigger models, someone might hear it running. But he was a half mile away from the nearest development—his—and with the high temperatures, people were keeping their windows closed and running their air conditioners, so he had that going for him. His development was also new and the only people who usually traveled to this area were residents of Whispering Pines. That was another thing he also had going for him.

Yes, he had this, and had no choice but to proceed. Shoveling a small grave would take him two to three hours, but with the skid steer loader, he could have the job done in forty-five minutes or less. In case he needed it, he took a shovel from the truck bed, climbed back on the digger, drew in a deep breath, and turned the key.

The machine fired up without issue, its motor drowning out the crickets and katydids. He drove it forward. The digger's tracks crushed the vegetation, which would leave signs that someone had come through here with heavy equipment. Even if the digger had wheels, it would have left impressions in the dirt. Damn, maybe he should've sucked it up and shoveled. But by the time he'd returned to Jim's body and dug the hole, he'd convinced himself everything would be fine. All would go well.

No one would ever know.

Wiping sweat from his brow, he hopped off the digger, then picked up the flashlight he'd left on the ground, the beam directed at the hole. He eyed the grave which was about four feet in depth and length, and around two to three feet wide. Jim was tall and lanky, but he should fit. He set down the flashlight and, facing the hole, pushed Jim inside. After folding the man's arms and legs until he was in a quasi-fetal position, he reached for the shovel.

As he began tossing dirt onto Jim, he stared at the man's face. Regret made him ache. Jim hadn't deserved to have his life cut short. Not by him or anyone. He would burn in Hell for this. He would—

Jim's eye slid open.

He jerked back and fell on his rear. Panting, heart racing, he reached a trembling hand for the flashlight, then shined it on Jim. The man released a groan.

"No," he whispered. "You're supposed to be dead. I…I swear I thought I killed you."

He was fucked. Why hadn't he checked for a pulse? Because he was drunk and stupid. Christ, he could have dumped Jim somewhere. When the man woke and tried to accuse him of being responsible for the beating, he could have simply denied it. But now…now he'd gone too far. He'd dug a grave, had already put him inside. Except, if Jim had suffered head trauma, maybe he wouldn't remember any of this.

What if he did? What if Jim has the camp roster or photos of me? He could use that as proof against me. The police could check the truck and find his DNA.

All true, yet how could he live with himself if he took another man's life? How could he hold his wife or kiss his babies with blood staining his hands?

"I could pay you. I'll give you money so you can move to Columbus. If I did that, would you leave me alone?"

He'll want more, his inner voice countered. *He'll extort me. Especially if he has proof I was at the camp and beat him. Jim has to die.*

If he were to save himself from humiliation, divorce and prison, Jim did have to die. Still.

He crouched closer to the hole. "Jim, can you hear me?"

"Yes," he rasped. "Why?" A tear cut a path through the dried blood and dirt on the side of his face. "What are you doing to me?"

Guilt ate at him. Jim was only a year older, had his whole life ahead of him. Who was he to decide if he should die today? "I... I'm sorry." The flashlight trembled in his hands as his stomach twisted and cramped with fear and worry. "I didn't want to hit you. But you just wouldn't stop. Why couldn't you let it go?"

Jim licked at the blood along his swollen lips. "Then it's true?"

He nodded. "But I'm not gay. My parents accused me of something I'm not, then you started to and...do you have pictures from the camp? Or a roster?"

"No."

Relieved, he stood, then flashed the light toward where he'd dropped the shovel. Killing a man during a fit of rage was one thing, but what he was about to do was premeditated murder. His throat tightened, clogged with mucus and the threat of tears. He didn't want to kill Jim, but there was no other way out of this mess. "I know you don't believe me." He picked up the shovel. "And I was worried that if you told, and my wife found out, she might not believe me, either. You could've cost me my marriage and ruined my reputation. Do you understand?"

"I wouldn't have told." Jim used his left arm to reach for the edge of the hole. "I won't tell." He clawed at the dirt. "Please believe me. Help me out of here. My legs are stuck and I can't move them." He grunted and tried to adjust his left leg, but he'd done a good job of stuffing the man in the hole, and had made it so his knees and soles of his shoes kept him lodged in place. "Please don't leave me in this hole. Don't bury me," he begged on a panicked sob.

"Don't bury me!" Fear cut him to the core. From inside the grave his father had dug, he looked to the heavy dirt covering his body and immobilizing him, then to his mother. She stood at the edge of the grave, her arms folded across her chest, and disappointment etched on her face. "Mama, help me. Please. I'm not gay. That stuff wasn't mine."

She snorted. "You disgust me," she said, then glanced to his father, who was breathing hard and coated with sweat. "Finish him."

Jim's pleas and cries snapped him back to the present. He focused the light on Jim's face, but didn't see his drinking buddy. Instead, he saw himself: sixteen, terrified, dirt surrounding every part of his body except his eyes, nose and mouth—which had been sealed with tape. He blinked a few times to ward off the image. It disappeared, only to be replaced by his father's face.

His vision blurred with tears. "Do you know what they did to me?" He set the flashlight on the ground, aiming it toward the hole, then used the shovel to scoop the dirt. "My mother couldn't handle the idea of having a homosexual son. She wanted me dead." He dropped the earth onto Jim's legs. "I should hate her for that, but I don't. She was an ignorant bigot. A God-fearing fool who took what the Bible and my preacher daddy said as fact."

"I believe you," Jim said, his voiced laced with terror as he piled on more soil. "I swear I believe you."

He chuckled and continued to shovel the dirt back into the hole. "You know when my father told me that? Just before cancer took him, and right after he admitted to being the one who was gay. Of course, Mama wasn't in the room at the time, so she never learned the truth. But I know. I know that my father beat and tortured me and gave those fucking whack-jobs at the camp the right to abuse me in order to keep his secret hidden."

"I'm sorry," Jim sobbed, except the voice didn't sound like Jim's. It sounded eerily similar to his father's. "Please don't kill me. Please!"

He stopped. More unwanted memories fell on him, surrounded and suffocated him. "I said the same thing to my parents the day my father buried me in our backyard."

Jim's eyes widened as he stared up at him. "Buried you?"

"It started as their version of hot box torture. They covered every part of me with dirt but my face, and taped my mouth. My mom wanted my father to bury me completely so I'd die, but I think his guilt kept him from doing it. Instead, they left me like that for two days. If I had to shit or piss, I had to lie in it. They gave me no food or water, nothing to protect my face from the hot sun. I think what worried me the most was the night. See, I could kind of move my head, and when I did, the dirt moved too and my head would sink a little deeper. Each time I did that, the dirt would get a little closer to my eyes and nose. Not much, but enough that it had me afraid of falling asleep. What if I moved in my sleep and it covered my nose?"

"If you know that kind of torture, then why do the same to me?" Jim pressed his fingers into the soil and once again tried to pull his body up and out of the hole. In his current position, and with the weight of the earth on his legs, he didn't have a chance. "Just let me go. I won't tell a fucking soul. I swear!"

Christ, he *was* torturing the man. While he hadn't planned for any of this to happen, he certainly hadn't intended to prolong the man's death. He looked down at the shovel blade. A quick blow to the head would kill Jim. If not, the dirt would finish the job. That would be the humane thing to do. After all, he liked Jim.

Determined to give the man a quick death, he raised the shovel and held it as if it were a baseball bat. His body trembled with fear and self-loathing. He wasn't a killer, wasn't a psychopathic murderer. He was a husband, father and friend. He was the neighbor anyone could turn to for help. The nice guy.

The guy who'll go to prison if Jim lives.

"Don't do it!" Jim sobbed and stared up at him. "Think about what you're doing. Think about who I am and what we've been through."

"Goddamn it, I know what I'm doing," he snapped. "And I don't want to kill you, but I don't trust you. Sorry, Jim, I can't go to prison."

"Wait!" Jim held up his hand. *"Lord Jesus Christ, give me the strength to fight Satan and expel the foul spirit of homosexuality from my body,"* he said, reciting a prayer his preacher daddy had taught the boys at Camp Hope.

His vision swam as rage rushed through him. He saw his father standing beside his mother, reciting the same prayer while he was held immobile by earth and terror. "Shut up," he demanded.

"Satan has deceived me," Jim continued, but, once again, he heard his father's voice. *"Lord God, help me repent, forgive me for my sins*

13

and wickedness. Cast Satan and homosexuality from me and—" Jim coughed and spat out the dirt he'd just tossed at his mouth.

"You are the sinner." He piled on more soil. "You punished your only son because you weren't man enough to stop living a lie."

"I didn't!" Jim coughed again. "Look at *me.* I'm not your father."

When he did, he saw Preacher Daddy. Mouth taped. Hands and ankles bound. Eyes wide with fear. And as he continued to shovel, he pictured his father suffering, dragging in that last, delightful breath of air before the earth swallowed him.

Ashes to ashes, dust to dust.

When he'd finished moving all the soil he'd dug up with the digger, his head cleared and his vision sharpened. He gulped in deep breaths and used his T-shirt to wipe the sweat from his face. With Jim now silent, the cricket and katydid symphony once again filled the night.

Other than the insects and night critters, no one knew that he'd just killed a man.

He'd killed a man. Murdered him. Buried him alive.

Though smothered by guilt, a strange sense of relief lightened the burden he hadn't realized he'd been carrying with him. He hadn't forgiven his father for what he'd done, nor had he under-stood that the resentment and hatred he still harbored had been wrapped around his throat like a noose. Choking him. Holding him back from being the man he was meant to be. He'd had higher aspirations than being a landscaper, and had wanted to go to college. But to prove to his parents he was straight, he'd had sex with the first decent-looking girl who would spread her legs for him, then got her pregnant. He resented his father for forcing him into marriage and fatherhood too early, for burying his dreams of college and, later, a high-paying career as an attorney. Instead, he was paid to play in the dirt.

While he moved brush, sticks and leaves around and over Jim's grave, he considered his next move. Because he was a nice guy, and because he liked his wife and loved his kids, divorce was not an option. He wasn't even sure why the thought entered his mind. Maybe imagining he'd been burying Preacher Daddy alive, rather than actually seeing Jim, had given him something. Not just the sense of relief he'd experienced once the deed had been done, but hope. For nine years he'd lived with nightmares of the year from Hell. He couldn't count how many times he'd woken sweaty and disoriented, his body shaking and tears streaming down his face. Burying his father with Jim, though, gave him hope that the nightmares would stop.

But what if they didn't? More importantly, what if someone discovered Jim's body?

Three months later…

The Hayloft, Akron, Ohio
Saturday, October 20th, 9:51 p.m. Daylight Saving Time

Nervousness made his stomach jumpy and his armpits damp. Never in his life had he been in a gay bar. Yet, here he was, a straight man looking to be solicited by a gay man. After he'd killed Jim, the nightmares had gotten better and he hadn't had any more until two weeks ago. And those nightmares were worse than any of the others before them. He wasn't just waking up sweaty and scared. According to his wife, who'd had the swollen lip to prove it, he'd become violent in his sleep. She'd claimed he'd screamed in his sleep—something unintelligible—and thrashed about as if trying to free himself. Which had led to him to accidentally hitting her in the mouth.

He'd met with his doctor the next day and was prescribed medication to help him sleep. It hadn't helped. Falling asleep wasn't the problem, his dreams were. Which was why he was here at The Hayloft in Akron—forty minutes from his home.

He needed to bury his father again.

Ignoring his twisting stomach, he walked over to the bar and sat on one of the stools. After ordering a beer, he glanced at his reflection in the mirror and almost did a double take. He wasn't used to seeing himself with a mustache and goatee or wearing glasses—all of which were fake. But he had to admit, the facial hair—which was one hundred percent real hair—and glasses didn't look bad, nor did the way he'd changed up his hairstyle with temporary color and gel. With how good he looked, someone was bound to hit on him tonight. He tried not to crack a smile at the ridiculous thought, and failed.

"Mind letting me in on the joke?" A young guy sat on the stool next to his. "Or is the joke between you and yourself?" he asked with a teasing grin.

He returned the grin. "Me and myself have an inside joke. You wouldn't get it."

"And would you and yourself prefer to be left alone? Or would you like company with me and myself?"

"I don't know. Between me and myself, and you and yourself, it sounds like a crowd."

"So maybe we should just stick with me and you." The young guy offered his hand. "Noah."

"Jim," he said, hoping to somehow honor the dead man. He and Noah bullshitted while they drank their beers, but the moment he discovered Noah had turned twenty-one last month, he tried to find a way to blow off the kid. Noah was too young to die. Except...the kid was gullible and clearly interested in him, making him an easy target. Besides, as of now, only the bartender and Noah had paid any attention to him. Did he want to troll the bar, have people noticing him and able to describe him to the police should they discover Noah's body? No. That wasn't an option.

Noah leaned in close enough that he caught a hint of the kid's aftershave. "I wouldn't mind getting out of here."

Damn, this was too easy. Now that the moment had arrived, though, he worried he wouldn't be able to carry out the plan he'd set in motion last night when he'd dug another hole near Jim's grave. Noah's death wouldn't be accidental. It would be premeditated. If the police arrested him for Jim's death, a good attorney might be able to convince the prosecutor to accept a guilty plea for manslaughter. Whereas Noah's murder could possibly have him sentenced to death. "What do you mean?" he asked, reconsidering his plan. What was he thinking? Murder? Manslaughter versus a death sentence? He had a family who depended on him. Who needed him. If he went to prison, his wife would probably divorce him, and he'd never know his sons.

"You know what I mean." Noah grinned. "Do you have your own place? I still live at home, otherwise I'd invite you over."

"I do, but I'm not into…what I think you're suggesting."

"Sex?" Noah's grin broadened into a big smile. "Why not? I happen to be very good at it."

This was a huge mistake, and he couldn't go through with it. He was not a murderer. If he wanted to stop the nightmares, he should go to a psychiatrist. The doctor would have to keep what was said between them. He wouldn't admit to killing Jim, but talking about the camp and what had happened to him might help him with his demons.

"I'm sure you are." He paid cash for his beer, then slid off the stool. "But I'm not into guys," he said, then left the bar.

Once in the parking lot, he inhaled the crisp October air. His stomach had been a mess since last week, when he'd devised a way to find another 'Jim'. Now that he'd made up his mind not to go through with it, he relaxed and let the tension leave his body.

As he approached his truck, Noah yelled Jim's name and jogged over. Shit. The kid needed to take no for an answer. If he only knew how close he'd come to being killed tonight. "Hey, man," he began when Noah caught up with him, "I told you I'm not into guys."

"Then what were you doing in a gay bar?"

He opened the truck's door. "I'm new to the area and didn't know."

Noah blocked him from entering the vehicle. "I don't believe you. You had to know I was into you. And I swear, you were into me." Noah touched his chest, sending a wave of rage through him. Why was it no one believed him? "So why don't we get into each other."

He knocked the kid's hand away. "I'm not gay."

"Wait a sec." Noah's eyes widened. "Holy shit. You are gay, but you've never been with a man, right?"

"Wrong. I'm straight. That's why I haven't been with a man."

Noah chuckled. "Pretending you like pussy makes you a pussy."

He shoved Noah out of his way. "Leave me the fuck alone," he said, turning his back on the kid. As he climbed into the truck, the other man reached between his thighs and grabbed his dick through his jeans.

"Are you sure you want to be alone?" Noah whispered. "Admit you want it. Admit you're gay."

Like a swarm of flies, Noah's whispered words buzzed through his head. They mingled with Jim's, his father and mother's, with the 'doctors' from the camp.

Tell us the truth.

Admit the porn and dildos are yours.

I know you...admit you were at the camp.

Admit you're gay...

The buzzing intensified to the point it drowned out all other sounds. His vision clouded as rage engulfed him and took over his body. "I'm not," he said, his voice muffled, tinny. "I'm not. I'm not. I'm not!"

Breath labored, he leaned against the truck. While his heart rate slowed, the buzzing waned and his vision cleared. Confused, he turned to see where Noah had gone, then decided it didn't matter. The kid had finally gotten the picture. When he reached for the partially opened driver's side door, he froze.

Noah's upper body was draped over the driver's seat, while his knees were on the concrete and keeping him from falling from the truck. "Noah?" Confused as to how the man had ended up this way, he reached down and lifted his head. The dim truck light revealed his closed eyes and the trickle of blood escaping his parted lips. After checking for a pulse and finding one, he inspected the lines of blood crisscrossing the back of Noah's white shirt, which had been torn along some of those lines. He lifted the hem up and over Noah's back, then quickly covered his mouth. Bruises and swollen tissue surrounded the vertical and horizontal cuts. Panicking, scared, he looked to the door near the handle and discovered bits of the white shirt had snagged along the metal.

"Oh my God," he muttered, and hung onto the door before his knees gave way. What had he done? And why couldn't he remember doing it? The last thing he did remember was Noah insisting he admit he was gay. Yes, it had angered him that the kid wouldn't take no for an answer, but violence wasn't part of his nature.

You throat-punched Jim, then bashed his head against the dashboard.

That had been different. He'd known exactly what he was doing, and had remembered every moment of the beating. A chill, that had nothing to do with the cool, night air, coated his skin with goose bumps. Had he experienced some sort of rage-induced blackout? The last time it had happened was the night he'd killed Jim. He could barely remember covering the man's face with soil. Even now, his father was the only person he could picture lying in that grave.

The grave.

"Damn it. Why wouldn't you leave me alone?" His already large frame and years of manual labor made it easy for him to lift Noah, who was probably about five foot nine and a buck-forty soaking wet, then move him to the passenger side of the truck. "You should've walked away when you had the chance," he said, turning the key. "Now..." He sighed as he brought to mind the hole waiting for Noah. "Now you have to die." Noah could ID him to the police. In turn, the police could try to link him to Jim's disappearance.

Although worried about getting caught, he *had* set out to find someone who could help relieve him of his nightmares and demons. And he had that someone right beside him. The grave was already dug and waiting to be filled.

As guilt followed him back to North Royalhurst, he hoped that ending Noah's life would end the nightmares. Even if it didn't, he would not kill again. He knew right from wrong. Knew what was immoral, sinful. And he vowed never to take another life.

Unless...

Chapter Two

Present day...

Cuyahoga County Sheriff's Department, Cleveland, Ohio
Friday, 2:08 p.m. Daylight Saving Time

"ARE YOU READY to walk down the aisle with a stranger?"

"It's not funny." Irritated, Whitney Russell walked ahead of fellow Cuyahoga County Sheriff's Department detective, Andrew Harris, and opened the door to the narcotics unit. "I am *not* comfortable living with a man I don't know." The only males she'd ever lived with had been her dad and three older brothers, and she'd always sworn she wouldn't live with another man unless she was either engaged or married to him. Which had been part of her 'life' plan: college, career, house, marriage, then babies. Besides, her overprotective and extremely Catholic parents would have a coronary if she—God forbid—shacked up with a guy.

"Might as well get used to it now," Andy said as he followed behind her and took a seat at his desk. "Since you have no luck with men, an arranged marriage is the only way you'll get hitched."

She flipped him the bird. "What number wife are you on

now? Third? Fourth?" Though Andy was in his early fifties, he treated her as if she were his kid sister. Which she never minded. Her older brothers had teased her—and still did—mercilessly. Since they'd all moved out of the area, she had chosen Andy as her surrogate brother and loved to banter with him. Just not about marriage or dating. Her brothers were married with kids, so were most of her friends. Yes, she had a great career and was proud to be the first female detective in the department's narcotics unit, but she wanted to finish checking off the items from her 'life' plan while she was still in her thirties. As of last pay period, she was only a few thousand dollars shy of having a down payment toward a home. Now she just needed the husband and children. Unfortunately, having high standards and a demanding career had made it difficult to find a man to fulfill that dream.

Andy pushed a hand through his brown hair, which was graying at the temples, and looked to the ceiling as if it held the answer. "Fifth." He held up a finger. "But this one is gonna last a lot longer than any of those guys you meet on the computer. Now that I think about it, online dating isn't that much different than an arranged marriage."

The man was old school and didn't understand how hard it was to not only meet decent men, but to find the time to do it. "Uh, yeah, I'd say there's a huge difference." She sat at the desk across from his.

"Okay, so you don't have Mom and Dad bargaining to marry you off, but don't you pretty much know a lot about the online guy before you meet? Where's the fun in getting to know someone if you already have a list of their likes and dislikes?"

Since she loved lists and checking them off, online dating was perfect for her. "That's what I like about using those services. I can find a match, or weed out the men who don't fit the profile of my ideal partner."

"If you could have a Hollywood husband, who would it be?"

"Well, that was random. Can we please change the subject?" She opened her computer browser, then the website of the real estate company the sheriff's department had gone through to rent the house for the undercover job. "I'd like to discuss how we're going to split up our team and follow our suspects."

"We will. But for now, humor me. I have a point."

Andy was a relentless man. When he wanted to know something, he never stopped questioning or searching for answers, which made him a great cop. Knowing him and that he wouldn't let up until she told him, and since she'd already had this silly Q & A with her teenaged nieces, she didn't have to think about her reply. "Hugh Jackman, but only when he's Wolverine," she said, glancing at him.

He raised a brow. "Claws in or out?"

She grinned as she remembered her nieces asking her the same question, their noses wrinkling in disgust. Not because of the claws, but because Whitney was interested in a man who was in his late forties—the same age as the girls' dad. "Depends on what we're doing."

"Pervert." He chuckled. "Then let's say Wolverine shows up on your dating service, but he doesn't meet your ideal profile. What do you do?"

He had her there, because she wouldn't turn down a date with Wolverine. While facial hair wasn't her thing and she preferred men to have a clean-cut look, Wolverine was a big, muscular, badass animal. Which made him incredibly sexy for a late-night fantasy. "Looks aren't everything, and Wolverine isn't real. Frankly, I don't need to date your typical hot guy." She made quotation marks with her fingers to emphasize *hot*. "The few I have dated were more interested in who was looking at them, than paying any attention to getting to know me."

"I get where you're coming from," he said, and tapped a few buttons on the keyboard in front of him. "But can't you find something in between your version of hot and your current boyfriend, Clifford, the big red dipstick."

She smothered a smile and tried to act offended. Instead of cracking up, she should be defending Cliff. He was a good person who met seventy-five percent of the bullet point qualities from her 'potential husband' list. "Don't call him that."

"Clifford, or big red dipstick?"

"Both. He prefers Cliff, and he's a nice, normal guy with a good job. He's also not my boyfriend. We haven't established that we're in a committed relationship yet."

"Good. You could do better. He's shorter than you and his hair is so bright, I need sunglasses to keep from burning my retinas."

Cliff was only an inch shorter, and his hair was more auburn than red. "Most men are shorter than me."

He shrugged and looked away from the computer screen to meet her gaze. "I'm not, unless you wear heels."

Which she rarely did, since standing at six feet was already tall enough. Between her height and career in law enforcement, it had been difficult to meet a man who wasn't intimidated by her. Cliff hadn't been, which was what had drawn her to him. He accepted her for who she was and what she did for a living.

"And Clifford is vanilla. Even Morgan thinks so," he said, referring to her best friend who owned a salon and cut Andy's hair every four weeks. "Me? The only vanilla I like is ice cream but you better believe I want chocolate syrup and whipped cream on top."

"Cliff is *not* vanilla." *He's safe, easy and nice.* After having dated a cheater, she needed safe. As for easy, Cliff was laid-back and didn't create drama, which she had enough of with her job. "I'm worried this undercover gig is going to cause a problem between us. I'm sure he wouldn't like knowing I'm going to be living with another man."

"You didn't tell him, did you?"

"Of course not. I told him I couldn't see him that much over the next few weeks because of work," she said, leaving out that the undercover job, which Andy had dubbed *Operation Kravitz* after the nosy neighbor from the television show, *Bewitched*, had thrown a giant wrench into her 'life' plan. Her biological clock was ticking —loudly—and she didn't want the budding relationship she had with Cliff to end before it had the chance to blossom.

She released a frustrated breath, and longed to set her hair free from its tight bun and slip into her comfy jammies. Her head ached just thinking about the operation, the time commitment and how uncomfortable it would be living with a stranger. Two months ago, when they'd originally planned to go undercover, she'd welcomed a change of scenery and had looked forward to swapping out the lower-level duplex she rented in West Park, an older neighborhood located minutes from downtown Cleveland, to live in a newer home in suburbia. But the suspects who lived across the street from the rental house had gone south for the winter months, forcing them to put *Operation Kravitz* on hold. In the meantime, she'd met Cliff, but now she had to put *him* on hold.

"I wish Dan's wife wasn't on the verge of giving birth." Cliff had met Dan, who was also a detective, and they'd gotten along... okay. Cliff thought Dan was great. Dan thought Cliff was a boring tool. Cliff wasn't boring. He was fun in a quiet, predictable, nerdy way. She thought it was kind of cute that he was still into playing Dungeons and Dragons, and that he also liked to put on a headset, fire up his PlayStation and play World of Warcraft with friends. "I don't think Cliff would be bothered if he found out I had to work undercover with him."

Andy grinned. "Dan's wife is selfish for choosing now to have their baby."

Her cheeks warmed. She hadn't meant to sound selfish, whiny or inconsiderate. Especially considering how much she liked Dan and his wife. "Stop it. You knew what I meant." She stared at the monitor and studied her temporary home, a small, two-story traditional with a cute front porch. "I don't want to talk about Cliff, marriage or babies. Campbell should be here any minute with my new...*partner*," she finished, and hoped her fake husband wasn't a boring tool.

As it was, she didn't like that Lieutenant Ken Campbell had agreed to bring in someone from another agency to help them. There were other male detectives and deputies here who could have worked undercover with her. But the department's counterparts at the Ohio Bureau of Criminal Investigation, who were also involved with their case, suggested they think outside the box and ask CORE (Criminal Observance Resolution and Evidence), a private investigation agency, for assistance. The case had been open for over two years and neither BCI nor the sheriff's department had been able to gather enough evidence to make an arrest. Now people were dying. Their suspects needed to be apprehended before more deaths followed, and Lieutenant Campbell was hoping CORE's research and forensics capabilities would help them.

When the door opened, she looked toward it just as Lieutenant Campbell entered the room. Behind him stood a giant, hairy beast, covered in leather, denim and chains. The man stepped inside, dropped two small bags on the floor, then set a motorcycle helmet on one of the empty desks.

Please don't let this be my fake husband. Good God, they were going to be living in the middle of suburbia, and this man looked as if he were a member of the Hells Angels. Then again, with the ridiculously big beard he sported, someone could mistake him for a wannabe mountain man or lumberjack—a guy trend she understood just about as much as the man bun.

"Afternoon," Campbell greeted them, then closed the door and introduced them to CORE agent, Sloan North. "Sloan, find a seat. With the cooperation of BCI, Detectives Harris and Russell have been working this investigation from the beginning."

"Two years and three months, to be exact." She turned to Agent North, who sat at Dan's desk, staring at her, his dark eyes unreadable, his expression bored. "Have you read through the case file I sent CORE?"

"Didn't have the chance." He slid his gaze to Campbell. "I need a quick rundown, the address where I'll be staying, and then you can consider your suspects as good as caught."

"Detective Russell has been the lead investigator. She can give you that information."

North smothered a yawn. "That's okay. I've got the case file. I just need that address."

"And then you'll swoop in and make an arrest?" Hoping he'd lose the attitude, Whitney forced a smile. "You must be very good at your job as a private detective."

"I've very good at just about everything I do."

A small tilt to his lips. Maybe? All that beard made it difficult to say with certainty. Regardless, if he was trying to intimidate her, he could kiss her butt. She'd grown up in a cop family and, though aware law enforcement was a male-dominated field, had never once dealt with any insecurity when it came to performing her job. She'd worked damned hard to prove her worth to her bosses and peers, and owed the hairy beast nothing.

"Well," she began, "that's fantastic. I'm looking forward to living with a humble man who can do just about anything."

He quickly looked to Campbell. "What's she talking about?"

"Operation Kravitz," Whitney answered for the lieutenant, while hiding her irritation. She'd given CORE an extremely detailed report that had taken her hours to write, and this *agent* hadn't bothered to read it? Insulted, she turned her attention to him. "If you'd read the file you would know that you and I will be posing as a married couple and living across the street from our suspects, the Eastons. We believe this family of five works for Reuben Morales, a suspected drug kingpin. BCI first learned about Morales when they busted a drug ring in Youngstown. Since then, his name has come up during other arrests and from various CIs."

"But we're not even sure if he exists," Andy added. "We've checked every Reuben Morales living in Northeast Ohio. All of them are clean. CIs either won't ID him or say they don't know what he looks like or where he lives."

Campbell rested his rear against a desk. "He's become a legend among the drug community. Like he's a ghost who can fade in and out and never get caught."

North's dark eyebrows pulled together. "If his name is being whispered on the street, then he exists. What makes you think this family is associated with him?"

Whitney glanced to the far wall where she and the other detectives had taped local maps—with areas of high drug activity highlighted in yellow—and photos of suspects and victims. "Six months ago, we saw a significant rise of marijuana and cocaine use in Cuyahoga County's west side suburbs. With the coopera-tion of those police departments, we had undercover officers pose as high school students. One of the officers, who was with the

North Royalhurst PD, told his captain about the Eastons, and claimed their seventeen-year-old son, Cameron, was dealing pot and coke out of North Royalhurst High. This officer also reported Cameron had hinted he'd have something new to offer him soon. We'll never know what that was because the officer went missing the next day."

Andy nodded. "We're suspecting it was heroin or fentanyl, maybe both."

Whitney motioned to the wall. "That's a photo of the missing officer. See the thirteen pictures on the left side? Nine boys and four girls overdosed on opioids this past January. All of those teens were living in or near North Royalhurst. Interestingly, the Eastons went south for the months of February and March. Guess what? There were no strings of overdoses, and the number of drug-related arrests in those areas declined."

"There's more," Andy added. "The two other Easton kids are in college. The girl, Blair, attends Miami University, and her older brother, Gage, goes to Ohio State. In January, there were dozens of opioid overdoses in Columbus and Cincinnati. Ohio State is located in Columbus, and Miami University isn't far from Cincinnati. We found out Blair and Gage had also traveled south with their parents, and once again, the ODs stopped."

North looked away from the wall and shifted his dark gaze to her. "What about the parents?"

"Dale Easton is a business coach, and his wife, Irene, is a photographer," she said. "We're not sure if they're involved or if it's just the kids, but we're leaning toward believing this is a family business."

"Because?"

"Eighteen months ago, the Eastons had a mountain of debt. Not only is it gone, but they've traveled—as a family—to Miami, Florida, six times over the past year and a half."

"So?"

She hung onto her patience. If he'd read the file, he would know all of this. His unpreparedness concerned her and had her questioning the use of CORE. She'd looked into the agency, and after reviewing some of their high-profile cases and the cutting-edge technology they used to help with the toughest investigations, she'd expected to meet an agent who paid attention to detail. Instead, they'd sent a cocky, inattentive barbarian. She hoped she was wrong about him, and that he was simply making a bad first impression. They had one shot at this operation, and with the department's budget, they had only six weeks to make an arrest. If that didn't happen, she had no idea how they would ever get this close to the Eastons again.

"When we began to suspect the Eastons were involved," she began, "we contacted the Miami-Dade PD to see if they had anything on them or Reuben Morales. They'd never heard of the Eastons, but suspect Morales was involved in a drive-by shooting that led to the deaths of five people—one of whom was a ten-year-old boy."

"But you said Morales was running a drug network here in Ohio."

"Right, but since we haven't been able to find him, we're wondering if he's living in Miami and has the Eastons running the Ohio network for him."

Campbell pushed himself off the desk. "Your boss, Ian Scott, told me when you were with the Chicago PD you worked Vice. Do you have a different theory?"

He shook his head. "Nope. Works for me. Your *Kravitz* thing doesn't." He held up a giant hand before she could argue. "Going undercover and living across the street from the Eastons will allow me to watch their activities and maybe get close to them. But I'll do it alone." When he looked at her, neither his face nor eyes held apology. "No wife."

Normally even-keeled, her face heated as her temper rose. This was *her* investigation, and she would not allow this man to bully her out of it. "I've been studying the Eastons for months and know everything about them down to the brand of toilet paper they use. I also researched the neighbors. You need me." She eyed his leather jacket, worn jeans and black boots. "Without me, suburbia is going to eat you alive."

His gaze incredulous, he folded his arms over his massive chest. "Lady, I've lived in the Chicago ghettos, run with street and biker gangs and have been up against the baddest of the bad. And I didn't always have backup around the corner to save my ass. I think the only thing I could die from in suburbia is boredom."

"Whitney is part of the operation." The lieutenant half shrugged. "If you have a problem with that, then head back to Chicago. I'm sure we can find someone to replace you."

Replace him? Instead of releasing a string of cuss words to let Campbell know he wasn't happy, Sloan North kept his mouth shut and jaw clenched. These people didn't get it. He didn't work undercover with a partner. Never had, and saw no need to start now. He preferred his partner to be waiting in a car or van, ready to help make an arrest or open fire should a situation turn deadly. Not because he wanted the glory, but because he'd rather worry about only one person—himself.

He also wasn't going back to Chicago without participating in this investigation. He loved working for CORE and Ian. Some of the other CORE agents thought Ian was manipulative. In his opinion, the man got the job done and that was all that mattered. Sloan also liked working normal hours, rather than the late-night shifts required by the Chicago PD. The pay and benefits were great, too. But he'd missed going undercover, pretending to be someone he wasn't, even for a few days. Lately, his life had become routine, mundane. Which was his own fault since all he ever did was work. But he liked staying busy and keeping his mind active. Many years ago, he'd learned that inactivity led to deep thinking and who had time for that crap? Besides, he'd only been with CORE for eighteen months. How would it look if he returned prematurely?

"No, Lieutenant, I'll stick around." When Campbell grinned, Sloan added, "But no one is going to believe Detective Russell and I are married. I mean, if I was going to have a wife—which I wouldn't—she certainly wouldn't look like Barbie." He glanced to the woman. "No offense."

While Campbell wiped a hand down his face, Detective

Russell laughed and turned to Detective Harris. "Now do you get why I prefer to weed out the bad ones?" She faced Sloan and gave him a pretty smile that didn't reach her ice-blue eyes. "Agent North, do you realize you look more like a drug dealer than any member of the Easton family? Between the clothes, wallet chain and all this facial hair," she said, smoothing her hands along her creamy looking skin, "you look as if you're having an identity crisis. What are you? A biker or lumberjack? No offense, of course."

The woman was hot, in a bitchy, prissy way. He loved women, but not mouthy ones. And based on what he'd witnessed to this point, he firmly believed Detective Russell had a mouth on her. "None taken. And I thought I was going to be going undercover in a seedy part of the city, not the burbs."

"If you'd read the file, you would have known. Do you have other clothes?" she asked, her focus on his beard.

How many times was she going to point out that he hadn't read her frickin' file? "Nope."

"Great." She rolled her eyes. "I hadn't planned on wasting the rest of the day doing this, but we need to go shopping and to the barber. We have to be at the rental house first thing in the morning. That's when the moving truck is arriving with our things."

Damn, she was bossy. He hoped to Christ she didn't plan on making this fake husband and wife deal too realistic. While he appreciated a strong, independent woman, there was a reason he wasn't married to one. He liked to do what he wanted, when he wanted, how he wanted, which had been why he was attracted to sweet, passive women.

Yeah, and that worked out well.

"What things?" he asked, ignoring that last thought. He didn't want to think about the two women he'd once dated or how both had rejected him. There was no point in dwelling on a past he couldn't change.

"The house came furnished, but we have to make it appear as if we're legitimately moving. I've taken care of filling the truck with the things we'll need while we're living there, including weapons and equipment we can use to observe and monitor the Eastons."

"It all sounds good, except the barber and shopping."

When she stood and flashed him a smile, he clenched his jaw again to keep from gaping. The woman was the Amazonian version of Barbie, and had to be close to six feet tall. He'd never been with a woman even remotely close to his six-foot six frame, and wouldn't mind giving it a go. Not with Detective Russell, of course. They were, unfortunately, partners and she obviously didn't have a biker or lumberjack fantasy.

"Don't you want to fit in with the neighborhood?" she asked, slipping on a suit coat. As she did, the buttons of her shirt opened slightly, giving him a quick glimpse of skin and lace.

He quickly looked away. "I...yeah. I mean... Look, lady, I'm not going to the barber."

She leaned close enough he caught faint traces of apples and vanilla. "If you call me lady one more time, I'm going to do something very terrible to you while you sleep," she said in a hushed, yet seductive tone that belied the threat. Smiling, she stepped back. "Starting tomorrow, we will be Mr. and Mrs. Sloan and Whitney Brown. Let's start talking to each other as if we're actually married."

Detective Harris grinned. "If I didn't know any better, I'd think you two were really married."

As the lieutenant chuckled, Sloan hid his frustration. He'd let her take him shopping, but he'd draw the line there. The beard stayed. Just because she was the lead didn't give her the right to order him to sit in a barber's chair. How would she like it if he told her he hated the way she wore her hair in that ugly, tight bun? He wouldn't. Not because he was a gentleman—far from it —but because there wasn't anything ugly about Whitney except her bossy, know-it-all attitude.

"My car is in the parking garage," she said, taking her purse from her desk drawer. After she said goodbye to the lieutenant and the other detective, she went into the hallway.

Carrying his helmet and the saddlebags from his motorcycle,

he met her outside the narcotics unit. "I rode my bike here. I'll follow you."

She frowned and shook her head. "I'd like to make a good impression on the neighbors, so you can leave the bike here." Her gaze moved from his head to his boots. "After we're finished making you more presentable, I'll drop you back off at my house. I took the liberty of securing you one of our vehicles to use while you're here and had a deputy leave it at my place."

"And what kind of vehicle would that be? Wait. Lemme guess. A minivan?"

"We don't have pretend kids, so I didn't think that was necessary."

"Lucky us," he said, then added, "I want my bike."

She gave him another one of those sarcastic smiles that didn't reach her eyes. For some reason, he wondered what she looked like if she genuinely laughed or smiled. Then decided she was so damned tense, it'd probably make her face crack.

"Let's see how things go first. I figured we'd tell people we're newlyweds," she said, leading him toward the filthiest and tiniest car in the parking garage. "That way if we screw up and say the wrong thing to the Eastons or the other neighbors on the cul-de-sac, we can blame it on that."

Cul-de-sac? Fucking great. They'd be living in a fishbowl. Which was fine for surveillance, but not good for privacy. If they could see what the neighbors were up to, then that meant those same people could watch them.

The little filthy car beeped and its lights flashed. "Tell me this isn't yours," he said, nearing the Fiat 500 hatchback that was probably gray, but with all the salt residue coating a good portion of the exterior, it could be white. "How do you fit in this thing?"

She straightened. "Just fine. You should, too. If not, I'll open the sunroof and you can put your head through there."

Laughing, he smoothed his hand along his beard and eyed the compact car. "Will I be driving something bigger than a Matchbox car? If not, I'm riding out of here on my bike."

"Yes, dear. I picked out a giant pickup truck."

"Thank you for being so thoughtful," he said, opening the

passenger door, then settling into the seat. To avoid riding around with his knees in his chest, he eased the seat back, and was surprised that he actually had plenty of leg room. "If we're going to pull this off with the neighbors, we need to give ourselves a history."

"I already did," she said, backing out of the parking spot. "And printed off a bullet point list that you can review later."

This was why he didn't like working with a partner. First, he preferred to be the lead and in control. If something went wrong, he only had himself to blame. Second, it wasn't always easy to keep made-up stories consistent. "Can I see this list now? I might want to make a few changes."

With a huff, she stopped the car, then reached into the back and pulled out a manila folder. "Here," she said, handing it to him, along with a pen. "I think you'll find that I've covered everything."

"You think, huh?" He skimmed through the list and shook his head. This woman might prove to be the most anal-retentive person he'd ever met. There had to be fifty-plus bullet points. "This isn't going to work for me."

She frowned. "All of it?"

"No, I like the idea that I'm a web designer. I need a job that'll keep me home. But why do you get to work for a law firm? I prefer to be the breadwinner."

They exited the parking garage. "Aww, that's so cute and 1950s of you," she said, her tone syrupy-sweet. "That's why I used my high-paying job to buy you a giant truck."

Smartass. "I wasn't trying to come off chauvinistic." He shrugged and continued to review their history. "Since we're only pretending to have these jobs, there's no point in arguing about it."

She wove the little car through the busy downtown streets and toward the freeway. "Agreed."

"How we met? We're changing that. Do I look like the type of guy who used to be a high school cheerleader?"

After momentarily glancing at him, she grinned. "Not in the least. In my defense, I didn't know what you'd look like when I came up with this. But I'll have you know, one of my older brothers was a cheerleader in both high school and college. He's about your size and always had a gorgeous girl on his arm."

"In his bed," he corrected, then chuckled when she wrinkled her nose. "No disrespect to your bro, but we need a new 'meet' story. How about this: you were working your way through law school as a stripper. I came in one night, saw you swinging around a pole—"

"Honestly?"

He half-laughed. "You don't like that idea?"

"Not at all," she replied, a small smile tugging at the corner of her mouth. "Let's just keep it simple. We met while we were in college."

"At a keg party?" he asked, hoping to get her to relax. They were going to be living together and he'd rather do that on friendly terms than worry about every little thing he said to her. Otherwise it was going to be a long six weeks.

"I've never been to one, so I don't think I should try to make up a story about it. Let's say we met at a coffee shop."

He stared at her perfect profile, high cheekbone, straight nose and full lips, and decided he'd buy a keg for their new house. His nerdy, prissy fake wife definitely needed to loosen up and have a few beers. "Fine. We met at a coffee shop." He refocused on the bullet points and was surprised she'd given them a beach wedding at an all-inclusive resort. "I figured you for the type who'd want a traditional church wedding followed by a big, expensive reception."

"All three of my brothers went that route, and I watched their fiancées turn from sweet to scary during the process. Plus, I think it's insane to spend tens of thousands of dollars for one day, even if we're talking about a fake wedding. I'd rather use that money for a down payment on a house." She slid her gaze to him as she exited the freeway. "Why don't you want a wife?"

"Because to get a wife, you have to get married."

"That's kinda how that works." Grinning, she slowed at a stoplight. "Why are you opposed to marriage?"

"Who said I was? Bachelor life works for me. Maybe I'll settle down and start looking for a wife when I'm in my seventies." By then, every person he'd arrested or wronged should be dead, and no woman of his would ever suffer because of him again. "How much longer before we get where we're heading?"

"We're going to RightWay and should be there in a few minutes."

"That's a department store, right?"

"Yes, you've never been inside one? I know they have locations in Chicago."

"I don't shop."

"Then where do you get your clothes?"

"Let me rephrase…I don't shop. I buy. And when I need something, I go into the nearest store and get it."

She turned the Fiat into a large complex that held several stores, one of which was RightWay Department Store. "Today, you have quite a bit to buy."

"Me? It's your investigation. Why should I have to pay for clothes I don't need or want?"

After parking the car, she faced him. "Because you didn't read the file I sent," she reminded him yet again, "you didn't pack accordingly. Now *you* have to purchase your own clothes to ensure that you look the part of a suburbanite. But you're in luck. I have a thirty percent off coupon and forty dollars in RightWay cash."

Money wasn't the issue. He didn't need her coupon or pretend cash. There was nothing wrong with his clothes. Even his boss didn't blow him crap for the way he dressed. The problem was, no matter how she dressed him, he knew once he moved to the cul-de-sac he'd be out of his element. He'd spent the first eighteen years of his life living on a dying farm near a small town in Indiana, then the next eighteen living in the city. He was used to crowds, traffic and rubbing shoulders with the scum of the Earth. Not white picket fences, neighborhood block parties and sharing cups of sugar with the neighbors. He'd worked his ass off at his parents' farm and could fire up a lawnmower, but he hadn't done that in two decades. Although he used to be handy, he had a maintenance guy who took care of any repairs needed at his condo. What if he couldn't man up and fix shit around their house? Whitney might think…what? And why the hell did he care?

He followed her into the store, then to the men's section. The place was crowded, mostly with women and small children. He ignored them and went straight for the display holding graphic T-shirts.

"Are you a double XL?" she asked, holding up a purple golf shirt.

He understood the woman had just met him, but of all the colors, why would she pick that one? "I am, and I don't wear purple."

"It's not purple, it's lilac. With your dark coloring, this would look nice on you. And, it's only fifteen bucks. Take thirty percent off and—"

"Do we belong to a country club?"

She shifted her blue eyes to him, and he couldn't help but notice how thick and long her lashes were. "No. Don't you think it'd be good for you to have a couple of golf shirts and a pair of khaki pants and shorts? What if we're invited to a neighbor's house for dinner?"

Unless it was a holiday, he saw no reason to dress up only to sit at someone's house, or to argue with her about it. There was no need to prolong the torture of having to shop. "Fine. Two golf shirts—I pick the colors—and one pair of khaki pants. It's April. I don't need shorts."

"The weather is supposed to change next week. I heard we should expect record temperatures." Her forehead furrowed as she held up the lilac shirt. "I don't know…I think you might need a triple XL. There's a fitting room around the corner and… Oh. My. God. What are you doing?"

He'd draped his leather coat over a clothes rack, then reached for the hem of his Henley shirt and was pulling it over his head. "Trying on your purple shirt," he said, taking it from her. Screw wasting time by going to a dressing room. He wanted out of the store before the clothes racks closed in and suffocated him.

Cheeks stained pink, her eyes wide, she stared at his chest and arms. "You're covered with tattoos." When the women near them began whispering and gawking at him, her face went from pink to red. She stepped closer. "People are staring," she whispered, averting her gaze from his chest.

"Apparently, they like what they see," he said just to needle her. If he had to wear these clothes, he deserved to have a little fun at her expense.

Her eyes narrowed. "I don't know why anyone would mark up their skin."

He finished putting on the shirt. "I don't know why anyone wouldn't."

"Well, they're concerning. What will our neighbors think?"

"Why do you care what anyone thinks? If you're happy with yourself, anyone else's opinion doesn't matter." Before she could respond, he turned away to check his reflection in the nearby mirror. Instead of focusing on the way the shirt fit, he met Whitney's gaze. "Besides, I'm sure there are plenty of housewives who have tats."

A cute young woman pushing a baby in a stroller stopped by the mirror. "I do, and I love yours."

"Me, too," another woman said. "You have so many though. Maybe you should remove your shirt again. I didn't get to see all of them."

As the two women laughed, Whitney cocked a brow and turned to them. "Excuse me. You're talking about my *husband*."

The young mom quickly walked away, while the other woman let out a sigh. "Lucky you. If my husband looked like yours, I wouldn't need to buy him clothes." She winked. "I'd keep him naked."

"Good God," Whitney gasped as the woman went back to shopping. "Who says things like that? And to total strangers?" She turned and handed him the other shirt. "Please. Use the fitting room. Or does your ego need women salivating over your bare chest?"

No, he didn't need that. And who was she to suggest such a thing? He hadn't taken off his shirt for attention, but for efficiency. He didn't understand why she was being so combative, or why she didn't like him—on a professional level. Everyone liked him. Hell, there were even a few people he'd arrested who would admit to thinking he was a cool guy. Whatever. Now that he thought about it, maybe he didn't like her. She wasn't very nice, cut on his clothes and beard and didn't like his tats.

As he finished letting her pick out his clothes, and he grabbed a few things on his own, it occurred to him that Whitney might not like men. Between her shot about his ego, her attitude toward him and how there wasn't even the tiniest flicker of interest when he'd taken off his shirt—not that he cared—it was a conclusion that made sense. He supposed it was a good thing. If she wasn't into guys, he wouldn't have to worry about her coming onto him while they lived together. She might be attractive, but she wasn't his type. His type didn't depend on bullet point lists, bossing him around or treating him as if he were a child who needed to shop for school clothes.

"We better pay for this stuff and get you to the barber," she said, heading for the registers. "It's getting late and I have to finish packing and closing up my house."

"I need to secure a room for the night."

She placed the clothes on the counter, then took the ones he carried and did the same. "I reserved you a room at a hotel near my house, which is only ten minutes from here, and there's a barber shop along the way."

"Just take me to the truck." He smiled at the cashier who'd been eyeing him between scanning the price tags. "I don't need you going to the barber with me."

"But I want to make sure you do something about that beard. It has to go. You should trim your hair, too. I noticed it touching the collar of the shirt I picked out for you."

When he realized both the cashier and the two women standing in line behind them were listening and watching, his face grew hot with embarrassment—something that hadn't happened in years—and his patience snapped. He'd tried to be nice, tried to be friendly, and instead of finding a way to get along and strike up a friendship, Whitney had made it clear she had no regard for him. At this point, he no longer cared if she liked him or not. What he cared about was making her understand he would not allow her to treat him like a child, especially in public.

"But I thought you liked the way my beard felt along your inner thighs," he said, going for the throat. Was it a prick thing to say? One hundred percent. Maybe next time she would pay attention to her surroundings when she was ripping on him.

"Gross." Her face twisted with disgust. "I can only image what's buried in all that hair."

His ears burned. Before he could respond with a comment meant to embarrass *her*, she handed the cashier her coupon and RightWay cash. Triumph spread over her face as she studied the register's monitor. "Look at that," she said. "I saved you almost two hundred dollars. And your bill is only around one hundred and fifty bucks."

Impossible. He had a ton of stuff, including running shoes, flip flops and socks. "That can't be right," he said, and, though still fuming over the way she'd humiliated him, he had to admit that he was impressed. If he ever became a shopper, he'd have start coming to this store.

Whitney took one of the bags and thanked the cashier. "It's the power of the coupon."

"She's right," the cashier said, then added in a hushed tone, "I like the beard."

He flashed her a smile he knew women loved—well, except for Whitney—avoided making eye contact with the ladies in line, and headed for the door. He and his fake wife needed to have a serious discussion regarding how they would treat each other in public, because how things had gone down in the store was not acceptable.

Once they were in the car and back on the road, he turned to her. "How's this husband and wife thing going to work between us?" he asked, deciding for a somewhat diplomatic approach, rather than lambaste her for the way she'd acted.

"I'm not sure what you mean, but to be clear: there will be *nothing* physical between us. The idea is…" She shook her head. "Ridiculous."

He chuckled. After the way she'd treated him, he had no

interest in her long legs or curves. "You're not my type, either. But to be clear: I wasn't talking about being physical, though we will have to act as if we like each other. And if any of the neighbors had heard how you talked to—"

Her phone rang. She glanced at the screen, then ignored it.

"Aren't you going to answer?" he asked, irritated by the interruption.

"I'd rather talk in private."

"Boyfriend?" he asked, mildly curious if he was right about her sexual preference.

She let out a huff of breath. "None of your business."

"Hey, it's like I told you," he began, "if you're happy with yourself, anyone else's opinion doesn't matter. You date who you want. Unlike you, *I* don't judge people."

She quickly glanced at him, her eyes widening with surprise. "You think I'm gay?"

Shit. He might've just fucked up. "I…no."

"Oh my God." She laughed and shook her head. "You do. You think I'm into women." She held up a hand. "Wait, let me guess why… Was it because I didn't drool over you when you took off your shirt?"

"I *never* said you were a lesbian."

"Or maybe it was the gross comment about your beard?" She parked the car along the curb in front of a craftsman style duplex, then turned to him. A playful glint brightened her eyes, while her mouth slid into a teasing smile. "You think that because I'm mildly nauseated by the idea of being physical with you, I must be gay."

Mildly nauseated? Whatever. She'd made her point—he was a douche bag who sometimes needed to keep his mouth shut.

"Do you know what this means?" she asked.

"Yeah, you have some imagination. Remember, I never said you were gay. But, if I somehow offended you, then I'm sorry. That wasn't my intent."

"This means you have got to be one of the most arrogant, conceited, pompous men I've ever met," she continued as if he hadn't apologized.

"Those all mean the same thing," he said. Fuck it. So, he'd made a mistake and had implied she was a lesbian. So what? He tried to right it. Instead of accepting his apology, she'd insulted him. Again.

"I know." She smiled. "I'm trying to emphasize my point."

"Which is?"

"You're a jerk."

"Because I'm confident? Why don't you take a look at yourself, Detective?"

"Are you now calling me a jerk?"

This argument was derailing, and he needed to get it back on track before he was sent home. He didn't want to have to explain to Ian that he'd been kicked off an operation before it had started. "No, just like I didn't call you a lesbian. But why don't you think about how you treated me at the store? Did you have a clue that people were listening to you talk down to me?"

She frowned. "I did no such thing. And, if I did, then I'm sorry. It wasn't my intent." She dug out a set of keys from her purse, handed them to him, then opened the car door. "The silver truck is the one you'll be using."

After grabbing his shopping bags, saddlebags and helmet from the backseat, he tossed them in the cab of the truck parked in front of Whitney's car. Still worried she'd request that he be sent back to Chicago, and how his boss would react to that, he caught up with her at her front door. "Why do you hate me?"

That pretty pink blush returned. She blinked and looked away. "I don't hate you."

Could've fooled me. "Then why are you so damned defensive?"

"Because I have many months and hours invested in this case. And it's aggravating that you just waltzed in and tried to take over."

He would admit that he might've done that. In his defense, he was used to being the one in charge. "I'm sorry if I made you feel that way. I don't always say the right things." He sighed, and decided to take the high road. "Look, we have to live together, so let's forget about today and start over tomorrow."

"Just go to the barber," she said, bossing him around one last time before shutting the door in his face.

Fucking awesome. She absolutely hated him.

And they had to spend the next six weeks pretending they were married and in love...

Chapter Three

The rental house, North Royalhurst, Ohio
Saturday, 7:28 a.m. Daylight Saving Time

A LIGHT MIST blanketed the green grass. The morning sun peeked through the fluffy clouds, while birds chirped from the budding trees. Yellow daffodils and bright red tulips had pierced the flowerbeds and were already blooming. At the end of the neighbor's drive, a gorgeous dogwood showed off its white flowers as an older man, wearing a bathrobe and slippers, fetched the morning paper from the box near it.

Welcome to the burbs.

Whitney blew on her coffee cup's sip hole and waved to the man, whom she recognized from her research into the street as Vincent Dietrich. Ironically, he was a retired Cleveland cop and his wife, Helen, a former schoolteacher. Though eager to finally meet all the neighbors—especially the Eastons—she did not want to engage in conversation yet. At least not without Sloan. While he'd taken their 'history' list back to his hotel room, she couldn't be certain whether he'd studied it or made more changes, and she wanted to be sure they didn't mix up their stories. Where was he anyway? Deputies, posing as movers, would be here any minute.

How would it look if her *husband* wasn't here to help with the move?

"Don't mind me," Vincent called from across the lawn. "And don't tell my wife you caught me in my robe. She'd die of embarrassment."

Whitney smiled. "Your secret is safe."

After he'd promised to come by later and properly introduce himself, she decided to head into the rental house. She'd only seen photos of the place and was anxious to settle in and unpack. The sooner they went to work and closed the investigation, the sooner she could be back in her own home.

When she reached the front door and slid the key into the lock, she hesitated. As a sign of unity and peace, she wanted Sloan to be with her when they entered the house for the first time. Yesterday hadn't gone as she'd hoped. She wanted to like Sloan—as a partner—and instead had ended up calling him a jerk, along with a few other names. As she'd finished packing and prepped for her stay at Shady Circle, she'd thought back to the time she had spent with him. Instead of irritation, she'd felt guilt. She could've been the better person, acted more mature and less judgmental. In her defense, he'd been annoying and arrogant. He hadn't read her report, was combative, had assumed she was gay, and *who* took off their shirt in the middle of a department store? The bigger question: why couldn't she stop thinking about his chest?

Bad Whitney. Don't go there.

How could she not? The man had layers of muscle. His chest. Those chiseled arms. She hadn't even minded the tattooed snake wrapping around his left bicep and shoulder, or the skull on his right arm—her favorite. She'd loved the flowers surrounding it and the butterfly, which looked as if it had escaped the skull's mouth, along his ripped forearm.

Yes, Sloan was not ugly. Yes, he had a body she'd love to climb on top of and ride. But she was not interested in him as anything but a partner. She preferred a man who didn't have an ego, didn't need it stroked, and wasn't so damned hot he made women stop, stare and salivate. She preferred safe, skinny, serious Cliff. He liked that she was organized and when she made plans for them.

During their second date, he'd told her that as a manager at an accounting firm he made decisions all day and wanted a break once he was home.

Sighing, she recalled last night's five-minute phone conversation with Cliff. She'd hated lying to him, but hadn't had a choice. *Operation Kravitz* was confidential. Plus, she imagined he'd be very worried about her safety if he knew she was working undercover to nail an extremely dangerous drug lord. Then there was Sloan. Cliff hadn't shown any signs that he was a jealous person, but she doubted he'd like for her to be sleeping down the hall from a man whose body made her girl parts come alive. Could *possibly* come alive, she amended. She'd have to fantasize about Sloan for that to happen.

A car door shut. She turned as Sloan left the truck parked along the curb and, carrying two cups with lids, headed up the driveway. "Morning," he greeted her with a smile that shouldn't have had an effect on her. But it did, along with everything else about the way he looked.

Yesterday, after he'd left, she'd figured he would skip the barber to spite her. He hadn't. His dark hair was now slightly shorter, and he'd styled it in a modern yet messy pompadour that she'd like to make messier as she directed his head between her opened thighs. While the beard remained, it had been trimmed enough to where she could actually make out the contours of his face and see his sexy smile. The things he could probably do to her with his mouth had her thinking back to what he'd said about the feel of his beard along her inner thighs.

Bad Whitney.

Damn it. All she'd wanted was for him to trim his head and beard so he looked less like a thug. Instead, and without knowing it, he'd given her a pornographic fantasy. Just as he had when he'd decided to take off his shirt in the middle of the department store. He'd shocked and flustered her to the point where she had, according to Sloan, been a jerk herself. When she'd replayed how she'd treated him at the store, she'd realized Sloan had been right. She'd been awful, and anyone who'd heard their exchange had probably thought she was a nagging, controlling bitch. That wasn't who she was, and she'd spent half the night lying in bed questioning why she'd acted that way toward him. Unfortunately, she still didn't have an answer.

"Morning," she finally said when he neared her. "Did you have any problems finding the place?"

"Not at all." He held up one of the cups and looked at the one she held. "I bought you a coffee, but I see you're all set."

"Thanks." She grinned, touched that he'd thought about her after how crappy she'd been to him. "I picked up one for you, too. It's in the car."

"You did?" A boyish smile tugged at his lips. "I'm surprised you'd do anything nice for me after the way we left things."

"Stay out of my head. I was just thinking the same thing." She stepped away from the door and toward him. "It's over, and I'm good. Are you?" she asked, hoping they could start fresh. Unlike her brothers and father, she was more like her mom and avoided conflict whenever possible. She preferred to think through a situation before reacting and liked to keep her emotions controlled. If no one knew what was going on in her head and heart, then they couldn't hurt her. Besides, drama was meant for the stage, not real life.

"Yeah, I'm good." He looked away to study the house and the two on either side. "These homes all look the same. I hope I remember which one is ours."

She chuckled. "No, they don't. There are a few ranches and not all of them are the same color. But I'll buy a lawn ornament so you'll know which house is ours." She motioned toward the house. "Ready to go inside? The moving truck should be here soon."

"You haven't gone in yet?"

"Since we're partners, I wanted to wait for you."

That boyish smile returned. He took her coffee and set it, along with his, on the porch.

"What are you doing?" she asked, then gasped when he scooped her in his arms as if she weighed nothing. Her girl parts came alive again as she hooked an arm around his neck. She hadn't been picked up since she was a child, and could get used to having Sloan's arms around her.

Stop! Bad Whitney.

Holding her with one arm, he turned the key and opened the door. "I'm carrying my bride over the threshold," he said, then brought her into the house. While she melted on the inside and longed for the day when her *real* husband said and did the same, he flipped a switch in the foyer. The chandelier above came to life, brightening the entrance. "Not bad." He took her into the living room which, like the rest of the house, had been decorated with a mix of modern and traditional furnishings.

The walls had been painted a neutral gray, and the floors were hand-scraped laminate, but the mocha hickory color made them look as if they were real hardwood. The sofa was dark gray. In front of it was a yellow bench table that could serve as an ottoman, and next to that was an oversized chair upholstered in a blend of the dark gray and yellow. White accent pillows matched the curtains, and the area rug had a mix of all the colors in the room.

"How many bedrooms does this place have?" he asked, side-stepping the couch to carry her into the adjoining dining room and kitchen.

She should squirm and make it clear that this was inappropriate. Dan, Andy, or anyone else she worked with, would never attempt to pick her up and carry her. But being held like this, by a strong man who smelled good, looked great and who'd brought her coffee was…fantastic, thrilling, something she'd never experienced. She'd been a virgin until she was twenty-two, hadn't been the type to throw herself at men, and because of college and her career, she hadn't truly involved herself in the dating game until four years ago when her biological clock had started ticking so damned loudly, it'd become her sole focus.

"Three, plus two bathrooms upstairs and a half bath on this level," she said, redirecting her thoughts, but refusing to squirm. Yet. Between Sloan's dark looks and build, she didn't have to close her eyes to experience her ridiculous Wolverine fantasy. Why not enjoy the moment?

Because this is inappropriate and you are in charge of an investigation. Act like it.

Right. She wriggled slightly.

He looked at her, surprise clear in his eyes, then immediately set her on her feet. "Sorry. I forgot I was carrying you."

Because she was far from petite, she didn't know how that was possible, but would go with it. She would not—no matter their differences in personalities—discount that she'd liked being in his arms. Cliff wouldn't be able to carry her around as if she weighed nothing and he certainly didn't smell as good as Sloan. Like soap and freshly cleaned laundry that had been hanging to dry on a warm, sunny day.

She cleared her throat. "I figured we'd each take a room and use the spare one to hold our equipment."

He walked toward the large island that sectioned off the newly updated kitchen, and looked out into the family room, where a sliding door led to the patio. "This is way nicer than my condo."

With the way he'd looked when they had first met, she pictured his place rivaling a college kid's and filled with empty beer cans, pizza boxes, a futon and TV hooked up to a gaming system, along with clothes scattered across a filthy floor. Not that she should judge. No one would be handing her an award for keeping a clean house anytime soon. For some reason, scrubbing toilets and sinks never seemed to make it on any of her lists.

"Have you always lived in Chicago?" she asked.

As he stood in front of the glass door and stared at the back-yard, there was a small flicker of...something. Longing? Regret? "No. I grew up on a farm. From there I moved to Chicago and—"

The doorbell rang. "That's probably the deputies." Relieved, she headed for the foyer. Part of her wanted to hear what he was going to say. The other part suggested she keep their relationship superficial. She was physically attracted to Sloan, and whenever she became attracted to a man, she tended to say the wrong things or lose the capability to say anything at all. In general—and although she was raised and worked with males—when it came to good-looking men, she was socially awkward.

But, she was also an adult and a professional. She needed to ignore Sloan's clean and masculine scent, that he looked incredibly sexy shirtless and could carry her around without the veins in his neck popping. He was, without a doubt, a gorgeous walking muscle, but he was also arrogant and, with his early assumption that she was a lesbian, he likely considered himself a ladies' man. In her limited experience, womanizers weren't safe and knew how to shake up her confidence and trample her heart. Which was why she currently dated Cliff. He didn't shake up anything and that suited her just fine. She didn't need passion or to fall so deeply in love with someone she'd be left devastated if the relationship ended—once was enough and something she didn't want to go through again. She needed a husband to help her cross off the last item of her 'life' plan: a baby.

As deputies brought in boxes from the truck, she left Sloan to help them and retrieved her bags from the car. Without bothering to discuss their sleeping arrangements, she mentally called dibs on the master bedroom which had its own bathroom. She wanted privacy, plus the master had a bigger closet and she'd brought enough to fill it. Once she'd emptied her last bag, and had stowed her toiletries in the bathroom, she decided to go downstairs and check on their progress. Before she made her way down the steps, she heard Sloan's voice coming from the spare room she'd planned to use for their surveillance equipment, and went in that direction.

Sloan stood in front of the window overlooking the cul-de-sac and shook his head. "I don't think this is going to work," he said without facing her.

"How did you know anyone was in the doorway?" she asked, and entered the room, which was small and would do well as a nursery.

"Not just anyone. I knew *you* were there. What kind of perfume are you wearing?"

"I'm not." She pushed up the sleeve of her sweatshirt and gave her arm a sniff. She certainly didn't smell as good as Sloan, but thought the apple vanilla scented lotion she wore was subtle and nice. "It's probably my lotion."

"Well, no offense, but it kind of reminds of my grandma. She was always baking and smelled like apple pie."

She stiffened. The man might be good looking, but he was still a jerk. "Thank you. What a sweet and rude thing to say."

"I said no offense."

"You've said that a couple times right before you've insulted me."

He shrugged and glanced over his shoulder. "Just trying to help you. You're not going to land a man smelling like an eighty-year-old woman."

"I'm doing just fine without your help."

"You have a boyfriend?"

"None of your business," she said, determined to keep their relationship superficial.

"Whatever." He moved the drape aside. "Come here and tell me what you see."

She didn't need to go anywhere near him, and could already tell the newly budding tree blocked their view of the homes across the street. Damn. The room Sloan was supposed to use faced the backyard, leaving the master the most suitable place for their equipment.

"I noticed you'd already commandeered the master," he said.

She held up a hand. "I know where you're heading with this, but I'm not switching rooms. I've unpacked—"

"Move it. Since I'm the one who'll be watching the Eastons, and there are two windows overlooking the street, it makes sense for me to take that room."

She folded her arms across her chest. "The guest bathroom doesn't have a tub."

"So? It has a huge shower."

While he was right, she was a bath person, and loved a long soak at the end of a stressful day. "I know, but I like taking baths."

He let out a huff that could've almost been a slight chuckle. "Then you can use my bathroom whenever you want."

"I don't want to use the bathroom if you're right outside the door."

"Christ, Whitney, don't be so damned stubborn and unreasonable." He pushed a hand through his hair, messing it up even more. "If you're worried about me coming into the bathroom and ravaging you, don't. I told you, when I smell you I—"

"Think of your grandma. Yeah, I heard you the first time." Disappointed with herself for thinking that being held by him was remotely nice, she started for the door. "I'll move my things," she said, because she wasn't stubborn or unreasonable, and because he was right. It made sense for him to take that room, and it wasn't as if he'd be in the master twenty-four seven. He could also view the Eastons' house from the downstairs living room and office, just not as well.

Two hours later, after she'd moved her things to the back bedroom, and had helped Sloan unpack the items they'd use for the operation, the doorbell rang. The deputies had left with the moving truck about thirty minutes ago, and she now worried one of their neighbors was stopping by to welcome them to the street. She wasn't ready for a meet and greet or to pretend Sloan was her husband. His granny comment still rubbed her raw, especially after she'd allowed herself the luxury to admit he was a good-looking guy—at least when he kept his mouth shut.

"How do you want to do this?" she asked him, and set one of the cameras they planned to aim at the Easton house on the bed.

He placed his laptop on the dresser, then headed for the door. "Do what?"

"Deal with the neighbors." She followed behind and grabbed his forearm when they were halfway down the steps. "We need to make a good impression and stick to the story I created. I want us to come off unassuming and friendly."

"Hey, I'm a friendly guy. And when it comes time to meet the neighbors, I'll make sure I don't embarrass you."

"Which is now."

He let out a sigh. "No. There's a delivery guy at the door. I've been expecting him."

Expecting him for what? She'd begun planning the operation months ago, had taken care of bringing in everything they would need, and had the itemized list to prove it. Out of curiosity, she kept quiet and waited for Sloan to take the large box from the driver. Once he was back inside and closed the door, he carried it upstairs.

"What's in the box?" she asked.

"Spy gear. Last night, after I read through your file on the Eastons, I put a list together of additional equipment I might need and had Rachel and Hudson send it to me."

She followed him into the bedroom. "I don't know who those people are or what additional things you'd need. I have it all, and if I don't, I'm sure we could've gotten it from the sheriff's department."

"Do you have one of these?" he asked, pulling out a black baseball cap with a gray Indiana Hoosiers logo across the front.

"Yes, but mine has the Ohio State block O on the front. Don't forget, we met in college...at Ohio State. You can't wear that hat."

"Why couldn't I go to OSU but still be a Hoosier fan?"

"I don't know. Because."

"Good reasoning, Detective," he said with a tilted grin, and handed her the hat. "Study the bottom of the logo right where the I intersects the U. See anything?"

"No, I...wait." She turned the hat over and ran her finger along the inside. "Is this a spy cam?"

He dug inside the box. "Yep, and I have more in here. Need a case for your cell phone? This one not only protects and charges your phone, it secretly records video and audio." He took out a key fob, then handed it to her. "Looks like a key, but this also records video and audio."

"This is all great, James Bond, but did you concern yourself with Ohio law?"

"Of course. It's legal as long as one party consents to the surveillance and doesn't plan to use the recordings to engage in criminal activity. Plus, I read your files, remember? A judge gave the sheriff's department an interception warrant that allows you, and me, to become walking cameras."

All true, but she hadn't been sure if he knew any of this. Then again, Lieutenant Campbell had mentioned Sloan used to work Vice for Chicago PD. She looked through the box and picked up a pen. "Let me guess: this is a listening device. You plan to leave it at the Eastons so you can eavesdrop."

He took the pen from her. Studied it. Clicked it a few times, then grinned. "Nope. It's just a plain old pen that must've dropped in the box when they were packaging it."

She fought an eye roll and moved for the door. "I'm going to let you play with your stuff. One thing that wasn't on the moving truck was food. I'll head to the grocery store so I can stock our fridge and pantry. Any requests?"

"Can you cook?" he asked, still looking through the box.

Although she wasn't much of a housekeeper, her mom had taught her a few culinary skills. "I can, but I'm not your maid, and don't plan on serving you five course meals every night. Actually, while we're on the subject, I also won't clean up after you or do your laundry. I'm not sure if you noticed, but the laundry room is on your way to the garage."

He set a gadget near his laptop. "I did notice and never expected you to do any of those things."

"But you asked if I could cook."

Rising, he walked toward her. Crowded her space in the doorway, but she refused to move and let him intimidate her—if that was what he was trying to do. She couldn't figure out this man. One minute he was rude and overbearing. The next, he was thoughtful and treated her with respect. Regardless, this was her investigation. He was the hired help, and she had no problem reminding him of that fact.

"I asked because if you can't do more than make scrambled eggs, I'll cover meals. My mom made sure I knew my way around a kitchen by the time I was eleven. Give me a crockpot and I'll make you..." He leaned closer. "Happy."

She ducked away from the heat of his body and moved into the hallway. "Good. Then we can take turns making dinner. Again, any special requests?" she asked, proud of herself for keeping her cool. She'd seen his bare chest and knew what it was like to be held by him. In a platonic, professional way. Still, she'd enjoyed his touch and looking at him. Probably because it'd been a long time since she'd had sex. With a hot guy.

Think about Cliff. He's safe and…nice.

And played Dungeons and Dragons.

Sloan thinks I smell like his grandma.

That last thought had her reevaluating her relationship with Cliff. During the two months they'd been texting and dating, he'd barely kissed her because he was sweet and shy. Next time she saw him, though, she'd make a move that would make her forget about Mr. Slabs of Muscle and Biceps of Steel.

"I told you," he began, "in my past life I was a farm boy. A poor one at that. I'll eat just about anything."

"Noted," she said, and started down the steps.

"Except Brussels sprouts and peas."

Good, she had an aversion for both veggies, too. She took a few more steps. "Got it."

"And liver."

Cringing, she stopped and turned. "I've never had liver."

"Then you're lucky. Is our grocery bill on the department's dime?" After she nodded, he added, "I could go for some popsicles. A bag of jelly beans would be cool, too."

She eyed his chest. *Again.* The man clearly worked out on a regular basis. She wouldn't have thought he'd waste calories on junk food. "I'll add them to the list."

"Beer, too. You know, in case a neighbor comes over and we need to get friendly." He leaned against the doorjamb. "Maybe I should just go with you."

"Are you hungry?"

"Starved."

"Then you stay home. Otherwise our bill will be astronomical," she said, then rushed down the steps. She didn't want to go to the store with him, and didn't want to live with him, either. Playing house was too intimate. Yes, she'd reminded herself repeatedly that she was a professional, that this was an operation and they were here to do a job, but—and she was only going by looks—Sloan was her Wolverine.

If his profile had showed up on one of the dating sites she belonged to, she would have dismissed him for being too… animalistic. Too much for her to handle. The kind of guy who had to be the hero, the breadwinner and decision maker. Growing up in a large family, having her brothers' friends always over had made for an extremely loud, active and chaotic household. And she'd loved every minute. But because she was so much younger than her brothers, there'd come a time when it had been just her and her parents. Without her brothers around, their house had become quiet and boring. At that point, she'd been a gawky, shy teen, and had had a hard time making friends. To keep busy, she'd begun helping her mom around the house, organizing her brothers' items for when they finished college and moved into their own homes. She'd become addicted to making lists and checking them off, to organize and control.

Yesterday, within ten seconds of meeting the man, she'd suspected Sloan also craved control. He'd wanted to run the investigation on his own, hadn't wanted a partner and had fought every one of her suggestions. He was the opposite of Cliff, who let her essentially run their relationship. Unlike Sloan, Cliff never argued, never complained, wasn't insulting and went with the flow.

Get Sloan out of your head and focus.

Right. That was exactly what she'd do. Why she found him remotely attractive surprised her. First, he'd thought she was a lesbian. Then he'd told her she smelled like his grandma. He was also uncivil, unrefined and high-handed. She also didn't peg him as the type of man who would romance a woman, woo her with flowers, soft kisses and barely-there touches. Instead, like an animal, he'd probably tear off her clothes and push her up against the wall. Kiss her until her lips were swollen and...

Her body hummed with need. Damn it.

Bad Whitney.

Whitney's scent still hung in the air, making him regret taking this assignment. She smelled nothing like his grandma, whose diet consisted of bacon, Marlboro Reds and Wild Turkey. Instead, Whitney's apple and vanilla scent made him want to strip her naked and lick her skin. After all, he had a sweet tooth. And he was sweet on the detective. When he'd lifted her in his arms—as a joke—he hadn't been ready to let her go.

No, he hadn't been ready to let go of the fantasy.

The wife. The kids. The house with the white picket fence. That'd been what he'd wanted eighteen years ago when he'd left Indiana to follow his high school sweetheart, Shannon, who'd gone to college at Northwestern University in Chicago. His mom had already been gone for a few years, and the farm had been dying a slow death for even longer. When his dad had passed during the fall after Sloan had graduated high school, there'd been nothing left for him there. No family. No money, since his father had owed money to creditors and had been on the verge of bankruptcy. But he'd loved Shannon, and she'd loved him. So he'd thought.

Whatever the fuck. Why was he thinking about any of this?

Because the house was awesome and Whitney was out of his league. Just like Shannon. He'd guarantee Whitney had a college diploma hanging on her wall next to her life's bullet point 'To Do List'. He knew her type: strong, confident go-getter, and avoided women like her. Unlike Whitney, he wasn't a planner. He liked spontaneity, to wake up one morning and ride his Harley without having a destination in mind. He couldn't do that if he was saddled to a woman. Marriage was not a synonym for freedom. And yet, twice in his life, he'd wanted marriage, to make a lifelong commitment and he'd been rejected both times.

There hadn't and wouldn't be a third time. After he'd followed Shannon to Chicago, only to have her tell him that she'd met a well-educated, sophisticated city guy, and that they were now an exclusive couple, it'd hurt. He'd been lucky to make it through high school and was far from sophisticated. He'd survived, and shortly thereafter, had begun his career in law enforcement. Being a cop and assigned to the worst neighborhoods in Chicago had changed his life, had stripped him of small town naivety, made him jaded, harder, edgier. Ellie, a sweet waitress he'd met after he had been promoted to detective and was working Vice, had softened him. She, like him, hadn't had the best education, come from money or had expected to eventually rub elbows with the rich and famous. She was a good girl, quiet, passive, and he'd loved her. Had been ready to ask her to marry him, until she'd wound up in the hospital.

Vengeance was an ugly thing. A drug dealer he'd arrested, and who'd later made bail, had found out that he and Ellie were a couple, then had broken into her apartment. He'd beaten her, breaking her nose, jaw, arm and several ribs, then had sent Sloan a message taking credit for the beating without incriminating himself. After multiple surgeries, months of recovery, and fearing she could be attacked again, Ellie had ended their relationship.

Once again, it'd hurt, but he'd survived and walked away a better man for knowing Ellie. She'd taught him to laugh again, and to remember to have fun, something he wasn't sure Whitney knew how to do. He'd also made a conscience choice to remain a bachelor and, unless it was a sex-only relationship, he refused to become involved with another woman. He never wanted anyone to be injured because of him again.

He emptied the box from CORE, then unpacked his bag. Since he'd started working for the agency, the paranoia of being followed by an ex-con or a suspect who'd made bail had subsided to some degree. He'd legally changed his name after leaving the Chicago PD, had moved, got a new phone number, email address, done everything to create a new life. Except, he couldn't change who he was on the inside. Not that he thought there was anything wrong with him. Whitney had called him arrogant. He wasn't arrogant, he was like her—confident. And he resented her know-it-all attitude and for knocking his confidence level down a few notches. Yeah, he'd made a few dick moves yesterday—they both had—but at least he'd acknowledged them and had apologized. And, yeah, he had to admit the haircut and beard trim made him look better. He hung up the khaki pants she'd forced him to buy with her damned coupon and fake cash. The pants and all the other clothes he'd bought would be donated after the job ended. She might've been right about the hair and beard, but she'd been wrong about the clothes. Nothing looked right on him except the new jeans and graphic T-shirts, and he wasn't comfortable wearing a golf shirt and khakis. He'd do it, though. Not for her, but for the investigation.

Once his things were put away, he went through the upstairs level and broke down the empty moving boxes. He'd noticed a fire pit out back and could use the cardboard for kindling. Since he figured today was going to be spent getting settled and meeting neighbors, he wouldn't mind opening a cold beer and relaxing next to a fire before the real work began. Whitney would probably object because fires weren't on her To Do list, but she'd have to get over it. In his experience, undercover work required time and patience. He wasn't sure about her, but he had plenty of both. There was no one waiting for him in Chicago, and he was on CORE's dime.

He made his way downstairs, then went to work cleaning that level. As he moved from room to room, and sunlight spilled in through the front windows, the house grew stuffy. He pulled his new sweatshirt—a purchase he didn't mind—over his head, folded, then set it on the kitchen island. After gathering the boxes, he slid open the glass doors and stepped onto the large, stamped concrete patio. The fenced yard was three times the size of what he would have if he'd ever decided to buy a home in Chicago. Flowerbeds—in need of maintenance—bordered the fence, a shed sat in the right corner of the lot, along with a few mature trees. He could hang a hammock from those trees, and when the weather warmed, nap in the shade. Except he didn't own a hammock and this wasn't his house. He wasn't on vacation, he was here to do a job.

When the doorbell rang, he dropped the boxes, then went back inside. He hoped Whitney was on the other side. She'd probably have a fit if he engaged with one of the neighbors without her. Frankly, he wasn't prepared to meet anyone yet. Last night, he'd read over the 'history' list Whitney had created for them, and he wanted to make more changes. Saying they'd met in college, but that they were newlyweds made no sense. If they stuck to her story, that would mean they had been dating or engaged for twelve to fifteen years.

He reached the door and looked through the peephole. No one was there, and Whitney's car wasn't in the driveway.

The bell rang again, making him lurch back and release a string of swearwords. He hated the fucking jump scare. Irritated and ready to let the neighborhood kids know not to screw with him, he whipped open the door and scanned the front yard.

"Hi."

He jerked back again and into the door. "Motherfu—" Sloan stared down at three sets of curious eyes and cleared his throat. "Were you ringing my doorbell?" he asked, while hoping to God Whitney came home. Now. The only kids he was used to dealing with were the street-smart ones who lived in the ghetto or projects.

"Uh-huh." A young boy with sandy blond hair nodded. "Two times."

A smaller, female version of the kid used her left hand to form a peace sign on her right. She was cute, maybe around three or four years old, and looking at him as if he were a freak. "Two time," the little girl repeated.

"Do you play basketball?" the other boy, this one with dark hair and brown eyes, asked. "You're really tall."

"Like a giant," the sandy haired kid added.

The little girl's blue eyes grew big and round as she nodded a headful of curls. She held onto both boys' hands. "I scared."

Fucking great. He'd been in Whispering Pines for less than four hours and had already scared the neighbors' kid. "I'm not scary. What's scary is that you three are roaming the neighborhood without adult supervision. How old are you and what are your names?"

"Oh my God!" A woman from across the circle, and two doors down from the Eastons', rushed from her front porch and toward the cul-de-sac. The man raking leaves from the flowerbeds along the front of the home on the left of hers stopped and watched her race over to them. "I'm so sorry," she called, breathless, and hurried up the driveway. "I didn't know the kids left the house." She dropped on one knee and took the dark-haired boy by the upper arms. "You know you're not allowed to leave without my permission."

He shook her off and stared at her with defiance. "You're not my mom."

"No. Her Step Mommy," the little girl said.

The woman sighed and stood. She offered Sloan a smile and her hand. "Becky Wagner. And this is Lucas." She rested a hand on the boy she'd just scolded. "Alex and Chloe."

Chloe once again used her left hand to make three fingers stand up on her right. "I three year old."

"And I'm six," Alex said. "Lucas is seven."

Whitney's tiny clown car pulled into the driveway. Thank God. He was drowning in a sea of children and wanted to retreat to the safety of the house.

"Hi," Whitney called, pulling a tote bag from the trunk.

"Hi." Becky smiled. "I was just apologizing to your husband about the kids. They were so excited to meet the new neighbors, they couldn't wait for me and their dad."

Whitney's face momentarily took on a blank expression.

Becky looked from Whitney to him, then back to the detective again. "I'm sorry. I just assumed you two were married."

"My Aunt Amanda isn't married and she has four kids with four dads," Alex announced.

Becky put a hand over the boy's mouth. "Hush."

Whitney's cheeks turned that pretty shade of pink he liked. She chuckled as she approached and he took the bag from her. "No, Sloan's my husband. We're newlyweds and the whole husband-wife thing has been hard to get used to." She held out her hand. "Whitney North."

"Good to meet you," Becky said. Then after reintroducing the kids, she asked if they'd met the other neighbors yet.

"No, but we're hoping to get acquainted with everyone on the street once we're settled. We heard this is a quiet neighborhood, which is good since my husband works from home."

Becky cocked a brow and eyed him with interest. "Oh, and what do you do?"

"Web designer."

"What's that?" Lucas asked, screwing up his face.

"Like Spiderman. He spins webs," Alex answered as if his stepbrother were an idiot.

Sloan grinned. "Close, but I make stuff for the Internet." When they both looked at him as if he'd spoken Greek, he added, "You know, the stuff you see on the computer."

Both boys sighed. "I wish you played basketball," Lucas said with disappointment.

Alex nodded. "Or were a ninja warrior. Do you got any kids?"

"No, honey, we don't," Whitney said, then she gave Sloan a wistful smile that—if he didn't know any better—was almost believable. "Maybe someday."

When Becky looked at them expectantly, he wrapped an arm around Whitney and kissed the top of her ponytailed head. Damn, even her hair smelled good. Like flowers and sunshine.

Grinning, Becky ushered the kids off the porch. "We'll let you get to work on that and catch up with you soon. We used to love hanging out with the Smiths—they were the previous owners— and hope to have you over for a cookout once the weather gets a little warmer."

As Becky and her brood crossed the street, the tension stiffening his body abated. He let go of Whitney, then carried the bag into the kitchen. "Is there more?"

Without a word, she nodded and began unpacking the tote.

Whatever. She was probably mad about the kiss, but would have to get used to those little signs of affection. Besides, it'd been her idea to pose as a married couple, not his. Plus, if they were newly married, shouldn't they have their hands all over each other? As he grabbed another bag from the trunk, along with a case of beer, wicked ideas filtered through his dirty mind. He could kiss that sassy, bossy sexy mouth in front of the neighbors and she couldn't knock him upside the head without looking bad. Though amused by the idea of terrorizing her now and then, chances were, he wouldn't bother. Why allow himself a taste of a woman he couldn't have? Why would he want her anyway? If they went on a date, she'd probably make a list of what they should do and check it off in the process. Same if they'd had sex. The bullet points would probably read:

- Kissing
- Heavy petting with clothes on
- Remove clothes
- Oral sex
- Missionary style
- Orgasm

After a final trip to the car, and still amusing himself by creating other lists for her, he came back into the kitchen. Whitney's brows were furrowed with irritation as she stowed groceries in the pantry.

He set a twelve-pack of pop on the lower shelf of the fridge. "What's with you?"

"I introduced myself as Whitney North *not* Brown. Why didn't you correct me? If anyone looks up your real name—"

"It's not my real name."

She faced him, confusion in her eyes. "Sloan North isn't your real name?"

He shook his head. "I changed it after I left Vice. And I know for a fact that you won't find my name anywhere on the CORE website or in articles about the agency." He put away the eggs and milk. "Just tell Becky you goofed and that North was your maiden name."

"Again, a name you didn't correct? No. It'll look suspicious."

"Only if someone is suspecting us of something."

"True." She shrugged. "I suppose it doesn't matter at this point and I'd like to keep minimal contact with Becky anyway."

"Why? She might know the Eastons well."

"Because I think she'd like to get to know you better than well."

Was his fake wife jealous of the cute mom from across the street? "Look, I know you think I'm an arrogant jerk, but I'm definitely no cheater. I will honor my fake vows and stick to business."

"I told you I was sorry for calling you that, and it's not you I'm worried about." She put his popsicles in the freezer, then slammed the door. "Did you see what she was wearing?"

"I guess." He brought the woman to mind and recalled the

tight leggings, equally tight zippered top which revealed a hint of cleavage, and tennis shoes. "Workout gear."

She released an impatient sigh. "Did she look like she just finished exercising? Her hair and makeup were perfect and there wasn't an ounce of sweat on her."

"Maybe she's going to the gym later. Why do you care?"

"Oh, come on. She dressed in that little outfit on purpose."

"That's crazy. The only reason Becky came over was because she didn't realize her kids had come here. I doubt she did anything on purpose."

She released a sarcastic half-laugh. "I do. I bet the ruse of her kids escaping without her knowledge was a bunch of crap. She saw my car wasn't there, and sent the kids over to get you outside."

"I pity your future husband."

The pretty pink returned to her cheeks. "Excuse me?"

He took her by the hand and led her to the stool by the island. "You're paranoid. Men don't like to be around paranoid or jealous women. We want to be trusted and given the benefit of the doubt. You're not married to me, you don't even like me, and here you are throwing a fit over a woman who may or may not be interested in me. Do you hear how...psychotic that sounds?"

She stood, reached up and ran a palm along his jaw. Her touch, the intimate gesture, the fire in her ice blue eyes should've had tension returning to his body. Instead, he wanted to pull her close, kiss her, ease her worries.

"Sloan. My adorably ignorant fake husband. You don't know anything about women, do you?"

The word ignorant penetrated the sensual spell he'd momentarily been under and had him hardening his jaw. "Trust me. I *know* women."

She drew to her tiptoes, making it so her lips were only inches from his. "You know how to satisfy a woman?"

"In more ways than one."

"You can give her pleasure."

"*Exquisite* pleasure."

"Mmm. I bet you're proud of that, aren't you?" she asked, her fiery gaze now darkening with desire.

And yet, he didn't just smell apples and vanilla, he smelled a trap. "I am," he replied with caution. "Mind telling me where you're going with this?"

"My vibrator can give me exquisite physical pleasure, but a humble, intelligent man who respects me and my psychotic opinion can rock my world." She pushed the stool back and stepped away. "Becky is on her second marriage. Her first husband caught her in bed with his best friend and filed for divorce. She still retained custody of their two kids. And, yes, she does go to the gym. But one of the deputies who I had helping me follow and research the people from this street discovered Becky's personal trainer has been giving her a workout that requires condoms, not weights."

He folded his arms across his chest. "Instead of making me feel like a dick, why didn't you say that in the first place? Or maybe you like cutting me down and making yourself look superior?"

"I don't have to do anything to make myself look superior to you."

Another fucking shot. "You're a ballbuster. It's no wonder you're single." God, the woman was both infuriating and sexy. He should fucking hate her, should do something to get himself kicked off the investigation so he didn't have to spend another minute alone with her. Instead, he wanted her back on her tiptoes, her mouth inches from his. Why? He had no clue. It had either been too long since he'd had sex or the air in the suburbs was rotting his brain.

She tightened her ponytail and lifted her chin. "Who said I'm single?"

Whitney had a boyfriend? How could she go into this... marriage, live with him, pretend to be his other half when there was someone else? "Well, he's got to be a wussy if he allowed you to do this with me," he said, an unfamiliar ache blossoming in his chest.

The fire returned in her eyes. "I don't need his permission to do my job."

"Does he know?"

She held his gaze. "No. When this is over, if I'm still talking to you, maybe I'll introduce you to him. Meanwhile, let's just do our jobs without killing each other," she said, leaving the kitchen.

He followed behind. "Where are you going?"

"To shower. Why?"

"We need to talk about our *history*."

An exasperated sigh escaped her parted lips. "Do you really want to be around me?"

Whitney's personality wasn't as straightforward and boring as he'd originally thought. She was intelligent, amusing—in an annoyingly sarcastic way—passive aggressive and a know-it-all ball-breaker. "Yes," he replied, because he'd never had this much fun with a fully clothed woman. "Come on, *wife*, let's go for a walk."

Hand in hand, the dark warrior escorted his snow queen down the street. Between their striking contrast in coloring—him dark, her fair—that was my fairy tale interpretation of the new neighbors.

I let go of the drapes and stepped away from the window, melancholy settling around my heart. While the couple was probably nice, they weren't Jackie and Brett, the previous owners of the house. Jackie... She'd been one of my closest friends. If Brett's job hadn't taken them to St. Louis, Missouri, I wouldn't be spying out of my window like our neighbor, Nell. Jackie and I would be making plans for when I finished my shift at work. A couple glasses of wine around her fire pit sounded heavenly.

With a sigh, I made my way to the kitchen. My husband and kids would be home soon, but not before I left for work. Guilt grabbed hold of me. I could have gone to the soccer games, but had used work as an excuse. Mingling with the other soccer moms, listening to my husband shout from the sidelines, and dealing with 'Mommy, I'm bored, can I have a snack?' from our youngest, was more than I'd wanted this morning. The grieving process wasn't over yet, and I wasn't sure when it would end.

Grieving.

Jackie hadn't died, she'd moved away. When Jackie's husband had found out he would be transferred, Jackie had cried. God, how many nights had I held her, consoled her, told her it'd be okay? At least a month's worth. Jackie and Brett had just finished remodeling their house. Had it exactly the way they'd wanted it, minus finishing their basement, and were trying for a baby.

Tears blurred my vision. Jackie's call last night, the news that she was expecting had made me happy and sad at the same time. They'd had such a hard time getting pregnant, and now I wouldn't be there to help her during the pregnancy, or to hold her new baby.

I prepped salami and cheese sandwiches for the kids to make things easier on my husband. Last night, the melancholy had momentarily slipped when he'd promised to budget for a plane ticket to Missouri once Jackie had the baby, and encouraged me to go visit my friend then. Still, it wasn't the same as living right across the street and being able to bring her casseroles, give her a break so she could nap, or help out in general. And her husband made many promises he couldn't keep.

The house phone rang. Inwardly cringing, I reached for it. Friends and family knew to call our cell phones—the kids tended to leave the cordless phones off the chargers and they were almost always dead—so any calls coming into the landline were usually telemarketers. Except for some of our neighbors. I checked the caller ID. Yep. That'd be Helen, who lived on the right of the dark warrior and snow queen. The woman was sweet, but had perfected the art of being able to talk nonstop without having to breathe. Plus, she was almost as bad as Nosy Nell.

Ignoring the call, I set the phone back on the charger and worked on the sandwiches. Since I had to be at work in thirty minutes, I didn't have time to gossip about neighbors I hadn't met, and would catch up with Helen tomorrow. Unfortunately, my husband's landscaping business demanded that he work on

Sunday. Or rather, Cleveland's unpredictable weather demanded it. With the exception of January, we hadn't had much snow this past winter, which had hurt the plowing side of the business. But my handyman husband and his business partner had kept money coming in through remodeling jobs. The problem was, people were slow to pay.

Which had been why I'd picked up today's shift and missed my kids' soccer games. I finished the sandwiches, bagged them, then placed them in the fridge. They were set for dinner since I'd thrown a chuck roast in the slow cooker, but I hated having to go to work and miss out on what meteorologists predicted would be a warm, sunny day.

Purse in hand, I headed for the door and opened it. I glanced across the street to my friend's old house and, once again, ignored the sadness. Jackie might no longer live there, but maybe another woman, who was just as kind, could be just as good of a friend, now did. I'd find out eventually.

If my husband let me...

Chapter Four

Five days later...

The rental house, North Royalhurst, Ohio
Thursday, 9:08 a.m. Daylight Saving Time

SUBURBIA WAS KILLING Sloan. Why would anyone choose to live here on purpose? The chirping birds, barking dogs, kids' laughter, the hum of a lawnmower, the pounding and banging coming from the construction going on at the new subdivision near their street...it was enough to drive him insane. To think that at one point in his life he'd wanted this. Not anymore. He missed the noise from the traffic outside his downtown Chicago condo, missed the conveniences of city living. Now, if he needed bread or wanted takeout, he had to climb in the truck and drive a full ten minutes to get to a store or restaurant. Nightlife— not that he was here to bar hop—consisted of either a bonfire out back, television or staring out of a window at the Eastons' house. If he were inclined to enjoy a night out, a trip into downtown Cleveland would take him thirty minutes, plus he'd have to pay twenty bucks for parking. Again, why would anyone live in suburbia?

The biggest mystery of the universe: why would anyone live with Whitney?

The Eastons' garage door opened, and Sloan became alert. He watched Dale Easton pull his Audi out of the garage, then drive out of Shady Circle—his personal Hell. He sent a text to Whitney, letting her know Dale had left. She and a few plain-clothed deputies had been following the husband and wife—Irene had left an hour earlier for her photography studio—but had yet to witness anything out of the ordinary. The Easton kids were harder to track. The two older kids had gone back to their respective colleges on Sunday afternoon. BCI had their people watching them. As for the youngest kid, Cameron, after the North Royal-hurst cop had gone missing, the city police had refused to risk another officer, forcing Lieutenant Campbell to plant a deputy at the school. The deputy wasn't posing as another student, but as a custodian. The hope was he'd overhear kids talking or find something in either Cameron Easton's locker, or in one of his buddies'.

On it, Whitney texted back. Typical. Since she'd gone back to work Monday, there hadn't been a single time when she'd called him during the day. She might send the occasional text, wondering if he'd seen any activity at the Eastons', but that was it. She never asked how he was doing, if he needed something from the store, if he was bored, lonely...horny.

His stomach grumbled, replacing the disgust he had for himself for being remotely turned on by a woman who disliked him. With no action happening across the street, he rose from the uncomfortable folding chair he'd found in the basement, along with a card table that served as his desk, and stretched. In need of breakfast, he headed downstairs and into the kitchen, which smelled fantastic, then shook his head. As if someone had thrown up confetti, small, neon yellow sticky notes were stuck to the counter in front of the slow cooker, on the dishwasher, patio door, fridge handle and pantry. He had grown accustomed to Whitney leaving the notes behind, but she'd never left this many.

He lifted the note off the counter: *add noodles at 5*. Noodles? What noodles? He turned to the refrigerator and read that note next: *cooked noodles in bag*. Ah, okay. Made sense. She'd mentioned cooking beef stroganoff at some point this week and that must be what was simmering in the slow cooker.

Not in the mood for eggs and toast, he pulled roast beef, horseradish sauce, lettuce, tomato and Muenster cheese from the fridge, then set what would eventually be his breakfast on the kitchen island. He opened the utensil drawer, noticed there were no knives, then read the note stuck to the dishwasher below the drawer: *Clean.* "Good to know," he mumbled, and retrieved a knife.

He went to the pantry for rye bread and read the note there: *garbage night.* Crap. He would've forgotten. Once he'd made his sandwich, he checked out the note on the patio door: *cut grass, see pantry.*

"Nag." He took down the note and crumpled it. Even when she wasn't here she was telling him what to do and being a total pain in his ass. While he appreciated efficiency and organization, the daily notes annoyed the crap out of him. She loved her damned lists, but why not leave one on the counter instead of a bunch of notes? Better yet, why not call him? He understood their situation was unusual, but they were living together, were supposed to be partners. After all, he kind of cared about how her day had been going, so shouldn't she care about his?

Tired of coffee, he grabbed a Coke from the fridge, his sandwich off the counter, and went into the small office off the foyer There, the furniture was more comfortable than the folding chair in his room, but the view of the Eastons' house wasn't as good, otherwise he'd stay in here. Hell, he'd even sleep in the office, anything to avoid what had become Whitney's nightly ritual. Her need to soak in the tub was becoming a problem for him. Not because it forced him to vacate the room and use the office in order to give her privacy. No, the issue was her damned lotion, soap and girly-smelling stuff. When she'd finished her soak in the evenings and headed for the family room or her own room, she'd leave behind her signature scent, along with a wet towel on the floor, her toiletries on the counter, toothpaste in the sink and, damn, if the woman didn't shed her long blond hair like a dog in Spring. He couldn't believe she still had any hair left on her head.

Even more unbelievable, for as organized as she was, he would've never guessed she'd be such a slob.

Becky's beige minivan backed out of her driveway. He checked his watch. "Right on time." During the past three days, Becky had left at exactly nine twenty-four to take her daughter to preschool. And if it was almost nine-thirty, that meant Vincent would be leaving any minute to walk his little Yorkie, which he, and sometimes Helen, did four times a day—once in the morning, twice in the afternoon, and again in the evening. The rest of the time, if the weather was nice, the dog stayed outside. Barking at squirrels, birds or whatever the hell came near its yard, and driving him nuts.

As Vincent and his dog strolled past the house, Sloan ate his sandwich. One thing he'd take away from this investigation was that the burbs were more fucked up than the ghetto or projects— his usual haunts when he'd been with Vice. This small cul-de-sac held a multitude of personalities, and they all swam together in a collective fish bowl. There was the slut—that'd be Becky Wagner. He hated to admit it, but Whitney had been right about the woman. Monday, after Becky had dropped Chloe off at preschool, she'd stopped by for a visit. He'd made the mistake of answering the door, and had been stunned by not only the way she had been dressed—more skin hugging, cleavage revealing workout wear— but that she'd suggested, with a wink, that they do lunch some-time. Whitney might think he was arrogant, and maybe he was, but he knew women and knew Becky hadn't been referring to getting together to share a sandwich.

Shady Circle also had its gossip: Nell Malinowski, who lived at the corner house across and at the end of the street. According to Whitney, her husband had passed eight years ago, she had a few kids who all lived around the area, and was in her early eighties. He hadn't met Nell yet, but Vincent and Helen Dietrich claimed she was the eyes and ears of the street, making her someone of interest. If she spent her days spying on the people of Shady Circle, she might've seen something of value coming from the Easton residence.

The dickhead neighbor, Joe Griffith, lived on the left of

Becky. While he and Whitney had managed to avoid meeting anyone but the Dietrichs and Becky, he'd had this guy figured out since the day after they'd moved into the rental. He had to give it to the man. His grass looked as if it were carpet, and he liked to sit in his garage, smoking cigarettes and watching that carpet grow. He also enjoyed yelling at any kid who dared to walk on his lawn, retrieve a ball from it, or laugh and yell too loudly. Whitney had informed him that Joe had called the local police to complain about the kids next door to him playing basketball, and how it was too noisy. Apparently, he'd called North Royalhurst PD so many times, they'd told him that unless those boys were vandalizing his property or worse he shouldn't call again.

Nestled between the dick and the Dietrichs lived a family from the Ukraine. Whitney had learned that Pavlo and Oksana Zelenko had been in the States for twelve years, and had moved onto the street six years ago. They had two little girls—Klara was ten and Mila was eight. The Dietrichs had told them the girls were sweet and always outside playing, but that their parents didn't mingle much with the other neighbors because of their broken English and inability to communicate properly—at least that had been their assumption.

Between Becky and the Eastons were Nolan and Vanessa Ainsley, who had three sons—ages twelve, ten and six. Nolan owned a landscaping and handyman business, together with another Shady Circle resident whose family lived diagonally from the rental house. Travis and Amy Murphy also had three sons who were the same ages as the Ainsleys'.

Between the Eastons and the Murphys sat a good-sized colonial that belonged to the Wolffs, a retired couple who also lived in St. Petersburg, Florida, for half the year. Helen said the Wolffs wouldn't return to the Cleveland area until mid-May, which could be good for him and Whitney. Or not. With Rachel's help, he could easily break into their home, disarm their security system and set up video surveillance from the windows facing the Easton house. But by-the-book Whitney probably wouldn't allow him to do that. Which he understood. If they obtained pertinent information about the Eastons illegally, and an arrest was made, they wouldn't be able to use it during a trial.

Quint Oliver, a forty-five-year-old bachelor lived in the house to the rental's left. All Whitney had found out about him was that he was former military—Army—worked for a car dealership, and didn't have a criminal record. Helen had informed them that, other than an occasional wave, the man rarely socialized with the neighbors.

Sloan didn't care about any of these people, except the ones they were investigating. But he did care about making sure the lawn was mowed and the garbage was on the curb before Whitney came home. He'd had enough of her nagging. Since the Eastons weren't around, now was a good time to take care of his chores.

Fifteen minutes later, he had the mower out of the shed, gassed up and ready to go. He hadn't cut grass in nearly two decades, and as he eyed their lawn, he thought about the dick, Joe Griffith, and his emerald green grass. The rental's lawn wasn't exactly brown, but more of a beige olive with smatterings of yellow. If he could make it as green as the dick's, then added brightly colored flowers to the beds, their house would rival Joe's. As he mowed the back, he noticed, at the left corner of the house, a small garden overgrown with weeds. If this were actually his house, he could plant cucumbers, tomatoes, green beans and peppers there. Whitney ate salad with every dinner. He could also plant lettuce in a pot, giving her access to fresh salad fixings all summer long.

When he moved the mower to the front yard, he also considered adding hooks to the porch columns. Colorful hanging baskets, and maybe a couple of giant ferns, would look nice, along with wicker furniture. Now that he thought about it, they didn't have patio furniture, and he'd been forced to use one of the folding chairs when he'd sat by the fire Sunday evening—by himself. A trip to Home Depot or Lowes would solve his problem. And maybe if she had something comfy to sit on, Whitney might join him next to the fire one night. Which would be nice. In Chicago, he had cop buddies, acquaintances from the bars or restaurants he frequented, and a few lady friends. He rarely sat at home and was always busy. Here, he had no one, and had never experienced this kind of isolation—and he lived with a living, breathing human being. The only time they truly talked was during dinner—those conversations were forced, shallow—or when they bickered. While he loved the way she looked when they argued—the passion in her eyes, her flushed cheeks, the way she'd toss that long blond hair over her shoulder or run her fingers through it—he was tired of arguing.

Damn it, he was tired of being alone. He hated it here and saw no need to invest the sheriff's department's money into flowers and furniture. Then again, if they could at least sit on the front porch, they'd be able to watch the Eastons without the family suspecting anything. And if they invited the couple over, they'd need a place to sit out back. Plus, buying and putting together furniture would give him something to do. Decision made, he finished the lawn, then headed for the store.

Three hours later, he returned home with a truckload of furniture, as well as a few large outdoor planters, soil and ferns. The lady at Home Depot had told him to hold off on planting or hanging flowers, since it was only the end of April and they could still see cold weather. Wanting to impress the neighbors, he'd bought them anyway. Because he wouldn't be there long enough to enjoy the plants and flowers, it didn't matter if they died. What mattered was making it appear as if he and Whitney were there to stay, and to build trust with the neighbors. And maybe the flowers would put a smile on Whitney's face. A genuine one. Not the fake, sarcastic smile he'd come to loathe.

"Whatcha have there?" Vincent asked as he and his Yorkie approached.

"Outdoor furniture. When I was growing up, I lived in an old farmhouse with a wraparound porch. I used to love hanging out there and doing my homework." All true, even the homework part. Though he'd never been book-smart and had struggled in school, his mom had worked with him, helped him study, and used to reward him with his favorite dessert when he'd passed a tough test. God, how he missed her. He'd give anything for one of her hugs. He cleared his throat when he realized Vincent was staring at him expectantly. "Anyway, I haven't had a place with a porch since, and want to enjoy this one."

Vincent nodded. "We love ours. Nothing like sitting outside on a nice evening, drinking a beer and watching the kids play a game of kickball in the cul-de-sac."

That sounded about as boring as watching golf or professional baseball. "I'm looking forward to doing just that."

"You and Whitney better get to making babies before all the kids on the street are grown and they have no one to play with but each other." His neighbor grinned. "Children were scarce where we used to live, and our son and daughter hated it. We did, too. Helen used to bitch about having to chauffeur them to friends' houses or the mall." He shrugged. "But we all survived."

Sloan hauled the wicker loveseat from the truck bed, then set it on the driveway. "Your grass is almost as green as Joe's," he said to derail the conversation from kids, since that wouldn't be happening. "Do you have a company fertilize it?"

"That'd be the one Travis and Nolan own." Vincent winked. "We all use them, and get a nice Shady Circle discount. Pop over to Nolan's place and talk to him about it. He's the one who sets the schedule."

After thanking Vincent, and making a mental note to do that this week, Sloan took the loveseat to the porch. Ninety minutes later, he stood in the backyard and admired his handy work. The table and chairs he'd put together looked nice, but the patio needed planters potted with flowers. Since it was getting late in the afternoon, and the Eastons would be arriving home soon, he'd take care of that tomorrow.

He gathered the packaging the table and chairs had come in, then went to the front to put it in the trash cans he'd left at the curb. As he finished, a black pickup truck pulled into the Murphys' driveway. Seconds later, both Travis Murphy and Nolan Ainsley climbed out of the truck. Figuring now was a good time to ask about lawn service, Sloan called to the men, then crossed the street and met them on the sidewalk.

"Vincent told me you guys take care of fertilizing the lawns on the street," he said after introducing himself to them.

"That's right." Travis nodded. "We mow Nell's grass and take care of her flowers and mulch, too."

"I won't be needing help with that, but I'd like my grass to be as green as Joe's"

Both men grinned. "Good luck with that," Nolan said. "See, your grass, just like mine and everyone else's on the street, is called Bentgrass. It's not the greatest and if it's not watered enough during the summer or fertilized properly, it'll go dormant and start turning brown. That's what happened to your yard last summer, and because no one has been living at the house since the fall, it s why your grass looks like Hell."

"But," Travis added, "Joe doesn't have Bentgrass. Last spring, he had us tear up his entire yard and seed it with Kentucky bluegrass, which is heartier and thicker."

Sloan highly doubted the sheriff's department would pay to have his lawn replaced. As it was, he had a feeling the outdoor furniture would be on his dime. Since his condo offered zero outdoor space, he'd probably end up selling it, or maybe he'd give it to Whitney as a parting gift. "Sounds like a big project. I don't think my wife will want to get into it this year, but maybe next spring."

"Besides the watering, making sure birds don't eat your seed or deer leave prints on the ground, it's more of a hassle than anything." Nolan rested a hand on Travis's shoulder. "Now if you want to talk about a big project, just look at my buddy over here."

Travis adjusted his ball cap. "No shit. I wish I'd let you talk me out of it."

"What's the project?" Sloan asked, curious. The other day, Vincent and Helen had mentioned having their home painted in May, and had also told them they'd heard the Eastons were having their basement waterproofed next week. Being a homeowner involved major expenses. Hell, the crap he'd bought today had cost him over a grand, even on sale, which was why he'd stick to renting. After growing up poor and watching his parents work themselves to an early grave, he preferred easy and low-maintenance.

"I'm in the process of putting in a pool and new patio out back," Travis said, thumbing toward his house. "It's destroying the yard, so when I'm finished I'll be planting Kentucky bluegrass. I'm hoping to do the same for the front before the end of the summer."

A pool would be a nice addition to the rental property. Which had him wondering if Whitney would wear a one or two-piece bathing suit. With how prissy and prudish she was, she'd probably hide her long legs and curves beneath a wetsuit. "In-ground or above?" he asked.

"A bit of both. I'm actually taking an above-ground pool and dropping it so it looks as if it's in-ground. I've got the equipment, so I figured why not do that and make the pool less of an eyesore? Then I'm going to have a concrete patio poured around it."

"I'm looking forward to barbeques and pool parties at your house," Nolan said. "If you help me finish my basement, I'll help you finish the pool."

Did everyone on the street have a freaking house project? "What are you doing to your basement?"

"Have you met the Eastons? They live next door to me." Nolan pointed to the house three doors down. "We both ended up with water in the basement, the Wagners, too, so I'm having it waterproofed."

"Construction workers building that new development next to ours hit a water line," Travis explained as sirens wailed in the distance.

Nolan frowned. "Bastards. Water damage ruined my carpet and drywall. Now I have to replace everything."

Travis chuckled and looked toward the new subdivision he'd mentioned as more sirens made their way in that direction. "He's not just replacing, he's adding walls and putting in a three-quarter bath. It'll be a great guest suite."

"If I ever finish it. And, yeah, that was a hint that I could use help breaking up concrete." Nolan sized up Sloan. "You're a big guy. How about you come by this weekend and lend a hand? A beer for every swing of the sledgehammer."

"Oh, hell." Travis grinned. "We do that and nothing will get done." His smile fell and he looked back toward the neighboring development. "I wonder what's going on over there," he said as a North Royalhurst school bus stopped at the end of Shady Circle and in front of Nell's house.

"Maybe someone was hurt at the construction site," Nolan replied, while the ten school-aged kids who lived on their street exited the bus.

"Dad!" A brown-haired boy, who looked about eleven or twelve, rushed toward them, his backpack bouncing. "Guess what?"

"Wait up," several other boys shouted.

"What is it, bud?" Travis asked, and ruffled the kid's mop of hair.

Excitement brightened the boy's eyes and face. "Did you hear the sirens?"

"Yeah, did you?" Another little boy caught up with the older one, while the littlest trailed behind them with the other kids. "You should've seen how many police cars passed our bus. There were, like, fifteen or something."

"There were not, dummy," the older boy said.

"Knock it off," Travis scolded him.

"Well, there weren't." The boy squared his shoulders. "I counted nine."

"And they all drove into Potter's Field," the youngest of the three said, while Travis laughed.

The little boy frowned. "What's funny about that?"

Sloan hoped Travis was laughing because the kid had messed up the name. Considering Potter's Field referred to a cemetery for criminals, the poor and unclaimed bodies, there wasn't anything about funny about calling a subdivision after a graveyard.

"Nothing son, but it's called *Otter's* Field. Now go inside and get yourselves a small snack. And I mean *small*. I don't want your mom mad at me." As the three boys raced off and then another three surrounded Nolan, Travis laughed again. "That boy is something else."

"Was he talking about the new subdivision?" Sloan asked.

"Yeah, Otter's Field at Whispering Pines is the official name."

"Which is dumb," Nolan said. "I don't think there's been an otter spotted in this part of Ohio since the early 1900s."

"What's an otter?" the little boy standing next to Nolan asked.

"Come on, let's go home. I'll pull a picture of one up on my phone and show you." As he walked off with his three sons, he glanced over his shoulder. "Think about that sledgehammer and beers," he called with a smile.

Laughing and squealing, Becky's boys, along with the Ukrainian girls, raced past Nolan and his kids, just as a car sped down their short street. Anger shot up Sloan's spine. Cameron Easton had a fucking lead foot, and if he wasn't careful, he could kill one of those kids.

"Little bastard," Travis murmured, then, when Cameron had parked on the apron of his driveway and got out of the car, he shouted, "Slow down or I'm calling the cops."

Cameron gave Travis the finger.

"Prick." He sighed and shook his head. "I should call the police. I'm not the only one on the street who's said something to his parents about his speeding."

"And?" Sloan prompted him, interested in anything he had to say about the Eastons. "Did they talk to him?"

"They said they would, and maybe they did, but the kid still keeps doing it. Unless Mom or Dad is home." He released another sigh. "I better get inside and make sure those monkeys aren't destroying the house. And, hey, even if you don't feel like working, you should stop by Nolan's on Saturday for a few beers."

Considering Whitney kept to herself and he spent most of his time alone, the idea of hanging out with the guys appealed to him. Sloan told Travis he'd have to make sure his *wife* didn't have any plans, then headed back to the rental. Now that Cameron was home, it was time to get back to the real reason he was living in suburbia.

The rental house, North Royalhurst, Ohio
Thursday, 5:36 p.m. Daylight Saving Time

A delicious aroma wafted from the kitchen. Whitney's stomach growled and her mouth watered as she shut the laundry room door and made her way into the house. She'd been stuck in a car all day and, other than a yogurt and banana for breakfast, she'd had nothing but a packet of cheese crackers. When Sloan had let her know that Dale Easton had left his house, she'd assigned another deputy to watch Irene's photography studio, then had used the GPS tracking device they'd placed on Dale's car to find his location. She could've stopped at a fast food restaurant at that point, but hadn't been in the mood for processed grease.

When she reached the kitchen, she pulled a water bottle from the fridge, then drank half of it. She also hadn't had much to drink today because she hadn't wanted to deal with finding a place to go to the bathroom. After another sip, she lifted the lid on the slow cooker. "Damn it," she muttered. Sloan had had three jobs: add the noodles, mow the lawn and take out the trash. He'd done two out the three, which she appreciated, and had apparently gone shopping. Why would he buy furniture without talking to her first? He couldn't expect the sheriff's department to pay for it. As it was, the operation had already cost the department quite a bit of money.

After adding the noodles, then setting the timer for twenty minutes, she made her way to her room to change. When she reached the top of the steps and heard Sloan talking, she went to the master bedroom.

"Call me when they're heading our way," he said, then set the phone on the card table.

"Who was that?" she asked.

"Andy. I let him know the Eastons left. He's going to have a deputy follow them."

"All three left?"

He nodded. "I'd love to get inside their house and plant a few bugs. We need audio."

"We wiretapped their cell phones months ago and that's resulted in no new leads."

"Which is why we need to put listening devices within their home and vehicles. How much do you want to bet they're using burner phones for drug transactions? That's probably why your people aren't getting anything from them."

"I don't need to take that bet because I agree with you. The problem is, we have no proof they have burners." She glanced toward the window and at the Eastons' house, where the sun began to dip behind it. "Our wiretapping software enables us to activate the microphones on any of their known cell phones and, if the phone is on standby and a conversation takes place near it, we can hear what they're saying. Unfortunately, they all turn off their phones when they're home."

"Then they're paranoid, or know someone is watching them."

"But they don't act paranoid. At all. My gut says they have no idea we're watching them, and that they're being overly cautious. Think about it. Less than two years ago, these were regular people, not drug dealers. If they're working for Morales, I'm sure he's schooled them on the art of caution." The timer beeped from the kitchen. "Crap."

"What's wrong?" he asked, closing the blinds.

"Dinner's done and I didn't have a chance to make a salad."

His face fell with apology. "I forgot about the noodles. Sorry. You go change, and I'll make your salad," he said, ushering her toward her room.

"That's okay. You don't know what I like."

"I've watched you eat one every night since we've been here. Trust me. I know."

As he walked off and she went into her room to change, she considered Cliff. She'd had dinner with him at least a half-dozen times or more over the past two months. Would he know what she liked in her salad? Now that she thought about it, did Cliff even eat salads? She knew Sloan didn't mind them, just not every time they sat down for dinner. He was definitely a meat and potatoes guy and loved his sweets. Like her, he preferred his coffee black. She couldn't remember whether Cliff used cream or sugar with his. Sloan loved listening to classic rock and watching action movies or comedies. He had no use for social media unless he was monitoring a suspect, and still preferred to read an actual newspaper. Who still did that? Cliff? Not likely. She couldn't say what type of music Cliff listened to because if they drove in his car, he always had on a news station.

She stowed her shoulder holster and weapon in the closet, but kept the ankle glove and gun tucked beneath her lounge pants. After freeing her hair of the bun she'd had knotted on her head since six this morning, she massaged her scalp, then her temples where a slight headache had been bothering her all day. Lately, she'd lost her ability to concentrate on anything but...Sloan. While following one of the Eastons, she would sit in her car wondering what Sloan was doing and if he was just as bored as her. All week, there'd been numerous times throughout the day where she'd dialed his number, then ended the call before it had connected. Sloan was a capable investigator, and she didn't want him to think she was checking up on him. And if she'd called him just to say 'hi' then he might think she actually cared. Which she did, but strictly as a partner.

With a sigh and her stomach growling, she left the bedroom. What she needed was to stay focused on the investigation and stop thinking about Sloan and comparing him to Cliff. She'd never been the type to let a little man-candy screw with her head, so why was she allowing that to happen now? She wasn't lonely, wasn't looking to escape her regular life, and she certainly wasn't looking for a hot, sensual fling. She wanted marriage, friendship and trust. To build a life with a man who accepted her for all her faults, who was reliable, caring, humble and yet strong. The only one of those qualities Sloan possessed was strength. But, to her, muscles weren't the only things that made a man strong.

Stop thinking about him.

But it was so damned hard to stop herself from thinking, imagining, fantasizing...

"What do you want to drink?" he asked as she entered the kitchen.

She stopped near the counter and stared at the table he'd set

Sure enough, he'd made her a salad just the way she liked it, and had also placed her favorite dressing on the table, next to a glass of ice water. "Water is good. Thanks for making my salad. Why don't you sit down and let me plate the food?"

"Nope, I've got it." He spooned beef stroganoff and noodles onto a plate, then set it by her salad. "How was your day?" he asked, filling his own dish.

God, she was a shit. She hadn't even said hello to him when she'd come home. Instead, she'd immediately discussed the case. What was wrong with her? She was usually more polite than that, and considerate of others. She wanted to blame Sloan for climbing into her head and scrambling it, but knew the fault lay with her. She had a crush on her partner and couldn't do anything about it. "Good. Yours?"

His dark eyes twinkled as he grinned. "Boring as hell at first. But then——"

"You went shopping." When his smile fell, regret had her wishing she'd kept her mouth shut. "Shopping always makes me happy," she said to clarify.

His smile returned. "Spending over a grand on everything I bought didn't make me happy, but my purchases definitely did. Do you like the furniture?"

"I only saw it when I was pulling into the garage, but it's a dark wicker, right?"

His eyes flickered with disappointment. "Yes, and the cushions are red. I figured since the house is white and the door and shutters are black, that the red would look nice."

Impressed, because she wasn't bold enough to buy anything red, she was now anxious to finish dinner and check out what he'd bought. "That does sound like it'll add a pop of color, but you realize the sheriff's department probably won't pay for that, or whatever you spent on the hanging baskets. They do look great, though."

"I figured as much," he said, then ate a forkful of stroganoff. "This," he motioned toward his plate, "is awesome. Everything you've cooked so far has been just as good. If we don't wrap up this investigation soon, I'm going to end up getting fat."

"Not when you're up every morning to go for a five-mile run."

"I'm only working out to burn calories so I can eat what you make."

He needed to stop being sweet, otherwise she would never be able to get the man out of her head. "Then maybe on Saturday I'll make something with tofu. That way you won't have to run as many miles." When his face screwed up, she laughed and promised she wouldn't do that to him. "Thanks for taking care of the grass and garbage. I'll unload the dishwasher after dinner."

"Yeah, I didn't have time to get to it. After I finished putting the patio furniture together, I met Travis Murphy and Nolan Ainsley."

"Wait, you bought stuff for out back, too? Sloan, it's too much. We should've talked about this first."

He half shrugged. "Why?"

"Because that's a lot of money and we're…" What? A couple? "Let me talk to Campbell. Maybe he'll be able to get the department to reimburse you. I'll suggest they donate the two sets to a charity."

He rose, then helped himself to more stroganoff. "Don't worry about it. I'm not loaded, but I do okay. I was thinking about giving the sets to you. I noticed you didn't have any on your porch, so consider it a wedding gift," he said with a grin.

Now she really wanted to see the furniture. She wasn't exactly cheap, but she was most certainly frugal. The old patio set on her own small back porch had been purchased at a garage sale. With the exception of her bedroom set—a college graduation present from her parents—even the furniture inside her house was secondhand. For the past ten years, she'd been saving for a house, and was close to reaching her goal. The main reason she'd been able to save so much on her own was because she'd been careful with her money, hit thrift stores and garage sales, and cut coupons.

"I can't accept the patio sets. It's just too much," she said, setting her fork on the empty plate.

"Too bad." He sat back down. "It's not like I'm going to rent a truck and haul it back to Chicago. I don't have anywhere to put it anyway."

"Maybe you'll buy a house someday soon."

He speared a piece of meat. "Nope."

What was wrong with him? Who wouldn't want to be a home-owner? "Why not? I've been saving for years. I'm sick of renting and paying down someone else's mortgage."

"I agree with you on that point, but I don't want to deal with the maintenance that goes along with owning a house. Vincent and Helen are having their house painted. I looked up the average cost and it came in around twenty-five hundred. The Eastons and the Ainsleys are having their basements waterproofed because of a busted pipe coming from the new subdivision. I looked that up, too, and it's about four grand. Plus, Nolan is adding a bathroom to the basement, new carpet and drywall—which can't be cheap. Then there's Travis who is putting in a pool, new patio and yard."

"Did you look up the cost for that, too?" she asked, amused by this strange side of him. She took a drink of water. For a man who wanted nothing to do with owning a house, he was taking great interest in the price of projects.

"I didn't have time, but I will. Speaking of Travis and Nolan...I'm thinking about having their company take care of fertilizing the lawn. Ours is embarrassing and the worst on the street."

She choked on the water. When the coughing jag that followed had subsided, she wiped her watery eyes. "Sorry about that, but, um, what's going on here? For someone who hates suburbia and doesn't ever want to be a homeowner, you're taking pride in living here."

"No. I just want it to look like we're here to stay. We need to build trust with these people. Which I plan to do Saturday when I go over to Nolan's."

"The neighbors invited us over? Did you ask what we could bring?"

"No, just the guys." After wiping his mouth with his napkin, he leaned back and let out a sigh. "Yeah, we're going to break up the concrete in his basement to make way for the bathroom he wants to build. It'll be cool to hang out with them."

How nice for him. While he had fun with the guys, she'd be stuck working. "So, you can build trust and maybe find out a little more about the Eastons, correct?" she asked, not bothering to hide her irritation. If he were going to be in the Eastons' basement, she wouldn't complain. After all, they were the reason why they were here.

"Exactly." He brightened. "Did you hear about what happened at the new subdivision? The kids said nine police cars went in there this afternoon."

The man was either clueless or didn't care about how she might feel about his spending Saturday with the boys. She picked up her plate and stood. "What kids?"

"Travis's." He chuckled. "The youngest one...how old is he?"

"Six, and his name is Parker."

"That explains it. Anyway, the kid called the subdivision Potter's Field, when it's actually *Otter's* Field."

"I don't know, I think Parker had it right the first time. Workers unearthed a body there." Anxious to be alone, preferably in a tub filled with hot water and bubbles, she took her dish to the sink. She didn't know what switch had been flipped, but this talkative Sloan was confusing and frustrating. While she understood they were undercover and needed to insinuate themselves amongst the people of their small circle, where did she fit into the mix? Had he bothered to consider her and how she might spend Saturday?

"Really?" He also rose and began clearing the table. "What'd you hear about it?"

"That's pretty much it. Andy mentioned it to me when I talked to him during the drive home. I mean, to here," she amended. This wasn't her home, even if she'd love it to be hers. The previous owners had her taste and style. If she were to buy this place, the only thing she would do—eventually—was finish the basement. Maybe make it a playroom for future children.

"Just one body?" he asked, his forearm rubbed against hers as he rinsed his dish.

His close proximity, heat and masculine scent had her stepping back and toward the slow cooker. Damn it, she hated and loved when that happened. The accidental touch, the occasional brush. Skin on skin… But this was business. A job. Since he'd made plans for Saturday without talking to her, he clearly didn't think much of her, or care. "I don't know anything more than that. Andy heard about it and mentioned it because the dump site is less than a mile from our house."

"If he's suggesting it's a dump site, that tells me he knows more about it."

She let out a breath and dried her hands with a paper towel. "That's all I know, and I honestly don't care. What I care about is getting something viable from the Eastons so we can wrap this up and leave."

His brows lifted. "What's with you? Why are you all snappy?"

She turned to the fridge and opened it. A glass of wine to go along with her bath would be wonderful. Until they somehow bugged the Eastons, this was nothing but a watch and wait game. And she'd like to do that relaxed. "I'm not snappy, but I'm not happy. Did it ever occur to you that I'd made plans for Saturday?"

He leaned against the kitchen island, and she hated that he could make a casual stance so damned sexy. Hated herself for wanting to explore his body, for memorizing his tattoos and wanting to run her fingers along them. Even more, she hated that because he didn't like her, she'd been spending the past five days wondering why. Was it her lists? The notes she left for him? Or maybe he preferred smaller women with voluptuous bodies. Damn it, she hated herself for caring what he thought about her. This was business, and it was wrong—on so many levels—to be attracted to her partner.

"I…you mean for us?" he asked. "What kind of plans did you make for that day?"

"I don't have any, I'm just saying. It was rude of you to agree to do something without talking to me first. For the record, I wouldn't do that to you."

He swiped a hand along his forehead and released a sigh. "I wasn't trying to be rude. I was trying to—"

"Hang out with the guys," she finished for him. "Got it."

A grin tugged at his mouth. "Are you jealous I have something to do?"

Yes. "No. But if we're going to get anywhere with the Eastons, *those* are the people we need to befriend."

"Don't you think that *they'd* think it was weird if we came on strong?"

Of course she'd thought about that. "I do, but having beers with…" God, she *did* sound jealous. "You know what? It's all good. I'll make my own plans. Maybe I'll get together with my boyfriend."

He pushed off the counter and invaded her space. "Who's going to monitor the Eastons?"

She loved and hated when he stood so close, that he was within reach, but couldn't touch him. "I will. I'll tell him I'm house-sitting and watch them."

His eyes narrowed. "From where?"

"The office, living room…your bedroom. I'll make it like I'm giving him a house tour. Don't worry. I promise we won't mess up your sheets," she said, wanting him to wonder, to be jealous, to actually see her as a woman and not a partner. Which was stupid. And she didn't do stupid. He didn't even like her.

His face hardened. "I can't picture you doing that anyway, so that's not what I'm worried about. What worries me is that you're bringing a man into the house while I'm not here. What will the neighbors think?"

He couldn't picture her doing what? Having sex? God, the man truly was a jerk and knew how to strip away her confidence. And she'd thought she could make him jealous. Apparently, she did do stupid. She wouldn't any longer, and would have to remember moments like these when images of him invaded her late-night fantasies. "If anyone asks, I'll tell them he's my brother."

"Whatever." He left her space. "If you're going to take a bath, you might as well do it before the Eastons get home."

She pulled a bottle of wine from the refrigerator. "That was my plan."

"Good. By the way, I got another delivery today from CORE. Rachel—she's the research person I told you about—sent me an infrared device that will trigger the video camera I have aimed at the Eastons' house. I placed it in one of the hanging baskets. If someone comes or goes, it'll trigger the camera and record them." His mouth slid into a small smile. "I'm tired of watching these people sleep during the night. Now I won't have to do that."

Guilt gave her a quick jab. Sloan had mentioned the other day that he would sleep an hour, check the camera, sleep some more, then do it all over again. She'd offered to take shifts with him, but he'd declined, saying when they were gone during the day he could catch an hour or two's nap.

"That's great. I know it's been rough on you," she said, shaking off the guilt and trying to infuse sympathy into her tone. Which was hard considering he'd just insulted her. She also didn't know why the *hanging with the guys* thing bothered her. Maybe, on some level, she'd expected him to spend time with her, like he had last Saturday after they'd unpacked. While she'd understood that the walk they'd taken, and how they'd held hands had been for show, she'd...liked it. Liked that they'd joked around about their fake lives, and the stories they would tell the neighbors. Mostly, secretly, she'd loved the way his big hand had swamped hers. The way he'd brush up against her, and how it had conjured up daydreams of what she had wanted for the future...marriage, kids, the house on the cul-de-sac. "I'll get my bath out of the way so you can sleep."

With a glass of wine, she left the kitchen before he could say anything else. He and this operation were messing with her head. She'd always been focused on the future, had her plan mapped out with the sheriff's department, had money saved for a house, had been dating a nice guy who was potential husband material... so why did she keep thinking about Sloan? Why was she suddenly longing for passion in her life?

While she soaked in the tub, she called Cliff, hoping he'd help take Sloan off her mind. Unfortunately, he was in a heated battle of Dungeons and Dragons with his friends. That used to be kind of cute to her, but now... "I won't keep you," she said, stretching her legs and loving the way the warm water enveloped her body. "Are you free Saturday?"

"Sorry, I'm not," he replied, then said something to one of his friends. "Maybe we can get together Sunday."

Surprised she wasn't disappointed, she told him she'd let him know, then ended the call and dialed Morgan's number. Fortunately, her friend was available Saturday, and she wouldn't have to be stuck at the house alone, pathetically wondering if Sloan was having fun *hanging with the guys.*

A knock came at the door as she was exiting the tub. Knowing Sloan was on the other side and only a few feet from her naked body had her nipples hardening. Damn it. She was upset with him, which was ridiculous. They weren't married. He didn't have to ask permission to go to Nolan Ainsley's for a few beers, and besides, he might discover useful information that could help their investigation.

"I'm almost finished," she said, applying her granny lotion. Once finished, she slipped into her bathrobe. When she stepped on her wet towel, she retrieved it and placed it on the wall hook. She'd noticed Sloan was a neat freak, and didn't want him thinking she was a slob. She shouldn't care what he thought about her. He certainly wasn't perfect. After running a brush through her hair, she gathered her clothes from the floor, then opened the door.

Sloan looked sexy and inviting lying on the center of the bed, pillows propped behind him. "Did you pick up your towel?" he asked, and used the remote to turn on the television.

The steam from her bath made the room hot and had her anxious to get to her own room so she could remove her robe. "I did," she said, moving toward the door.

"Is your boyfriend coming over Saturday?" he asked, and she couldn't be certain, but she swore there was bitterness in his tone.

"He is," she lied. Morgan was a good-looking man, and this wouldn't be the first time he'd pretended to not be gay and acted as if he were her boyfriend.

"For the record, I think it's a mistake." He kept his focus on the TV and cruised through the channels. "I certainly wouldn't bring one of my many women here. It's…inconsiderate. I mean, look how jealous you were over Becky, and I'm not remotely interested in her."

Jealous? She hadn't been jealous of the petite, curvy woman or her abundant cleavage. Not really. Maybe a little. Becky was an attractive woman who oozed sensuality, whereas, with the exception of a blister, she didn't know how to make anything ooze.

"I wasn't jealous of Becky, and I wouldn't be jealous of one of your *many* women." God, the man was arrogant and knew how to aggravate her. "Since you're the one acting weird about my boyfriend coming over, maybe you're the one who's jealous."

Within seconds, he was off the bed and crowding her at the doorway. "I'd have to be attracted to you for that to happen." When his gaze dipped to her breasts, she clutched the lapels of the robe. "But if I *was* interested, I'd make it so you wouldn't be able to remember your boyfriend's name."

"Why? Would you drug me? Because that'd be the only way you'd ever be able to get me into your bed."

She ducked under his arm and stepped into the hallway. He was being such a major prick today, and she didn't want to be around him or talk to him for the rest of the night.

"Trust me, I wouldn't need drugs to seduce you," he said, leaning against the doorjamb and looking way too cocky.

"Do you realize the things you're saying border on sexual harassment?"

He covered his mouth and yawned. "Do you realize I could accuse you of the same? Remember, you're using my bathroom."

"So what?"

"You're the lead on this investigation and I work for you. And you have forced me to be outside the bathroom door while you're naked. It's very sick and twisted and it will probably scar me. At least that's what I could tell your lieutenant."

"You know what? I take it back. You're not just a jerk, you're an asshole."

He grinned. "I know. Good night, *wife*." He started to close the door, then stopped. "Don't be surprised if I lock the door tonight. I don't want to have to worry about you ravaging me."

She gave him the finger, then turned toward her room. His laughter chased her down the hallway and infuriated her. *He* infuriated her. He was also right, in a ridiculous and ignorant way. Neither of them were acting like professionals and they both had said and done inappropriate things. Plus, being around Sloan had dropped her maturity level and had her acting as if she were in middle school. Having Morgan pretend to be her boyfriend in order to make Sloan jealous was a stupidly ridiculous idea and she had no intention of going through with it. What would be the point?

I'd have to be attracted to you for that to happen.

She slumped on the bed and tried to tamp down the hurt. Because, despite that he could be a condescending jerk, Sloan also had a funny, sweet and considerate side to him, which she found very attractive. Add on his hard chest, muscular arms, sexy mouth and...

Give up, Whitney. He's not into you.

She convinced herself that it was a good thing he didn't like her. She wanted a safe, nice accountant, not a barbaric, lustful animal.

Well, maybe she did, but only for one night. One glorious, orgasmic night.

She let out a sigh.

Bad Whitney...

Chapter Five

S LOAN INHALED APPLES and vanilla, then pressed on his arousal. His heart still beat hard from having to call on every ounce of his willpower and not wind up being slapped by either Whitney, or a major sexual harassment suit, or both. Damn, he'd wanted to shove that robe off her shoulders, then drop to his knees and press his mouth against her heat.

He grabbed the air freshener from the sink and sprayed the bathroom to rid it of her signature scent. After closing the door behind him, he paced in front of the bed. He'd worked tough undercover assignments in the past, had been shot, beaten and up against some of the baddest, meanest motherfuckers out there. Right now, he'd rather be dodging bullets or fists, than under the same roof as Whitney. He had no right to want her, no right to be jealous that she had a boyfriend, yet he couldn't help himself. Until the investigation closed, she was his fake wife, and she needed to honor their fake vows. He wasn't sure how he planned to convince her of this, but would figure out a way without letting her know the effect she had on him. Physically, of course, because she wasn't a nice person. After all the money he'd spent today and the work he'd put into the patio set, she hadn't even gone outside to look at the furniture.

And why had it bothered her that he planned to go to Nolan's on Saturday? He supposed he could've asked. After all, he'd told Nolan he would have to check with the wife, but had only said that because he figured it was a good 'husband' response. Clearly it *was* the right response, and he'd made a major error by not talking Saturday over with Whitney first.

Now he had to deal with her boyfriend coming into their home, eating their food and sitting on their furniture. And if he smelled the slightest trace of her lotion on his sheets after the boyfriend left, he'd... He didn't know what he would do, but it would probably be ugly and immature. Which was exactly how the princess down the hall made him feel. Ugly, unwanted, useless and childish. Damn it, he was a grown man, and they were running an investigation. This wasn't a vacation, or a time to think about sex. This was about stopping drug dealers before more kids died.

Thinking about death had him considering the body found in the subdivision. How long had it been there? Was it a male or female? Old or young? How had the victim been killed? All morbid questions, but he'd rather focus on murder than Whitney —her long legs, round ass, curvy hips and...

He needed to be out of the fucking house and away from her. After putting on his tennis shoes and grabbing a sweatshirt from the dresser, he pocketed his cell phone, then left the room. He stopped at the top of the steps and debated whether he should tell her he was leaving. That would be the considerate thing to do. What if she came to his room, saw he was gone and worried something had happened to him? *Would* she worry about his safety? Other than his boss and coworkers, no one else did.

Because there is no one else...

Maybe that was the crux of the problem. He'd been living alone since he was eighteen. Other than answering to his superiors, he enjoyed the freedom to do as he pleased. Unlike his married neighbors and coworkers, he didn't have to ask for permission or call anyone to say he'd be running late. No one nagged him or left To Do notes all around the house. No one stole his covers, messed up his bathroom or snuggled next to him during the night. He might like the snuggle thing, but not enough to strap himself to a woman. He'd tried commitment twice, and both times had ended in rejection, which was why he didn't want a relationship. He'd never be smart and sophisticated—like Shannon had wanted—and because of his career choice, Ellie could have been killed. While she was now fine, married to a good guy and raising two kids, he still couldn't shake the guilt, just as he couldn't shake the past, couldn't go back in time and take a different, less dangerous job.

With a sigh and regret needling him, he approached Whitney's closed door. He hadn't been nice to her, and said many shitty things because he could picture her having sex—only with him, of course—and because he was jealous. Now he'd do the right thing, take her feelings into consideration and let her know he was going for a walk. Before he could knock, the door opened. Whitney gasped and held her robe closed. "You scared me. Is something wrong? Are the Eastons home?"

"Sorry. Nothing is wrong and they're not home yet. What were you going to do?"

"Get a water." Frowning, she tossed her long blond hair over her shoulder. He loved her hair and wanted it draped along his body, teasing his bare skin. "Why were you at my door?"

He cleared his throat. "I need fresh air and thought I'd go for a walk. I wanted to let you know in case you came to my room looking for me." He held up a hand. "Not that you would for anything other than the investigation."

A small grin played along her kissable lips. "I get it. Thank you for being thoughtful enough to tell me."

"You're welcome." He took a backward step. "I won't be long, and I'll lock up behind me."

"I have two guns," she reminded him. "Other than drug dealers and the dead body in the subdivision, this is a safe neighborhood."

"Right. Drugs, murder, no big deal." He inched closer to the staircase. "So…I'll see you in a bit."

"Okay, enjoy your walk," she said, disappointment in her eyes.

Had she thought he'd stopped by her room to apologize? *Should* he apologize? Probably, but, once again, they'd *both* said nasty things to each other. When he reached the front door, he decided he'd think about how to handle their argument during his walk. Whenever Whitney was around, he had a hard time concentrating on anything but her scent, curves and smile. Which needed to stop. They were almost a week into the investigation and had yet to obtain any new leads. He needed to come up with a way to get inside the Eastons' house, and he wouldn't be able to come up with a plan if all he kept thinking about was Princess Nag-a-Lot. He also took pride in being a solid investigator and wanted to please his boss by helping the Cuyahoga County Sheriff and making CORE look good.

When he reached the sidewalk, he glanced at their house. Light glowed from the second story side window—Whitney's room. Keeping his gaze on that part of the house, he took a few more steps, until Whitney's faint silhouette darkened the blinds. When she took off her robe, he inwardly groaned and was grateful the damned blinds were in the way. If he saw her naked, the next five weeks wouldn't just be rough, they'd be hell. She'd already crawled under his skin, made his stomach twist with need, his head ache and his dick hard. He looked away from the window and continued along the sidewalk.

The last time a woman had that kind of effect on him had been...never. Yes, he'd loved Shannon. But he'd been young, immature, on his own for the first time and terrified he wouldn't be able to support himself. He'd had no direction, and with no skills or college education, he'd had no confidence. Shannon had been smart to dump him for the city guy and to prefer to be with a man with a plan. He'd loved Ellie, too, but knew in his gut he'd loved the idea of being in a relationship even more. At that point, his career had been going great, he'd had money in the bank and was tired of being alone, especially during the holidays. That hadn't been fair to her, just as she hadn't deserved to be nearly beaten to death because a man he'd arrested wanted to hurt him.

He hadn't thought about Shannon or Ellie in years, and

didn't know why he was now. Living in a house in the burbs and pretending he was married had probably unlocked those memories. But he'd like to lock them up again. He wasn't destined to have this lifestyle, to have a wife and children. He was too stubborn and set in his ways to live with someone, and he wouldn't know what to do or how to act around a kid. Mostly, he never wanted anyone to be hurt because of him again.

His cell buzzed from the back pocket of his jeans. He retrieved it and read Andy's text: *They're heading your way.* Sloan quickly walked back to the house. But as he approached the front door, dread pooled deep within his gut. He wasn't ready to go back inside, didn't want to run the risk of seeing Whitney, and wished he'd had more time to walk around and clear his head. What he wanted—needed—was to pin something on the Eastons so he could get the hell out of suburbia before he did something stupid...like fall for his fake wife.

Somewhere on Shady Circle, North Royalhurst, Ohio
Wednesday, 10:34 p.m. Daylight Saving Time

Rage and worry cut through him, had panic clawing at his insides, making his stomach sick. He swallowed back the fear with a swig of beer, then inhaled the cool spring air. From the darkened porch he tried to relax, watch as the new guy, Sloan, entered his house, and wondered why the man had been out walking instead of inside fucking his hot wife. Anything to take his mind off the body the construction workers had unearthed. Which one had they found? Would they find the rest? More importantly, would they link them back to him?

Headlights momentarily lit the porch, and he recognized Dale Easton's Audi. The cheap bastard still owed him for the custom work he'd done on their walk-in closet. If the man could afford the fancy cars he, his wife and kids drove, he could cough up the fifteen hundred for the closet.

After taking another drink, he leaned into the chair and forced himself to relax. No one would suspect him. He had no criminal record, paid his taxes, his bills and was a good family man.

But the bodies...

So many of them.

Guilt no longer kicked him in the ass. Regret had become a meaningless word to him. The men he'd buried, they'd been nothing more than a pill he might swallow. An antidepressant that'd helped him over the rough months. A necessity.

Although he no longer believed in God, thanks to his prick-ass preacher daddy, he'd thanked coincidence for placing him at the right place and time last summer. That had been when he'd heard the large property butting up against Whispering Pines had been sold to a developer, and why he hadn't buried a victim there since.

It had been nearly eight months since he'd killed a man. Eight months of either sleepless nights or violent nightmares.

Eight months of real therapy—not the killing kind—had proven useless. His therapist had wanted him to be open, and that hadn't been an option. By the time he'd gone to see the counselor, he'd put eighteen, or maybe it was twenty-something men in the ground. He couldn't be sure. Many nights he'd been drunk when he'd dumped soil over their bodies. Except for his first two kills, he'd kept his victims' wallets to make identifying the men harder for the police. But they were stashed in his secret hidey-hole, and it wasn't as if he spent his evenings going through them in order to take a trip down memory lane. To tell his therapist the truth, how his parents had tortured him, about his time at the camp...he'd feared those were things that would connect him to the men buried in the field. If they were found.

He took another swallow of beer.

Which they were. So...

So, he'd been smart by being cautious. By not telling the truth.

He lifted the bottle in a mock salute.

Except...the nights were bad. The demons haunted him and he needed to watch as his father took in a mouthful of soil, preventing his screams, constricting his airways and killing him.

Eight months. The longest he'd gone between killings had been about five months. The urge was there, the hunt...he missed the hunt, and was itching for another. Finding the willing victim who would replace his preacher daddy. A victim who would give his life so that he could sleep peacefully.

Because of his violent nightmares, his wife had taken to sleeping on the couch. That wasn't acceptable. Their kids were getting older, would notice and question, maybe worry they were having problems. He didn't need that, didn't need them saying something to their friends. If his oldest boy said anything to his best buddy, and that kid told his folks, word would spread that all was not well in their house.

Suspicions would arise.

People would wonder.

"Honey?" His wife turned on the living room light, taking away the darkness he'd come to crave, and held open the screen door. "Are you going to bed?"

"In a minute," he said, then took another drink. "But by bed, do you mean ours, or the couch you sleep on every night?"

Wearing fuzzy pajamas and slippers, she stepped onto the porch and hugged herself. "Our bed. Put that away and come cuddle with me?"

He stared at the empty street. "All night?"

"Sure. Unless..." She released a sigh. "Honey, I'm worried about you."

"Don't. I'll be fine. The new meds are helping me sleep through the night." He glanced at her. "Which you wouldn't know, since you're not by my side."

Light from the living room windows revealed her guilt and fueled him. His mother had had no remorse for what she'd encouraged his father to do to him. His preacher daddy...that bastard had tried to cleanse his own soul with a deathbed confession. Had told him the truth, then died, leaving him with no satisfaction. He'd wanted his father to make that same admission to his mother, put it in writing, tell anyone who'd known about Camp Hope that he'd lied. Tell them about the torture, the beatings...the burial.

"If you say they're working, then I'll sleep with you," she said.

"I'm tired of using the couch. I wake up every morning with a sore back and neck."

Frankly, he was tired of her. She'd lost her looks, had allowed the gray to show, making her brown hair mousy. She didn't bother with makeup anymore, and had put on at least ten pounds. But she was the mother of his children and, for that, a part of him loved her. The other part? If he'd thought he could get away with it, she'd be buried in the subdivision, and he'd be free to continue on with his therapy without having to worry about her discovering the truth.

She was married to a serial killer.

"I dunno," he said, raising the bottle to his lips. "Maybe you should stay on the couch through the rest of the week. I've only been on these meds a short time." If he truly loved her, he'd take the couch. Bitter that he was forced to have to kill around her schedule, and that he hadn't buried a man in eight months, had him wanting her to suffer.

She eyed his beer. "Should you be drinking?"

"Probably not. Are you going to take my alcohol away?"

She looked to her slippers and shook her head. "I was just wondering, is all." She hugged herself tighter and looked onto the street. "I saw on the news that the police plan to go back to Otter's Field tomorrow to look for more bodies."

"I heard that, too. Crazy, huh?"

"Scary. I don't want the kids riding their bikes over there."

He drained his beer. "Why? Do you think there's a killer on the loose? Maybe he lives in our neighborhood." He nodded toward Joe's house. "My money is on the prick."

Bristling, she dropped her arms to her side and fisted her hands. "Joe is not a murderer, and you can't let the kids ever hear you say something like that. It's bad enough none of the children on the street like him. We don't want them afraid of our neighbor." She drew in a deep breath. "I don't want the kids going over to the field because of what they might see. They'd have nightmares."

"They'd be fine, but whatever."

She glanced longingly at the new neighbor's house. "Have you met them yet?"

"Just the guy. Seems nice enough."

"I thought I'd bake brownies this weekend and take them over there, so I can meet them."

He shook his head. "That's probably not a good idea. I hate to break it to you, but your brownies are dry. Plus, the wife's an attorney and the husband's a web designer."

"So?"

"So, I get the feeling those people might be a little too… worldly for you."

She blinked several times. "I see," she replied, sadness in her tone.

Had that been a shitty thing to say? Of course. But he preferred that his wife have few to no friends. Women talked, were nosy and secretive. They liked to plant ideas in people's heads and cause drama. Jackie had been that way, which was why he was glad she and Brett had moved to St. Louis. One of the reasons he liked his wife was because the woman had no backbone. No drive. But Jackie, meddlesome Jackie, had put it into his wife's mind that she should do something more with her life than work at a crappy retailer for minimum wage. Jackie had suggested that, since the kids were all in school fulltime, his wife could go to the local college or take online courses so she could find a higher paying job.

When his wife had approached him about going to school, he'd told her they didn't have the money. A lie. He had a couple grand stashed away, she just didn't know about it. He was the one who paid the bills and controlled the finances, and he didn't want her knowing how much they had. What if she wanted a divorce? She'd take half, get custody of the kids, get alimony. He'd be left with jack shit. Or, what if she went to school, landed a job making more money than him and then divorced him? He couldn't have that. Those were *his* kids, and after what his own parents had put him through, he couldn't trust anyone but himself to raise them. Their mother was simply a supervisor who worked for him.

"But not for you?" she asked.

The beers he'd drunk tonight had his head fuzzy. "What are you talking about?"

"You said the new neighbors are too *worldly* for me. But they're not for you? You don't have a college degree, either."

"I'm a businessman," he reminded her, then hiccupped.

"Of course." She reached for the handle of the screen door. "My sister is going to be visiting my parents next weekend. I'd like to go see her."

She had an older and a younger sister. And he'd ended up with the most unattractive of the three women. "Which one?"

"Lucy."

The youngest and prettiest. "You can go. This is the last weekend for soccer, so it works for the kids."

Worked for him, too. By next weekend, he'd have a better idea of what the police had unearthed, and maybe what they knew. Vincent had always been a wealth of knowledge when it came to anything that had to do with crime stories, and he liked to share what he might've heard from old cop buddies. If the police hadn't put it together that the men in the field had been gay—the only thing linking them all together—then he could hunt. If the cops realized the men were homosexuals, though, he would expect them to warn the gay community, which meant he couldn't stalk gay bars for his next therapy session. Since he'd never killed a straight man, he wasn't sure if the killing therapy would work with them. He needed the men to accuse him of being something he wasn't, to push him, to anger him until he snapped and unleashed his inner demons. To rid himself of the nightmares, he was willing to try anything.

But where would he bury the body?

"I was hoping to go alone," she said, trampling all over his thoughts.

"No. If you don't take the kids, you don't go."

"But I haven't had a weekend away since…ever. I always take the kids when I go to Columbus and give you a break. I'm asking for the same. Please."

"Next time. I'm working on a lot of my own projects and business is picking up again. I can't be worrying about who's watching the kids." If the kids were around, how could he hunt for his next victim? "Like I said, they go, or you don't."

Without another word, she entered the house. Taking his empty beer bottle with him, he also went inside, then closed and locked the door. After he'd tossed the bottle into the recycling can, he turned toward the family room, where his wife was placing blankets on the couch. He knew the old furniture was lumpy and uncomfortable, and he should probably give her a break and take the couch for the night. Especially since he'd just told her she couldn't go away for the weekend without the kids.

She finished with the blankets, then glanced up at him. "On your way upstairs, can you turn off the kitchen light for me?"

"You can do it. I'll take the couch."

Her dull eyes brightened. "You're sure?"

When he nodded, she quickly gathered her cell phone and water bottle, then walked over to him. She rose onto her tiptoes and kissed his cheek. "Thank you."

Giving her the bed was the least he could do for her. After all, without knowing it, she'd given him two nights to find and bury his preacher daddy.

Parking lot of Mom's Kitchen, North Royalhurst, Ohio
Thursday, 10:51 p.m. Daylight Saving Time

From the passenger seat of the Pontiac Grand Am, Austin Goldhirsh stared at his younger brother, Laredo. "I don't know about any of this, dude. I think we should head the fuck back to Chicago."

Laredo passed him the joint he'd just hit. "But Dallas told us—"

"She ain't here, and it's not her ass that's gonna end up in prison." Their sister was determined to get even with the cop who'd put away their brother, Antonio. When Antonio had died of a knife wound while serving his time, and their mom had passed a week later from a weak and broken heart, they'd all wanted revenge. But after being away from home, and having too much time to think, he wasn't sure about going through with a plan created out of grief and vengeance. "The lady living with him has got to be a deputy or something. Why the fuck else would he be here?" he asked taking a hit.

A month after their mom had died, they'd found the man. Sloan North—as he was now calling himself—had changed his name, job and address, but he hadn't changed the way he looked. Thanks to a tip from a cop they'd bribed, they had discovered North was still in law enforcement, but as a private investigator. When they'd told Dallas, she'd had them follow him. But the man was hard to track, especially when he'd boarded a private jet.

Luck had been on their side, though. Friday morning, when he and Laredo were just about to arrive at North's place to follow him to work with the intent to kidnap him, North had raced out of his parking garage on a sweet Harley Davidson. As they'd followed him out of the city, then out of the state, he'd called Dallas and asked her what they should do. They didn't have any extra clothes with them, had forty-three dollars between them, and his credit card was a few hundred shy of hitting its limit. Dallas had taken care of them by depositing two hundred dollars into his bank account. Where she'd gotten the money, he couldn't say and hadn't cared. He'd wanted to make sure they wouldn't run out of gas and could buy a few things once North had stopped riding.

Which ended up being in Cleveland at the Cuyahoga County Sheriff's Offices.

From there, they'd spent the past five days either stalking North, or the tall blonde living with him. And sleeping in the car. The only reason the Pontiac didn't smell like ass was because they'd found a truck stop with a public shower, and a thrift store where they were able to buy clothes.

Laredo drummed his fingers along the steering wheel, before taking the joint. "I want to go home. This place is creeping me the fuck out. Call Dallas and tell her about the dead body and all the cops crawling around here."

He'd never been in trouble with the law, but Laredo had done some time in juvie for selling weed, same for Dallas, only she'd been busted for prostitution when she was sixteen. But his brother was right about this place. It creeped him the fuck out, too. From the outside, the dozens and dozens of nice homes looked like something out of a magazine. He'd grown up with nothing, and when he was a kid, he'd spent nights dreaming about and wanting to live in a place like this. But he realized there was something kind of scary about the suburbs, as if something dark and disturbing was hiding behind manicured hedges, and brick and vinyl sidings. Or maybe the pot was making him paranoid.

"I gotcha, dude," Austin said. "And I'll handle Dallas."

Laredo glanced away from him to look at the dashboard. "You don't think I'm bein' a pussy?"

"Nah, I don't like it here." He took the joint from him, then hit it. After a slight coughing jag, he said, "And I'm done with showering at the truck stop. We're gonna run out of money if we stay much longer, so Dallas is gonna hafta deal. No way I'm going to be stranded in fucking zombie land."

"That's exactly what this place is." He tapped Austin's arm with the back of his hand. "No, wait, it's like that stupid ass movie. Shit, what's it called? You know. It has to do with snatch."

Austin laughed. "Are we talking porn or a regular movie?"

"No, dude." Laredo grinned. "But if we had a hotel, I'd watch porn."

"While I'm in the next bed? Fuck that. I don't want to know what you do." The phone rang and they both jumped, then laughed. Until they looked at the screen. *Dallas.* "I got this," he said, now wishing he'd waited to get stoned. Dallas could be one bossy bitch.

"What's going on?" Dallas asked when he answered.

He put the call on speaker. "Some fucked-up shit."

"I'm listening."

"North lives on a circle street—"

"You're such a dummy," she said with a mocking laugh. "Those streets are called *cult-ve-zacs*. It's Russian."

Russian? He looked to his brother, who covered his mouth to keep his laughter quiet, then quickly looked away before he ended up with a case of the giggles, too. How Russian sounded French, he didn't know. "Whatever. Just listen to what's been going on here," he said, then explained about the cops, the dead body near the circle street, and how North never left the house.

"He doesn't leave the house? At all?" she asked.

"Maybe he goes outside and sits on his porch, but we wouldn't know. We can't find a good place to park the car and watch him." He gave the joint to his brother and let him finish it. "I told you, there are too many homes, too many people that would notice us."

"So, let me guess…you two assholes have been sitting in your car smoking dope, right?"

"No!" he and Laredo exclaimed in unison, then burst into laughter.

"It's not fucking funny. Hang on…you better go the fuck to bed or you're gonna get it!" She sighed. "Goddamned kids are a pain in my ass."

Austin sobered slightly. He didn't have a steady job or a steady future. But the one constant he had in his life was family. He didn't always love Dallas, but he adored her kids, and hated that she was their mother. They deserved better, deserved kindness, hope and the chance to actually have a decent future. Laredo's sidelong glance said he was on the same page as him.

"Anyway," she continued, "I got a way you can get into North's place and take care of him."

His stomach twisted with concern as he looked to the beaten-up glove box housing the gun and bullets they'd brought—illegally. Neither he nor Laredo had a license to carry a weapon, same with Dallas. But she'd gotten it off one of her baby daddies, and expected them to use it on North. He and his siblings were half Jewish and half white, lived in a predominantly black and Hispanic neighborhood, understood people sucked, and had no problem beating or harassing a person for being a minority. Despite hating the haters, he'd never once fired a gun or provoked a fight. And his sister wanted him to kidnap and murder a man? While he wanted payback, too, he wasn't sure if he could go through with it. Not anymore.

They'd all grown up on the west side of Chicago in Garfield

Park, near the 4400 block of West Monroe Street, where violence was high and drug dealers flourished. Just last year, there had been three, fatal drug related shootings that had taken place not far from the apartment he'd been raised in and still shared with Dallas, her kids, and Laredo. If their mother hadn't died, she'd be with them, too. Although it would have been so easy for him to be lured by the quick cash he could pocket by selling drugs or stealing, his mom had raised him to be a better man, to want more for himself. Maybe it was the weed or wishful thinking, but he swore his mom was with him now. Sitting on his shoulder and telling him this was all wrong. That she wouldn't want them to do this for her or Antonio.

"Getting into North's house won't be easy," Laredo said before their sister could continue. "And what are we supposed to do once we're inside?"

"Beat, torture, then shoot him," she said as if rattling off items from a grocery list. "That's what we agreed to do."

"No, that's what *you* want us to do," he reminded her. "We just wanna scare him. I can't kill a person." He glanced at his younger brother, who was only eighteen. Their mom always said to never give up, and to find a way to climb out of poverty without breaking the law. He wanted that for both of them. They weren't college material, but if they quit doping, found a couple decent jobs, maybe they could do something with their lives. "I dunno, Dallas, I think we should let this go. I don't know that Mom would want us to do this."

"North is the reason she's dead. Are you telling me he *shouldn't* be punished?"

"For what? Antonio got busted, and it was his own frickin' fault he ended up in prison."

"So, are you saying he deserved to have a blade shoved into his gut?"

He sighed and wondered why he bothered to argue with her. Dallas always had to be right, even when she was dead wrong. "No, but I still don't think this will work. Have you seen the size of North?" Unfortunately, none of the Goldhirsh children were tall, and had inherited their Jewish father's height. At five foot six,

Austin suspected North had him by a foot and maybe one hundred pounds. "Going after him will be like us trying to wrestle a gorilla."

She let out a breath. "Okay, I'll agree with you on that." She gasped. "Ooh, ooh! Wait, I've got an idea," she said, then scolded the kids again. "I'm back. I swear, these kids... Anyway, skip killing him and take the woman. He took from us, so it's only fitting we take from him, right?"

Laredo frowned. "And do what with her? I...I'm not...forcing her—"

"Shut the fuck up, dumb butt," Dallas snapped. "If I ever find out you two raped a woman, I'll slit your throats in your sleep. Now, what I'm suggesting is you kill her instead of North. But we have to make sure he knows she died because of him. Otherwise, what's the point?"

He still didn't like the idea of murder, but the woman *would* be easier to kill. She had him and Laredo by half a foot, but wasn't built like a WWE wrestler. "I don't know that there's a point to any of this. But since you're so smart, how do you think we should get to the woman?"

"She's got to be a fucking deputy or something," Laredo said, his voice laced with panic. "We kill her, and the cops will come after us hardcore."

"He's right. Fuck it. I'm out," he said, tension rolling off his shoulders. He'd wanted out about a week ago, but had gone along with it because he honestly hadn't thought it'd come to this point. Plus, looking for North, then following him, had taken his mind off losing both his mom and brother.

Dallas let out a sarcastic laugh. "Really? Well, if you don't kill her, then you don't have a place to live. Remember, Mom's apartment is now in my name."

"So, we'll find somewhere else to crash."

"You do that, and don't ever show your face around here again. Neither of you will be allowed to see my kids."

Bitch. Dallas didn't act as if she even liked her own children, but she knew how much he adored his three young nieces. It would kill him if he wasn't able to see them, or make sure their slut of a mother hadn't neglected them, or had brought around a lowlife scumbag who might try to hurt them.

"You're just sayin' that." Laredo shook his head. "She wouldn't do that to us."

"There's only one way to find out," she said, her tone sweet yet threatening. "Or, you can go along with my plan."

"Which is?" he asked, curious.

"Jehovah's Witnesses."

He and Laredo laughed. They hadn't been raised Christians, and had never once been practicing Jews. What they knew about God or Jesus came from television. And growing up poor, they hadn't had much to watch on TV, when they'd had one that had worked.

"I'm dead serious," she said. "All you have to do is go door to door on their *cult-ve-zac*, talk about God or whatever, and when you reach her house, you take her. Does she park in the garage?"

"Not sure," he answered honestly. They'd been nervous about visiting the circle street too many times and being noticed by North or his neighbors. "When we parked on the street behind North's, we were able to see her car come and go, but not what she does with it at home."

"Find out. Because if you can get to her when North ain't home, you should be able to force her into her car, then drive out of there. Before you go, leave North a note telling him it's fucking payback, baby."

Laredo raised his brows and met his gaze. He hit the mute button. "It's actually a good plan," he whispered, even though Dallas couldn't hear him. "We can try it, and if it looks like we're gonna get caught, we'll bail."

"I dunno…it's risky."

"We don't have to kill her." Laredo released a breath. "I don't want her taking the girls away from us. We're the only stable people they have, and that don't say much, you know?"

He did. If he'd had the power and authority, he would have made it so his sister never had custody of those girls again. It'd kill him to never see their faces anymore, but he'd rather they lived in a good home with a family who loved them than with his bitch sister.

"Are you two still there?" Dallas asked.

Laredo took the phone off mute. "We're here. I...like your plan, but we don't look like Jehovah's Witnesses."

"Get a suit from the thrift store, then go to the barber. And I'm mostly talking to you, Austin. I can't stand that stupid man bun."

He touched the top of his head where the floppy knot rested. "I'm not cutting it. You know how long it took me to grow."

"So you can wear it up? That's dumb. I'm tellin' you, it's frickin' ugly and went out of style the moment toy makers slapped one on top of Ken doll's plastic head."

The long hair was a hassle to maintain, but it should be his decision, not Dallas's, as to whether he should cut it or not. "I'll think about it."

"No, you'll go first thing in the morning and take care of that and the clothes. Then you're going to find a way to get the woman. Understand?" One of the girls began crying in the background. "Damn it. I gotta go see what she's wailing about now. I'll call you in the morning."

The call ended, and he looked to Laredo. "Well? What do you think?"

His brother started the car. "I don't think your hair is stupid," he said with a grin.

He chuckled. "Thanks, dude, but you know what I'm talkin' about." He leaned into the passenger seat. "I don't like her plan. The woman will see our faces and be able to ID us. If we take her, she can't live. And I don't wanna kill anyone."

Laredo pulled the Pontiac out of the parking lot. "Same. What if we break into the garage, then her car, and kidnap her that way. If we wear ski masks, we won't have to kill her."

"Now, *that's* a better plan." He stared out the window, while longing to be home and in his old bed. "But...do you think this is what Mom would want? Or even Antonio?"

"They're dead, so why would they care?"

"Why does Dallas? She and Antonio couldn't be in the same room with each other without fighting."

Laredo made a turn. "Don't know. Guilt? You know, 'cause he's dead and she was a bitch to him."

"She's a bitch to everyone, but I guess that makes sense." His stomach rumbled. "Let's hit a drive-thru before heading to the truck stop for the night. I got the munchies."

"Are we gonna try for the woman tomorrow?"

"The sooner we make this go away, the sooner we'll be home. So, yeah, tomorrow we're kidnapping North's girl, or whatever she is to him."

Chapter Six

The rental house, North Royalhurst, Ohio
Friday, 9:23 a.m. Daylight Saving Time

S LOAN STARED AT the clock, waiting for the appropriate
moment to FaceTime Rachel Malcolm, CORE's computer
forensic analyst and top researcher. She was an hour behind him,
and he didn't want to come across too pushy. Rachel, he'd
learned, resisted pushiness.

Last night, after making sure the video camera he'd had aimed
at the Eastons was operational, he'd texted Rachel about the local
murder, and asked her if she could find out anything about it.
Whitney had made it clear that they had nothing to do with that
investigation, and they needed to focus on their own. Only, *their*
investigation sucked. Here it was, the start of day six, and all he'd
discovered was that he had a few strange neighbors and a crush
on Princess Sticky-Note.

When Ian had first approached him about the undercover job,
he'd assumed he would be working the streets, not the burbs.
Once he'd realized what the job had entailed, he'd adjusted and
adapted, and had considered the operation a solid one that could
lead to an arrest. Now he wasn't so sure. There was absolutely
nothing out of the ordinary about the Eastons, and he'd begun to

wonder if Whitney and her counterparts at BCI had been wrong. They had no proof the family was involved with Morales, no real evidence that the drug lord even existed, and nothing to link them back to the North Royalhurst cop who'd disappeared. What they had were coincidences.

Unlike his past and present coworkers, he believed there were such things as coincidences, along with bad timing and luck. Random shit happened, and that could be what they had here—a family caught in the middle of random shit. Whitney would likely tell him he was wrong and bring up the *coincidence* and timing of the opioid overdoses. While he agreed it was strange, and that it didn't help that they knew—thanks to the missing cop—Cameron had sold marijuana and cocaine, but they needed more evidence. And how did that make the whole family involved?

The video camera pinged, letting him know there was movement across the street. He looked out of the window just as Irene Easton made her way down the driveway. When she didn't stop at the mailbox as he'd expected, he tensed and watched her cross the street, her strides long and determined and taking her straight to his house.

Before he had the chance to text Whitney, the doorbell rang. Again, random shit. There was no way the Eastons had a clue they were watching them, and Irene was probably doing the new neighbor thing.

He left the bedroom and headed downstairs. When he opened the door, Irene smiled. She was trim, attractive, in her late forties and in no way looked as if she were a drug dealer. "Good morning," she said, offering her hand and introducing herself. "I'm a terrible neighbor. I wanted to bake something and bring it by, but I can't really bake so consider yourself lucky."

He chuckled. "Thanks for the warning," he said, and introduced himself. "I wish my wife was here. I know she's anxious to meet everyone on the street. Between the move and work, we just haven't had time."

"I'd love to meet…"

"Whitney."

"Yes, I'd love to meet Whitney, but, honestly, I'm here to talk to you. Gotta sec?"

Shit. Had he made a suburban faux pas at some point? "Sure. Do you want to come inside?"

"No, I was hoping you'd come to my house. If not today, maybe another time." Worry lined her face as she wrung her hands. "I own a photography studio and my website crashed last night. I'm beside myself. We're in the thick of the wedding and graduation season. If people can't access my site, review my services, packages and portfolios, I could lose a lot of business. Plus, there are the people who've already paid for my services and have codes to access their photos. I can't have people leaving negative reviews for that." She gave him a sweet and sheepish grin. "I heard from both Helen and Becky that you're a web designer, so I was wondering if you would have the time to help me?"

Fan-frickin-tastic. He knew nothing about web design. "What about the company that created your original website?"

"He's a one-man operation and is backed up with other clients. He can't get to my site for another two weeks. I understand if you're too busy, but I thought it wouldn't hurt to ask."

"Actually, your timing is perfect. I'm in between projects, so I should be able to help you," he said, hoping Rachel could create a website on his behalf, since he didn't know the first thing about it.

She gave him a big smile, and her eyes lit with relief. "Thank you. Do you have time to come over now? I have screenshots of how my website looked before it crashed. Those will give you an idea of the original format. But I'm up for any creative suggestions you might have. I also thought you'd like to look at my portfolio. It'd be great to incorporate my new photos."

The woman not only rambled, but talked fast. He was still digesting the invite to go over, and wondering how to handle the situation. He could bullshit with the best of them, and had spent his adult life pretending to be another person. He could do this and had to, now that he'd finally been given a *legal* way inside the Easton house.

"Sure, I can come over. I need to finish an email. Can you give me ten or fifteen minutes?"

She beamed. "Perfect. Thanks so much. I'll see you soon."

The moment Irene left, Sloan went upstairs, taking the steps two at a time. As he opened the drawer containing his James Bond-like devices, he phoned Rachel.

"Good morning, sunshine," she said, her tone chipper. "I'm surprised it took you this long to call me. You must be getting patient in your old age."

"Morning, Red. I was going to call you earlier, but Irene Easton just stopped by the house." He pocketed the key fob. "And you and I are the same age."

"Really? But I look so much younger," she said, her voice teasing. "So, what did Mrs. Easton want?"

"A web designer," he answered, then explained Irene's situation.

"I'm not a web designer, I'm a computer analyst."

"Who can also put together a website, correct?"

"In my sleep, but I've got other things—*important criminal investigatory things*—that need my attention. For example, someone requested information on a dump site less than a mile from your house."

"Have you found something for me?" he asked, and placed the pen Rachel had sent him into his pocket with the fob. He'd joked with Whitney about it being a regular pen, but it wasn't. Instead, it was a voice-activated recorder that had a twelve-hour battery. The nice thing about that was the battery only ran if the recorder was activated.

"A little, but I'll have more for you later. Jag is friends with the Cuyahoga County deputy medical examiner, Lee Polowski. He put a call into Lee and is waiting to hear back."

Jagger Stone was a former Cleveland detective and had been employed with CORE since last October. Since he knew the area, Jag would've been the ideal person for the undercover operation in North Royalhurst. But his wife had just had a baby two weeks ago, and he'd come to notice Ian was a softy when it came to family. Considering Sloan didn't have any family or any attachments, and had spent the majority of his career working undercover, of course he was the perfect candidate for the job.

"Great. Thank him for me." Sloan snagged a notebook off the card table. "Got any pointers for me before I head over to meet with Irene Easton? She told me she took screenshots of her last website, so that'll give you something to work with, right?"

"Ugh. You're really going to make me do this for you?" Rachel sighed. "Have her email you those screenshots," she said, then told him what else she'd need. "You're going to owe me for this. I would've charged her fifteen hundred to two grand to design her site. Maybe more."

He thanked her, then, after ending the call, considered texting Whitney. Deciding to call her after the meeting when he actually had something to report, he left the house. Vincent waved as he walked his little Yorkie, Fritz, along the sidewalk. From her passing minivan, Becky waved too. He glanced to the left and crossed the circle. Joe sat in a chair just outside the garage, a coffee mug in one hand, a cigarette in the other. When Sloan waved, the man gave him a simple nod. Maybe after he'd finished with Irene, he would stop by Joe's. The man's house was in a location where he could view every home on the street, and Joe always sat out front. In a way, he wished he could simply flash a badge and question the neighbors. But he also enjoyed unraveling a mystery. If there really was one here.

When he reached Irene's front porch, she smiled and opened the screen door. "Thanks again for coming over, and on such short notice, too."

He glanced around and realized her house had the same exact layout as his and Whitney's. Only the rooms were flipped to the opposite side. The Eastons also hadn't made many updates to their home, not that he was comparing or judging. But the carpet was worn, the beige walls and furniture were dated and tired. Which surprised him, considering the expensive vehicles they drove and that they frequently traveled to Miami. Then again, they did have two kids in college and one about to graduate high school. Drug money could only go so far, he supposed.

"My husband, Dale, uses the office, so when I work from

home, I'm forced to go to whichever room is quietest," she said, leading him to the kitchen where she had an opened laptop and portfolio book resting on the peninsula. He wasn't sure if that was what it was called, but if he and Whitney had a kitchen island, and Irene's was connected to the main counter, what else could it be?

"I get it. Before we moved, my office also served as Whitney's closet and the guest room."

"Where were you living?"

He thought back to the bullet point list detailing their history, but couldn't remember if there'd been anything about that. "West Park," he said, deciding to go with where Whitney currently rented. He'd learned early on in undercover work that building off the truth was easier than from a lie. "It was the lower half of a little duplex."

"Dale and I used to live in one of those," she said, her smile wistful. "It only had two bedrooms. Can you believe we had two kids while we were living there?"

"Had to have been hard," he replied, while trying to figure out the best places to leave the listening devices.

"It was, but those were good times. Money was tight, but life was simpler." She let out a sigh. "I don't want to keep you. Let me show you what my site *looked* like."

She spent the next twenty minutes showing him screenshots and newer photographs she'd taken, along with old favorites. He asked the questions Rachel had given him, and jotted the answers in the notebook he'd brought—using a regular pen, since the other with the recording device was a fake. He'd hoped to leave *that* pen in Dale's office, and because the kitchen and family rooms, which were adjacent, tended to be the hub of most homes, he hoped to plant the key fob somewhere in one of those rooms. Except, what if Dale and Irene had nothing to do with selling drugs and it was solely the kids? Cameron's room would be a perfect place to catch audio. But how to get in there?

"Well, what do you think?" she asked him. "Is this something you can do for me?"

He nodded. "Absolutely. Email me those screenshots and any

photographs you want to use. I should have an idea of timing by this evening or the morning," he said, and hoped he was right. He didn't need Rachel bitching at him. Not when he lived with Whitney. Then again, Whitney had been pleasant to be around both last night after he'd returned from his walk, and again this morning. While he'd prefer the next five weeks to be argument-free, he worried if she was too nice, he would have a harder time keeping her out of his head.

After he and Irene had exchanged numbers and email addresses, he turned toward the patio door, noticed an above-ground pool with a wraparound deck, and stalled for time. "Nice pool. That's a great deck, too."

She moved alongside him, then slid the glass door to the right, letting in a mild breeze. The yard was fenced and about the same size as his and Whitney's. Even with a pool, there was plenty of grass, enough for kids and maybe a dog. While she looked at her yard and explained how—with her husband's bonus—they'd had the pool and deck installed last summer, he stayed behind her, edged back slightly, then slipped the key fob beneath the leaves of the medium-sized fern sitting on a plant stand near the door. Although risky, they needed something, anything, to indicate that the Eastons were indeed dealing drugs.

He stepped further into the kitchen when Irene came back inside. "Nolan said you're having your basement waterproofed."

"Unfortunately." Irritation lined her face. "Had we known that we'd get flooded, we wouldn't have put in the pool." She shrugged. "If only we'd had a crystal ball. On the bright side, our basement wasn't finished and we keep our important things in the safe or attic.

Like opioids, marijuana and coke? "That's good," he said, grabbed his notebook off the peninsula and started for the foyer. Once there, he glanced at Dale's office. "Those built-ins are nice. Mind if I take a look? I'm considering doing the same in my office."

"Sure," she replied. As she stacked mail on the desk and explained that the built-ins were one of the few updates they'd made since moving into the house, he slipped the pen behind a picture frame sitting on one of the shelves.

"I'm glad Whitney insisted on buying a turn-key house." He met her at the screen door. "We're both so busy, I don't think we could deal with anything more than a few, smaller projects."

After promising to call or text soon, he left. When he reached the end of the driveway, he looked toward Joe's house. The man was still sitting just outside the garage, smoking and drinking from a mug. Sloan walked toward him. The moment he did, Joe tossed his cigarette into a coffee can, stood, then went inside the garage.

Well, fuck you, too.

Shoving the dickhead from his mind, he went home and immediately to his room. Once there, he checked the software he'd installed on the computer to make sure the listening devices were syncing. Unfortunately, he couldn't be one hundred percent sure until they were activated. Rachel, along with Hudson Patterson, who was also a CORE agent and dealt with various security measures, had both assured him the devices would connect up to one hundred yards apart.

As he worked on the software, Rachel texted, telling him to call when he had the chance. Anxious for an update on the body found in the subdivision and to tell her about Irene's website, he dialed her number.

"How'd it go with the drug dealer?" she asked.

"I don't know that she is one. Back in the day, I dealt with plenty of dealers, and she doesn't fit the mold. It doesn't mean she's not involved, though," he added, because in his experience there wasn't necessarily a mold. Rich, middle class or poor...he'd busted people from all social levels for selling.

"But your spidey sense isn't giving you any signals," she said. "Oh, and by *back in the day*, do you mean about eighteen months ago?"

He chuckled. "Seems longer than that, but yeah. Now about that website..." He went on to explain Irene's needs, then asked Rachel when she could have a draft ready to show his neighbor.

"You suck," she replied. "But if you email me all her crap, I should be able to have a draft completed sometime tomorrow or Sunday."

"Thanks. I appreciate your hard work, and I'll buy you dinner when I get back to Chicago."

"I have a better idea. You can send Owen and me to dinner, and babysit our kids for us. For free."

Owen was also a CORE agent, and the two had met through the company. "Since I'm not good with kids, I'll pay for your babysitter."

"Deal. Are you ready for the scoop on the dump site?"

"Jag heard from the deputy ME?"

Keyboard tapping clicked away in the background. "Construction workers unearthed the skeletal remains of *two* people. The clothing found in the graves indicated they were likely male, and their wallets confirmed it."

"Graves?"

"I'll get to that," she said. "Lee, the deputy ME, told Jag they autopsied the remains of Jim Montgomery and Noah Vance. They're waiting on dental records for confirmation, but both men have been missing for over ten years."

"Cause of death?"

"Undetermined. There was no trauma to the head, no broken bones or cut marks to the bones, and CSI didn't find any bullets or casings."

He stared out the window and noticed Vincent returning from his walk with Fritz. He glanced at his computer's clock. Vincent had been gone for over thirty minutes. Normally he was back within fifteen, which had Sloan wondering if the retired cop had gone to nose around the new subdivision. "Maybe they were strangled," he suggested.

"Possibly. The hyoid wasn't fractured, though."

"And that would be?"

"It's the U-shaped bone that's about midline in the neck. But Lee said the hyoid doesn't always fracture during strangulation, and that it depends on the force and instrument applied to the neck."

"Then maybe the men were drugged."

"Possibly. Lee extracted bone marrow from both men and is waiting on toxicology results."

Craving a Coke, he left the room. "You said they were found in graves?" he asked, bypassing the staircase and moving to the window located in a useless nook. The upstairs was stuffy and needed some air.

"Yeah, interestingly, they were only a few feet from each other and were both the same size. A third body was found this morning, but you didn't hear that from me. This one didn't have a wallet, but the clothing indicated the remains were of a male."

"So, either the killer smartened up, or hadn't thought he'd continue with his streak, and wanted to cover his tracks."

"That's what I'm thinking. I don't know why, but I don't see him as one of those types who keep trophies. The first two victims had jewelry and car keys on them. A wedding ring was found with Jim Montgomery's body, along with keys. Noah Vance didn't have a ring, but he also had a set of keys on him."

"But Montgomery and Vance have no connection?"

"Not that I've found. And, it appears, North Royalhurst PD is keeping all of this to themselves. They've only told the media about one body, and they're not revealing the victim's name."

He opened the window to let in the cool breeze. What was happening in Otter's Field beat the hell out of his investigation. He'd much rather work on a case dealing with a serial killer, than watch the grass grow on Shady Circle. "The police have to realize they've discovered a serial killer's dump site," he said, and watched as Vincent's Yorkie dug up the flowerbed running along the fence line at the back of the property.

"Fritz," Vincent shouted. "Get out of there."

The dog stopped, then ran to the back patio.

"I believe they do," Rachel replied. "And, you can't tell your wife this—"

"Partner," he reminded her, then made his way downstairs to the kitchen.

"Same difference. Anyway, I didn't get all this info from Lee. Some of it I got from the North Royalhurst PD. They really need a more secure server."

The woman had balls. Hacking into any law enforcement agency's system was a major offense that could land her butt in prison. "Don't worry about Whitney. I don't want her knowing I was looking into the murders."

"Why? Other than the fact I've broken laws, what's the big deal?"

"Because I'm *supposed* to be focusing on *our* investigation," he said, not bothering to hide his irritation.

"Which is a yawner, and forcing me to develop a website."

"You got it. Plus, Whitney and I don't exactly talk much."

"Uh-oh, is the honeymoon over?"

"Before it started. She's a perfect example of why I never wanted a partner or roommate. She's a know-it-all nag, controlling and a complete slob. Don't get me started on all the sticky notes she leaves around the house to remind me of things, or all the lists she makes."

"Sounds annoying."

He pulled a can of Coke from the fridge. "It can be. She also made me go to the barber and forced me to buy new clothes."

"You're kidding me. What kind of clothes?"

"Golf shirts and khakis, you know, like what your husband wears. Anyway, she's driving me nuts. You're a woman."

"Last I checked."

"You're a frickin' riot." He opened the pop. "How often do you take a bath? I'm talking soaking in the tub for twenty or thirty minutes."

"My kids are four and two. The only time I'm near a tub is when I'm bathing them. Why are you asking? Are you planning on sending me to a spa? Because you should, since I have to make you a website."

"I'm sending you and Owen to dinner and paying for your babysitter. No spa day for you." He opened the kitchen window. "I was asking because Whitney soaks in the tub every night."

"Good for her. I wish I could do that."

"Not helping. The *only* tub in the house is in *my* bathroom, which is attached to *my* room. So, every night I have to go to bed smelling her girly stuff and...what?" he asked when Rachel laughed.

"Sloan's in *lurve*," she teased.

His face grew hot. He wasn't in love. He was in lust. "You know, sometimes I truly hate you," he said, not meaning it. Rachel was a kickass, ballsy woman, who knew her shit. "I was venting. Next time...never mind. There won't be a next time."

She laughed again. "Oh, stop. Come on, admit you like your fake wife."

He went to the patio door, noticed a sticky note on the floor and retrieved it. "No," he said, and read the note. *Water plants.* He'd forgotten, but would take care of it after he got off the phone. Which would be within seconds if Rachel didn't back off. He was on assignment and didn't want any of his coworkers over-hearing her and thinking he was screwing off or around with his partner.

"Chicken."

"I am not."

"Bawk, bawk."

"Fine," he snapped, because he knew she wouldn't leave him alone until he'd admitted the truth. "I like her, but she hates me. Happy?"

"Really? Who could hate you? You're not hard on the eye—don't tell Owen I said that—you're rude, overbearing, arrogant and—"

"It's settled. I do hate you." He went to the front of the house to open those windows too. When he reached the office, Irene's Mercedes was backing out of the garage, which meant he had to get off the phone and let Whitney know. "I gotta run."

"Because of what I said? I'm sorry. You know I was just teasing you."

He did, except how Rachel had described him was exactly what Whitney thought of him. But what did his *partner* know? Had she bothered, she'd realize there was more to him. He was loyal and honest, had a good sense of humor and...there were prob-ably other good qualities, but he was too distracted to think of them at the moment.

"I know you were," he said. "Irene's on the move and I need to tell Whitney."

"One more thing before you go... How can you be sure she hates you?"

"She avoids me most of the time, and when we're together, the conversation might start off okay, but then one of us says something that ticks off the other and we end up arguing." He rubbed a hand along his beard and thought back to last night. "Here's an example: yesterday, dinner was going along just fine until I told her I'd made plans with a couple guys from our street. She got bent out of shape about it, then said she'd invite her boyfriend over, since I wasn't going to be home."

"She has a boyfriend? Well, that complicates things, doesn't it? I bet it made you jealous."

Rachel had no idea. He tightened his grip on the phone. "Are you planning on making a point?" he asked, willing to listen, especially because he had no one else to talk to about Whitney and the irritating emotions she evoked.

"I am. How did you react after you found out about the boyfriend?"

He rested his rear against the desk. "I was a dick," he admitted, regretting the things he'd said. "Later, after her bath, we got into it again. This time she started in on me. She actually said that she would have to be drugged to sleep with me."

Rachel laughed.

"I need to go before I really do hate you."

"Not yet. You know, for a smart guy, you're kinda clueless."

Him, smart? Hardly. He'd barely graduated high school. "Because?"

"Your fake wife likes you."

This time, he was the one laughing. The idea was ridiculous. "Not a chance, and not in the way you're thinking."

"Does she go out of her way to do anything nice for you?"

"Sometimes, and I do, too. We're partners and we live together. It's not as if we're constantly bickering."

"Hmm... In that case I'm probably wrong."

"I know you are."

"It's just...well, if you start arguments with her because you're jealous and don't want her to know you like her, did it ever occur to you that she might be doing the same?"

Was that possible? Maybe if they were twelve. The idea sounded incredibly immature and juvenile. "Whitney's too smart to act dumb like me. Plus, she has a boyfriend."

"But—"

"I need to let Whitney know Irene left." He didn't want to discuss the subject any longer, and regretted opening up to Rachel in the first place. He didn't open up, didn't share *feelings*. He hadn't depended on anyone since he'd been eighteen, and prided himself for being strong, for being able to cope with life's shit on his own. Except…strength and pride were all he had going for him. That thought, as many had since he'd moved to Shady Circle, depressed him. He didn't know what it was about this place, but all he seemed to do lately was self-evaluate. It made his head ache and gave him reasons to want to go back to being his regular self, where his only concerns were work, riding his bike and having fun. "I appreciate the advice," he said. "But I'd also appreciate it if we forget this conversation ever happened."

"Why?"

"In five weeks or less, I'll be back in Chicago, and none of this will matter."

"You mean Whitney."

Now his chest ached, too. "Let me know if you hear anything else about the subdivision, and when Irene's website will be ready." He ended the call, then sent Whitney a text. After she replied with *ok thx*, he pocketed the phone. Restless, itching for something to do, and needing to shake off the conversation with Rachel, he decided to plant the flowers he bought yesterday before he watered them.

As he hauled the bags of soil from the garage, the rev of a motorcycle had him longing for his Harley. The skies were blue and the temperature was supposed to top at seventy-five degrees. A perfect day for a ride. He turned in the direction of the revving and, for the first time, finally saw the bachelor who lived next door. Quint Oliver killed the motor, then climbed off a Victory Boardwalk—a kickass ride with whitewall tires and wide handlebars. If Sloan hadn't been a loyal Harley Davidson man, that bike would've been his second choice.

"How ya doin'?" Quint asked, taking a cloth from the back pocket of his jeans, then using it to wipe down the motorcycle.

Looking for a distraction from his conversation with Rachel, he crossed their adjoining lawns. After introductions had been made, and they'd talked about bikes, Quint said, "If you're ever in need of a car, let me know. I can get you and your wife a great deal." Then he explained what he did for a living.

"Thanks, man, I appreciate it, and might take you up on the offer when we start having kids. There's not much room in Whitney's little clown car."

Quint laughed. "Yeah, I noticed what she's driving, but, hey, it's good on gas." He draped the cloth over his shoulder. "I need to head out and pick up my girlfriend." He hesitated. "How nervous were you when you asked Whitney to marry you?"

"I…are you going for it today?" he asked, and that memory bank unlocked again, took him back to ten years ago when he'd been ready to propose to Ellie. He'd been a nervous wreck, had kept questioning himself, wondering if he was settling. Wondering if he'd convinced himself he was in love with her so he wouldn't have to be alone anymore.

Quint dug into the pocket of his jeans and revealed a tiny box. When he opened it, Sloan let out a low whistle. "Nice," he said, then realized something major, something his efficient, bullet point and list-making wife hadn't—neither of them had wedding rings.

"I'm hoping Tammi thinks it is, too." He shoved the box back in his pocket. "And, yeah, I'm asking her today. We've been together for four years." He took the cloth off his shoulder, and started wiping the bike again when it didn't need it. "I should've asked her sooner. But I wanted to hit certain goals first."

"What kind of goals?" Sloan asked, curious, because he didn't have one. The only things that concerned him were making sure there was money in the bank to pay the bills, and that whatever investigation he'd worked had ended with an arrest.

"Tammi has a couple kids from a previous marriage, so

owning a home was a big one. I also wanted to make sure I had enough cash saved to take her on a nice honeymoon and give her the wedding she'd never had." He half shrugged. "She'd married young and didn't get that." He looked at his house, pride evident on his face. "Before I met Tammi, I was doing just fine, living in a condo downtown, eating up city life, you know, doing my thing. But after I met her, and then eventually her kids, city life wasn't as important. So, I sold my place, bought this one and put more into retirement." He grinned. "Realized it was time to start acting like an adult so I can achieve my ultimate goal."

Sloan had money in the bank, enough to put a hefty down payment on any one of the homes on Shady Circle. Between his 401K with CORE and his pension from the Chicago PD, retirement wouldn't be a problem. "What's the ultimate goal?"

Quint looked away. "I...ah..."

"Sorry, wasn't trying to get personal on you."

"No, it's okay, I walked into that." He tossed the towel over his shoulder again. "We're neighbors, and it'd be cool to be friends."

"That would be cool. I own a bike, too. It's in the shop. But I heard from Vincent and Helen you keep to yourself."

"Have you noticed how many kids there are on our street? It's hard to fit in when you don't have any. And I spend a lot of time at Tammi's. I'm sure once she and her two daughters move in, we'll be getting to know the neighbors better."

"Nell and Joe don't have little kids. And the Eastons' children are older," he said, fishing for information now.

"Nell's Nell, and Joe's...I don't know what to do with him. I *will* be telling Tammi's girls to make sure they stay off his lawn. As for the Eastons... I know Dale well, at least on a business level. A year ago, the dealership wasn't doing well. I'd just been promoted to general sales manager and was worried we were going to have to close. I suggested to the owner that we bring in a business coach, which is what Dale does for a living."

"I take it you hired Dale."

He nodded. "He was great, got our team motivated and, within six months, the dealership was back on track."

"Nice. I haven't met Dale, but I did meet Irene today. Sorry to say, but I already don't like their son. I'm sure you've seen how he speeds down the street."

"I have." Quint glanced at the Eastons' house. "Cameron's a punk. He's one of those kids who thinks he's entitled to whatever he wants, which I don't get. Dale and Irene work damned hard for their children."

"And cars," Sloan added.

Quint grinned. "They're used. I got them a great deal. Otherwise they couldn't afford them. I'm not looking forward to helping put Tammi's girls through college. I'll probably have to sell the condo I have in Miami to pay for it. Speaking of which, if you and Whitney ever want to get away, if it's not being rented out, you're welcome to the place. Dale and Irene use it all the time."

Son of a bitch. They were watching the wrong people. They drove used cars, their home was average and in need of remodeling and, other than her wedding ring, he hadn't noticed Irene wearing any other jewelry. In his experience, dealers, especially those running a network, and who had people selling for them, had cash—lots of it—and no problem spending it on cars, clothes, jewelry and homes. Plus, their frequent trips to Miami could now be easily explained.

"Thanks, man. We love Florida and might take you up on that."

"Yeah, just give me a date and I'll see if it's available. Whenever Dale and Irene use the place, I only charge them a few hundred bucks, just enough to cover my costs."

"That's very generous."

He shrugged. "I inherited it from my parents. It's paid for and I make quite a bit during the in season, so I'm not up for gouging my neighbors. You never know when you'll need a favor, right?" Quint glanced at his watch. "Sorry, I need to run. There're a few things I need to do before I pick up Tammi and the girls."

"I thought you said you were proposing today?" Sloan asked, when his mind was still wrapped around everything Quint had revealed. Whitney wasn't going to be happy, not after the amount of time she, her unit and BCI had invested in this case.

"I am. But I want the girls there. I'm not just asking their mom to marry me, I'm asking them to let me adopt them and be their dad."

Sloan momentarily forgot about the Eastons and shook Quint's hand. "You're a class act. And now I get why you're so nervous. You're not just proposing to one girl, but three," he said with a smile.

After they parted ways with the promise of getting together and having a couples' night out, Sloan bypassed the pots, flowers and bags of soil and went inside the house. He sat at the kitchen island and stared at his phone. Once they verified the information he'd obtained from Quint, Lieutenant Campbell would likely pull the plug on the operation, and he could be home in a matter of days.

Instead of relief, his stomach coiled with disappointment. Not because he wouldn't return to CORE with another home run— he knew every investigation wouldn't turn out as expected. The problem was Whitney. Although she drove him crazy, distracted him, had his thoughts scrambled or teetering, he'd miss living with her. He'd been alone for so long that, even when they weren't on good terms, he liked knowing she was in the next room or down the hall. He'd miss her sticky notes, and how they let him know she'd been thinking of him when she'd written them. He'd miss stepping over the things she left lying around and how they reminded him of her as he went about his day. He would miss being surrounded by her apple and vanilla scent as he drifted off to sleep. Most of all, he'd miss her face.

He rubbed his beard, then shook his head. No, he wouldn't miss *her*. He'd miss not being alone. Maybe there'd been a reason he had been given this assignment. Being planted in suburbia, away from his routine and surrounded by people he wouldn't normally associate with had opened his mind, given him time to think and want to make a plan for the future, since he had none. Maybe that had been what his life lacked. A goal. Whitney was working toward buying a house. Quint worked to be able to give the woman he loved, and her daughters, a home and security. Soon, the man would achieve his ultimate goal and have a family.

So, what was his goal? What did he want out of life? Where

did he see himself in ten years? He hadn't a clue and was tired of being in his head, dealing with complex questions and emotions. Life didn't have to be that hard, and there was nothing wrong with how he'd been living his. A week from now, when he was home, and going about his usual routine, he'd be back to normal. Working, riding his Harley and having fun.

As he called Whitney, Vincent's shouts floated in through the window. While his neighbor yelled at Fritz to stop digging, the phone rang. When Whitney answered, the tension coursing through him intensified, had him hesitating, had him wishing for one more week in his personal Hell. Because the idea was ridiculous, he quickly tried to picture himself on his Harley, or hanging out with acquaintances or lady friends at his favorite restaurants or bars. Instead, he saw Whitney on the back of his bike, imagined her smiling at him from across the dinner table, and swore he caught a hint of her scent.

"Is something wrong?" she asked.

"Yeah," he said, his stomach growing sick. "I think we're chasing after the wrong people."

Chapter Seven

Minimart & Petro, North Royalhurst, Ohio
Friday, 12:17 p m. Daylight Saving Time

THE RUSTED PONTIAC Grand Am sat in the parking lot of Mom's Kitchen, facing the road. As he pumped gas, he stared at the car and tamped down the paranoia. He'd first noticed the vehicle in his development last Saturday, when he'd been bringing the boys home from soccer. The car had been slowly driving through Whispering Pines, as if the driver were looking for an address or casing the neighborhood. He hadn't thought much of it until he'd seen the Pontiac again on Sunday. That time, the car had been parked on Willow Drive, the street behind Shady Circle, but he'd once again dismissed it. The driver and passenger were young, probably high school age, and he knew there were several families with teens living on Willow Drive.

But today marked the seventh day in a row that he'd seen the car. Sometimes it was parked at Mom's Kitchen, other times on Willow Drive, or outside the minimart where he was currently fueling his truck. He knew Cameron Easton smoked dope. The idiot and his buddies liked to hang out behind the Eastons' shed and get high, and he'd smelled pot on several occasions while fertilizing the yard next door. The two guys in the Pontiac could be interested in the weed Cameron had at his house and had been looking for an opportunity to break inside. They looked like the types who were into drugs. Then again, there were plenty of young guys who had long hair or wore their jeans so saggy that their underwear showed. Neither of which meant they were potheads.

Still, it was odd that he'd never seen these people or their car until a week ago. Other than the North couple, no one new had moved into Whispering Pines in the last six months. He'd been tempted to contact the police, but didn't want the cops cruising around his neighborhood at random times looking for the Pontiac and its occupants. A week from now, the hunt would begin. He planned to bury his next victim close to home and wanted nothing to interfere with his killing therapy. Instead, because it had been eight long months and he couldn't be sure when he'd have the next opportunity to hunt, he wanted to savor the moment. Prolong the kill.

The gas pump clicked, indicating the tank was full. As he replaced the truck's gas cap, the guy with the ugly bun on his head exited Mom's Kitchen carrying a bag—likely lunch. It occurred to him that if he had noticed them, they could've just as easily noticed him. For the past week, he'd been working a job in Whispering Pines, had been driving in and out of the neighborhood to buy additional supplies or fill gas cans for his landscaping equipment. What if they were still around next weekend?

He climbed into the truck and decided that maybe he should call the police. If the cops questioned the two, they might stop hanging around the area and he wouldn't have to worry about them. Better yet, he'd stop at Vincent's after work and mention the boys to him. Now that he was always out walking the dog, Vincent probably saw them, too. He could tell Vincent his concerns and talk his neighbor into making the call, in order to keep his own name out of it. Stopping by Vincent's would also give him the chance to bullshit about what the police had discovered in the subdivision.

He'd caught the news this morning, and was surprised only one body had been discovered. When he'd first learned the property had been sold, and plans had been made for the subdivision, he'd tried not to panic. He couldn't exactly move the bodies, and had known all along there was a chance the property would eventually be developed, which had been why he'd dug the graves in close proximity to one another. He'd hoped if the property ever sold that the area where his Preacher Daddies rested would be spared from undergoing construction, and that maybe they'd leave it as green space. Since that hadn't happened, more than one body should've been unearthed. Was it possible the police were keeping their discoveries from the media? He'd love to head over to Otter's Field and see for himself. Instead, he left the gas station and drove toward Whispering Pines.

A few minutes later, he parked in front of the Milsons' house. They were a nice couple who lived on the street behind his. Their backyard butted up against Nosy Nell's, but with the way the homes were laid out on this particular street—Maple Lane—the lots curved, and from the Milsons' yard he could view a few of the homes on his own street. As he exited the truck, his business partner called to let him know that the job he and the rest of their crew were doing in Brunswick, a city not far from North Royalhurst, would eat up the rest of the day. Meaning he would have to work at the Milsons' solo, which wasn't a big deal and would get him home early. The Milsons' had hired them to add a small pond in the corner of their yard, grade the lot, create flowerbeds along the house, then add sod, rather than plant seed. Earlier in the week, he and their crew had taken care of clearing the property and marking off the areas for the beds. All he had to do was finish digging out the area where the pond would go. Since their skid steer loader was already on the property, he could have the hole dug, and the soil moved to the new beds, within a few hours.

Once he'd ended the call with his partner, he went into the backyard, climbed on top of the digger and went to work. After two hours of digging and moving dirt, he killed the motor and took a break, relaxing and leaning on the side of the house with a bottle of water. He needed to check the depth and width of the hole he'd created. But after years of digging graves, he'd become an expert on what four feet deep looked like and was sure he'd done just that today. As he drank from his bottle, he caught movement out of his peripheral vision. Turned his head slightly, then watched as one of the young guys from the Pontiac snuck through the neighboring yard.

The saggy pants kid crouched behind a tall, conical, evergreen bush and stared toward the street. He did, too, scanning the areas between houses. Tension moved through him as the guy with the knot on his head stood just outside the new neighbor's opened garage, and near where Sloan had left his truck parked on the right side of the driveway. With a cell phone to his ear, Knot Head entered the garage, touched the handle of the service door, then rushed out from where he'd been and ran along the fence line sectioning off Quint and Sloan's yards.

Little fuckers. He'd been right. These two had been casing the neighborhood, and he'd guarantee Knot Head unlocked the service door so they could access the garage and house when Sloan and his wife weren't home. Or maybe robbery wasn't the motivation. Sloan's wife was a beautiful woman, and it was possible that she was their target. Regardless, the Norths usually left the garage door open when they were home. What if these two shitheads had done this to his house? What if they'd come in during the night while his family slept, were surprised by one of his kids and reacted? If they were armed, they could shoot one of his boys. Hell, they could do that to any of his neighbors.

Angry that they'd have the balls to come into *his* neighborhood, he decided to involve the police. He reached into his pocket for his cell phone, then remembered he'd left it in the truck. Though worried the kid in the next yard was armed, he didn't want him to get away. If he subdued Saggy Pants, he could then call the police and get these guys out of his development.

His heart beat hard as he set down the water bottle. He picked up the shovel he'd left on the ground, then edged around the skid steer loader. The Milsons had a fence, but he and the crew had taken part of it down to bring in their equipment. If they hadn't, he would've never noticed Saggy Pants, or have been able to see Knot Head.

Using the remaining fence for cover, he peeked around it.

Saggy Pants had his back to him, a phone also to his ear. He sized up the kid, who couldn't have been more than five-six or seven. Since he topped out at six-three, he had the size advantage. But height would do him little good against a loaded weapon. Drawing in deep breaths to slow his racing heart, he tightened his grip around the shovel handle, left the Milsons' yard and quietly approached from behind.

"I'm two streets over," Saggy Pants said, his tone hushed. "You see me, right? Come pick me up so I don't have to cut through the yards."

As the kid shoved the phone into the pocket of his jeans, he rushed forward and knocked him to the ground. Saggy Pants released a grunt, pressed his hands against the grass and lifted up his body.

"Stay down," he ordered, and raised the shovel. "Roll over."

The teen quickly complied, then stared at the shovel, his eyes wide and filled with fear. "Whattaya doin'?"

"Funny, I was wondering the same."

"J-just goin' for a walk," he said, his voice panicked.

"Bullshit." He reached down and easily hauled the skinny kid to feet with one hand. "I know you're not alone. I've seen you and the other guy casing the neighborhood for the past week."

"Chill, dude." Saggy Pants raised his arms as if surrendering to the police. "We ain't doin' nothing like that. I swear. Me and my bro are new around here. We're just learnin' the neighborhood."

"You and your *bro* don't belong here," he said, and still holding the shovel, patted the kid's front pockets for any weapons.

"Fucking fag. You ain't no cop." Saggy Pants knocked his hand away. "Get the fuck off me."

His vision momentarily blurred. "What did you call me?" he asked, now gripping the shovel with both hands.

"Exactly what you must be, since you were feelin' up my junk."

Outrage made him lightheaded, but he had to curb it, couldn't let the kid goad him. Not here, not in broad daylight, where anyone could see him. "I'm not gay. I'm a concerned neighbor who plans on calling the police."

Saggy Pants spat onto the grass and glared at him with defiance. "Coulda fooled me."

"You're not fooling anyone," his mother shouted, her voice shaking with anger. She kicked the box of porn and dildos. "Admit that these disgusting things are yours."

"They're not. I swear!"

Wearing a scowl, his father stepped forward and backhanded him. "We won't tolerate lying or you wanting to be homosexual. Tell your mother the truth. Admit you're gay, then we'll find a way to drive the demon out of you."

He blinked and thrust his parents from his mind. He couldn't allow his emotions, his need to punish Preacher Daddy, to screw with his judgment. Next weekend, he would hunt. Today, he'd make sure the authorities kept their neighborhood safe.

He took the kid by his scrawny arm and hauled him toward the Milsons' yard. "We'll let the police decide if you belong here."

"Flaming fudge-packing turd burglar," Saggy Pants said as he struggled to free himself from his hold. "I ain't done nothing wrong, so get your gay-ass hand off me."

Rage, so sweet, raw and beautiful, blackened his vision, his soul. Gave him the exquisite pleasure he'd been craving for eight long months. That familiar swarm of flies invaded his head, buzzed loudly, drowned out everything but his father's words...

"You like boys?" Panic clawed at his insides as his father tossed a pile of dirt over his immobilized body. "Tell me how much you like it when they touch you. Tell me. Tell me! Admit the truth. Tell me..."

"No!"

Breathing hard, his own voice snapping him back to reality, he shook his head until he could once again see clearly. Then, with dread balling up his stomach, he looked to the ground. Sickened by what he'd done, by his lack of self-control, he turned away and vomited.

He would not be burying the kid alive, and didn't need to bother with checking for a pulse. After all, he'd hit the boy with the shovel enough times to smash in his face and make him unrecognizable.

Paranoia returning, he quickly looked around, searched for anyone on the street, in the yard, watching from a window. Not seeing a soul and terrified he'd be caught, he quickly bent, grabbed Saggy Pants by the wrists, then dragged him toward the hole he'd recently dug for the Milsons' pond, and left him near the fence behind a wheelbarrow. He then rushed to his truck. Along the way, he noticed spots of blood along the legs of his jeans and work boots. When he checked his T-shirt, he found more stains on his chest and knew he would have to burn his clothes in the fire pit later this evening. When he reached the truck, the Pontiac drove past slowly, its knot-headed driver glancing out the window and between the yards. More concerned with the bloody corpse than Knot Head, he pulled a tarp from the truck bed, then again, having searched his surroundings for anyone who could be watching, he hurried into the backyard.

After draping the tarp over the kid, he fired up the skid steer loader and went to work. To accommodate the body, he attacked the hole and took it down another three feet. Two probably would've been enough, but he'd rather err on the side of caution. If the Milsons, or a new homeowner, ever decided to get rid of the water feature, he wouldn't want them discovering bones beneath the pond's lining.

He climbed off the digger, shifted his paranoid gaze to the neighbors' windows, then dragged Saggy Pants to the hole. He removed the teen's phone before folding him into the tight space, pulverized the device, then dumped it on top of the boy. Using the digger, he moved soil over the body. After he made sure the trench was once again four feet deep, he checked the time. He had an hour before the school bus arrived. His wife would be home to take care of the kids, so he wasn't worried about them. What concerned him were the Milsons' son and daughter. They were his two older boys' ages. Knowing how curious kids could be, he decided to cover the surface of the four-by-seven-foot hole with the thick pond liner he had in his truck. Along the way to retrieve the liner, he realized Saggy Pants had left a pool of blood in the dirt, and that there were drag marks from the blood to the hole.

Fuck, he'd made a mess. Within less than an hour, the blood

and marks were cleaned, the liner was in place and he had a large piece of plywood covering the trench. Tomorrow he'd fill it with water, install the pump and add the rock border the Milsons had chosen.

And no one would know there was a body decomposing beneath the pond.

Yeah, I've got this.

Or did he?

Knot Head would be looking for his *bro.* When he'd driven by, the guy had to have seen his face. But why would Knot Head think *he* had anything to do with his brother's disappearance? Who would he tell anyway? If Knot Head went to the cops and explained his brother had gone missing while they were casing the neighborhood and unlocking service doors, he'd implicate himself.

He doubled-checked the backyard, took the shovel to the spigot on the side of the house, then washed away the blood and hair stuck to the metal. When he noticed he'd turned the dirt beneath the faucet into mud, he used his gloved hand to wipe the sludge over the bloodstains along his jeans, shirt and boots, then he climbed in his truck and headed home.

"Hi, honey," his wife greeted him as she dropped a trash bag into the can in the garage. "How was your day?"

"Great. After tomorrow morning, the Milsons' pond will be ready for fish."

"Oh, my gosh, are you filthy. If you leave your clothes in the utility sink, I'll take care of them for you."

The fire would take care of them. "There're oil stains underneath the mud. These clothes are old and beat-up anyway. I'm just going to toss them."

"Dad," his oldest son called as he rode his bike onto the driveway. "Wanna play catch?"

"Your dad just got home," his wife said. "Let him clean up and relax."

"I'm relaxed." He grinned, and realized the tension was gone. Why wouldn't it be? He was fucking Super-dad. He'd worked all day, killed a man and was about to play ball with his son. If he could talk his wife into sex later, this would end up being one of the best days he'd had in over eight months. He turned to his son. "Go get a ball and our mitts. See if your brothers want to play, too."

As his son ran into the house to search for his brothers, and his wife went inside to make dinner, he headed down the driveway. Vincent and Helen stepped outside with Fritz. He waved to them, then Sloan, who was potting flowers. Clearly the man didn't know what he was doing. A cold snap, which they could get well into May, could kill the flowers. While he waited for his sons, he looked down the street...just as the Pontiac Grand Am slowed at the stop sign. The car idled. The driver stared at him, but Knot Head was too far away for him to see his face, the worry in his eyes. And he should be worried. If the kid thought to come after him, he was sure he could find a special place to bury him, too.

Parking lot of Mom's Kitchen, North Royalhurst, Ohio
Friday, 4:51 p.m. Daylight Saving Time

Austin Goldhirsh dialed Laredo's cell. Once again, the call went straight into voicemail. He didn't know what could've happened to his younger brother. He'd been on the phone with him when he'd snuck into North's garage, hoping like crazy that Laredo wouldn't tell him a neighbor was coming by, or that North was heading out of the front door. As he'd left the garage and run to the car, Laredo had told him to come pick him up, then ended the call. What could've happened in the five minutes it had taken him to drive to Laredo's location?

He considered the landscaper. Except that made no sense. Why would he do anything to Laredo? And yet...when he'd been looking for his brother and had driven past the man's truck, the man had stared at him, his gaze suspicious, as if he knew what they'd been doing. Later, when he'd been stopped at a stop sign, he had seen the same guy. While he was far away, Austin swore the landscaper stared at him now, a small smile curving his mouth. Which again made no sense. If the man had thought they were up to no good, he would've probably called the police. He was being paranoid. But how could he not be when he couldn't find his brother?

He jumped when his cell rang. Hoping it was Laredo he quickly looked at the screen. Disappointment washed over him when he saw the call came from Dallas. He wasn't ready for his sister, wasn't even sure what to tell her. But with worry eating at him and uncertain what to do, he needed someone to talk to, to give him advice, guidance…too bad it would come from his stupid sister. Then again, maybe Dallas had heard from Laredo. He hoped that was the case, because he refused to leave Zombie Land without his brother.

"What's happening?" she asked after he finally answered.

"I'm not sure," he replied, then told her everything.

"How can an eighteen-year-old guy go missin' in less than five minutes?"

"How should I know? But I'm tellin' you, I can't find him." He let out a breath and wished he could smoke a joint to help ease his fears and concerns. "I don't know what to do."

"Where are you now?"

"Parking lot of a restaurant. It's about a mile away from where North lives."

"Would Laredo know to come there if you two were separated?"

He rolled down the window to catch some breeze. "I think so." He sighed again. "I don't know. We never *planned* to separate."

"Well, dumbass, you did separate when you went to North's house."

He wiped a hand across his forehead and tried to keep his temper in check. "He was on the next frickin' street. Look, I'm not going to fight with you about this. I need to figure out what to do. It's not like I can go to the cops and report him missing. What if it makes the news or something? If North recognizes our last name, he might figure out that we were here for him."

"You absolutely can't go to the cops. They're gonna want to know what you two were doing there, and that ain't no good."

The TV in the background blared a kids' show. He wished he

were there, hanging with his nieces, Laredo with him, making plans to go out later. Instead, he was stuck in Zombie Land and scared shitless something bad had happened to his brother.

"Maybe he hurt himself or something," Dallas suggested. "You know, fell and bonked his head."

"It's been over three hours since I talked to him. Do you think that's possible?"

She huffed. "I ain't no doctor, how should I know?"

"You suggested it."

"'Cause I don't know what else to think. Who has the money and gun?"

He shifted his gaze to the glove box. "Me."

"Good thing you had the keys, too, or you'd be screwed. Here's what you need to do...go back to that neighborhood tonight and search the yards. Unless he's wandering around with amnesia, he has to be there. You guys didn't get into a fight?"

They rarely fought. Laredo wasn't just his brother, he was his best friend. "No, that's why I'm tellin' you something happened to him."

Dallas shouted for someone to turn down the television's volume. "Still don't make sense to me. Why don't you go ask the landscaper guy? You said he's the only one you saw out when you were driving around, right?"

He thought back to the maze of streets he'd driven through while looking for Laredo. "There was also a guy walking a little dog. He was on the street behind the one where I was supposed to pick up Laredo. I've seen him before and think he lives next door to North. The landscaper lives on North's street, too. And I'm not asking the landscaper if he saw a guy hiding in the neighbor's yard. That'd go over well."

She sighed. "Let me think...wait, so you know where the guy was working?"

"Yeah, it was a house or two from where I think Laredo was keeping watch for me."

"What if you go check out the property? Maybe he buried Laredo there."

And his sister thought he was the dumbass. Dallas had said

and done plenty of stupid things in her life, but this suggestion ranked in the top ten. "Now, why would he bury Laredo? C'mon, Dallas, this shit is for real. I'm scared something bad happed to him. I think I should check the local hospitals. Maybe he's allergic to bees or some shit and got stung. I could also call the police and ask if he's been arrested. I don't have to tell them why I'm wondering."

"If that don't work, whattya gonna do? Besides, kill North's girl."

"I am not killin' anyone," he snapped, furious she was still on her revenge kick when they had a bigger problem. "What is wrong with you? Our brother is *missing*." He drew in a shaky breath. "I'm gonna go and call the hospitals and police. If I can't find him, I'll search the neighborhood."

"Then what? I can't keep supplying you with money. Luther would kill me if I knew I already stole two hundred from him."

Luther was one of her piece-of-shit baby daddies, who made his money selling dope and gambling. He had a mean streak ten miles long, and would beat the crap out of Dallas if he busted her. His sister might be a bitch, and he might not like the way she parented his nieces, but she was family. Deep down, he loved her. Why, he wasn't always sure. "I don't know. I can't stand the idea of leaving without him. Laredo wouldn't leave me."

"That's because he's a dumbass like you." She swore, yelled for the television to be turned down again, then said, "Let me know if you hear anything. Give it the weekend, then...I don't know. I'll have to think about it. Listen, if you, um, have to go searchin' for him tonight, watch your back, okay?"

Was that actually concern in her tone? Not good. The only person Dallas was concerned about was Dallas. "I'll be fine."

"You need to be. Who else do I have to watch my girls for me?"

Okay, there was the old Dallas he knew and sometimes loved. He ended the call. His data was just about done for the month. Not wanting to use it up searching for phone numbers, he decided to head into Mom's Kitchen. He'd find the numbers for the police and hospitals the old- fashioned way—the phone book. While he hoped to God Laredo wasn't hurt or in jail, it was better than what Dallas had suggested.

Buried somewhere. He shook his head. Now that was dumb.

The rental house, North Royalhurst, Ohio
Friday, 5:26 p.m. Daylight Saving Time

Whitney shut the car door with her hip and left the garage to enter through the front door. This morning she'd made a point to check out the furniture Sloan had bought, but she wanted to see it when the sun was brighter. Especially because the stuff might be on the front porch of her rental sooner than she'd planned. How could they have been wrong about the Eastons? Between BCI and their narcotics unit, hundreds of hours had been put into the investigation, and a good chunk had been used on the Eastons and Rueben Morales.

She admired the planters Sloan had placed at the porch entrance. He'd potted bright red begonias, white impatiens and yellow marigolds, and had also added spike plants for height. She glanced to the black door. She would love to see a spring wreath there, imagined it having similar colors, along with a pretty white bow to give it a classy touch. Deep melancholy settled in her chest. She'd fallen in love with this house and wasn't ready to leave.

Even more, she wasn't ready to part ways with Sloan.

She'd spent the day either at the office or on the road following one of the Eastons. When she'd been sitting in her car, she'd had plenty of time to reflect on her relationship with Sloan. While he could be high-handed and infuriating, she supposed she could act the same way. Actually, she knew she did, and had been told as much by her mother, brothers and even Andy. Not her father, though. In his eyes, she was his tomboy princess.

She smiled at the thought, and wondered what her dad, her family, would think of Sloan. Her mom would adore him simply because the man was a proud member of the clean plate club. She loved feeding people, and Sloan was a big eater. Since he was a man's man, a hard worker and a former cop, her brothers and dad would instantly like him. Why wouldn't they? He was a likable guy. He could be funny, sweet and thoughtful one moment, and rough, sexy and badass the next. Not that her family would be interested in the sexy part. She also hadn't witnessed the badass side of him and was okay with that. Knowing what he'd done while with the Chicago PD was enough for her. Having been with the narcotics unit, she didn't have to imagine what he'd experienced. She'd lived it. Not necessarily the undercover aspect, but she understood the danger involved when working the streets.

"Afraid to go inside?" a man called.

She turned and forced a smile. Vincent and Helen were walking Fritz to their own front porch. "Hardly. I was just admiring what my husband did today."

"I hope we don't get a cold snap," Helen said. "The frost could kill your flowers. I never plant mine until after Mother's Day."

"They can be replaced. We're both so excited to have our own home. Sloan couldn't wait until then."

Helen grinned. "That's adorable. You two are a lovely couple. We loved the Smiths, and were hoping our new neighbors would be just as wonderful." She glanced up at her husband. "I think God answered our prayers."

Vincent wrapped an arm around his wife as Fritz pulled on the leash and toward their front door. "That He did." He chuckled when the dog whined. "Fritzy wants his cookie for being a good boy. We'll catch up with you later."

After wishing them a good night, she finally went inside. The house smelled...zesty. Eager to find out what Sloan had cooked, she went into the kitchen. She placed the container she'd been carrying onto the counter—a little something for Sloan—and opened the oven.

Lasagna. Yum.

Before she headed for her room to change, she went out onto the porch. The furniture Sloan had purchased was incredibly nice. He definitely had great taste. He'd also potted more flowers and had placed planters around the patio. As she gazed at the yard, she instantly pictured having family, friends and neighbors over. Saw Sloan holding a beer at their imaginary grill, a fire going in the pit, a game of corn hole at the center of the yard.

And wanted to cry.

This operation had given her a taste of her goals—of being a homeowner and having a husband—and it was coming to a swift end. Although Andy and BCI were still verifying the information Sloan had obtained from their neighbor, Quint, she suspected—based on their lack of evidence against the Eastons—that the info would check out, leaving Campbell no choice but to have them move in a different direction.

Move Sloan back to Chicago.

She should be happy that she would soon return to her regular life, to dating...Cliff.

Clifford, the big red dipstick.

She itched her head, then released her tight bun. After living with Sloan, she wondered what she'd ever seen in Cliff.

He's safe.

No, he was easy to be around because he'd allowed her to dictate their relationship. Unlike Sloan, he'd never once challenged her, never argued, never showed a single side of passion.

Passion is bad. You've gone down that road and it broke your heart.

True. But...

She went back inside, then to the living room, her favorite place in the house. The room wasn't a typical, formal living room. Instead, it was small and cozy. If this were her house, she'd add a fake fireplace for their long, cold Cleveland winters, and would spend time here reading. If she made the space cozy enough, and if Sloan were into playing board games or cards, they could hang out here and...

Oh my God, she'd taken the fake marriage thing to a psychotic level. What was wrong with her? A week ago, she'd been level-headed Whitney Russell. She'd had her crap together, goals in place, and was dating a marriageable man. If she'd played it right, she could have a child in a couple of years. She drew in a deep breath, inhaled the aroma coming from the kitchen and tried to find her way back to last week's Whitney.

The sensible, goal-oriented woman who had her life plan set in stone.

"You're home."

Sloan's familiar voice washed over her, soothed her, had her once again longing to be *home*. Not the duplex she rented, but a real home, where she could put down roots and raise a family.

"Yeah, I just got in, but was checking out everything you did today," she said, and turned, watched him walk down the steps. Her stomach and heart both did a little flip. Sloan wore the lilac golf shirt and khaki pants she'd picked out for him. He'd also brushed his hair and trimmed his beard. This should please her. He fit the mold she'd set out to create a week ago. Instead, she wanted him back in his graphic T-shirts and jeans, wanted to mess up his hair and climb on top of him.

Bad Whitney.

Yes, very bad. As handsome as he looked now, this wasn't him. This wasn't the man she'd...oh, hell. Who was she kidding? Even in lilac Sloan was still her Wolverine. He couldn't hide the tattoos or the muscles that filled out his clothes in a way that made her want to tear them off him. She'd bet he could rock a tux, a suit, a bathing suit...anything, because he oozed the confidence she had strived to gain since she'd been a gawky, leggy teenager.

"Hungry?" he asked, and she wanted to groan. Yes, she was hungry. While lasagna was a favorite, she had a hankering for something else.

Sloan.

Naked.

On top of her.

Stop! Don't go there. He's leaving. The operation is just about over. You'll never see him again.

Which, in her mind, made the situation perfect. She'd never had a one-night-stand, and if she hooked up with Sloan, it wouldn't exactly qualify as one since they'd been living together for six nights. Still...what if she did let him know she was interested? If he were game, they could have a hot night. Of course, that'd mean she would have to stop seeing Cliff—she wasn't a total jerk—but she could enjoy a night of passion, then wave bye-

bye to Sloan and go back to her life plan: find a husband and have kids.

Except, for some reason, her life plan sounded so…stale, life-less, unappealing. As if something was missing.

She cleared her throat. "I took a peek at what you have in the oven. Lasagna is one of my favorites."

He grinned, finished making his way down the steps and joined her in the living room. "I got the recipe from Helen. I hope I did it right."

"You made it from scratch?" she asked, impressed, considering he'd planted listening devices at the Eastons', potted flowers, and likely proved the investigation was a bust, too. "You've had a busy day." She eyed his clothes again. "You look nice. Why are you dressed up? I'm also wondering why you bothered to pot the flowers when we're probably leaving."

"The flowers would've died if I hadn't done something with them. According to everyone around here, they probably will anyway." He half shrugged. "I thought you could take the planters with you, too. We can use the truck to transport everything to your place."

"Sloan, I don't think I can accept them and the furniture as gifts. It's too much money. I'd like to pay you for them."

He held up a hand. "I'm not going to argue with you about it. I bought the stuff knowing I wouldn't be reimbursed. Since I can't take it with me, I want you to enjoy it."

She would. She'd also likely think of him every time she sat on the furniture. "Thank you. It's very generous. So…what's with the clothes?"

He plucked at the front of the shirt. "I won't wear this once I'm home. I figure I'd put them on at least one time before I donated them."

She reached up and adjusted his shirt's collar. "That's too bad. You look very…handsome."

Giving her that boyish grin she'd come to love, he looked away. "I look ridiculous."

"Stop it. You do not, and I'm betting you know it, too. I'm also starting to think you're fishing for compliments."

"Maybe." His grin broadened. "Go change while I make your salad. Helen gave us a bottle of Cabernet Sauvignon to go with dinner. Do you want a glass?"

"Sounds good, thanks. I'll be down in a few," she said, then went to her room to change. Normally she'd put on a pair of sweats or her go-to lounge pants. But with how good Sloan looked tonight, she decided to forgo her usual evening attire and slipped into black leggings, paired with a denim shirt and black flats. After she'd put her weapons in the portable gun safe she kept in the closet, she checked her reflection. Wanting to impress him, she put on gold hoop earrings and a necklace, touched up her makeup, added on lip gloss, then ran a brush through her hair and pulled it back in a low ponytail. Satisfied she looked pretty good, she left the room.

Nervousness ping-ponged through her. She didn't know why. This wasn't the first time they'd had dinner together, and she doubted she would do anything with her idiotic idea of coaxing him into a one-night-stand. That wasn't her style anyway. She'd always carefully chosen her sexual partners. Yes, there'd only been three of them, but she'd still been…choosy. Well, at least two out of the three times. Wes, guy number two, had swept her away with his looks, charm and sex appeal. He'd had her going against her 'no sex for three months' rule and into his bed within three weeks. He'd been passionate, had showed her she could be uninhibited and desirable, and had had her falling hard for him. Two weeks later, she'd run into him at a bar and caught him kissing a beautiful woman. That had been when she'd sworn off dating charmers and womanizers.

When she reached the bottom step, she wondered why she was thinking about any of this. Probably because all she'd been able to think about for the past week was Sloan. His rock-hard body, his bad boy appearance, that boyish smile and those dark eyes.

Not wanting to think, but to have a glass of wine and eat, she pushed aside her foolish nervousness and went into the kitchen. Once again, he'd set the table and made a perfect salad. For some reason, his salads tasted better than hers. She would miss his cooking, the way he kept her aware of how she tended to not pick up after herself, seeing his clothes in the laundry room, his toothbrush next to hers on the bathroom counter. His clean, masculine scent. The way he...she needed to stop torturing herself and admit the truth. She would miss him.

"Looks delicious," she said, eyeing the lasagna bubbling in the casserole dish.

"Thanks." He handed her a glass of wine. "Hear anything from Andy about what Quint told me?"

She blew out a frustrated breath. "I did, and it's incredibly annoying. The BCI investigator who looked into the Miami connection didn't dig deep enough. Quint's rental property is under an LLC, and the investigator assumed, since Morales is an alleged criminal, a drug dealer wouldn't leave a paper trail with his name on it."

"A bad assumption."

"No kidding. I chalked it off to laziness."

"But, isn't it possible that the Eastons looked at Quint's place as the perfect excuse to meet up with Morales? No one would suspect them of being big spenders if they're staying for practically nothing. Something that bothers me, though, is they spent January and February down there. That's the in season, and I think it's odd Quint would let them stay there for next to nothing."

"I thought the same and had Andy pull the Eastons' bank records again. They paid six grand for the two months they were there. You said Quint keeps a car at the condo, so they wouldn't have to worry about renting one. What's sad is, we were so busy focusing on their activities in Miami, no one realized they had a couple renting their home here. Andy found a check made out to Dale Easton for five grand. The person who paid him works for the same company Dale does and was in town to help with a consulting job. Essentially, the Eastons didn't pay much to spend two months in Miami. Plus, while they were there, Irene earned income from half a dozen photo gigs, and Dale continued to be paid his salary because he was coaching a business down there."

"But you knew that."

"We did, and assumed it was too convenient." She sipped the wine. "All this assuming has wasted time and money."

"Hey, you wanted the Eastons to be the connection to Morales. I get it," he said, plating the lasagna. "I've been there myself many times."

"Thanks, but that doesn't make me feel any better."

"You should feel fine about it." While he carried their plates to the table, she brought over their glasses. "We know Cameron Easton is selling drugs, and we still have the missing cop to consider."

"True. And Andy and BCI are following up on the other things you discovered, along with digging deeper into their finances. Maybe something will pop up and give us a new lead." She sat across from him. "Wait, have you changed your mind about the investigation?"

"I still don't believe Dale and Irene are involved, but I do think it's smart to stay here for another week or two and keep an eye on Cameron. I've already planted two listening devices. Now that I'm working with Irene on her website, I might have another opportunity to go into the house. I'd love to plant a bug in Cameron's room." He raised a forkful of lasagna to his mouth. "How do you feel about contacting your lieutenant and recommending that we stay?"

Excitement replaced her earlier nervousness. She'd been sad over the prospect of leaving Sloan and their Shady Circle home, but might now have the opportunity to prolong the fantasy of playing house with this man. Other than the investigation, what would be the point, though? The longer she remained here, the harder it would be to leave.

The home, or Sloan?

Both, damn it. This was her dream house, and Sloan... She'd told Morgan about her issues with the man, and her friend had pointed out that when Sloan became defensive or said obnoxious things to goad her, it could be a sign that he was fighting his attraction for her. She'd scoffed at the idea, then later, when she was alone in her car, she'd examined their arguments, how they'd started, and how he'd reacted to knowing she was dating someone. While she hadn't come to the conclusion Morgan had, she'd realized Sloan was more than muscle. He was an emotionally complex man, and she'd been a horrible person to judge him for his hair and clothes. She hadn't been fair, hadn't considered his background, what might have happened that made him hide behind superficial conversation or sharp barbs. Then again, fearing she'd end up wanting more from him—an emotional and physical connection—she hadn't been open, either. Now they could have the chance to truly get to know each other. Did she want that?

"I've been all in from the start," she finally replied. "You, on the other hand, hate living here and…well, you don't exactly like me."

He looked away, set his fork on his plate and rubbed a hand along his jaw—a habit whenever he was frustrated or irritated. Clearly, she'd managed to say the wrong thing again, and given him a reason to be one or the other.

"Sorry," she said. "I wasn't trying to start another bickering match."

He looked at her, his gaze dark, intense, as if he wasn't sure whether to swallow her whole or push her away. Her face heated, because she didn't know if she could handle either of his reactions. Sloan made it clear he knew women, and she didn't doubt that. When it came to men, she wasn't the most experienced, and she worried that should they…become involved, she would mistake sex for something more than a physical act. If he told her she was right and he didn't like her in the least—as a person or partner—it'd hurt. She liked Sloan, and also respected him on a professional level. Now that she really thought about it, she'd save herself from embarrassment or hurt, and continue to wonder what he was thinking, rather than know the meaning behind the look in his eyes.

When he opened his mouth to speak, she pushed her chair back and stood. "I'm not hungry right now and am going to save this for later," she said, taking her plate and salad bowl to the counter. Within seconds, his masculine scent surrounded her.

"What's in the container?" he asked, his arm brushing hers as he reached for the box she'd brought home.

She finished covering her plate and bowl with plastic wrap. "When I was getting a sandwich at the grocery store, I went past the bakery and thought of you. I know you like your sweets, so I thought I'd bring you home a couple of slices of cake."

He stared at the closed box. "You...ah...you thought of me?" he asked, uncertainty in his tone.

Confused, she touched his forearm. "I think about you all the time." Though true, he didn't have to know in what way.

"How?"

Crap. So much for that. "How what?"

"How do you think of me?"

"I don't know. I just do. Leave the dishes. I'll take care of them later. I'm going to take a bath," she said, turning away to make her escape.

He gripped her arm and forced her to face him. The undeterminable intensity still darkened his eyes, yet his gaze was probing, questioning. "Why did you buy the cake?"

"Oh my God, Sloan. This is ridiculous. I thought of you and wanted to do something nice, okay? That's it. You do nice things for me, I wanted to do a nice thing for you."

"Even though you think I don't like you?"

"I don't think you hate me, but I do think you'd prefer to be alone or with someone else," she said, deciding to be honest. If they were going to continue to live together, they needed to quit skirting the truth. If she knew with certainty that he wanted nothing to do with her, in any capacity, she would rather pull herself from the undercover portion of the operation, than torture herself by living with, liking and lusting after a man who didn't want her.

His grip became possessive, as he moved her closer to him. "I don't know how to hate you," he said, his gaze drifting to her mouth.

Confused, turned on, and scared he would eventually hurt her, she gripped the front of his shirt. "I don't know how to hate you, too," she admitted.

When his gaze met hers again, her stomach did another nervous flip. Though naïve when it came to men, she understood desire and it was clear in his eyes. "Does that mean you like me?" he asked.

She wanted to tell him the truth. Wanted to tell him how she'd lusted after him from the moment she'd seen him without his shirt, that he made her body come alive just thinking about him, that she loved living with him, seeing his face in the morning and before she went to bed. How he'd erased the loneliness she hadn't realized she'd been harboring, and that she thought he was sweet, interesting and funny.

And, damn it, that she liked him more than she should...

Chapter Eight

S LOAN DREW IN a deep breath and held it. Waited for this beautiful, classy and intelligent woman to either laugh in his face and tell him to fuck off, or to wrap her arms around his neck and kiss him. He'd prefer the latter. After he'd called her this afternoon to tell her what he'd learned from Quint, he'd been down and upset that his time with Whitney was coming to a swift end. He'd then spent the afternoon trying to come up with a reason why they should continue the operation. He hadn't been ready to return to Chicago, hadn't been ready to walk away from this woman without at least tasting her lips.

Rachel might've been right about Whitney. But he wouldn't know unless she answered him. And if she didn't talk soon, he was going to pass out from lack of oxygen.

"Sloan, I…I don't want to say something that could jeopardize the operation and drive a wedge between us."

Fuck. She didn't like him.

He exhaled and nodded, but didn't release her. There'd never be another chance to be this close to her, and he wasn't ready to let her go. "Understood. If I made you uncomfortable by asking, I apologize. It was stupid of me to turn the slice of cake into something more than a nice gesture."

"You don't need to apologize, and it wasn't stupid of you."

She was wrong. Wanting to know how she felt, how she thought of him had him coming off as needy and desperate. But it'd been a long time since anyone had bothered to care, to think about him, and he wanted her to care. He wanted to be someone she'd miss, think about at odd times of the day, long to kiss and hold. He wanted this fake life to be real. Maybe not the wife part, since they'd only met a week ago. Still, he'd love a shot at something with Whitney, the chance to have a steady person in his life, someone he could turn to, who accepted his faults, and stood by his side during both the good and bad times. He'd never truly had that, but his parents had, and the example they'd set, of how to be there for each other, was something he'd admired and wanted.

He let go of her arm. "Go take your bath. I'll clean the kitchen."

She took a fistful of his shirt and tugged. "That's it? That's all you have to say?" Her eyes narrowed. "My insides are a mess because I don't want to admit something that could humiliate me. I didn't hear you say whether or not you like me."

Her insides were a mess? He didn't want that, but it gave him hope. "I told you I couldn't hate you."

"So what? I said the same thing, and we're both still left without an answer." She released his shirt. "You know what I think? You're just as afraid of rejection as I am."

He caged her against the counter before she could walk away. "I'm not afraid of anything."

"Nothing?" She tilted her head and studied him, her gaze inquisitive, thoughtful. "Then why won't you say how you feel?"

"Because I don't want to be slapped with a sexual harassment suit."

"Not buying it."

He'd taken risks all his life, had left Indiana with barely enough money to pay for the gas he'd needed to make the drive to Chicago, and had dove head first into a dangerous career. But he'd never taken an emotional risk. Shannon hadn't been one. They'd been together all throughout high school and he'd assumed they'd wind up being a couple. Ellie hadn't been much of an emotional risk, either. He'd loved the idea of being married more than he'd loved her. Whitney was different. She was the go-getting type of woman who would expect him to live up to his full potential, and it scared the shit out of him that he might not be able meet her expectations.

She sighed and her eyes filled with disappointment. "If you're not going to respond, then I'm going to take my bath. Please let me go."

"I can't do that," he admitted.

"Can't do what?" Her forehead furrowed. "Let me take a bath?"

For such a smart woman, she was clueless when it came to herself. There'd been times over the past week where he'd wondered if she was purposefully torturing him by using the bathtub, by wearing tight fitting yoga pants that hugged her ass and had his mind going to dirty places. Now he knew for certain she had no idea the effect she had on him.

Unable to resist, and once again ready to take a risk, he touched her cheek. Her skin was as soft as he'd imagined. "Let you go."

Her eyes widened slightly. "Oh."

"If we start something, I have a feeling it's going to be hard to stop." He inched closer, loved that she was tall and he didn't have to hunch over to reach her lips—the direction he was heading. "So, either tell me to stop now, or I'm going to kiss you."

She speared her fingers through his hair and drew his mouth even closer to hers. "Not a chance," she said, and kissed him.

He expected a soft, demure kiss. Instead, she set him on fire. Parted her lips, slid her tongue along his, clumsily gripped his hair and deepened the kiss. When she leaned her body into his, he moved his hand over her back and held her. Breathed in her scent. Loved the way her breasts pressed against his chest and slowed her pace.

"Savor it," he whispered against her lips. "I know I am."

"Sorry." She kissed him again. "I've been holding this in for a while."

"Since when?" he asked, curious if they'd been on the same page all along.

"Since you took your shirt off at the store."

"Is that so?" he asked, figuring as much. The women he'd 'dated' had been only interested in what was on the outside, not him personally, and he'd thought Whitney was different.

She ran her palm along his beard. "What about you?"

Easy question. "When I picked you up and carried you into the house." She'd been a perfect fit, and holding her had been as natural as breathing.

"I loved that."

"You did?"

She nodded. "And when we held hands during our walk later that day."

"Me too."

Her gaze was probing. "What's wrong? I get the feeling I said or did something I shouldn't have."

He kissed her, then leaned back. "Nothing. Why don't you take your bath while I clean up the dishes?"

"You're dismissing me. Are you trying to tell me I can't kiss?"

Hell, no. He'd loved having her lips on his, her eagerness and passion. He was accustomed to being with women who were experts at the art of seduction, who liked sex without attachment. Based on what he knew about Whitney, her need for control, for everything to be listed then checked off later, he'd expected her to be the type of woman who didn't have relationships based on sex. If Campbell allowed them to continue with the operation for another two weeks, he didn't want to spend that time just fucking. He could do plenty of that when he was back in Chicago. No, he wanted more from her. While he wasn't exactly sure what that was, he'd like to explore the possibilities, but supposed it wasn't a good idea anyway. None of this was real. They were playing pretend, and in a couple weeks, he'd leave this fake life behind.

"I'm not dismissing you," he said as his phone chimed. He glanced to the kitchen island where he'd left it. "Somebody at the Eastons' activated one of the listening devices."

"How do you know?"

With reluctance, and wishing they could go back to kissing, he stepped away from her and reached for the phone. "I rigged the computer software so it would send a notification signal to my phone whenever the device is in use." He started for the staircase. "But it's only a notification. I have to use the computer to hear what's being said."

"Dale and Irene aren't home." She followed him up the stairs and into his room. "If we can confirm Cameron is using a burner phone, I'll put in a request for our Stingray. We only have one, and it was being used for another investigation, but I'm sure Campbell will let us have it for a while."

The Stingray, also known as a cell-site simulator, posed as a legitimate cell phone tower in order to 'trick' nearby cell phones into connecting with the device. Once a connection was made, they could obtain the phone's International Mobile Equipment Identifier. If they had the IMEI numbers of the burner phones they believed were being used by one or all of the Eastons, they could easily tap and trace their calls.

"CORE has one if we need to go that route." He sat at the card table and opened the recording device software. "We can listen in right now, or start at the beginning."

She unfolded one of the extra chairs and positioned it next to his. "Right now."

He clicked away at the keyboard, then gave the software the necessary commands. "Here we go," he said, then turned up the monitor's volume.

"No, you let him know. I'm going out with Lexi."

"That's definitely Cameron," Whitney said. "We know he has a girlfriend by that name."

"But tell him he has to be on time," the kid continued. *"I know three a.m. sucks ass, but we don't have a choice."* He was silent for a moment. *"That's not gonna work. You have to come home that weekend. He's going to be expecting his money."*

"Do you think he's on with the sister?" he asked when Cameron stopped talking again.

She shrugged. "And maybe one *he* is his brother?" When her cell phone chimed, she checked the screen. "I just got a text from the deputy following Dale and Irene. They're on the way home and should be there in about five minutes."

"Yeah, well, he's not going to care about a frat party." Cameron continued. *"Make sure Gage knows he has to come home, too. It's Mom's birthday that weekend anyway. Dad will go apeshit if you guys blow it off and pull a no-show."*

Whitney hiked a brow. "I guess that answers our questions."

"Hey, did you hear about the dead body they found in the new development? Me and my boys went to check it out, but the cops have been there night and day. There's police tape everywhere." He quieted for a moment, then said, *"I haven't met them yet. The dude is a fucking giant and his wife is supermodel-tall and smokin' hot. I keep having to wash my sheets because of the wet dreams she's been giving me."* Cameron laughed. *"I'm just messin' with ya. I know how you get all grossed out."*

"Lovely," Whitney said, her cheeks turning pink.

While Sloan didn't appreciate the kid's crude remark, Cameron was right: his fake wife was smokin' hot. "He's an ass. But, if I'd had you for a neighbor when I was seventeen—"

She wrinkled her nose. "Please don't go there," she said, then looked at the video camera when it activated. "The Eastons are back from dinner. I'm surprised they have any money. Did you notice how much they go out to eat?"

"Fourth time this week," he replied, and wondered if Whitney would want to go to dinner with him. Then again, if she wanted to keep it physical between them, dating probably wouldn't appeal to her.

"Gotta go. I just heard the garage door. I'll call tomorrow night around eight. Mom said they're going to a fundraiser then."

"Honey?" Irene called.

"In here, Mom."

The clinking of keys filled the background. *"I brought you home a burger,"* she said.

"Thanks, but Lex and I are going to the mall. I was gonna grab something to eat with her."

"I'll put it in the fridge then. Maybe you'll want it later."

"Hey, Cam," Dale greeted his son. *"How was school today? Did you ace your Spanish test?"*

"Si, señor."

Cameron and his parents talked a little more about their day, then everyone left the room. The device went silent.

"We need the Stingray for tomorrow evening," Whitney said as he rewound Cameron and Blair's conversation. "If we can get his number, we can tap the phone. What's the battery life on the pen and key fob?"

"Twelve hours."

"Then we definitely need the Stingray. The listening devices won't last long."

They listened to the thirty-plus seconds they'd missed between Cameron and his sister, but gained nothing new from that short portion of the call.

"I need to let BCI know Blair and Gage are picking up something—I'm assuming a shipment of drugs." She drummed her fingers on the coffee table. "I need to look at my notes and check when it's Irene's birthday."

"But that's when they're supposed to deliver the money, not get the shipment."

She released a sigh and pushed her fingers through her long hair. "True. We don't know *when* they're supposed to make an exchange, but at least we have a time."

He nodded. "Three in the morning."

"Hey, it's me"

Tensing, Sloan looked to Whitney. "That's Dale's voice."

She picked up her phone and placed a call.

"Sorry I missed you earlier," Dale continued, his voice hushed.

"They got him." She beamed. "I have a detective listening in to the conversation. Guess who he's talking to?"

"No clue."

"Becky, just be patient."

Sloan grinned. "Becky?"

She rolled her eyes. "Too easy. Just like Becky," she added with a smug smile. "I was totally right about her."

"I know you were. She came over Monday and suggested we have lunch sometime. Wink, wink."

Whitney's eyes narrowed. "The witch hit on my fake husband? I should march over to her house and—"

"I don't know when I can see you again. If Irene catches us...I can't have that happen."

"I wish we could hear what she's saying." She sat on the bed, tempting him to turn off the computer and pin her to the mattress, forget about the neighbors and focus on giving them ultimate pleasure.

Except that was all she wanted from him. Nothing more. That should make him happy. Yet, it didn't. He could go home to Chicago, make a phone call that would lead to guaranteed sex. While he wanted to eventually have sex with Whitney, he didn't want it *guaranteed*. He didn't know why, but he wanted her to feel something for him first.

"I'll call you again tomorrow," Dale continued. *"We have that fundraiser to go to, but maybe we could get together for coffee in the morning. I'll tell Irene I need to meet with a client."* There was a short pause on his end of the conversation. *"She has a photo shoot, so we should be good."* He was quiet for a moment. *"Perfect. See you then."*

The device went silent again. Sloan saved the recording, then looked to Whitney, who snatched up her ringing cell phone, then answered it. After a few minutes, she said, "Okay, thanks. Make sure we have a deputy ready in the morning anyway." She ended the call, disappointment evident on her face.

"What?" he asked.

She puffed her cheeks, then released a breath. "They've got nothing. Even if they'd heard anything about an affair, who cares? We're not here to bust Dale for cheating on his wife."

The camera signaled them again. He glanced at it. "Cameron just left."

She made another call and let one of the members of her team know so they could track him, then dropped her cell on the bed. "I'm tired of these people. We need new neighbors."

He smiled. "No doubt." The folding chair groaned when he stood. "Since there's nothing more we can do tonight, you go take your bath. I need to put the lasagna in the fridge."

Her eyes filled with guilt. "You went through all the trouble of making it and I didn't even take a bite. I'm sorry."

Earlier in the week, when Whitney had mentioned lasagna

was one of her favorite meals, he'd looked up recipes online, but was overwhelmed by the amount of them and the mixed reviews. Which had been why, when he'd run into her the other day, he had asked Helen if she had a go-to recipe. "If you're still hungry I can heat it up for you."

"I wish I was, but my stomach is jittery from listening to the conversations. I feel like we're close to...*something*. You know?"

Yeah, he did know. Only the *something* she referred to wasn't the same as his. Her mind was on the investigation, while his was on her. He needed to stop that shit before it distracted him from the reason why he was here. She was only interested in him physically, and he needed to remember that. Now that he thought about it, he should probably pretend the kiss hadn't happened and keep their relationship professional. Because he liked her—too much—if he kept kissing her and those kisses led to something more, he wasn't sure if he could maintain a *this is just sex* attitude. It'd been years since he'd faced rejection from a woman, and he saw no reason to face it again.

"Go relax," he suggested, wanting to distance himself from her.

"No, I should get on my laptop and look up Irene's birthday."

"Run the water while you do it. I'll get your glass of wine."

She pushed herself off the bed. "You've already done too much. I'll skip my bath and shower in the morning. Let's go eat your lasagna. Don't forget I brought you spice cake for dessert."

He froze. "Spice cake?"

Worry deflated her face. "No good?"

Memories washed over him, had him thinking of his mom. "It's..." He cleared his throat. "My mom used to make that for me. It's my favorite kind of cake."

She sat back on the bed. "Used to?" she asked. "Is your mom gone?"

He nodded. "She died when I was fifteen. Breast cancer."

Sadness filled her eyes. "I'm sorry."

He rubbed a hand along his beard and considered what he'd told Vincent about the front porch. "I was never good at school stuff. My dad used to say I didn't need to worry about knowing who was president and when, or about geometry and chemistry, just so long as I could bale hay or milk a cow. But my mom was adamant about education." His mother's image rose to the surface and brought with it bitterness, pain and joy. "I loved my dad, but my mom could've done better than marrying an uneducated farm boy who quit school at fourteen."

"What?" Her brows furrowed. "Why would his parents have allowed that?"

"Because farming was all they knew. Same with my mom, only she finished high school and had plans for college. She was a smart woman, but her parents couldn't afford to pay for her education. So, she did what all the women in her family had done...she got married and became a farmer's wife."

"Do you have siblings?"

He shook his head. "I pretty much broke my mom. I guess she had all kinds of complications during her pregnancy with me and her doctor recommended she shouldn't have more children."

"I'm sorry," she repeated.

"Why, because you come from a big family?" He shrugged. "It's no big deal. I don't know what that's like, so how can I miss something I've never had?"

"I understand that, but...never mind." She rose from the bed again and moved toward the door. "Come on, let's go eat."

"Never mind what?" he asked, following her to the kitchen.

She took the plastic wrap off her plate and salad bowl. "Nothing. When did your dad pass away?"

"About twenty years ago."

After she put his dish in the microwave and started it, she turned to him, her eyes holding sympathy. "Do you have anyone? Aunts, uncles, cousins?"

"I have an aunt still living, and two cousins. She's my dad's sister, but they had a huge falling out before I was born. I've never met her or her kids."

The microwave beeped. She removed the plate in exchange for her own. "What do you do for the holidays?"

When he'd been with the Chicago PD, he'd either volunteered to work or locked himself in his condo until the holiday had ended. Over the years, cop buddies, who knew he was alone, would invite him to their homes, but he hadn't wanted to intrude on times that were meant for family. "I have plenty of friends and always have a bunch of invites," he said, not wanting to make himself sound like a loser, and to take her off the subject.

"Well, that's good. No one should be alone during the holidays." She brought their plates to the table, while he topped off their wine glasses. "I couldn't imagine being by myself, especially at Christmas."

"What's the big deal? It's just another day."

"I disagree. And Christmas isn't just one day, it's a whole season." She sipped her wine. "At the beginning of every November, I always go to my parents' and help them decorate. As the month goes on, we bake cookies, make candy, shop, wrap and plan meals. My brothers and their families live out of town, but within driving distance." She then told him her brothers' names, what order they were born in, rattled off the names of their wives and kids. How, during any major holiday, the youngest of the three sons, along with his family, stayed with her at the West Park rental, while the rest went to her folks'. "It's a ton of work, but I love every minute of it. Until, my brother and his family began staying with me, I didn't realize how quiet and lonely it was at my house."

She finally stopped talking and tried the lasagna. "Mmm, this is fantastic. I need this recipe. I want to make it for my parents." She took another bite, then lifted her glass. "I'd love to invite them over to see the house."

"But it's not ours."

"I know. It's what I eventually hope to own, though."

"I understand that, but what's the point of showing them a place that you're using for work and will be leaving in five weeks?" Because they had something more on Cameron, he doubted Lieutenant Campbell would end the operation. "Don't become attached, I know I won't. I can't wait to be back in my own space."

What a jerk. Whitney masked the hurt and disappointment by taking a long drink of wine. Thirty minutes ago, they'd been kissing and talking about starting something between them. Either he'd lost complete interest after they'd kissed, or he had a split personality. Unfortunately, she was certain he had no mental illness and it boiled down to her not being able to deliver a decent kiss. She finished the wine in two swallows, realized he was watching her, then set the glass on the table.

"I was thirsty," she said.

"I see that." He placed his napkin on his empty plate. "Would you like more?"

"I'd like to know why you're suddenly anxious to get back to Chicago. If I recall, you were worried that if we start something, you'd have a hard time stopping," she said, not interested in spending the rest of the operation trying to figure out this man and his motives. "Was the kiss that bad?" she asked. Sure, she'd been a little overzealous, but she'd been so turned on by him and his words, any worry about finesse had fled her mind. Her sole focus had been on touching and kissing him. On finally making one of her fantasies real.

When he didn't say anything, she brought her glass to the kitchen island, then picked up the bottle of wine. "If you have to think about it, then don't bother answering." She filled her glass to the very top, leaned over and gave it a sip, then topped it with what was left in the bottle.

"I didn't want any more wine," he finally said.

"Good thing." She kept her back to him. "I'm thinking that since we're both great at faking it, let's just pretend the kiss never happened and go back to the way we were."

"That'd probably be the smart thing to do."

Her throat tightened. One lousy kiss and he was done with her? So, she wasn't very experienced, had been a little too excited and hadn't given her best performance. What was wrong with that? What was wrong with giving it another try?

Worried she'd tear up in front of him and make a fool of herself, she carefully picked up the full glass. "It would. I'm going to my room." Tonight, of all nights, she'd love to soak in the tub and to wash away the humiliation, but decided the next time she set foot inside the master bedroom, it would be for business, not bath time. "I'm also moving my stuff out of your bathroom and into the guest bath. I think we should stop doing intimate things like eating together and talking."

"Christ, Whitney, are we back to being childish again?"

She faced him. "Might as well be, since you're back to being a jerk."

His brows pulled together. He stood and approached her. On to him, and familiar with his games, she put out a hand stopping him before he could invade her space. "Why am I a jerk?'" he asked.

"You tell me? You acted like you were into me, into us, and now…nothing. Because you won't tell me why you changed your mind, I'm going to assume that it's because I can't kiss."

"That's not true." He rubbed his beard, then pushed a hand through his hair. "I enjoyed kissing you."

"Enjoyed," she repeated. "That sounds so…hot. Okay, you *enjoyed* the kiss, but changed your mind about us. Was it because I was talking too much or asking too many questions?"

"No, I enjoy…I mean, I like talking to you."

Frustration settled in her chest and, thanks to the wine and lasagna, so had heartburn. "This is ridiculous. If you're too afraid to admit what your problem is, then I definitely think it's best we keep our relationship professional. I don't want to be with a man who can't be honest with me, or himself."

His eyes narrowed. "I told you, I'm not afraid—"

"Of anything," she finished for him. "Yep, heard you the first time."

"It's true. After years of working Vice, facing the barrel of a gun or the sharp edge of a blade and surviving, nothing scares me." He took her glass, then drained half of it. "I don't know why you're acting hurt when you made it clear you were only interested in a purely physical relationship." He set the wine on the island. "But, hey, if that's what you're looking for, I'm your guy. I can bend you over the island right now if you'd like. I'm sure you'll *enjoy* it," he finished, and she didn't miss the bitterness in his tone.

"What are you talking about? At what point did I say or even hint that I just wanted sex? To be clear, I don't do *purely physical*."

"But the no shirt thing."

"At the store? What about it? I liked what I saw. You said you wanted to kiss me after you carried me into the house. Are you saying that you actually liked me then, or were you attracted to how I looked?"

He stepped close. "I dreaded living with you." He cupped her cheek with one hand. "The night before we moved in together, I couldn't sleep. I kept wondering how I was going to make it through six weeks under the same roof with one of the sexiest and meanest women I've ever met."

Her cheeks grew warm. No one had ever told her she was sexy. She had no sex appeal, had no idea how to flirt or flaunt her body, which she knew wasn't bad. But even though she was in her thirties, it was hard to shake off teenage insecurities, to not look in the mirror and see the tall, gawky, flat-chested, skinny teen she'd once been. "You thought I was sexy?"

"Don't forget mean," he said, softening the insult with a grin. "I still wanted you. Even when you were driving me nuts with all your sticky notes and lists, leaving your clothes around and messing up my bathroom, I wanted you. I also began to realize I liked you, too."

"Why?" she asked, not understanding why he was attracted to her. The picture he painted was rather ugly, and made her sound as if she were a nagging OCD slob.

"Because."

"That's not an answer."

He leaned in until their lips were inches apart. "It's the only one I'm ready to give right now."

While she'd have loved to have heard what was truly on his mind, she understood. What was happening was too new and they were partners. Exposing true feelings would leave them vulnerable and embarrassed if they became involved and it didn't work out—especially if they were still working the operation.

"Okay, so now what?" she asked, hoping they could finally move forward. A little kissing would be nice.

"First, I'm going to apologize. I've said things I didn't mean.'

She twined her arms around his neck. "I did, too."

When he brushed his lips along hers, goose bumps coated her skin. "You don't smell like my grandma."

Relieved, because that was her favorite lotion, she gazed up at him. "And I don't think you're a hairy barbarian."

"When did you call me that?"

"At least a thousand times—in my mind. You really know how to get in my head and blow all rational thought. There's been a few times this week where I've acted like a defensive twelve-year-old."

"I can say the same. Apparently, we bring out the best in each other."

"Apparently." She glanced at his chest. "So…"

"We're having an awkward moment, aren't we?"

"It doesn't have to be. We could kiss again. This time I'll let you control the pace so I don't accidentally swallow your tongue."

He laughed and rested his forehead against hers. "I want to kiss you… Honestly, I want to do more than kiss you, but—and I'm not trying to start an argument—we have a problem." He tilted his head and met her gaze. "You have a boyfriend."

Cliff. Damn it, she'd forgotten about him. "He's not my boyfriend," she said, then explained their relationship.

His brow furrowed. "Then why did you tell me you have a boyfriend?"

"Because I was upset you made plans for Saturday without me, and I didn't want to look like the loser sitting at home alone," she admitted. "Again, you bring out the twelve-year-old in me."

He released a breath. "I was jealous."

"You told me you couldn't picture me having sex with him."

He sifted his hand through her hair until he cradled her head. "Because I could only picture you having sex with me."

Her body tingled and hummed. Her nipples hardened and her sex grew heavy with need. It'd been almost two years since she'd made love, and it hadn't been that great. The guy she'd been dating back then had been nice and a gentleman, but also a total bore—in and out of bed. Weird, too. They'd had to have sex in the dark, he'd thought oral sex was unsanitary and he'd always worn his socks to bed. During the nine months she'd wasted on dating him, she had never once seen his feet. Not that she was complaining. She hated feet. Still, had his been webbed or something?

"I have dating rules," she said, pressing her body against his.

"You have a list of dating rules? This doesn't surprise me, since you have lists for everything else." He kissed her cheek. "Why is your face getting pink? I wasn't trying to embarrass you."

"I know, but you think my lists are strange."

"You like to be organized. I get it. But sometimes you need to go with the flow." He moved his hands to her hips, then angled his head and kissed her neck. "Tell me your dating rules."

More goose bumps rose along her arms as she tried to remember them, while his warm breath and beard tickled her skin. Drove her crazy, had her wanting to throw away her rules and have fun with him. "No kissing until the third date. Second base comes after sixth date, third base after the ninth."

"And sex?"

He was going to think she was a total prude, but didn't care. She'd set high standards for herself, and if men couldn't respect that, then there was no point in dating them. "Three months of solid dating."

He brought his mouth near hers again. "Since we're fake married, why don't you pretend we fake-dated for three months?"

He'd come up with a tempting suggestion, except she wasn't sure if she could pretend away her rules and standards. To her, actually dating, building a relationship and trust, experiencing her first kiss with a new partner were not things she could fabricate.

"I don't know if I can."

"Let me help you. I'll need you to play along and use your imagination, though. Okay?"

"I don't have a very good imagination, but I'll try."

He held her hand. "I'll never forget our first date at the coffee shop. You were so smart and beautiful, I was nervous I'd say something stupid. I kept telling myself that you were too good for me and nothing would happen between us. But then you agreed to go out with me again."

She liked where he was going with this. She could pretend and trick herself into justifying why she should toss out her rules this one time. Nothing would come from this anyway. Sloan lived in another state and wasn't the marrying kind. Plus, a brief affair—one that was hot and passionate—might do her good. Even though he'd cheated on her, she'd loved the passion and intensity she'd experienced with Wes during their brief relationship and missed those lustful, all-consuming emotions he'd evoked. Why not treat herself to an affair with a man she wouldn't normally date? After all, once Sloan left for Chicago, she planned to cannonball into the dating pool again and continue her search for a safe man, who would not only be a good provider and father, he wouldn't be ruled by sex and desire. He wouldn't be a cheater.

"You took me to the theater," she said, playing along with him.

He furrowed his brow. "Theater? Do I look like the kind of guy who would enjoy something like that?"

"No, but when we were having coffee, I'd mentioned how much I loved musicals, so you took me to one. When I realized you hated the theater, I was so touched that you went just for me."

He grinned and led her to the foyer. "What can I say? I'm a thoughtful guy and was hoping for a third date."

"Which was wonderful. I loved the restaurant you took me to, and then how we went for a long ride on your motorcycle."

"I purposefully took the bike that night because I wanted you to be forced to hold me and press up against my back," he said, opening the front door and bringing them onto the porch.

"I had no idea. But I do know that I was secretly glad you brought the bike. I'll also admit to holding onto you tighter than necessary."

"You didn't hear me complaining." He closed the door. "Especially after we came back to your place. Remember? I walked you to your front door and we had our first kiss."

Their first kiss was in the kitchen of the rental house. Although she hadn't delivered the sexiest of kisses, being with Sloan at that moment had been special to her, because they'd both just admitted they liked each other. She'd continue with the make-believe, though. If the memories weren't real, then maybe her feelings for Sloan wouldn't be, too. Not that she anticipated becoming attached or having deep-seated emotions that would mess with her head and break her heart. She liked Sloan, but he didn't fit into her life plan, or what she looked for in a man. He was too quick tempered, too overbearing and, from what she could tell, he had no goals, no drive and absolutely no desire to live in suburbia.

"I remember being very nervous," she said, her stomach doing a little flip. She suspected he was going to kiss her, which she wanted, except now she was self-conscious and worried she would screw it up again.

"It didn't show." He shifted her until her back faced the door. "It was as dark as it is now. The porch light wasn't very bright, but I didn't need it to be. I'd memorized the curve of your face, the fullness of your lips and depths of desire in your eyes."

Holy crap. She had no idea Sloan could be so romantic and poetic. Then again, he probably used similar lines on his multitude of women.

"And how we fit so perfectly together." He cupped her head and angled his mouth closer to hers. "Let's see if we can recreate that kiss," he said, then brushed his lips against hers. Gently, leisurely, he coaxed her mouth apart.

Aroused, anxious to touch him, she twined her arms around his neck, then released a low moan when his tongue caressed hers. As she feathered her fingers through his hair, he wrapped his arm around her lower back and pulled her close. She forced her breasts against his hard chest, as he deepened the kiss. The intimacy, the way his masculine scent cloaked her, how his big, strong hands held her, had her nipples tightening and her sex aching for his touch. Growing bolder, wanting more, she gripped his hair and held his head in place. Tangled her tongue with his until, breath labored, Sloan broke away, only to kiss her temple, cheek, then neck. As her heart continued to beat hard and fast, he dragged his lips back to her mouth, then gave her a chaste kiss.

"That was the best kiss I've ever had," she admitted, bringing her hands to h:s shoulders.

"Same." He rested his forehead against hers. "I'll never forget that night."

A night they'd invented.

Because what they were doing was meant to be fun, and a way to help her OCD mind let go of her rules, she wouldn't allow herself to be cisappointed. No man had ever kissed her the way Sloan just had, and it didn't matter if kissing her meant anything to him or not. They would hopefully be lovers, maybe even friends, but ncthing more. Nothing more than a fun distraction while working an investigation together.

He reached behind her and opened the door. Keeping her body pinned to his, he walked her backwards and into the house. "I'll also never forget the first time you let me get to second base." He nudged the door closed with this foot, then continued to move her until her back was against the foyer wall that separated the space from the office. "We'd just gotten back from our sixth date and you'd invited me inside."

"We had a drink." She breathed in his scent and melted into him. "Then you had to leave."

He lightly kissed the corner of her mouth. "I didn't want to go."

"I didn't want you to leave, either. We'd been kissing and cuddling on the couch."

He smiled against her lips. "I think we kissed all the way to the door."

"Kind of like now?"

"Mmm-hmm." He moved his hands from the small of her back to her hips. "What was it you did that gave me a sign that I could be...bolder?"

He was letting her lead, but she didn't want to be the one who controlled this stroll down fake memory lane. If she was going to have an affair with a man who she wouldn't normally date, then she also didn't want their relationship to be how the majority of hers had been, where she dictated what they did, when and how.

Since she wasn't ready for the fantasy to end, she'd still play the game, though.

She placed his hands on her rear and pressed herself against his erection. "I believe I did this," she said, then gently nipped his lower lip.

He squeezed her bottom, then shifted his leg until her sex cradled his thigh. "What happened next?" he asked, kissing her neck, then jawline.

"You put your hand on my breast," she said, and hoped to God he'd do it. Other than her annual gynecological visit—which in no way was hot—she hadn't been touched there in over a year, maybe longer.

"Like this?" He cupped her right breast, grazing his thumb over her nipple. "Or was it more like this?" he asked, and gave her nipple a gentle pinch.

Desire shot straight to her sex. "Maybe both ways. You should keep alternating to help jog my memory," she said, then sought his mouth. When their lips met, she swept her tongue along his and ground herself against his thigh, creating an exquisite friction. Between that, the sensual kiss and what he was doing to her breast, she was going to come. Hard and fast. She didn't know whether that would turn him on or off and didn't care. At the moment, all she cared about was the overwhelming pleasure he was giving her.

He moved his lips from hers, then once again dragged them along her neck, then lower, where he placed open-mouthed kisses along the exposed flesh above the lace of her bra. For a millisecond, she wondered when he'd undone the top two buttons of her denim shirt, then dismissed it from her mind. If it hadn't been for her rules and lists, they'd already be naked and in one of their beds.

"Come for me like you did the first time we did this," he murmured against her breast. "I know you're close." He nudged the denim aside and pulled a lace-covered nipple into his mouth, then used his big hand to help move her sex along his thigh. "Come for me."

When he kissed her again, her vaginal muscles clenched, her

belly coiled, then burst. As her orgasm shot through her body, she stiffened and released a groan. Didn't care about the noise, and whether he thought she was gawky or clumsy. Instead, she focused on the pleasure he gave her.

"Yes," he hissed. "It's all coming back to me." He slipped his hand beneath the waistband of her leggings. His fingers brushed the hair above her sex, but didn't go lower. "Then it was after date nine when you let me do this."

Another groan hummed from her throat when he pressed a finger inside her. Allowing a man she barely knew to do this to her went against so many of her rules. But, again, she didn't care. She wanted this. Wanted Sloan. Not for the Wolverine fantasy—she didn't need a superhero—not because he was ridiculously good looking, but because she liked him for him. He was more percep- tive than she'd given him credit for, understood and accepted her quirky lists and rules, and was determined to make this good for her without making it about him.

When he added a second finger, then pumped his hand, she reached down and stroked his thick arousal through his khakis. Another orgasm neared. *She* made this man hard. Knowing he was used to being with plenty of women, knowing *she* turned him on...empowered her. Made her want to be reckless, to let go of her staid lifestyle, her lists and live her life off a blank page.

"You're so fucking wet." His mouth hovered near hers. "Come on my fingers."

The way he talked, it was so...dirty. She loved it. Hadn't known she would. Dirty talk wasn't on any list she'd ever created, but they were pretending. Except the coiling returning deep within her was real. *Very* real. As he kissed her, the rhythm of his tongue matching the thrust of his fingers, that coil sprang out to every part of her body, giving her another fantastic orgasm that left her breath labored and her heart pounding.

"You're gripping my fingers," he murmured against her ears. "Do you have any idea how hot you are?"

She hadn't a clue, and his words barely registered her sex- fogged mind. "We should find a bed and reenact the first time we had sex."

He slipped his hand from her pants. His gaze hungry, he brought his fingers to his mouth, then licked them. No one had *ever* done that. The sight of him enjoying her essence on his tongue aroused her to the point she was prepared to let him take her on the steps.

"We can't," he said.

A bucket of cold water washed over her. "Why not?"

"I have no condoms."

Chapter Nine

"**N**O CONDOMS?"

Sloan didn't know whether to be pleased or upset by her disappointment. She'd just come all over his hand—which had been fucking hot—but did she think he would carry around a box of condoms during an investigation?

"What makes you think I'd have some with me?" he asked, not wanting an answer. He knew Whitney well enough to guess her response. She'd assumed he was a womanizer, which would be a correct assumption and his fault. He'd purposefully mentioned having many women in his life—whether to make her jealous, turn her off or have her think he was *the man*—the reason didn't matter at this point. Sabotaging the rest of the night was what mattered. The things he'd said to her before they'd kissed weren't lines, hadn't been part of the pretend version of their past. He'd meant every word. Now that he'd tasted and touched her, walking away from her would be difficult.

The corner of her mouth curved into a small smile. "Nope. Not taking the bait." When she pushed herself off the wall and moved past him, her body brushed his.

He took her by the arm and stopped her. "What are you talking about?"

"I've lived with you for a week. And I know how you are. If

you think things are going good, you do or say something to ruin them and start an argument."

"How do you know?"

"Because I've been doing the same thing. I don't get why you want to drive me away now, but that's fine. I'm sorry if I hurt your feelings by assuming you had condoms." She pulled her arm free. "If we're not going to have sex, I'm going upstairs to do the next best thing—take a bath."

Hell, no. Not going to happen. He didn't want to drift off to sleep with her scent lingering in his room, reminding him of the way she kissed, how her body had responded to him. "You said using the tub was too intimate."

"You made me orgasm twice. I think that's more intimate than using your bathtub."

She started up the steps, then tossed her long hair as she glanced over her shoulder. The fire in her eyes told him he should run, grovel or head to the drug store for a box of condoms. Kiss her before she said something that could cause a fight. Yes, he'd wanted to sabotage the night, and he'd accomplished that. But after kissing and holding her, he didn't want to hear any nasty comments coming from her pretty mouth.

"It's interesting. You've mentioned several times that you're not afraid of anything."

"Not taking the bait," he said, repeating her words.

"Then don't. I'll say what I want anyway. I think you're afraid of being close with someone."

"That's not true."

"Deny it all you want, but that's the vibe I'm getting from you." She turned and held the stair rail. "I didn't expect for us to get close and fall in love, if that's what has you worried." She motioned between them. "I was ready to do this, have fun while you were here and hoped to make a friend in the process. But I can't be *intimate* with a man who can't make a decision."

"About what? You and me? I know exactly what I want."

That small smile returned. "Let me guess…sex?"

"Exactly."

"If you wanted it that badly, you wouldn't be standing here

talking to me, you'd be in the truck and driving to the nearest drug store," she said, then turned her back on him and went upstairs.

Fuck. He hated when she was right. He didn't know what to do with her, with the emotions that were driving him crazy.

He went into the kitchen, finished the glass of wine left on the island, then proceeded to clean up the dinner mess. She wanted a fun fling with a friend. What she wanted *should* have him driving to the store for condoms. Whitney was giving him a fantastic offer: sex with a buddy, no strings attached. Except, he liked her as more than a friend. The pretend thing they'd been doing earlier, and coming up with the fake dates they had been on, their first kiss, first touch, had left him longing for it to all be true. He could picture her on his bike, her breasts pressed against his back as she held him. He saw them standing on the front porch of her West Park rental, where he would lean in and coax her into their first kiss.

The imagining and pretending weren't healthy. At least, not for him. Over the last week, he'd been in his head, thinking about things that had never occurred to him or had never bothered him in the past. Until he'd moved in with Whitney, being alone hadn't been a big deal. Now, the idea of being in his condo with no one to talk to, no one to eat dinner with, no one to think or care about, depressed the hell out of him. Now, because he liked Whitney, the fear of rejection was real. Shannon had brushed him out of her life because, at the time, he couldn't offer her much of anything. Ellie had left him because she feared his career could get her killed. If he were honest with Whitney, told her how much he liked her, how he didn't want to just be friends, and then she rejected him, the hurt would cut deep. He had a good job and financial security. While working for CORE had its elements of danger, the job was a cakewalk compared to his time with Vice. He couldn't see Whitney dismissing him for those reasons, which left only one: him.

He couldn't change who he was, and didn't see a reason why he ever would. He liked himself. Maybe if he opened up a little, Whitney could discover that he was a good guy. But if he did that and she fell for him, she might expect him to make a commitment. And he knew Whitney had plans for the future that included a home, husband and children.

Christ. He leaned against the counter. He really was indecisive, which was unusual for him. Normally, he always knew what he wanted, and never had a problem achieving whatever that might be. Except, what he wanted now was something incredibly unfamiliar and slightly scary.

"Well, how about that?" he murmured, and opened the fridge to retrieve a bottle of chardonnay—Whitney's preference. Apparently, he was afraid of something: falling in love with Whitney, the white picket fence, the two-point-five children. Marriage and kids weren't him. He didn't know how to be a husband or father. All he knew was how to be a badass detective.

As he opened the bottle, he decided he was fucked in the head, and had been from the moment he'd stepped foot in this house. Because he'd enjoyed the rush, and wasn't afraid of dying, he'd spent his adult life working a dangerous job. Yet, for the first time, he was afraid of taking a risk, of having to consider someone else's feelings and expectations, of being forced to evaluate his future, and actually set goals for himself. He was afraid of failure.

"Yep, fucked in the head," he said, taking two clean glasses from the cabinet. Carrying them and the wine, he left the kitchen and went up the steps. When he reached the second level, he noticed Whitney's room was empty, so he went into his hoping he'd find her on the computer, not in a robe. His room was also empty, which meant she was still in his bathroom.

Damn it. He'd taken his time in the kitchen, hoping she'd finished her bath and was hanging out in her room—clothed. The wine was a peace offering, an icebreaker that would help him lead into an apology. His head might be fucked and filled with uncertainty, but his body knew what it wanted during the time he was living with Whitney. She wanted sex, too. Other than her possibly hurting him, and making him insecure and depressed, he saw no reason to deny either of them *physical* pleasure. He also saw no reason to let her know that he'd been having a hard time navigating their relationship and his emotions. Then again, how could he have any real feelings for her when their relationship was based on a bogus marriage and pretend dating?

The bathroom door opened, sending steam and her apple and vanilla scent into the room. She jumped, grabbed the doorjamb and clutched the lapel of her robe with the other. "You scared the crap out of me."

"Sorry. I thought you'd be done by now."

"The water helps me think."

"What were you thinking about?"

"You. Me. I don't know what to do with you. But it's like I told you: I can't keep dealing with the hot, then cold business. It's not fun. If anything, it'll distract me from the reason why we're here." She drew in a deep breath. "Which is why I need you to promise that, since we're both very good at pretending, you'll pretend nothing happened between us."

His muscles tensed. He should agree. Take intimacy out of their relationship, stick to being partners, and focus on the investigation. "I can't pretend I didn't touch you."

She rolled her eyes and walked past him. "You can't do that, but you don't know if you want to touch me again. This is frustrating and stupid." She stopped at the doorway, turned and took the bottle and one of the glasses from him. "I'm going to my room."

He followed her. "I brought *two* glasses with me."

"You don't even like wine," she said, entering her room, which was surprisingly clean.

"Since I've been living with you, I'm learning to like a lot of things."

She poured wine in her glass, then set the bottle on the dresser. "Such as?"

"Taking care of a house, being around neighbors...living with you."

"See? There you go again." She placed her glass on the night-stand, then sat on the edge of the bed. "You throw out these things that make me think you like me. You actually tell me you like me. You helped me get rid of my dating rules so I could justify having sex with you, and just when I thought, *hey, we have something cool between us*, you pushed me away." She let down her long hair, then picked up the brush resting next to the wine glass. "I don't know what you think I want from you, but a long-term relationship isn't one of them."

"Why not?" When she quickly looked at him, her eyes widening with surprise, he added, "Just curious. I'm not into that either."

She relaxed and began brushing her hair. "I have a list detailing my ideal life partner."

Of course. "And I don't meet any of the bullet points, correct?"

"I'm not trying to hurt your feelings, but no."

He couldn't believe he didn't possess a single quality that matched her ideal life partner. "What's on the list?"

"It's personal. You've never really opened up to me, so I see no need to do the same."

"Fine. What do you want to know?"

"What's your real name?"

He'd rather tell her women always rejected him. "It's not important. Next question."

She set the brush aside in exchange for the wine. "You tell me your name, and I'll tell you one of my bullet points."

He poured himself a glass of wine and kept his back to her. "It's a family name. And don't forget I grew up in an extremely rural area." He met her gaze in the mirror. "Stacy Eugene Northowski," he said, then took a big drink. "Since I was a kid, everyone except my folks called me North. When I left the Chicago PD, I was worried about being targeted by perps I'd busted, and decided to change my name. My mother's maiden name was Sloan."

"You said Stacy was a family name?"

He nodded. "Don't worry, I would never subject our fake son to it. Now, how about one of those bullet points."

"If I'd met you as Stacy, I wouldn't think you were any less… manly. It's just a name. Based on your size, I doubt anyone made fun of you for it."

"The size helped, but I also went to school with kids who had names like Huck, Vern and Zeke. I'll take Stacy over any one of those. No more stalling. Because you dragged out the name Q&A, you have to give me two bullet points."

"Financial stability and good career."

"I have both of those."

"But are you goal oriented, or ambitious without being aggressive?"

He was neither of those, but could change that if he were inclined.

"My ideal partner would be honest, dependable, chivalrous, generous and caring," she continued. "He needs to have a good sense of humor, be able to cook and...I don't want to do this anymore."

He faced her again. "Because I *do* have qualities on your list."

She crossed her legs. "No, because it's personal and none of your business."

Grinning, he leaned against the dresser. "Face it. I meet your ideal."

"Wrong. I want a man who can compromise, and who can apologize and communicate his feelings."

"Which I've proven I can sometimes do."

"*Sometimes* being the operative word." She sipped her wine. "He has to be smart, faithful and have a pleasing disposition."

"Sounds like the mutt we used to have when I was a kid."

She cracked a smile. "Us too. Anyway, my ideal husband will also want a home and children. He will have no problem letting me make decisions and he's not argumentative." She looked to the ceiling for a moment. "I think that's it."

"Interesting list. Other than the last few items, I'm a possible candidate."

"Now that I've said it out loud, yes, I'm aware." She held up her index finger. "But the qualities you don't have are deal breakers."

"I see. So, you want to marry a doormat who won't argue with you and allows you to dominate every aspect of your relationship, correct?"

"No, I don't want to live with a controlling jerk who likes to pick fights with me."

He knew she referred to him, but she couldn't look in the mirror and realize they were alike in that regard. "I noticed your missing quite a few items on that list."

"Like?"

"Do you want to marry an ugly guy?"

"Looks aren't important. It's what's on the inside that counts."

"That's what ugly people say."

"Nice." She shook her head. "I'm going to add *not a rude person* to my list."

"Okay, so you don't need to have a good-looking husband, but what about physical and emotional chemistry?" He pushed himself off the dresser and approached her. "Passion and love? Or would you prefer to marry a cardboard sperm donor?"

"If the chemistry and love aren't there right away, it will grow in time. As for passion, it's overrated."

Whitney was a highly passionate woman. For her to leave that *and* love off her list, someone must have hurt her. Badly. While he understood rejection, he couldn't wrap his head around why she would marry a man she wasn't necessarily attracted to or in love with. What bothered him the most was how she'd easily dismissed him as an ideal partner when they had great chemistry, were attracted to each other and he had the qualities she looked for in a man. Apparently, he was good enough to have sex with, but that was about it.

Jealousy and irritation quickly moved through him as he realized she was using him. Using him for a fun fling, getting the passion out of her system, then once he left, she could go on the hunt for a boring partner who wouldn't demand a fucking thing from her.

The hell with that. No one used him.

He set his glass on the nightstand. If she wanted fun, he'd give it to her, show her what she'd be missing once she was married.

To another man.

"I predict you and your future, ideal husband will be divorced within the first five years of marriage," he said, kneeling in front of her.

"What a lovely thing to say. Thank you." Her brow furrowed. "What are you doing?"

"Just being honest." He uncrossed her legs, then ran his palms over her calves. "I don't think marriage should be based on sex, but it's important."

"First of all, it didn't seem that important to you earlier. Secondly, I never said I wouldn't have sex with my husband."

"Right. Can't make a baby without your husband sticking it in you," he said, not bothering to hide his bitterness. "And would you rather I be that guy who didn't care about making sure you're protected. Don't forget, I've been with a lot of women."

"Why would you say such a crass thing when you're touching *me*?" She held her robe together, while trying to drape the material over her knees. "Why *are* you on the floor and touching me?"

"Why would you talk about another man after you came all over my fingers?" he countered.

Her cheeks turned pink and her eyes darkened with desire. "I wasn't talking about any particular man, and you wanted to know about my list."

He untied the sash of her robe and held her gaze. "Spread your legs. I want to show you why I'll never make that list."

"After what you said about all of your women? No thanks."

"But doesn't knowing that I'm a player make it easier to use me."

"Use you? What are you talking about?"

"For sex. In particular, hot, raw, erotic, and yes, passionate sex."

"I would never use you."

She knocked his hand away and started to rise, but he quickly stood and wrapped an arm around her back. "That's right," he said, "while we fuck, you were hoping we'd become BFFs."

"Why are you being so crude?" she asked, struggling to free herself from his hold.

"Because I'm jealous of a man you've never met, and angry that you can only see me as someone to make you orgasm, not someone in your future." The admission stung, and his ears grew hot with embarrassment. He released her and stared at the closed window blinds. He'd said too much, and needed to find a way to get her to pretend he'd never come to her room. "That came out wrong. We've only known each other for a week, and I think all of this pretending is starting to get in my head."

"Mine, too. I wanted the dates we made up to be real."

Surprised, he faced her, then became instantly aroused by the sight. Her robe hung open, revealing a hint of her breasts, her flat stomach and the small patch of dark blond above the split of her sex. She was more stunning than he'd imagined, and he'd done plenty of fantasizing about her over the past week. Still, this was wrong. He was afraid of falling in love with her. If they continued with a physical relationship and became closer, his fears might come true. Since she was adamant about her list, where would that leave him?

Back in Chicago. Alone.

"We shouldn't…you should close your robe," he suggested, and couldn't believe the words had come out of his mouth. But he respected himself too much to allow his dick to rule his head. Good God, what the fuck was happening to him? Respect, jealousy, love…he needed to escape the burbs before he completely lost his mind, then have sex with a total stranger and push Whitney out of his head.

"You're the one who untied it." Her face flushed a deeper shade of pink. "If you don't like what you see, *you* close my robe."

Although he wanted to stare at her body, he held her gaze, which was uncertain, yet challenging. "When I opened it, I was trying to prove a point about the importance of passion. I had no intention of taking things any further," he said, the lie easily rolling off his tongue.

"That's disappointing. I thought I was going to find out how your beard feels along my inner thighs."

Even though he kept his eyes on hers, the image she conjured made his dick hard. If he didn't leave the room, he'd end up tossing his self-respect out the window and tearing the robe from her body. "I don't think that's a good idea."

"Probably not." She moved close to him, leaving a few inches between their bodies. "I want you to know that I would never use you. I'm sorry if I gave you that impression. But I'm not sorry for wanting to have fun with you, or for liking you and wanting to be good friends." She took the sash of her robe and placed the ends in his hand. "You tie it."

A short time ago, they'd been in the kitchen, where he'd attempted to seduce her, coax her into having fun with him and pretending they'd dated so that fun could happen while they lived together. She'd now reversed the roles on him, and she was doing it in a passive-aggressive way that was annoying and hot. He was supposed to be the seducer, the badass loner who didn't need a woman for anything but sex.

"No," he said, determined to get back to the old Sloan, the one who didn't agonize over pussy feelings and emotions, and prove to himself he could have Whitney and still remain emotionally detached from her. He'd done that plenty of times before, and could do it again. He let go of the sash, then, using his fingers, traced a path from the base of her throat, between her breasts, over her stomach and stopped just before he touched her curls. "Do you really want to know what I was planning on doing when I untied your robe?"

Her breath quickened and her eyes glittered with excitement. She licked her lips and nodded.

"I'll show you, but it'll require you to sit on the bed again. Before you do…" He spread the robe, then shifted his gaze to what had been hidden beneath it. "Perfection," he said, staring at her breasts. "I haven't even touched you and your nipples are already hard." He bent his head and swept his tongue along one stiff peak. Worried about coming in his pants before he did anything more, he slid the robe from her shoulders, then sat her on the bed.

He knelt in front of her and began caressing her calves. "Lean back on your forearms," he said, placing her feet on the mattresses edge, spreading her legs open, and exposing her completely. "Beautiful."

Her sex pulsed with need. Her heart raced as she fought to

keep from closing her legs. She wasn't a prude and, though it'd been a while, was familiar with oral sex. But she'd never bared herself in this way. "Can you turn off the light?" she asked, embarrassed and yet aroused.

He curled his arms around each of her thighs, placed his thumbs along her swollen labia and spread them. "I want to watch you come," he said, then ran his tongue along her heat. He did it again and again. She'd wanted what he offered: hot, raw, erotic, and yes, passion. And he was delivering. Drew her clit between his lips and sucked.

Her head fell back and she closed her eyes.

"Uh-uh," he murmured, his warm breath fanning along her sex. "Keep watching."

She opened her eyes as he kissed her inner thigh. His thick beard tickled the sensitive area. Goose bumps rose over skin, and she decided it would be criminal if he were to shave off his beard. He kissed a trail from her inner thigh to her labia again. Delved his tongue between the folds, then dipped it in her heat. Kissed her sex as if he were kissing her mouth, before focusing on her clit.

Her breath coming in short bursts, her body tensing and inner muscles coiling with the need for release, she reached out and ran her hand through his hair. As he flicked his tongue over her clit, she gripped his hair and held his head in place. Stared down the length of her body and watched him. He'd closed his eyes, his dark lashes leaving shadows beneath them. Even with his facial muscles working, he looked relaxed, as if this gave him as much pleasure as it did her.

"I love the way you look right now," she said, breathless.

"More than what I'm doing?"

"Yes."

While focusing on her clit, he looked up and met her gaze. She loved his dark eyes, too. Over the past week, she'd memorized his face, his body language, knew when he was retreating into himself, when he was putting up a wall to block her out, and when he was allowing her to truly see him. Right now, the intensity in his eyes, the intimacy, the way he made love to her with his mouth, was almost too much. She'd expected the lust and hunger in his eyes, but there was something else there. Something beyond like and caring, and something she wasn't prepared to deal with at the moment. Her orgasm was nearing, and she focused on that, not whatever emotions might be running through him—she was having a hard-enough time trying to figure out her own.

She was having a hard time keeping herself from falling in love with Sloan. From picturing them being this way, or kissing, hugging, loving each other's bodies. She imagined him taking off his clothes and climbing on top of her. Saw him hold the base of his erection as he rubbed her inner thighs just before he filled her.

A groan escaped. Her inner muscles clenched then released, sending waves of pleasure throughout her body. While her sex pulsed during the aftermath of her orgasm, he kissed her thighs, moved forward and kissed his way up her body until she was forced to lie on her back. He used his arms to brace his body above hers, leaned in and kissed her.

As she tasted herself on his tongue, erotic thoughts—something she'd never experienced—wandered through her mind. She wanted more experiences with this man. Not for the pleasure he could give her, but because she trusted him, cared for him. Hoping to show him how much, and to please him, too, she reached between their bodies and began unbuckling his belt.

He stopped her, then took her wrists and pinned them above her head. "This was about you."

"And proving that I need to add passion to my list."

He kissed her again, open-mouthed, possessively. "Fuck your list," he whispered against her ear, just before nipping it. "I don't want to hear about it again."

Because she'd told him he didn't qualify as her ideal partner. She still couldn't believe he'd become so upset, but supposed it shouldn't surprise her. Sloan was the type of man who had to win, to come out on top. Even though he wanted no part in her future, he was competitive enough that he'd want to be in the running. There was no way she'd allow that to happen. Sloan was more than she could handle. He didn't know what he wanted out of life, and she needed a man who had direction. She needed a man who understood his own emotions, and knew in his gut that she was the one for him.

He dragged his lips along her neck before releasing her wrists and moving off her. "Sorry, I didn't mean…after what we just did, I didn't want to go back to that." He picked up the robe from the floor, then handed it to her. "I'm going to check the listening device program to see if there's been any other activity."

She slipped into the robe. "Want me to join you?" she asked, torn with needing to be alone so she could digest the entire evening and wanting to spend more time with him.

"No." Releasing a breath, he looked toward the door. "It's been a long day, and I'm about ready for bed."

"Okay," she replied, and not knowing what else to say, she added, "Night."

"Night."

Without looking at her again, he left the room, left her disappointed and confused. Since she still had wine, she decided bullet point therapy was necessary. After she found her journal in the dresser drawer, she sat on the bed and opened the book to a blank page. She took a sip of wine and thought about what to title the list, then chose to go with the main issue: Sloan.

She stared at the page. Normally she could easily come up with bullet points to help her work through and organize a problem. For some reason, she didn't know what to write. Pros and cons? Maybe. She made two columns and decided to start with the *pros*.

- Thoughtful
- Considerate—sometimes
- Good cook
- Clean
- Hard worker
- Smells fantastic
- Hot

She considered everything that had transpired tonight. The pretend game, the kissing, touching, the orgasms. Then added:

- Sexy and fun
- Imaginative

Her list for an ideal husband came to mind, and how he'd checked off many of those traits. While she trusted him enough to fool around with him, she didn't know if he could be faithful, which led her to moving on to the *cons* column.

• Indecisive
• Argumentative
• No goals?

She wasn't one hundred percent sure about that one, and placed an asterisk next to it. From their conversations though, it hadn't sounded as if he had any plans for the future. Even if he didn't want a wife, family and house—she jotted those down as cons—he should have something he wanted later in life. A place to retire. A once-in-a-lifetime vacation. Did he have any hobbies? Other than bullet pointing, did she? She scratched the hobby side-note off the list.

• *He wants me—but doesn't*

Since that fell under indecisive, she scratched it from her list. The push and pull, the hot and cold, made her crazy. How could he not know what he wanted from her? Either he liked her or he didn't. He'd said he did, so she wasn't sure what the problem was or why he fought the attraction between them. Had he, like her, been burned in the past? Or maybe he didn't want to get involved knowing they'd never see each other after the investigation. She added *Lives in Chicago* to her con list, then, as she took another drink of wine, reread her words. Her bullet points didn't soothe her as they normally would. She set the journal aside and stared at the closed door, wondering what he was thinking about right now. Did he regret leaving her room? Did he want her in his bed? To sleep, since they didn't have condoms. Remembering the condom bit irritated her. Why did he constantly throw his many, many women in her face one minute, while attempting to seduce her the next?

The man drove her crazy. She opened up her journal again and added that to the list. Cliff hadn't made her nuts. Thinking of him had her checking the time. After having another man between her legs, she really should let him know that they couldn't see each other anymore. She hadn't necessarily cheated on him—

his profile was still on the dating site where they'd met—but closure was just another part of scratching things off her various lists. Still…had Sloan been right about her? Had she been looking for a cardboard sperm donor? Had she allowed one cheating man, one passionate relationship, to ruin her? Maybe. But boring was safe. Easy. Mundane.

She fell back against the pillows and closed her eyes. Tried to imagine life with a guy like Cliff and saw him wearing a headset and gaming with his buddies while she took care of the kids. Saw herself paying the bills, grocery shopping, cooking, doing the laundry and dealing with the lawn service. Sloan wouldn't expect her to do all of that. He had no problem making decisions, helping around the house and being a solid partner.

She curled on her side and hoped sleep would claim her. Nervous energy bubbled within her, instead. Made her restless. In a matter of a week, Sloan had turned her neat little life upside down. He'd had her rethinking her ideal husband list, had her not focused enough on the investigation.

Had her wishing their fake marriage were real.

Pathetic Whitney.

Somewhere on Shady Circle, North Royalhurst, Ohio
Friday, 10:37 p.m. Daylight Saving Time

Releasing a ragged breath, he climbed off his wife. Still half hard, he glanced over his shoulder at her. When she gave him a shy smile, he remembered why he'd been attracted to her all those years ago. The dim glow from the nightstand lamp hid the fine lines on her face and the gray in her tousled hair. When she lay on her back, her stomach was as flat as it had been before the first pregnancy. She looked sated and sexy. If he were back in his twenties, he'd take her again. Unfortunately, he wasn't and needed to recuperate.

"That was great," he said, rising to retrieve his underwear. "It's been a long time." Too long. She hadn't been interested, and he'd been too preoccupied with thoughts about his killing therapy to seduce his wife. Tonight had been different. Killing that saggy pants kid had breathed new life into him and had erased the tension he'd been carrying. Saggy Pants' death hadn't proved that he could deviate from his normal killing therapy while still finding the release he needed, though. The kid had inadvertently goaded him by calling him derogatory names and accusing him of being gay. Either way, his murder had taken the edge off the need to kill, and would hold him over until next weekend's hunt, when his wife took the kids to Columbus.

"It was very nice," she said, curling on her side and bringing the covers over her nude body. "I'd like to do it later, or in the morning. Maybe I can sleep here again tonight?"

She'd gone from sexy to pitiful in less than thirty seconds. Her name was on the deed to their house, she worked and helped pay for the bills and groceries. She shouldn't be asking if she could sleep in her own bed. Instead, she should grow a damned backbone and do it.

But they had just had great sex and he'd like to do it again too, so he saw no reason to be a dick to her. "You're not worried about my nightmares? Because I'm not sleeping on the couch again."

"I am, but I…I miss you. Since last summer, I've been feeling like we're drifting apart."

Last summer had been when he'd learned the killing field was going to be developed into a neighboring subdivision, and the last time he'd been on the hunt. "I didn't know you felt that way."

"I know the nightmares aren't helping, and that you're tired and stressed about money. Sometimes I think we get so wrapped up with the kids and their activities, we forget why we married."

"We got married because you were pregnant," he said with a grin. Even though he *had* married her because she was carrying his child, he'd also loved her.

She smiled, too. "You know what I meant."

"I did. So, what are you saying? We don't spend enough time together? If I'm not working, I'm always around and I certainly don't ignore you and the kids."

"We don't spend *quality* time together. When was the last time we went on a date?"

"Babysitters are expensive, and money's been tight," he said with bitterness, and once again thought about the fifteen hundred Dale still owed him. Sure, he had a couple grand in the bank, but he wanted more security for his family.

"What if we have a date at home? I can put the kids to bed early, make us a nice dinner and we can pretend we're at a restaurant."

He walked to her side of the bed, then sat on the mattress. When she rolled toward him, he caressed her bare shoulder. "That's too much work for you and not a real date. Next weekend you'll be in Columbus, but let's plan on going out the following weekend. See if you can get a sitter."

"But the expense…"

"Don't worry about it. We don't have to do anything fancy. It'll be nice to get out of the house and spend time together," he said, and honestly believed she was right. She hadn't changed during the twelve years they'd been married, he had. Before his first kill, he'd been happy being with her and starting a family. The nightmares had been there, but they hadn't been as bad then. The killing therapy had brought out a negative change in him. He'd become like a drug addict. He knew murder was wrong, but craved the high, the pleasure and peaceful dreams it gave him afterward. Yes, that was it. He was a killing junkie, and when he couldn't get a fix, he took his anger and frustration out on his wife.

She smiled. "I'm excited. It'll be fun. I know it's not in the budget, but I'd like to pick up hair color the next time I'm at the store. I can get it for around ten dollars. The gray is making me feel old."

If he'd known plans for a date were all it took to get her to dye her hair, he'd have asked her out months ago. "You don't need my permission to color your hair. But don't go crazy and get a manicure or something. That's definitely not in the budget."

The covers fell away from her body as she reached up and hugged him. "Thank you."

He couldn't believe that she thought she needed his permission to buy her hair stuff. And he'd thought she was pitiful. No, that was him. A pitiful asshole. Sure, he'd wanted to limit her friendships, along with her comings and goings. That had been done out of self-preservation. He couldn't have her friends here, snooping into their business, couldn't have her going back to school and possibly finding a better job than him. He couldn't stomach a divorce that would have him losing half of his money, his business and full custody of his kids. His paranoia, his killing therapy, would destroy their marriage if he didn't change his ways. One day, she could develop a backbone and leave him, put the kids in the van, head to Columbus and move in with her parents. Then what would the neighbors say?

He leaned back and met her tender gaze. "I know I'm not always easy to live with, but you don't spend anything on yourself. You don't even wear makeup or earrings anymore."

"There's really no point. I don't go anywhere except to work, the store or one of the boys' games."

"But if it makes you feel good…go for it."

She smiled again. "You're sure?"

"Positive." He kissed her and eased her against the pillows. "Get some sleep. I'm going to make a sandwich and watch the news before I head to bed." He kissed her again. After putting on a T-shirt and a pair of sweats, he left the bedroom.

While he was in the kitchen making a bologna sandwich, he realized he'd had a major breakthrough today. Killing Saggy Pants hadn't just put him in a good mood, it'd made him realize that he had to own his killing addiction, but not forget about the important things: his wife, family and friends. Conversion therapy and his parents were the root of his demons, were the stuff that made up his nightmares, but maybe treating his wife badly, not enjoying her, not finding room in his heart to love her were what had made those nightmares violent.

After his first kill, out of guilt and shame, he'd distanced himself from her. Within months of that, he'd hit her while he'd been sleeping. Was it possible that the solution to the violent dreams had been in front of him all along? Could finding happiness with his wife again help take him back to the man he'd been before his first murder?

He used the tie wrap to close up the white bread, then stowed the bologna, American cheese and ketchup back in the fridge. As he took a bite of the sandwich, he glanced around the kitchen, then moved into the darkened family room. Thanks to a strict budget, they had no debt, were able to add money to the kids' college fund every month, had a retirement account and small emergency fund. Light spilled in from the kitchen and touched on the dated furniture. The room could use new carpet and the walls needed a fresh coat of paint. But they had three little pigs posing as their sons living with them. Still, his wife had worked with what they had, and had made their house a home. She kept the place clean, was a good cook and mother. Even after the way he'd treated her, she still stood by his side and loved him.

Regret made it difficult to swallow the last of his sandwich. In need of water to wash it down, he went back into the kitchen and filled a glass from the tap. After draining it, he turned off the kitchen light, but kept the one over the sink lit—in case one of the kids ventured downstairs during the night. He passed through the dining and living rooms. When he made his way to the staircase, he stopped and the anguish over what he'd done returned. He'd considered his wife a doormat for not standing up to him, and had been wrong. She'd never been a confrontational person, yet he'd wanted her to fight him. Maybe he'd wanted to drive a wedge between them. After all, how could he be allowed happiness when he was guilty of killing so many? His therapist would be proud of him and his new revelations. Too bad he couldn't share this epiphany with him as well.

Too bad none of tonight's journey into self-discovery would change who he was: a serial killer. But he was determined to be a happy one.

He couldn't give up the hunt, the thrill or burying his demons alive. He'd come to enjoy it too much, depended on the rush and high. And today's kill had definitely been a rush. He'd never murdered anyone in broad daylight, let alone in a location where anyone could have seen him. But he'd gotten away with it. He'd protected his little corner of the world from possible thieves or rapists. He'd—

A shadow momentarily crept up the steps. He quickly turned

and looked toward the living room's picture window. Specifically, at his neighbor's lamppost.

Someone was out there. He'd seen the shadow. It hadn't been his or an animal's.

Staying close to the wall, he walked to the window and scanned the street and yards. When he didn't see any of his neighbors out for a late-night stroll, he wondered if Knot Head had returned and was looking for Saggy Pants.

He hurried to the laundry room, slid his bare feet into a pair of tennis shoes, then went into the garage. After grabbing one of his sons' baseball bats, he walked to the service door and looked out the window A silhouette yawned across the neighboring yard. Determined to find out who was lurking around his street, he slipped out the service door. Using hedges for cover, he moved in the direction where he'd seen the last shadow, then stopped and smiled.

Knot Head.

He'd never killed two people in one day. Going after Knot Head could be risky. But he'd taken dozens of risks during the past ten years, and this punk was on *his* turf, fucking with *his* neighbors. Since he couldn't call the police or have them find out Knot Head had a missing saggy-pants partner, he'd have to take care of business on his own.

Chapter Ten

AUSTIN STOPPED BEHIND a tree to catch his breath. Twenty minutes ago, he'd worked up the nerve to search for Laredo. He'd run from Mom's Kitchen—where he'd left his car— to the development, and had been combing the yards since. He *had* to find his brother. He'd already lost Antonio and his mother. He couldn't lose Laredo, too. Something bad had happened to him. His gut told him so, and it was usually right. Why hadn't he listened to his gut when he and Laredo had been following North to Zombie Land? Why had he stupidly let Dallas talk them into going after North in the first place?

Dallas… He'd caught up with her an hour ago. Talk about stupid. Dallas had now convinced herself that North was to blame for Laredo's disappearance. North wasn't at fault. Not for his missing brother, or for Antonio's and their mom's deaths. Antonio had chosen to break the law and had paid the price. Their mom hadn't died of a broken heart, but of a heart attack, likely brought on from being two hundred pounds overweight and smoking two packs of cigarettes a day. Laredo was missing because they'd been dumb enough to listen to Dallas and follow North. Still, it'd been their choice. And he had no choice now but to keep searching for his brother.

Dallas wanted him to return to Chicago on Sunday—with or

without their brother. She also refused to send him more money, which meant he'd have to leave Zombie Land. Otherwise, he couldn't pay for gas and food.

Fuck, where was Laredo? No longer panting, he glanced around the circle street to gain his bearings, then shifted his gaze to North's home. He'd been standing on the side of North's garage the last time he and Laredo had talked. Looking at North's house, then to the approximate location of where Laredo should have been, would put his brother at one of a few locations. Austin looked behind him. The guy he'd seen working on a yard lived in the house across the lawn from where he was hiding. There was a home behind the landscaper's, a street, then the property the guy had been clearing or whatever.

He looked back to North's house. If Laredo had been able to see his movements at North's place, the direct line of sight would have come from either the yard Austin was currently in, the one behind him, or where the landscaper had been working. Plus, Laredo had said to pick him up on the next street over from Shady Circle, meaning his brother had to have been watching him from somewhere near where the landscaper had been. But he'd checked that area. Not once, but twice.

His stomach grew sick as he remembered driving past the landscaper when he'd gone to his truck. The man had watched him, as if *he'd* been watching him. But he and Laredo had also smoked a joint before setting out on their mission, so paranoia could've come into play. Except...later, when he'd cruised through the neighborhood looking for Laredo, he'd seen the guy again.

Austin stared at what he assumed was the man's house. That afternoon, the landscaper had been standing in the driveway, watching him idle at the stop sign, and he'd sworn the guy had smiled. Not a happy smile, but an *I know something you don't know* one. What could he know though? Had he seen him unlock North's service door off the garage? Possibly. But if he had, wouldn't he have called the police?

Austin itched his scalp and tried to come up with an answer, or where else he should look for his brother. Nothing made sense. Laredo *should* be somewhere between the two streets.

Worried, his stomach twisting with fear and panic, he didn't know what to do. Though he was older than Laredo by barely two years, his brother was his best friend. The one person he could count on, and, now that Mom was gone, the only buffer he had left against Dallas. Yeah, they smoked dope. Yeah, they'd made mistakes. But—

Dead leaves rustled. He tensed as a cool breeze blew against his heated skin. Zombie Land sucked ass. The unfamiliar sounds had him edgy. Back in his neighborhood, which was nothing but concrete, shitty apartment buildings, stores and equally shitty houses, the night noises consisted of people yelling, traffic, music and beeping horns. Here, though, it was too quiet, too many unknowns. He'd never believed in the boogeyman until coming to this place, and now wished he'd never watched *Halloween*. Crazy stuff went on in Zombie Land, and he firmly believed the suburbs were like the Bermuda Triangle, where weird shit happened that no one could explain. But this wasn't the fucking Bermuda Triangle. Laredo should be somewhere close.

The rustling happened again. *Behind him.* Scared, totally out of his element, he held his breath and looked over his shoulder. A bunny hopped from a flowerbed, stopped and looked at him. He relaxed, released the breath he'd been holding, then shook his head. He needed to pull it together, remember his environment and that little critters lived in Zombie Land, too.

The bunny hopped forward, stopped again, then bounced off between yards. Good. He'd hoped he had spooked the rabbit and maybe his rabbit friends. Considering he was scared and spooked himself, he didn't need the bunny making him anymore paranoid.

Something cracked—a twig?—from the hedges at his back. Knowing Laredo wouldn't disappear only to scare the shit out of him, and being in unfamiliar territory, the city boy in him said to run. He launched from his hiding place, then was immediately jerked back and fell on his butt.

"Not in my neighborhood," a man said as he dragged him by his hair.

Heart beating fast and hard, Austin reached up and gripped the man's wrists. His scalp hurt like a motherfucker, causing his eyes to water and blur his vision. "What the hell, man?" Fear had him digging his heels into the ground to stop the progress, and looking for a chance to land back on his feet.

Pain shot through his skull as the man hit him in the head with his fist. Terrified, freaking the fuck out, he writhed, kicked, punched at the air, tried to do everything he could to free himself.

Another punch to the head left him dazed, wondering why he was here. But, as the man dragged him by his stupid bun—one he swore he'd cut off after this—he tried to shake the haze clouding his head.

"What the hell? I'm just going for a walk," he said, still gripping the man's wrist.

"The fuck you are. I saw what you and your saggy pants *bro* were doing today. Sorry, but we can't have that around here."

He knew about Laredo? Relief momentarily settled over him. This guy must've called the cops on his brother. But he'd contacted the North Royalhurst police himself. Why didn't they tell him they had Laredo in a jail cell?

"Can't have what?" he asked, still using his heels to stop the man from dragging him by the hair.

"We can't have criminals in the neighborhood," the man said when they reached the landscaper's fence, then pain shot through his skull again.

And his world went black.

Austin's head throbbed and ached as if he had a hangover from Hell. He tried to recall what party he'd been to last night. Had he and Laredo gone to DeAndre's and smoked too much pot, maybe done too many whiskey shooters?

Something moist and cold hit his chin and a heavy weight encased his body. Groggy, he opened one eye. Stars lit up the black sky and he remembered where he was: Zombie Land. Both eyes wide open, he jerked up, but couldn't. The darkness made it difficult to know what kept him pinned. Whatever it was, he couldn't shove it away. His arms were bound behind his back and his ankles were tied together, too. Panicked, he tried to wriggle free and knock the weight from his chest, but he was encased in something.

Hot breath coated his face. "Don't move. Don't make a sound," a man said. "It's almost over."

"What the fuck is—"

A hand slammed down on his mouth, silencing him. "My wife, kids and neighbors are sleeping. If you try to wake them up by screaming, I'm going to smash your head in with my shovel.. just like I did to your saggy pants buddy."

Tears filled Austin's eyes, and he momentarily wondered if he'd been wrong about his mom's cause of death. A deep ache filled his chest with overwhelming sadness. Laredo couldn't be gone, couldn't be dead. It made no sense. Why would this man have killed his little brother?

The man pulled his hand away. A low, slow ripping sounded right above his ear. Tape? He'd grieve over Laredo later. He might be a city boy, but he recognized the fresh, earthy odor surrounding him. The gritty soil was in his ears, inside his clothes, and making his skin crawl with fear and desperation. Now he knew why he couldn't find Laredo, and what his own fate would be if he didn't find a way to escape...

The crazy landscaper had buried his brother.

"I won't scream," he whispered, worried that if the man had tape, he'd use it to cover his mouth. He *needed* to talk the landscaper out of doing this to him.

"I don't believe you." There was another rip. "There's no such thing as an honest criminal."

"Criminal? I ain't no criminal and never been in trouble with the police."

"Shut up. It's late, I'm tired and I want to finish burying you so I can go to bed," he said, confirming Austin's fears.

"But I'm still alive." His heart raced with panic and he grew lightheaded. Tears slipped down the sides of his face and into the soil. "Is that what you did to Laredo?"

"I already told you—he got lucky. A couple whacks to the head with my shovel killed him."

Austin's throat clogged with mucus and misery. "Are you going to do that to me?"

"Whack you? Nope. But no worries. I've done this twenty or so times, and all of my victims died in less than five minutes. At least that's what I'm assuming. I couldn't exactly confirm when they died since they had a pile of dirt on their faces, know what I mean?"

Oh, God. Twenty or so times? He was going to die, and no one would ever know where to look for him or Laredo. And now he knew why North had moved to the circle street: the sick fuck was a serial killer.

"I...me and my brother, we didn't do anything wrong," he said in a rush. "I swear. Please. You don't have to do this. I won't tell anyone."

"Really? I found your brother working as a lookout from behind the bushes. I also saw you go into my neighbor's garage and unlock their service door. I'd say you two were definitely up to no good."

Hope buried its way into Austin's chest. He and Laredo had assumed North and the woman were doing undercover work, but hadn't been able to confirm it. Knowing the landscaper was a killer was more than enough of a confirmation and gave him leverage, a chance to barter, trade the info he had for his life. "We weren't going to rob North. We were gonna scare him, is all. I swear."

"Scare him? Why?"

"I have something on North that you'll want to know. But I'm not talking until you get me out of...this."

"This, meaning your grave." The man released a breath. "Why would I want to know?"

"If you've buried twenty plus people, that'd make you a murderer, right?" Austin asked, glad he had the landscaper's attention, and praying to God he could talk himself free. "Well, North isn't who he says he is. Free me and I'll tell you everything I know, then I'm gone. I won't go to the police, and I won't ever come back here again."

"I'm not freeing you until you talk. If I like what you tell me, I'll let you live. If I don't…you'll end up like your brother. Deal?"

A shitty one. "Will you give me your word?"

"I swear to God. Now talk."

He didn't trust the man, but what choice did he have? Austin explained who North and the tall lady were, and why he and Laredo had wanted to scare North. Not thinking it was wise to tell this guy they were going to kidnap the woman, he left out that part, along with Dallas's involvement. If this guy knew their names, he could be crazy enough to go after his sister and nieces.

"You're telling me North is a former Vice cop and now works for a private investigating firm?"

"Yeah, and we saw him and the lady leave the sheriff's department." His earlier hope took root and stretched throughout his body. "If you're killing people, they've got to be here for you. So whattya say, dude? Good info, right? I helped you. Gave you a head's up on North, and I could tell you more about the guy. It's worth freeing me, doncha think?"

He jerked his head when tape was slapped over his mouth. Terror and betrayal shredded those hopeful roots.

"Here's the deal, *dude…* First off, I don't believe in God, so I was going to kill you anyway. Secondly, your info does me no good. If it's true, which I doubt, North isn't here for me. You know the bodies they're finding in the subdivision? Yeah, I did that. And the first one wasn't discovered until Thursday. North moved in on the previous Saturday. Do you see where I'm going with this? If not, I'll be clear: North's here for somebody else."

Wretched despair had tears filling Austin's eyes and streaming down his face. Utter terror gripped him by the throat. Behind the tape he screamed his horror and was thrilled when his long wail echoed throughout the yard, causing a dog to bark in the distance. Before he could do it again, the landscaper pinched his nose.

"That was a mistake. I'm tempted to either stay like this until you die or ram the shovel against your neck. But, in all honesty, I need you to die with a mouthful of dirt. I want it clogging your nose and throat. I want you to suffer. Your apologies are worthless to me. The only thing that would be better than watching you die over and over is if I'd killed you myself."

Austin's skin burned as the tape was ripped from his mouth, then quickly cooled when the landscaper pushed handfuls of dirt in his face. Panicking, squeezing his eyes shut and holding his breath, he turned his head from side to side, trying desperately to shake the soil from his face. Dirt filled his ears, deadening all sound. Hysteria ripped through him. His lungs burned with the need to breath, to drag air into them. Fearing the landscaper would get what he wanted, he kept his mouth shut.

Instinct intervened, forced him to inhale through his nose. He snorted granules, which mixed with mucus and slid down his throat. He gagged, coughed and drew in a breath, but swallowed soil instead. The gritty, salty-tasting dirt coated his teeth, clung to the roof of his mouth. He tried to spit it out, but the heavy soil weighed him down, made it difficult to part his lips, to work any muscle in his face.

Trapped, smothered, breathless and powerless, the sheer terror making his head buzz, he searched within himself. He'd never meditated in his life, but knew Death would come for him soon. He didn't want to die with fear and dirt choking him, so he pictured what made him the happiest. As the heavy but cool soil cocooned him and his heart began to slow, he went back to the last time his family had been together. His mom and Antonio were there, so were Laredo, a pregnant Dallas and two of his nieces. It had been Christmas and, even now, he swore he could smell the turkey roasting in the oven, the evergreen scented candle Mom had next to the 1970s silver tree standing in the corner. They weren't religious people except at Christmas—Mom's rule. He and Laredo used to joke that Mom only went all holy on them at Christmas because baby Jesus was her favorite version of the man. He believed in God, wasn't sure about any of the versions of Jesus, but now prayed to Him anyway. Prayed that a miracle would happen and he'd survive. But as his mind grew fuzzy, he prayed there was an afterlife and he'd see his mom, dad and brothers there.

He stiffened. Made one final gasp, one more attempt for a lungful of air, then his world went black.

Sweating, panting, he finished covering the grave he'd made between the shed and back fence. The location was perfect, and had been where he stacked wood. He'd blown through a cord of firewood this past winter, and would need more for summer bonfires. While he wasn't keen on having a body buried in his backyard, at least he wouldn't have to worry about it being discovered. No one but him went back here. Occasionally his oldest son would help him carry the wood, but by the time that happened again, he'd have another cord covering the grave.

He used his shirt to wipe the sweat from his face and wondered what to do about the freshly turned earth. Though no one went behind the shed, caution told him to do more to cover his crime. He went into the shed, found a tarp and half a dozen two-by-fours and decided they'd make a good foundation for the cord of wood he planned to order tomorrow. He placed the tarp over Knot Head's final resting place, then the two-by-fours on top of it. Satisfied, he leaned against the shed and looked up at the starry sky.

This kill hadn't been as fulfilling as he'd hoped. He hadn't experienced that fit of rage, that moment where he would snap, almost black out, and go back to another time and place. He'd tried to force it, tried to make it about Preacher Daddy, but had failed. Regardless, killing Knot Head had been necessary. Even if the kid hadn't been creeping around in order to rob his neighbor, he couldn't have him running through yards looking for his brother. What if he'd had the balls to go to the police and report that Saggy Pants had gone missing right where he'd been digging the Milsons' pond? There would be no reason for the police to suspect him, but so far—according to the evening news—they'd unearthed three bodies at the subdivision. At this point, the cops would likely follow up on anything that had to do with holes and missing people.

As he stared at the sky, he waited for the guilt, for the shame. Nothing. What did that mean? Nothing? Everything? This had been the first time he'd killed without being provoked into denying he was gay. Instead, he'd killed to protect himself from being caught. Which meant he'd needed the goading, to be forced into denial to obtain that true fulfillment he sought. He needed the anger, that overwhelming rage to coil through him and explode, then to have that quiet moment, the soothing sound of the shovel scraping along the dirt, then hitting his victim as he buried him. While that hadn't happened tonight, he'd taken care of a problem and also had two new revelations: he could kill without remorse, and North wasn't a web designer.

He pushed himself off the shed. After stowing the shovel inside, he went into the house through the garage service door, locking it behind him. As he toed off his tennis shoes, he thought more about Sloan North. Vincent had been the one who'd told him Sloan was a web designer. He'd been surprised. Between the tattoos and his size, Sloan looked more like a bouncer for a night-club, or maybe an owner. Then he'd figured, who was he to judge? He was clean cut, a businessman, family man and serial killer. If Knot Head had been honest, and Sloan and Whitney really weren't a web designer and attorney, but working under-cover, then what the hell were they doing here?

He firmly believed they weren't after him. Even his paranoia agreed. The timeline didn't make sense. And he wondered...what neighbor were they after? He immediately knocked his business partner from the running. He and his wife were good people. Then again, they could say the same about him and his own wife. He didn't know much about the bachelor, Quint, or the Ukraini-ans. There was no crime in being a dick, so he doubted Joe was a target. As he dismissed the other neighbors, his mind zeroed in on Cameron Easton. Maybe the kid wasn't just smoking weed, but selling. Still, would the Cuyahoga Sheriff's Offices go through the trouble of placing people undercover to watch a seventeen-year-old kid who *might* be selling dope? For that to happen, Cameron would have to be moving a large amount of marijuana. Except, other than smelling pot a few times while mowing the neighbor's grass, now that the two older kids—namely the girl, Blair—were gone, there wasn't much activity at the Eastons'.

In need of a shower, and too tired to think about any of it anymore, he went to the kitchen for a glass of water, then jerked back. Swearing under his breath, he placed a hand over his racing heart and looked down at his six-year-old son. "What are you doing down here?" he asked, crouching and resting his hands on the boy's shoulders.

"I had a bad dream and went to your room to snuggle. When I couldn't find you, I came down here."

"Why didn't you just snuggle with Mommy?"

"Because you're big and strong, and I was scared."

"Nightmares aren't real. And you *are* strong. Let me see your muscles."

The boy flexed his tiny biceps.

He wrapped his hands around his son's little upper arms. "Well, look at that. I think these are bigger today than they were when you showed me them last week."

His son grinned. "Where were you?" The boy glanced at his sweats and T-shirt, which were filthy.

"I couldn't sleep, so I thought I'd get the back of the shed ready for a new load of wood. You know, so we can have fires this summer and make s'mores."

"I love s'mores."

"I know you do." He went to the sink, refilled the glass he'd used earlier, then gulped down the cool water. After placing the glass on the counter, he ushered his son toward the stairs. "Come on, let's go to bed."

"Do I hafta sleep in my bed? I don't want to be alone."

He and his wife had been talking about putting the six and ten-year-old in the same room to avoid nights like this, and to give their oldest boy his own space. Since their youngest hated sleeping alone and constantly crept into their room during the night, maybe it was time to make that happen.

"I need to take a quick shower, so why don't you snuggle next to Mommy and keep her safe with your strong muscles. I'll join you when I'm done. Deal?"

"Deal."

After he had his son tucked in, he went into the master bathroom and started the shower. Once he was under the hot spray, his mind drifted back to Knot Head, Sloan and the woman living across the street. Maybe Knot Head had been fucking with him to save his ass. But Knot Head had been quick with his story about Sloan. Either he was a good liar or telling the truth. Whatever the case, he still didn't consider himself a target—*if* they were actually working undercover. Vincent was a former cop, had been one for forty years before retiring. Even though he hadn't been with the Cleveland PD for three years, he still looked like a cop, still would go into that cop stance. Wouldn't Vincent recognize a fellow lawman?

As the thought rolled through his head and he toweled off his body, he decided that was a dumb assumption. He'd been in dozens of gay bars over the years, and none of the men he'd met had thought he was straight.

After he put on fresh underwear, he went into the bedroom. His son was snoring and sprawled across his side of the bed. He gently moved the hair from his boy's forehead. When he didn't stir —a solid sign he was sleeping—he lifted him in his arms to put him in his own bed. He kissed his forehead, then went back to his room. Once inside, he climbed into bed and curled against his wife.

"What's the matter?" she asked, her voice sleepy.

"Nothing." He held her close and remembered how much he missed this. The connection to someone who truly loved him, who'd never judged him and who had never, ever accused him of being anything but himself. "Go back to sleep."

And as she burrowed into him, her bottom nestling against his groin, her warmth comforting him and taking him back to when they'd first been married, he didn't think about Sloan or the knot head buried behind his shed. Instead, he thought about the woman in his arms. How he'd allowed his killing therapy, and the shame that came with it, to affect their marriage and how he'd treated her.

As he drifted off to sleep, a final thought filled his mind. Mended him. Gave him hope.

He was a good dad, could once again be a good husband. And he could still kill.

Somewhere on Shady Circle, North Royalhurst, Ohio
Saturday, 11:09 a.m. Daylight Saving Time

"Mom, I'm going outside!"

I glanced over my shoulder at our eldest son, just as the two younger boys rushed into the kitchen. "Keep an eye on your brothers and stay on our street."

"Okay, Mom," my two oldest boys said in unison, while the youngest sat on the kitchen floor and attempted to tie his shoe. Velcro was so much easier to deal with, but the boy had to learn to tie his laces.

"Honey, do you want Mommy to help you?"

"I got it," he said, sounding so much like his father. Then he let out a frustrated grunt. "I can't do it!"

"Learning to tie shoes takes time. Let me help you, so you can go play. We'll work on it later."

He released a disappointed sigh, and tried again. "Miss Cooper says I should know how to do this."

Miss Cooper, his first-grade teacher, was twenty-five, had no husband or children, and, outside of teaching, had no clue how to deal with kids. The young woman expected too much, and didn't understand that not every kid learned at the same rate. And I highly doubted my son would still need help with his shoes when he was eighteen.

"Don't worry about Miss Cooper. You're doing just fine." I sat next to him on the tiled floor. Wanting to just do it for him and anxious to try out the new hair color I'd bought this morning, I fisted my hands. "You're becoming a big boy and will figure this out soon."

He struggled with the looping process, and almost had it. "Cameron called me a baby."

"Cameron Easton?"

He nodded.

While I liked Dale and Irene, their children were idiots. The eldest used to throw parties when his parents were gone for the weekend, their daughter had become the talk of the street after the night she'd exploded on her boyfriend, and Cameron drove too fast.

"When were you anywhere near him?" I asked, concerned. Unlike his older brother, Gage, Cameron didn't throw parties. He also didn't create drama for their street to watch like his sister, Blair. But my husband had mentioned numerous times that he'd suspected Cameron and his friends liked to smoke dope when Dale and Irene weren't at the house—which was frequent.

He shrugged. "I dunno. The day we played kickball and I had to go get the ball from their yard. Cameron was outside and he kicked the ball at me and it hit me in my belly. It hurt bad and I started to cry. *That's* when he called me a baby." I hid my anger, and would talk to my husband about this later. Several of our neighbors, along with my husband, had said something to Cameron's parents about how fast he liked to speed down their short street, but he still continued to do it, and now he was picking on a six-year-old. *My* six-year-old.

For over ten years, I'd played nice with the neighbors. When Brett and Jackie Smith had moved in across the street, and Jackie and I had become close, she'd taught me that I'd been too nice. Had encouraged me to make waves. Two years ago, I'd been prepared to let Dale and Irene know that I'd had enough of their daughter's drama, how her screaming and ranting at her boyfriend—either in the driveway or the middle of the cul-de-sac —were too much, but my husband hadn't just discouraged me, he'd forbidden me. Had said they were good customers, and that I should keep my mouth shut.

"I'm not a baby," my son continued.

I rubbed his little arm. "Of course not. You're a big boy. Big boys sleep in their room," I added, hoping to plant a little seed in his head.

With the exception of last night and the night before, it'd

been weeks since I'd tried sleeping with my husband. His violent dreams had been too much for me to bear. The last one had resulted in a black eye, along with questions from coworkers. Not wanting people to know our business, I'd made up excuses —a baseball to the face had worked. But my main concern had been for our son, who randomly came to our room during the night. What if he'd got into our bed and my husband had had one of his nightmares, then accidentally hit him? Fortunately, our boy must have a sixth sense, some weird radar, because my husband claimed he only crawled into our bed when I was there.

"I don't like being in my room alone," he said, then stomped his feet when he failed at tying the shoelaces. "I can't do it!"

"Let me." I pushed his hands aside and went to work. "I know you don't like being alone, but you can't keep sleeping with Mommy and Daddy."

"Why not? I like snuggling next to you."

"I *love* snuggling with you. But it sometimes makes Daddy crabby, especially when one of your boney elbows hits him during the night," I said, reaching over, touching his elbow, then tickling him in the armpit, and eliciting a giggle.

"Stop!" He giggled some more. "Do it again." I did, and after another round of giggles, and an attempt to tickle me, he calmed, and said, "Daddy didn't mind last night."

"Oh?" I pushed myself off the floor. "Was he still up when you came to bed?"

He also rose and nodded. "Uh-huh. When I got up I was scared and went to your room. I had a bad dream about octopuses."

"Octopuses? Oh, my."

He nodded again. "When I couldn't find Daddy, I came downstairs. He was coming in through the laundry room."

"What do you mean he was coming *in* through the laundry room?"

"From the garage. He was *super* dirty. Like when he comes home from work," he said, widening his eyes as if that were explanation enough.

Except, that made no sense. It had been close to eleven when he'd gone downstairs for something to eat.

I bent down and tweaked his nose. "Maybe that was something you'd dreamed about, along with octopuses."

"I'm not lying! Daddy was dirty like after work. He came inside, got a glass of water and took me up to your room." He started for the door. "He said I could snuggle with you while he took a shower. I'm not lying," he repeated, and crossed his arms.

I walked over and ran my hand over his hair. "I didn't say you were. Go play, but stay with your brothers."

As he darted from the house, I went onto the porch to make sure he hooked up with his brothers, who were at the center of the cul-de-sac playing Wiffle ball with the other kids on the street. Helen was out and waved from her mailbox. Guilt gave me a nudge as I remembered that I hadn't returned her call from last week.

But Helen clearly wasn't upset. She smiled, then shouted, "Give me a call when you have time."

"I will!"

Once I was satisfied my boys were all together, I went back to the kitchen to grab the grocery bag filled with a few toiletries and the hair color, my youngest son's parting words still on my mind. Why would my husband be filthy late at night? The child had to be mistaken.

As I headed to our bathroom, my thoughts weren't on whether or not my husband was dirty at eleven or so at night, but on *him*. Yesterday had been wonderful. He'd come home in a great mood, had been sweet to me, praised my cooking, how the house looked, how *I* looked. Then later, after I'd put the kids to bed and I was in our bathroom, washing my face and getting ready for a night on the couch, he'd come up behind me. Kissed my neck. Run his big hands over my breasts...

I'd leaned into his strong chest, relished the caresses, his heated touch. The compliments he'd given me.

For months, I'd been depressed. I'd recently lost my best friend to a move, had put on a few pounds and hated looking at myself in the mirror. We were on a strict budget. To adhere to that, I'd avoided purchasing frivolous things like hair color and nail polish. One reason I hated going to the boys' soccer games was because all the other moms looked put together. Like our neighbor, Becky, they'd have their hair done, makeup applied, either wearing their expensive workout gear—even though they weren't anywhere near a gym and likely had no intention of being at one—or dressed in something I'd wear if we went on a date.

I used to be prettier—not as attractive as my sisters—and I would take the time to make myself look good for my husband. After years of being ignored by him, of being tired, working an unfulfilling job, of being treated as if I were the nanny and roommate versus wife and mother, I'd given up on trying to make myself pretty, thin, *modern*. Maybe by giving up, I'd driven my husband away. But he'd become so controlling, so critical, it'd been easier to withdraw into myself. To focus on my kids and home, not the way I looked, and hope that my marriage would change, go back to happier times.

When had that been? Eight, maybe ten years ago? And had the past eight or ten years been *that* bad? I'd had two more children during that time, and they'd been a blessing and created out of love. My husband hadn't always been distant or demeaning, but he had been controlling. He was also an excellent father, a hard worker and, despite keeping us on a strict budget, a good provider.

With a sigh, I set the bag on the bathroom counter, then put away everything except the box of hair color. I'm not sure what had changed from one night to the next, but I wouldn't complain or question it. Our sex life had practically been nonexistent. Because my husband was always worried about money and worked as many hours as he could, I'd assumed stress and exhaustion were the cause of his disinterest. As his attitude toward me had worsened, and he'd become even more distant, I'd begun to think the problem was me.

Last night, he'd made it clear he still desired me, had actually talked with kindness and had *listened*. He'd understood that I needed more, needed for us to spend quality time together. Yes, he was home every evening for dinner and rarely went out to bars with friends. But even when he was here, and the whole family sat around the table—the boys talking about their day, their dad joking around with them—oftentimes, I would sit and watch them, my food untouched, a sense of isolation, of loneliness, enveloping me. How could I feel lonely when surrounded by four other people? What did that say about me? Why hadn't I spoken up and forced my way into their conversations?

I stared at my reflection. "Because you have no backbone and you're afraid of being alone." I'd spent my childhood and teen years living in my sisters' shadows. The two were bubbly, outgoing and so much alike. The one time they'd force me out of my shell and taken me to a party located in the Georgia town neighboring ours, I'd met my future husband. He'd been my first and only boyfriend. The only man who'd kissed or touched me, and I'd fallen in love with him because he'd been charming, funny, handsome and had ambitious plans for the future. We'd been seniors at different high schools, but we'd planned to attend the same college in the fall—until I'd found out I was pregnant the summer before we were scheduled to head off for school.

His extremely religious parents—my father had called them fanatical evangelicals—had insisted we marry immediately and move in with them so they could help raise the baby. Between their strict rules and how they took the Bible literally, my future in-laws had always disturbed me, made me uncomfortable and uneasy. How my husband had ended up the total opposite of them—claiming to be atheist—I'll never understand. Thank God, my parents had refused to allow me to move in with them, and that my dad's company had promoted and transferred him to Cleveland. Worried that my in-laws would be too interfering, too domineering, he and my mom had offered to move us north and to have us live with them until we'd saved enough money for our own place.

I'll never forget how relieved and surprised I'd been when my husband had agreed, but he'd explained that he would go anywhere with me. While I'd believed him, and a small part of me still does, I've always privately maintained that he'd wanted nothing to do with his parents. There'd been a rift between them, whether because of his strict upbringing or their religious ways, I don't know. My in-laws had been one subject he'd never discuss, along with how he'd had to give up going to a four-year college to save for a house and raise a family. Instead, my tenacious husband had adjusted and adapted. Once we were in Cleveland, he'd bought used lawn equipment and started working on the neighbors' yards. After he'd saved money, he had slowly bought new gear and began taking classes at the local community college. Within two years, he'd earned a certificate in carpentry, joined forces with another small-time landscaper, and created a landscaping and remodeling business to keep money coming in throughout the year.

I was very proud of him then, just as I am now. His father's fruit farm and pastoral salary had been good. His parents had plenty of money, but as soon as they'd learned we were moving to Cleveland, they'd refused to help us. That'd been fine with me. I'd wanted nothing to do with those people, or have any obligations to them.

By the time my father had been promoted and transferred again—this time to Columbus—we'd scraped together enough money to buy our own home. But my parents' relocation had left a hole inside of me. I hadn't had many friends in the area, and depended on them, my husband and toddler for company. If something happened to my husband, or he divorced me, I wouldn't know where to begin. I could move to Columbus, but wouldn't want my kids and me to be burdens.

God, why was I thinking about this? *Because you love your husband and don't want last night to be a one-time deal.* No, I didn't. I wanted for us to spend kid-free time together, to laugh, enjoy each other's company, make love...

I leaned in front of the mirror to examine my graying roots. I'd never minded my brown hair until the grays had started to appear, making not only my hair dull and lifeless, but washing out my complexion. I could use a tan. Since it was only April, that wouldn't happen naturally for a couple of months. The bronzer I'd bought today should do the trick. Hopefully, my husband would think so and want a repeat of last night.

The ringtone I designated for my husband chimed from the first floor. Remembering I'd left my cell phone on the charger on the kitchen counter, I quickly made my way downstairs. "Hello?"

"Hey, honey, how are you?" he asked.

My cheeks warmed. It'd been a while since he'd used a term of endearment. "Great. Did you finish the Milsons' pond?" I asked, heading into the laundry room. I'd rather use rags than my 'good' towels to protect my clothes and bathroom counter from the hair dye.

"Yep, just finished. The truckload of sod arrived early, so the crew is just about finished laying it down in the front, and will work on the back shortly. I'm thinking I should be home in about an hour."

Oh, shoot. That didn't give me much time to do my hair, and I didn't want him to see me until it was styled and I'd applied my makeup. I leaned against the washing machine. "Will you want lunch before you work on the basement?" He'd made remodeling plans with his business partner and the new neighbor.

"It's too beautiful to be stuck inside."

"Then you're going to work on the pool project?" I asked, loving that he was a helpful and ambitious man, but wishing he could take the afternoon off and spend time with the kids and me. A picnic at the duck pond would be fun.

"Nope. We've decided we're done working. How about a neighborhood cookout? I saw Vincent this morning when he was walking Fritz. He's the one who suggested it, and said he'd roll his grill to the front. We can get a game of softball or kickball going in the street with the kids, have some beers and burgers...what do you think?"

"It's a great idea. Who's bringing what?" I asked, taking the rags from the cabinet. I'd better get a move on if I needed to run to the store or whip up a side dish.

"Call Helen. She's letting all the neighbors know and handling the food part."

"Do you think the Norths will join us?" I asked, anxious to meet them, but a little apprehensive, too. After all, my husband was right: I wasn't *worldly*.

"I don't see why not. Sloan was going to help in the basement anyway." He released a sigh. "What I said the other night…you know, about you not being able to fit in with them?"

And that my brownies were dry. But I wouldn't remind him of that, not when I sensed an apology coming my way. Besides, I knew for a fact that my brownies were moist and delicious.

"Well," he continued, "it was a crappy thing for me to say. I didn't mean it. I don't mean the majority of the jerky things I say to you. I…I've had a lot on my mind, been down and cranky. It's not fair of me to take that out on you."

My eyes filled with tears as my heart swelled with love and hope. Our marriage was still strong, and we'd fight to make it work. "It's okay. But I wish you would lean on me when you're feeling down. I love you, and you know I'm always here for you."

"I know you are and have been. I love you, too."

A tear escaped and slipped down my cheek. I couldn't remember the last time he'd told me that.

He cleared his throat. "Go call Helen, and plan on seeing me in about an hour. I think the party will start around three."

"Sounds good," I said, told him good-bye, then ended the call. I tucked the phone in my back pocket. As I took the rags from the laundry room, I caught the familiar odor of earth and mildew. I looked to the ceiling, where the laundry chute was, and hoped one of my sons hadn't left something wet and muddy in there.

I set the rags on the washer, then opened the chute. A small pile of clothes fell to the vinyl floor. As I tossed them into the hamper hidden in the closet, I came across the T-shirt and sweats my husband had put on last night just before he'd gone to the kitchen to make a sandwich. My son had been right. The clothes were filthy. Not muddy, but very dirty.

What could he have been doing last night? After tossing the soiled clothes into the utility sink, I grabbed the rags and made my way into the kitchen. I looked out of the patio window and scanned the yard, which was in major need of an overhaul. A green tarp behind and near the corner of the shed caught my attention. I left the rags on the peninsula and went outside.

When I reached the back of the shed, I looked down to where

two-by-fours were lined up on the tarp. I would rarely go back there, and had no clue if this was new or not. The freshly turned earth spilling from beneath the tarp, which was clean, along with the wood boards, suggested this was definitely new. As I bent to lift a corner, my cell phone chimed my husband's ring tone.

"Hey, hon," he began, "I forgot to tell you that I've got a cord of wood being delivered today. If the truck shows before I do, have him dump it in the apron of the driveway by the basketball hoop."

Now I knew why the wood and tarp were there. After telling him I'd take care of it, I went back into the house. First on the agenda: color my hair. Then, while the dye worked its magic, I'd call Helen.

It'd been a long time since I'd been excited about something. And it wasn't the neighborhood party that had me happy. No, it was my husband. Whatever had been holding him down lately was either on its way out or gone.

And I predicted nothing but happier times to come...

Chapter Eleven

The rental house, North Royalhurst, Ohio
Saturday, 12:14 p.m. Daylight Saving Time

SLOAN STOOD IN front of the closed bedroom door, contemplating his next move. Until he could be certain he'd rid himself of those pussy feelings Whitney had stirred in him, and knew in his gut that he was officially emotionally detached from her, he didn't want to be around her. Unfortunately, living together made avoiding each other difficult. Earlier, and unable to sleep, he'd risen at six. In need of coffee and figuring she would still be in bed, he'd gone to the kitchen. Unfortunately, she had been up and sitting at the island, coffee brewing, her laptop in front of her.

She'd been pleasant, had wished him a good morning, but had kept her focus on the computer screen. The moment had been awkward, had him regretting leaving her room last night. What else could he have done, though? Sleeping together would have made their situation too familiar, too affectionate, too much of a sign that he cared. And he did care. So much that it bothered the hell out of him that she had so easily dismissed him as an ideal partner. Which was dumb on his part. He didn't want marriage, so why should he give a shit that he hadn't made the cut?

He stepped away from the door, then sat on the bed. He couldn't continue to stay in his room, and wasn't in the mood to run another five miles—he'd already done that earlier this morning—just to avoid her. With regard to their investigation, he had nothing to do. The Eastons weren't home. After his run, Whitney had caught him before he'd been able to make it to his room undetected, and had explained that Campbell had listened to the audio they'd recorded. The lieutenant agreed that they should remain on the case, and had put in a request for the cell-site simulator, which was currently being used by another unit within the sheriff's department. Campbell hoped to have the Stingray to them by Monday or Tuesday.

Although either day worked, he and Whitney didn't want the Stingray coming to them later than Tuesday. They needed the device to identify Cameron's burner phone in order to place a tap on it. Irene's birthday was next Saturday. Her two older kids were supposed to come home for the weekend and, from the one-sided conversation they'd heard yesterday, he and Whitney believed there was a possibility that drug money would exchange hands. Even if Cameron ended up wiring the money to Rueben Morales, communication between the two could not only confirm Morales's existence, but might also lead to his location.

A knock came at the door. "Sloan? I'm going to the grocery store to pick up a few things for the party. Do you want to come with me?"

His mood soured even more. Thanks to Vincent and his brilliant plan to have a neighborhood party, he no longer had a place to escape to for the afternoon. Nolan and Travis had agreed it was too beautiful a day to spend it in the basement, so now he not only had to socialize, but he had to do it with his *wife* by his side.

"I would, but I have too much to do here," he said, glancing around the spotless bedroom.

"Like what? Can I come in?" she asked, her tone impatient. "I hate talking through doors."

"No, I'm not dressed."

"Whatever. You go ahead and keep hiding and being ridiculous. If I'd known letting you go down on me would have you scared to be around me, then I wouldn't have allowed it to happen."

Let him go down on her? Scared to be around her? Bullshit. He went to the door and opened it. "I'm not—"

"Scared of anything," she finished for him. "Wow, you sure got dressed in a hurry."

The smirk she wore should have him irate at himself for allowing her to goad him, but she smelled so damned good and he knew how she tasted. Right now, despite having berated himself all morning for having no will power where she was concerned, and no control over his emotions, he still wanted to kiss her. Remind her that she'd wanted him touching her, his mouth on her lips, on her body.

"That's right," he said. "I'm also not hiding, or being ridiculous. And you practically *begged* me to go down on you."

"That's not how I recall it."

His body was wound tight with the conflicting need to pull her in his arms or push her away. Trying for calm, he leaned against the doorjamb. "Let me refresh your memory…when I was ready to leave the room, you untied your robe and let it hang open so I could see your naked body."

"That was an accident."

"The untied robe?"

She nodded. "What came next was fun and I liked it, but not enough to do it again or deal with you creeping around the house trying to avoid me."

"First, I made you come with my fingers, then my tongue." He pushed himself off the doorjamb and entered her space. "Are you sure you don't want to do it again?"

Her gaze smoldered with desire as it drifted to his mouth. "Maybe. The evenings are kind of boring around here."

She was fucking with him, trying to get a rise out of him so he'd stop avoiding her. He should concede, tell her she'd won, that she was right, that he was being cowardly and ridiculous. Instead, he wanted a replay of last night. Not just the physical part of what had gone on in her bedroom. He liked her, respected her, wanted to prove that he could be decisive, that he went after what he wanted. That he deserved a place on her list. If, after the investigation ended, they went their separate ways—which, given they lived in different cities, would likely happen—he'd cope with losing her then, and probably get over her in no time. Especially because, then, she wouldn't be rejecting him. No, this time and location would be to blame.

"Why wait until it's dark?" He brushed his knuckles along the side of one breast, before grazing his fingertips over her stiff nipple. "There's a bed behind me." He moved his hand to her hip. "I want to strip you out of your clothes." Leaning close to her ear, he slid his hands over her rear. "I'd love to bend you over."

When she turned her head slightly, her cheek touched his. "We have no condoms," she reminded him.

He massaged her bottom. "For what I want to do, I don't need one."

Her breath quickened. "What do you want to do to me?"

His dick hardened as he imagined her naked, on her knees, ass in the air. "Exactly what I did yesterday, but from a different angle."

She speared her hands through his hair and captured his mouth with hers. With a throaty moan that had his balls tightening, she parted her lips. He did the same, and as their tongues glided over each other, he lifted her. After she wrapped her legs around him, he walked her into the bedroom, then set her feet on the floor.

As they kissed, he undid her jeans, then inched them over her hips. Too impatient to wait until she was completely naked, he slipped his fingers beneath her panties, along her sex, then between her wet folds. She groaned against his mouth and pressed her hips forward, forcing his fingers deeper.

"You're so fucking hot," he said, after she broke the kiss to catch her breath. She intrigued him more than any woman he'd ever met. She was strong, smart, driven, and an excellent detective. She knew what she wanted out of life, and had plenty of lists to prove it. There was also an innocence about her, yet she knew pleasure, and wasn't afraid to find it, or show him what made her body hum. She was an enthusiastic lover, naively aggressive, and he couldn't wait to have her mouth on him. To watch her take in his length.

His dick ached for release as her inner muscles gripped his fingers. She rested her forehead against his chest, just as her body stiffened and she came. Ready to see her naked body on his bed, and bring her to orgasm again, he pulled his fingers free to finish removing her clothes.

The doorbell rang. They both froze and looked at each other Then her eyes widened.

"Crap, crap, crap," she said, pulling her jeans and panties up and over her hips.

"Who is it?"

The doorbell chimed again. "I forgot to tell him not to come over today."

Jealousy weaved its way into his chest. "The guy you're dating?"

"No, not Cliff."

She'd been dating a guy named Cliff? No wonder his real name hadn't bothered her.

"My friend, Morgan," she continued, and headed for the door. "When Cliff couldn't come over, I asked Morgan to show up here instead."

"If I'd known hanging with the guys bothered you that much, and that you didn't want to be alone, I would've canceled."

"Coming," she called as they made their way down the steps. "I didn't mind being alone for the day. I...oh, I don't want to say because it's completely childish."

He stopped her in the foyer. "My dick is hard."

She blinked, then dropped her gaze toward his groin.

"It was kind of juvenile to point that out, don't you think?" he asked.

A small smile curved her lips. "A little." She sighed. "I asked Morgan to come here and pretend he was my boyfriend. I wanted to make you jealous, and for you to think men desire me."

A voice in the back of his head told him to run before he completely fell for her. Instead, determined to let her know where he stood and put her at ease, he cupped her face with one hand.

"That made my dick even harder," he said with a grin. "If I haven't made it clear that I desire you and that I like you, then I'll jot it down on sticky notes and place the reminders around the house."

Oh my God. Whitney caught her breath. She'd just fallen half in love with Sloan. Not because he desired and liked her—though that helped and was nice to hear—but because he'd diffused what should have been an embarrassing moment. And without judgment. "That won't be necessary. I've already made a mental note, and doubt I'll forget you said that."

"Whitney?" Morgan knocked on the door. "Are you okay?"

"Hang on, Morgan." She turned to Sloan. "I'm sorry about the interruption. Can we, ah... I'd like to do what we were going to do," she said, her face burning. Sloan made her want to be bold, but she wasn't used to talking about sex or various elements of it.

"Absolutely," he said, then opened the door.

Morgan leaned against the porch column. His clothes were usually in line with the latest male fashion trend. Currently, he preferred wearing skinny pants—not jeans, he loathed jeans—in a variety of colors and wore them with boots or loafers. He also loved button-down shirts and fedoras. Today, he'd clothed his lean, muscular, six-foot three frame in a pair of straight-leg jeans, a graphic T-shirt and black boots—all something Sloan would wear.

Morgan slipped off a pair of sunglasses, looked from her to Sloan, then back to her again. "Hey, babe, how's it going?" he asked, stepping inside and giving her a long kiss—thankfully, no tongue.

She moved back and, wiping her mouth, fought from cringing. She and Morgan had been best friends since the seventh grade. Kissing him was almost incestuous. "Morgan—"

Morgan offered his hand to Sloan. "What's up, man? Gettin' along well with my woman?"

Remembering where Sloan's fingers had been moments ago, she quickly grabbed his forearm before the two men connected hands. "Sloan North, this is Morgan Reese. Sloan was fixing the toilet and needs to wash his hands. I know how you are about germs."

Morgan snorted, widened his stance and crossed his arms over his chest. "C'mon, babe. Germs don't bother me. I eat cherry tomatoes straight from the garden—*without* washing them."

"Right," she replied, staring at the tattoos along his arm, none of which were there a week ago. "Nice tats."

He smiled at Sloan. "My woman has a thing for ink. It makes her freaky-naughty. When she told me you had a bunch, I thought I'd better come over and let you know what's up."

Sloan's brow furrowed. "Up with what?"

"You know." Morgan jerked his head toward her. "Whitney."

While she would honestly love to let Morgan continue to pretend to be her macho boyfriend, she had to bring this to a close before he made a fool of himself and ended up mad at her. "Morgan, he knows."

"Knows that we have raging hot sex?"

Sloan laughed.

"What? No!" She couldn't help laughing, too. "He knows you're my best friend, and why you're here."

Relief crossed Morgan's face as he dropped his arms. "Thank God. The whole way over here, I kept trying to come up with super-manly, heterosexual things to say."

"Telling him you eat cherry tomatoes without washing them helped with your whole machismo vibe." She went over to her best friend and took his hand. "You're going to have to scrub your arms raw to get rid of the fake tattoos."

"I'm going to keep them until they start to fade. I think they're kinda cool. So does Micah," he said with a wink. "We're thinking about going together and getting matching tattoos with each other's initials."

She led him into the kitchen. Sloan followed behind, then went to the sink and washed his hands.

"Wow, that's a sign of commitment," she said, taking a can of Coke and two bottles of water from the fridge. "Or would be, if you two didn't have the same initials."

Morgan grinned, took one of the bottles from her, then sat at the table. "True." He glanced to where Sloan stood at the sink, his back still to them, then looked to her and mouthed, "Hot."

"Shut up," she mouthed back, then said, "It's been years since I've seen you in jeans. Where'd you get them?"

"You know Laney from the salon, right?"

"Tall, rockin' the fire ombre?" Whitney asked. If they were talking about the same woman, the top part of Laney's long hair was a vibrant orangey red that faded to a pale yellow blond.

Sloan used a paper towel to dry his hands. "What's ombre?"

"A type of color shading," Morgan answered. "It's all the rage at my hair salon. Anyway, Laney let me borrow her husband's clothes."

"They look good on you."

"Interesting." Sloan joined them at the table. "I own similar clothes, and you told me I looked like a thug wearing them," he said, his tone teasing.

Morgan twisted the bottle top. "Whitney's very opinionated."

"I am not. And I told him he looked more like a drug dealer than any of the people we're investigating."

Morgan chuckled and looked to Sloan. "She's opinionated," he repeated. "But she means well. Does she leave notes all over the place?"

"I'm starting to regret having you drop the fake boyfriend role."

"Oh, stop it. I won't say anything bad about you. Not really."

She gave his arm a light slug. "Change of subject...what do you think of the house?"

He shrugged. "Gee, Mrs. Cleaver, it's just swell." Grinning he added, "Sorry, but I couldn't live here. If I didn't have to close the salon, I'd go straight home so I can wash the stench of suburbia clinging to my body."

"Could you be any more melodramatic?" she asked.

"Of course." He held up a hand. "I know this is your dream, but it's not mine. I love living closer to the city. Besides, creepy things happen in the burbs. You heard about the bodies construction workers found, right?"

Sloan thumbed in the direction of the new subdivision. "That happened a half mile from here."

Morgan's eyes widened. "What? I mean, I knew it was in this city, but *half a mile?*" He shivered and took her hand in his. "I don't like you staying here."

Whitney loved when Morgan went into brotherly protector mode, and how it gave her the warm fuzzies. "I have guns and you know I can handle myself in a fight."

He shifted his gaze to Sloan. "Before I hit my growth spurt during our junior year in high school, Whitney was my body guard. One time—"

"Sloan doesn't need to hear about this, and I have to go to the grocery store." She did not want Morgan telling Sloan about their high school years or any other humiliating stories. As it was, she'd already embarrassed herself a few times in front of Sloan—like asking her gay best friend to pretend to be her boyfriend. "Come to the store and keep me company."

"Hang on a sec," Sloan said. "I want to hear this."

Morgan grinned. "Well, we were in tenth grade, and these two guys from the JV football team spent the entire month of September pushing me into lockers, tripping me, calling me names."

Sloan frowned. "Why?"

"Because I'm gay."

"So those guys were homophobic dicks."

Yep, she was definitely halfway in love with Sloan. He hadn't even flinched when Morgan had admitted he was gay. And it was important to her to be with a man who didn't judge others.

"Exactly," Morgan said. "Anyway, they'd never done it in front of Whitney, but she knew about the bullying and kept telling me to have my parents talk to the principal about it. But I didn't want to be a snitch." When Morgan looked to her, there was love and pride in his eyes. "One day, those two guys started up on me again, but this time, Whitney was there. She told them to stop, and when they asked her what she was going to do about it, she walked over, sent a right hook into one kid's face, then did this awesome turn to deliver a back kick. She drilled the other kid right in the stomach with her heel. While he was on the ground coughing, the other guy tried to hit her back, but she blocked him, then let him have it with a few rounds of punches. It was epic."

She squeezed his hand. "Serving detention every Saturday for a month wasn't, but you were worth it. Plus, those boys never bothered you again."

"No." He faced Sloan. "We all ended up being friends. But who wouldn't want to be friends with Wonder Woman over here?"

"Now that you remembered that I can take care of myself, don't worry about the bodies the police found. Besides, I highly doubt the killer is going to be hanging around here when police are still excavating the field."

"Good point. I saw on the news that they've found six bodies so far. Your neighbors have to be worried about property values going down."

Sloan cracked a smile. "The developer who owns the subdivision is the one who's probably worried. I think it'll be hard to find people willing to buy a home where there used to be a mass grave."

"Mass grave? You exaggerate just as much as Morgan." When Sloan looked away and rubbed the back of his neck, she suspected he knew something more about the subdivision. But how? And why would he dig into what was happening there when they had their own investigation to run? "What aren't you telling me?" she asked. Then she remembered... "Rachel. Your research person was looking into the murders, wasn't she?"

"Maybe. Look, I was bored and curious. It wasn't as if I spent days discussing the murder case with her. I was still working our investigation and—"

"You don't have to get defensive. I don't care."

"Can you blame the guy?" Morgan asked. "You're kind of a freak when it comes to your lists and making sure everything is checked off and completed."

She rolled her eyes. Morgan loved to tease her about her bullet pointing, and commented on the subject whenever possible. "What does that have anything to do with Sloan trying to get info on the murders?"

"I'm just saying."

"Then please say something that doesn't involve making fun of my lists."

He blew her a kiss. "You're right, and I'm sorry." He glanced to Sloan. "She's also a freak about her sticky notes."

She half-laughed. "Oh my God. If you don't stop, I'm going to force you to come to our neighborhood party. And I'll make you eat potato salad and a hot dog, *after* you play kickball with the kids."

He exaggerated a swallow. "I just threw up in my mouth."

Sloan raised a brow. "What's wrong with hot dogs and potato salad?"

"Nothing, if someone else is eating it. But it was the kickball thing that got to me."

Laughing, Sloan stood. "Don't worry, man. I've got your back on this. Suburbia wasn't my thing, either."

Wasn't? As in past tense? Had the burbs grown on him, or had she?

"Thank you." Morgan pressed his hands together as if praying, then nodded. "You're a noble man."

"I wouldn't go that far." Sloan smiled, then looked to her. "I'll go to the store for you so you two can hang out together. Where's your list?"

Her cheeks heated. Panic squeezed her chest as she mentally berated herself for adding condoms to the list. "I didn't make one," she lied. And she'd been worried Morgan would tell embarrassing stories about her. She would rather have her friend do that than let Sloan know she'd intended to be prepared, should there be an opportunity for sex.

He looked at her as if she'd sprung another head. "Since when?"

Morgan leaned over and placed a hand against her forehead. "Are you sick? You've never gone to the store without a list. *Ever.*"

"Seriously," Sloan began, "give it up."

"I don't have one," she insisted. "And, it's okay. Morgan and I will go. He can help me come up with some ideas for what we can bring to the party."

A few minutes later, they were in her Fiat. She slowly backed out of the garage, checking her mirrors for kids. Once she was on the street, and the car was in DRIVE, she glanced over to Morgan and sucked in a breath. "Give me that," she demanded, reaching for the list he'd taken from her purse while she'd been worried about running over a neighbor's kid.

He quickly sat on it and, wearing a wry grin, shook his head, then tsked. "Whitney Joan Russell, you are a naughty girl."

Seething, she drove down their street. "I swear to God, I'm going to slash your tires so you're stuck here."

Chuckling, he pulled the list out from under him and began scanning it. "Let's see. We have stuff to make buffalo chicken dip, burgers and all the fixings for those, milk—I take it that's for Sloan since you don't drink it—and enough candy that your teeth should rot out…"

"Sloan has a sweet tooth, and yes, the milk is for him. Can you just stop now?"

"No, no, no, I'm not finished. Let's see…ice, beer, water and…this is random. Am I reading this right?"

Her face had become so hot that perspiration dotted her upper lip. "You're an ass."

He gasped. "For shame. What would your mom and dad say if they heard you talking like that, or saw that their daughter was buying…*condoms*?"

Mortified, she gripped the steering wheel. "*Now* do you understand why I didn't want to give the list to Sloan?"

"I mostly certainly do. So, who's going to wear them?"

She glanced at him. "Certainly not me." Sighing, she stopped at a red light. "You were right. Sloan likes me. I like him. We kind of fooled around and I'm hoping to…you know."

"What happened to your three-month rule? Since you've fooled around, you clearly gave up on it when you let a guy get to first, second and third base. Wait, why are you smiling?"

The light turned green, and she began driving again. "Because."

"Don't you hold out on me. Dish."

Needing to talk, she did, and told him how Sloan had come

up with the whole pretend dating thing, but she left out the sexy details. "I'm not sure what to do or how to feel. I…told him about my ideal partner list."

"And, so?"

"Other than being well educated, having future goals, wanting marriage, a family and to live in a place like this, he ticks everything on my list."

"You told me he has a good career and was a former cop, so you know he has a pension. Meaning we can take the education thing off the list. At this point, it doesn't matter."

She parked the car. "True. But he's made it clear he doesn't want a wife, and that he hates the suburbs."

He pursed his lips and nodded. "That is a problem. Except…"

"Except what?"

He shrugged. "You kill plants."

"Which is why I don't have any. What's your point?"

"My point is, I noticed all the pots on the front porch, and the ones on the back patio—which are probably going to die when we get a cold snap. I'd bet my Salvatore Ferragamo loafers you didn't plant them."

"The suede ones? You stupidly spent almost six hundred dollars on them."

He grinned. "Because I know it's a sure bet."

"Okay, what's your point?"

"If Sloan doesn't like living here or pretending to be a homeowner, why is he taking pride in his house?"

"To make it look like we're here to stay," she said, not wanting to get her hopes up that Sloan was possibly leaning toward the idea of liking suburbia. "That's what he said when I asked him why he'd bought the outdoor furniture, which he's giving me when he leaves."

"*If* he leaves."

She opened the car door. "He's leaving."

Morgan exited the car and met up with her. "Talk him into staying."

"His job is in Chicago."

"He can get a new job here."

Her stomach balling into a knot, she stopped in the middle of the parking lot. "I can't be with him. He's like Wes. A self-proclaimed womanizer, a charmer. He's too…" She grabbed his arm. "He gives me orgasms."

Morgan laughed. "And that's a bad thing?" He took her hands in his and looked at her, his gaze understanding. "Whitney, don't tell Micah, but you're my favorite person in the world. I love and adore you, but sometimes you're so damned rigid, I want to shake it out of you."

Was she? Yes, she liked her lists, but could be flexible with them. Sometimes. "I'm not rigid."

"Frigid?" She tried to pull her hands free, but he held them firmly in his grasp. "Listen," he began, his tone patient. "You've spent your life living by rules you made when you didn't know what it was like to be an adult. Yes, you've adjusted those rules over time, but not that much. You're too picky when it comes to men, too scared to let go of control and…not every charming guy who can give you an orgasm is going to cheat on you."

Tears filled her eyes. "Do you really think I'm frigid and controlling?"

He shook his head. "I think you're a beautiful, vibrant woman who is too scared to allow her passion and zest for life to show." He touched her cheek. "How many times have you been there for me when I've been hurting after a breakup?"

Unlike her, Morgan was a risk taker who followed his heart. "Too many."

"Those times sucked. But if I hadn't taken chances, I wouldn't have grown as a person."

He'd be like her. Stuck in a juvenile time warp, daydreaming about the ideal man who might not exist. She stared at his handsome face, one that was as familiar to her as her own. "I love and adore you, too. If you liked girls, you'd be my ideal partner," she said, throwing out a line they both liked to use when dealing with their love lives.

"Back at ya." Chuckling, he wrapped an arm around her shoulder, and they began walking toward the store. "He does like you."

"I know," she said. "But for a fun time while we're on assign-ment. And I'm okay with that."

"No, I mean he *really* likes you. I saw the way he looked at you. How the two of you interacted. There's this weird familiarity that I've never seen happen with you before."

She grabbed a shopping cart. "We've been living together for a week. It's kind of hard to *not* become familiar with someone."

"Yeah, but he looks at you as if he's starving."

After tossing celery into the cart, she eyed him. "I don't know what that means."

"He's hungry. For you."

"Of course he is. Before you showed up we were fooling around in his bedroom." A woman standing next to them glared at her. "Don't judge me," she said to the lady, then grabbed a few tomatoes.

While Morgan laughed, they made their way out of the produce section. "Are you sure you'd do well living in suburbia?"

"I think so. Honestly, Sloan knows the neighbors better than I do, and I researched the crap out of them."

"Research and lists will only get you so far. Human interaction is what counts."

She snagged a bag of tortilla chips for the buffalo dip. "Back to this starving and hungry thing…I noticed it, too. But don't you think that's simply an indication of a physical attraction."

He picked up a container of Oreos—which wasn't on her list —from an end cap and placed them into her cart. "Sure, but in this case, I feel like it's something deeper. Kind of like what went down with Micah and me. We resisted each other, tried to put up a front, until it was clear we were meant to be together."

She stopped the cart. Morgan had always been the one who wore his heart on his sleeve. She'd figured his relationship with Micah would, as many had in the past, start out flaming hot, then burn out after a few weeks. But the two had been together for nearly a year. "You really love him, don't you?"

"I do." His face developed pink splotches, a sign he was nervous or embarrassed. "He asked me to move in with him."

She embraced him. "I'm so happy for you. Please tell me you said yes."

He leaned back. "I didn't say yes or no."

Deflating, she stepped away, and began pushing the cart. "Why not?"

"He wants what you want. A house in the burbs, marriage, to adopt a kid or two. I don't know if I'm cut out for that."

"But you're so good with your nieces and nephews."

"Because they *go home* with their parents." He sighed. "I don't know. Micah has me thinking about things I haven't ever considered."

Which had her considering the irony of their conversation. "You just told me that I need to be more open minded, and deviate from my lists, yet you have a mental list of your own that you're not sure you can change."

He stopped. "We have issues."

She grinned. "So I'm discovering. At least we know we're not all there in the head. The question is: how do we stray from what we know?"

"You mean our safe places." He snapped his fingers. "Here's a thought… Our safe places really aren't so safe, they're self-imposed prisons that have held us back from where we're truly meant to be in our lives."

She wasn't sure if she necessarily agreed with him. Being cautious about the men she dated and expecting certain standards wasn't imprisoning, but smart. "Maybe for you. You're the one who has cold feet about exploring the world of marriage and children. I, on the other hand, know exactly what I want."

He laughed again. "Really? Let's talk about *Clifford*."

God, no. Morgan refused to say why, but he couldn't stand Cliff. "No need. You'll be happy to know that I won't be seeing him again."

"Miracles do happen. I will say my piece on this anyway. He's a manipulative user."

"Cliff? No way. How was he using me? When we went out, he always paid."

"I'm not talking about money. Besides paying for meals, what did the guy add to your life? Did he bring you any kind of joy?"

"I enjoyed his companionship."

"Why? What was it about Clifford that drew you to him? His looks? Charisma? Humor? Did he do nice things for you that made you feel special? Did he have you lying in bed at night thinking about all the fun things you two could do if he were there with you? Did his kisses make you melt? Did he make you feel alive?"

Not at all. Knowing where this was heading, she kept that to herself. "Your love for melodrama is showing again. And I still don't see how Cliff was a manipulative user."

"Because he knew you were so desperate to get married that he could get away with acting however he wanted. You went out when he decided, not when you suggested it, then he made you feel in control by letting you choose what you'd do on your date. Ever notice that he put his nerdy friends and games before you? And how often did he call or text? That's right…never. You were the one doing the calling and texting. You were the one trying to force a relationship to happen because the guy was an eighty-seven percent match to your ideal husband list."

Ashamed and furious with herself, she turned away and scanned the various brands of canned chicken. How could she have been so naïve? How could she have allowed her desire for marriage and children to cloud her judgment? She didn't have to evaluate the two months she'd been seeing Cliff to know Morgan was right. She'd been a desperate fool and had allowed herself to be led around by her biological clock, along with her stupid list of life goals.

"Hey," Morgan said, his tone concerned. "I'm sorry if I hurt your feelings. That wasn't my intention."

"You didn't. For the buffalo chicken dip…do you think I should shred up a rotisserie chicken or go with canned?"

"Rotisserie."

"Agreed," she said, setting the can back in place, then heading down the aisle.

"I can't stand when you shut down on me." Morgan caught up with her. "Please say something."

She stopped near the deli. "Cliff did nothing to or for me," she admitted. "*Nothing*. He was boring, I barely found him mildly attractive, and he had a horrible sense of humor. I lied to you about his match to my list. He didn't score an eighty-seven percent. He barely reached sixty." Her self-disgust multiplied. "I knew our relationship wouldn't go anywhere."

"Then why did you continue seeing him? Be totally honest with yourself."

"I don't know. Just like I don't know why I'm getting involved with Sloan." Her head began to throb. "I don't want to talk about this. I have obvious issues with men and dating. When the investigation is over and I'm back at my place, you'll have to come by, we'll get drunk and make a list of all my issues."

Guilt and sadness filled his eyes. "I don't think that's necessary, because I just realized you only have one real issue."

"What's that?"

"You're afraid to reach your life goals."

"That's absurd." She left his side to select a chicken from under the heat lamp. Although she and Morgan loved talking about life, this conversation had been blown out of proportion. "Afraid to reach life goals," she said when she returned to the cart. "How did we go from my buying condoms to that?"

"No clue. And I still stand by my assessment. You like to be in charge and are afraid of being hurt, so you date dipshits knowing —on a subconscious level—it'll never last. That way you can pat yourself on the back for at least trying to find a husband without actually landing one, not falling in love and having your heart broken or later dealing with a failed marriage."

"Your assessment is dumb."

"Is it? We've already discussed Cliff… Let's take a look at Wes the cheat. You knew he was no good. I remember one of the girls from the salon telling you he was a player. But you went out with him anyway. Why? For fun. Because he offered you an opportunity to let loose and break out of your usual routine."

"Not true. He really hurt me. Scarred me for men like him."

His brows lifted. "We've known each other for over twenty years. You can try to lie to yourself, but you can't lie to me. You didn't shed a tear over Wes. He just became another excuse to become even pickier about men. Now, do we want to discuss the guy who might have webbed feet?"

"Oh my God," she whispered, and stared at him. "Why did I even sleep with him?" As she pushed the cart to the dairy section, she thought back to the other men she'd dated over the years, which hadn't been many. Maybe Morgan's dumb assessment wasn't so dumb. Had she been sabotaging her own love life because she was afraid of truly falling in love? "None of this makes any sense." She opened the cooler and pulled out a gallon of two percent milk. "My parents have a wonderful marriage, my brothers all fell in love and have solid marriages, too. Why wouldn't I want that?"

"Maybe because you can't control love, can't bullet point or use sticky notes to keep your emotions neat and organized." He smiled. "But what do I know? I've only been in love about a dozen times."

As they finished shopping, Morgan thankfully remained silent. If what he'd assessed and suggested were true, then she'd never achieve her life goals. Sure, she could buy the house. She could even have a baby without being married. But she would be doing a terrible disservice to herself and her partner if she married a man she didn't love. They would simply be roommates who occasionally had sex, and her husband would be—as Sloan had suggested—a cardboard sperm donor. She didn't want that. She wanted the butterflies Sloan gave her, how she looked forward to waking up in the morning so she could meet up with him at the coffee pot. He consumed her thoughts, made her happy, angry or sad. Made her laugh, want to cry or long to be held by him. What did it all mean?

You know. Admit it to yourself.

"Did you just growl?" Morgan asked.

"I'm frustrated." She looked at her list. The last thing she needed were condoms. "We're done here. Let's head to the register."

"You forgot something," he said, and waggled his brows.

"I didn't. I took them off the list."

A huge smile practically split his face in half. "You love him."

"I do not, and I'm tired of using my grocery store to carry out this discussion you insist on having."

"You love him, and are worried that if you have sex you'll have an even deeper connection with him."

She glanced around to make sure no one had heard him, then leaned toward him. "I'm only half in love with him," she said, keeping her tone hushed. "I think it's a good idea to keep it that way, don't you?" Her eyes misted as her throat tightened. "He's going to leave and it's going to hurt."

"Give him a reason to stay," he said, then started walking away. "Go to the register. I'll meet you there in a sec."

She pushed Morgan's words from her head and busied herself with unloading the shopping cart. After she'd finished paying for the groceries, her friend met her near the exit, a bag in his hand. "You bought them anyway."

He grinned. "A belated fake wedding gift. Plus, I don't want the reason for him staying to be an unexpected pregnancy."

"How thoughtful," she said with heavy sarcasm. "*If* I wanted Sloan to stay, I don't know what I could do or say to convince him to give up his career in Chicago."

When they reached her car, Morgan helped her unload the shopping cart. "I wasn't suggesting that you say or do anything. *You* would be the reason. Not some list you've given him bullet pointing why he should move here." He put a bag in the car. "How is it that you managed to always do better in school than me?"

"Because while I was busy studying, you were out looking for your latest conquest."

He nodded. "I'll give you that."

They drove back to the house. Morgan surprised her and stayed for an hour before he had to leave to close the salon for the day. While he helped her prepare for the party, Sloan sat in the kitchen, talking with them. It amazed her how well her best friend and her...Sloan got along. Laughing and joking as if they'd known each other for years. Actually, it was Sloan who amazed her. He wasn't a chameleon—for her, that term had a negative connotation—he was smart, personable, adaptable and friendly.

When it was time for Morgan to leave, Sloan kept his hand on the small of her back as they walked him to his car. Their neighbors were already out, and had coolers on tree lawns. The two landscapers and their wives stood at the end of Vincent and Helen's driveway, where Vincent had parked his grill and set up a table for appetizers and side dishes.

The older man waved. "We have plenty for one more!"

"If I didn't have to get back to work, I'd be staying," Morgan yelled back, then, in a hushed voice he added, "when Hell freezes over."

Chuckling, Sloan shook his hand. "It's not so bad once you've been here for a while."

"You don't miss the city?" Morgan asked.

Sloan wrapped an arm around Whitney. "I miss the conveniences, but I figured out the time it would take me to walk to a store in Chicago is equivalent to what it takes to drive to one here. Plus, I don't have to lug my bags, I can just drive off with them." He looked at the Ford F-150 on loan from the sheriff's department, wistfulness in his eyes. "I'm going to miss driving that truck."

Morgan gave her a hug, then met her gaze. "Maybe I'll have to come out here a few times before you two leave. You know, to see if this grows on me."

"I think you should," she said. After another round of goodbyes, they watched him leave.

"Why does he need *this* to grow on him?" Sloan asked.

As they walked back into the house to gather the items they'd prepared for the party, she explained Morgan and Micah's situation. "What's silly is Morgan and I both grew up in the suburbs, so I don't know why he's acting as if this is a foreign country."

"I get where he's coming from on this. The first few days we were here, I thought I was going to lose my mind. I was so bored, it was too quiet...I entertained myself by clocking Vincent's dog walks, when Becky drove Chloe to preschool, how many cigarettes Joe would have in an hour…it was becoming my personal Hell."

Meanwhile, she'd been jealous of him for being able to sit in her dream house. "Why didn't you tell me?"

"When? You kept to yourself, barely talked to me during dinner, then you'd take your bath and disappear to anyplace but where I was hanging out for the night."

His tone wasn't bitter, but matter of fact. "I liked you then, and didn't know what to do with that, or want you to know how I felt," she said, deciding to take a risk and let him know what had been going through her head then.

He set the tray of lettuce, sliced tomatoes, onion and pickles he'd just pulled from the fridge onto the counter, then went to her. "Sounds like we were on the same page. Are we done with that?"

His nearness, the intensity in his eyes made her heart skip a beat. "What is *that*? Hiding that we like each other?"

He nodded. And that hunger that Morgan had talked about was there in Sloan's eyes, heating her from the inside out, making her wish they didn't have to go to the neighborhood party. "I know what I want. Do you?"

She nodded, too.

"Good." He stepped away. "How long do these parties last?"

"No idea, why?"

"Morgan showed me your grocery list."

She was *so* going to make him pay. "Oh?"

"I ran out while you two were gone and bought some, too." Carrying the tray toward the door, he glanced over his shoulder. "I plan to use them."

Chapter Twelve

Shady Circle, North Royalhurst, Ohio
Saturday, 3:17 p.m. Daylight Saving Time

THE SMELL OF propane filled the air, mingling with children's laughter and adult conversation. He stood near Vincent's grill, and in between his business partner and George Wagner, Becky's idiot husband, who hadn't a clue that he'd married *the* suburban slut. They'd all just placed bets on whether or not Joe would bother to move his cranky ass out of the garage and to the party. Since Joe rarely socialized, he had five bucks placed that said the man would sit on his lawn chair, smoke cigarettes, drink beer and watch from his hidey-hole.

But he couldn't care less about Joe or the bet. He had two reasons for wanting to be here. When his wife approached, carrying a tray filled with hot dogs and burgers for their family, he decided he had three reasons. For a week, she'd been anxious to meet the new neighbors, and he'd been a dick about it. Even before Knot Head had told him Sloan was a private investigator and former cop, he'd decided to loosen up, let his wife enjoy her life so he could enjoy his, and that maybe there was some truth to the whole *happy wife, happy life* thing. Now that he knew Sloan and Whitney weren't who they'd claimed—if Knot Head was to be believed—it didn't matter if his wife became friendly with them. How long could they stay undercover pretending to be husband and wife?

Plus, he wanted to be around his wife. She looked beautiful, radiant, and he now wished he hadn't been so blinded by his selfish needs and shame that he'd neglected her, or had made her think the budget was so tight that she'd had to neglect herself. Her hair looked fantastic, made her skin glow. And it'd been a long time since he'd seen her wear even a hint of makeup. Whatever she'd put on her face, her eyes and mouth had him wishing tonight was their date night, so he could take her out, show her off, and let her know she was something special.

He took the tray from her, then kissed her cheek. "I put the cheesy potatoes you made on the side dish table."

She glanced around him to the tables Helen had set near the garage, where the surface was the flattest. "Oh, good. I was going to bring dessert, too, but ran out of time."

"We already have too much," Vincent said, popping the top of a can of Natural Light. "I predict a mass sugar rush on the horizon." He eyed her, then smiled. "You look wonderful."

She blushed, reminding him of when they'd first dated and how shy she'd been then. Hell, she still was, which once again had guilt jabbing him. Just because he'd changed, had become darker, a killer, didn't mean that she should change, too.

"Thank you," she said, then after saying hello to the others, she went off to see if Helen needed any help.

Once she was gone, the other reason he'd wanted to come to the party arrived, carrying burgers and toppings. If Sloan and Whitney were here undercover, then one of his neighbors had not only been very bad, but extremely stupid. The question was, which neighbor?

"There're the newlyweds." Vincent set his beer can on the concrete to take the burgers from Sloan, then placed them on the table near the grill. Vincent and Helen had a thing about parties, had every imaginable item for one, and loved setting up tables, then designating them for particular items. "Whitney, have you met these bozos yet?"

She grinned. "I haven't."

"This is Nolan Ainsley, Travis Murphy and George Wagner," he said, then began pointing out their wives and kids.

"Nice to finally meet you." She shifted her gaze from them to the tray she held, then toward the garage where Helen and a few others stood. "Let me get rid of this, while you guys do your man-grill thing." She glanced to Sloan. "Hey, babe, can you bring the cooler over? I'm going to see if Helen has a plastic cup I can borrow for my wine."

"You got it," he said, then looked to them. "Glass and concrete don't mix well with my lush of a wife."

She elbowed him, then gave him a kiss. "Hush."

A few minutes later, Sloan returned with the cooler. Whitney came over, along with his wife and Becky, who'd changed up her dress code, swapping out her usual workout attire for skin hugging denim and a tight shirt which revealed a massive amount of cleavage.

"Who was that good-looking man we saw leaving your house?" Becky asked Whitney.

Vincent adjusted the knobs on the grill. "I think that's the first visitor you've had since you moved here."

"We've only been here for a week," Whitney said with a smile. "Trust me, you'll see plenty of visitors at our house."

"But who was there today?" Becky asked, her eyes probing.

Whitney's smile didn't reach her eyes as she looked at Becky. "My cousin, Morgan."

"Cousin? How nice." As Sloan filled Whitney's plastic cup with wine, Becky moved next to Vincent. "So...any word on what's going on at Otter's Field?" she asked, blowing off Whitney and bringing up the third reason he'd wanted to be here.

"You know I'm retired. No one tells me anything."

She nudged him with her shoulder and gave him a smile. "Oh, come on. After how many years you were on the force, the arrests you made and all the people you know, I don't believe that for a second. You're practically a legend with the Cleveland PD."

Vincent took a drink of his beer. He tried to act as if the

compliment meant nothing to him, but the excitement brightening his eyes gave him away. "I'm not supposed to talk about it."

"That development begins a half a mile from our house," his business partner said. "If you know something, talk. My wife's been sick over this. She's worried there's a killer living somewhere around us, and also about our kids trying to go over there."

"Well…" Vincent went conspiratorial on them, and lowered his voice. "You didn't hear this from me, but they've found *eleven* bodies."

My wife moved next to me and gripped my arm. "Eleven? During last night's newscast, the anchor said they'd discovered six."

"Wait until tonight's newscast. The tally will be higher." Vincent tossed burgers on the grill, then shut the lid. "Yep, way higher."

"Should we be concerned?" George asked.

"Until they find the killer, I know I am." Vincent picked up his beer from the driveway. "Well, look who's decided to join us."

George looked toward Joe's garage. "Did I just lose five bucks?"

"No, Joe probably went inside for another beer. Nell's on her way."

They all turned. Nosy Nell made her way toward them, handing out peppermints to the kids—not a good idea, since he didn't want his kids running around with hard candy in their mouths.

"Does she want every one of those kids to choke?" his wife asked, then shouted, "Hey, kids, save those for after dinner."

"Seriously." Becky shook her head in disapproval. "I know it's been a while since she's had little ones, but does the woman have any common sense?" She planted on a smile. "Hi, Nell. So good to see you."

"Good to be seen." She handed Vincent a grocery bag. "Two cans of creamed corn. My contribution," she said, glancing around. "Gotta beer?"

Sloan opened his cooler, opened up a Bud Light, then handed

it to her. "Here you go. I'm Sloan North, and this is my wife, Whitney."

Nell took the bottle. "I know. A little old to be newlyweds, wouldn't you say?"

"I don't think age is mentioned under the definition of newly-wed," Whitney said. "And we're only in our mid-thirties."

Nell sized up Whitney, who stood a foot taller. "I suppose you're right, dear. But if you plan on having kids, you better get on it soon before you get any longer in the tooth."

"Jesus, Nell." Vincent sighed, and set the bag of corn on the ground. "Don't scare off our neighbors. Their house sat vacant for too long, and we're happy good people finally moved in next door."

"Oh, Vinnie, I'm not trying to scare off anyone. Just stating facts. Speaking of which, what do you have on the murders?"

"That's what we were just talking about," George said.

"Yeah," Vincent began, "I was just telling them that eleven bodies have been found."

Nell's eyes widened. "You're sure? The news people…"

"Will have all the facts today. A detective I know with the Cleveland PD has been helping with the investigation. He told me North Royalhurst PD initially kept the number of victims from the press because they were worried how folks would react, and because they wanted more answers before the questions began. Now that they have a few, they're releasing a statement this evening."

"Do you know what they're going to say?" Becky asked.

"They've ID'd two victims. Both went missing ten years ago. I don't know names, but I do know that one of them was homosexual."

His business partner furrowed his brows. "What's that have to do with anything?"

Vincent took another sip of his beer. "If more homosexuals are ID'd, then this might be a hate crime. Since all the victims were male, that could very well be a possibility."

At the mention of homosexual, he tensed.

"Sounds like a big leap," Sloan said as the kids' kickball rolled to a stop at his feet. He tossed it their way.

Whitney nodded. "I agree. It could be a random coincidence. Do they have a cause of death for any of the victims?"

Becky's eyes widened. "That's right. You're an attorney. Do you deal with this type of stuff?"

"No. My focus is on real estate, but I'd originally planned to go into criminal law."

Wanting to participate in the conversation and get to the bottom of why they were here, he asked, "So you know enough on the subject to give us an opinion?"

"Honestly, criminal law isn't my forte, but if I were the DA, I wouldn't be jumping to any conclusions until I could confirm at least three of the victims were homosexual. That being said, I do think it's odd that all the victims were male. Which leads me back to my original question: do they have a cause of death?"

Vincent opened the grill. "They have skeletons that don't have a mark on them. No knife cuts to bones, no bullets or anything around the neck indicating strangulation. They're not even sure if Otter's Field was a dump site, or if it was where these men were killed. They're also not sure they've recovered all the bodies yet." He flipped burgers. "Word has it that they're bringing in the FBI and another company which has high-tech equipment that can penetrate the ground and help locate other bodies."

"First, our tax dollars will be spent on the police and FBI, now this company. How much is that going to cost us?" Nell drank her beer. "Then, *if* they catch the murderer, we'll be paying for him to sit on death row for the next twenty years."

Nell was so old, she wouldn't be around to see his execution—if he were caught. "This practically took place in our neighborhood," he reminded her, then, still paranoid about what he'd done to Knot Head and Saggy Pants, he added, "Speaking of *our* neighborhood, anyone notice a Pontiac Grand Am driving through here? Two young guys in it?"

Vincent finished flipping the burgers, then closed the grill. "I saw them a bunch of times when I was walking Fritz."

A car horn sounded. They all looked toward the street. As Dale slowly drove his car, the kids scattered to the tree lawn.

"I'm home by myself for a good part of the day," Becky said, watching Dale pull into his driveway. "Should I be concerned about these two young guys?"

Not at all. They're dead.

"I'm sure it's nothing," he said. "We've been doing a job at the Milsons and I happened to see them a few times. They're probably friends of one of the teens in the development."

Vincent nodded. "That's what I was guessing." He grinned. "Looks like the Eastons are going to join us." He waved as Dale and Irene walked over, carrying something store-bought. "I'm certainly not disappointed Cameron isn't with them. After a few more beers, I might go off on that boy over the way he drives."

After everyone agreed, they were all smiles when the Eastons arrived. From there, it was the typical neighborhood gathering. Chatting about what was going on with the school, the changes being made at the local grocery store, how a new restaurant was going in near them...stuff that meant nothing to him when he had a body rotting behind his shed.

Surprisingly, the Zelenkos, their Ukrainian neighbors who rarely came to their street parties, joined them. Oksana Zelenko brought along *golubsti*, which was basically stuffed cabbage and a strange dish to bring to a cookout. Since he thought it was extremely delicious, he wouldn't complain, and even suggested to his wife that she get the recipe from Oksana.

Once everyone ate, they brought out lawn chairs to watch the kids play kickball in the circle. Quint, who also wasn't a usual at their parties, showed up with his fiancée, Tammi, and her two daughters. While Tammi's girls joined the kids for team selection, the adults congratulated the couple on their engagement.

Nell held Tammi's hand and investigated the engagement ring. She let out a low whistle. "That a beaut." She looked to Quint. "How much did it set you back?"

"Jesus, Nell." Vincent chuckled and wrapped an arm around her. "Let's get you dessert. If your mouth is full, you won't be able to ask more rude questions."

"What can I say? I'm curious by nature."

"We all know," he said with an exaggerated sigh, then walked off with her.

"It really is a beautiful ring." Irene looked at her own hand. "Seeing yours makes me want to have mine redone, so it's a little more modern. But with Cameron going off to college in the fall, we've been saving like crazy."

"I'd love a new ring, too," Becky said.

Irene's brow furrowed. "You just got a new ring when you married George."

"Yeah, but that was *two* years ago."

"Two whole years." Irene rolled her eyes. "Your ring is practically an antique."

Becky huffed and turned toward Whitney. "Let's see your ring."

Whitney's face turned pink as she stared at her nude hand. "I forgot to wear it."

Becky raised a brow and looked to Sloan's hand, which was also devoid of a ring. "What newlywed couple goes without their wedding rings? Why, I haven't taken mine off since George placed it on my finger during our wedding ceremony." Irene choked on the wine she was drinking, while Helen turned away, covering a grin with her hand. Becky looked to where her husband stood talking to the Zelenkos, then at the two women. "Laugh it up, bitches. I don't give a shit what either of you thinks of me. At least I'm happy," she said, then walked away and joined her husband.

"Wow." His business partner and wife joined them, along with his own wife. "I can't believe she just said that."

He pulled another beer from the cooler. This one made three, and would be his last. He didn't like being drunk around his kids, but mainly he wanted to stay sober for his wife, and what he planned to do with her later when the kids were sleeping. "Becky drank almost a whole bottle of wine," he said, opening the can. "She's lit."

"That's not all she is," Irene said, directing her attention to Whitney. "And I sometimes forget to wear my ring, too."

Whitney and Sloan made eye contact, and he wondered what

they were trying to mentally communicate. Could it be that they just realized they'd fucked up and had forgotten to buy rings?

"We don't have wedding rings." Sloan kept his gaze on Whitney. "Instead of buying rings, we used the money we'd set aside for them to help with the down payment of the house. But one day, very soon, I'm going to give my beautiful bride her ring."

Whitney took Sloan's hand. "It's just an expensive symbol. What matters to me is that we love each other and are able to live in a great home surrounded by wonderful neighbors."

"Aww, that's so sweet." Helen embraced the couple. "If you don't have rings, what did you use on your wedding day?" she asked.

Sloan grinned. "We went to Walmart and spent a total of twenty dollars for both rings. Within a week, mine looked as if I'd been wearing it for decades. When the claw holding the cubic zirconia broke on Whitney's ring, we decided to get rid of them."

As the women gushed about how sweet, cute and blah, blah, blah all of this was, he began to wonder if Knot Head had been lying to save his ass from dying. Whitney and Sloan acted as if they were a married couple, showed an appropriate amount of affection, teased and looked at each other as if they were in love. Either they were great actors, or they really were married. Besides, after spending hours with his neighbors, other than the pothead, Cameron, he couldn't think of anyone on this street who Whitney and Sloan would be investigating. No one around here was living large. Even Dale and Irene bought their cars used and couldn't afford to pay him for the closet he'd built. Becky received alimony and child support from her ex, but her current husband was paying the same to his former wife. He didn't know enough about the Zelenkos to say much. Maybe they were part of some local Ukrainian criminal organization, if there was such a thing. Or maybe they were just a normal family trying to live the American dream. He immediately dismissed Vincent and Helen. After all, Vincent was a former cop. Then again, he could've been a dirty cop. But he'd known the couple for over ten years and couldn't fathom the thought. They were good, solid people, law-abiding citizens who performed plenty of charity work and never missed a

Sunday mass. He knew his business partner and could easily dismiss him. Hell, the man hadn't had a traffic violation since he was twenty. Since he doubted that eighty-five-year-old Nosy Nell had been running a prostitution, drug or money-laundering ring out of her house, he skipped over her, as well. Which left Quint, Joe and himself.

Quint was a nice enough guy, but that was all he could say about the man. During the four years Quint had lived on Shady Circle, he'd never had more than a ten-minute conversation with him. Maybe Quint was doing more than giving deals on cars. As for himself, again, the Norths had moved in five days after the first body was found. Until then, no one had been aware there was a killer who was hunting men. Leaving Joe as the last neighbor to consider. Before retiring, Joe had spent over forty years working as an electrician, and had run his own company for twenty-five of them. According to Vincent and Helen, Joe had also invested his money wisely and was worth millions. If that were the case, why would Joe risk stealing or selling something illegally to help expand his wealth? Unless Joe had turned his basement into a dungeon and had imprisoned sex-slaves, he doubted the man had done anything wrong. Besides, what were the odds that not one, but two twisted fucks lived on the same street?

When the kids began playing, the adults sat in lawn chairs along the sidewalks to watch. Just as Sloan was about to head into Vincent's garage to borrow a couple chairs from them, Whitney's cell phone rang. She excused herself to answer it, then came over to Sloan a few minutes later.

"Everything okay?" Sloan asked.

She sighed. "That was my brother, Campbell. Apparently, we have family drama he wants to discuss. And you know how quickly my family resolves their issues."

"Want me to come home with you?" he asked.

She looked onto the street, where the kids were playing. "I hate for you to have leave because my brothers can't get along. I'll be fine." She gave Sloan's forearm a squeeze, then went to one of the tables Helen had set up to retrieve what she'd brought.

After Whitney had entered her house, Sloan also watched the kids play. "I should go."

Becky sauntered toward them, swayed to the side, then righted her gait. Smiling, she walked over to Sloan, then hooked her arm through his. "Where'd your wife go?" she asked, her words slightly slurred.

He disengaged her. "Home, which is where I'm heading."

"Oh, pooh." She turned to watch the game. "Nice one, Alex," she shouted when her son scored, then walked off, mumbling something about Dale.

"You better get out of here before she opens another bottle of wine," his business partner suggested to Sloan. "Becky can get very…just trust me."

He cleared his throat. "What my partner is trying to say is, leave before she tries to invite you to a threesome with her and George."

His wife gasped and gave his arm a light tap, while Sloan laughed. "Don't spread rumors," she said, her voice hushed.

He placed an arm around her, then kissed the top of her head. "You're right. Let me rephrase: leave before she gets drunk enough to show you the before and after pictures of her boob job."

"Okay, now *that* I know she'll do," his wife said with disapproval.

"Since that's not what I want to see, I'll be heading home. Looking forward to the next time we can get together," Sloan said, then, carrying his cooler, he walked across the adjoining lawns to his house.

"They're a nice couple," his wife said. "I hope they don't move anytime soon."

He liked the Norths, too. But not knowing if Knot Head had been telling the truth about them being investigators made him nervous. He had a hunt scheduled for next weekend, and planned on burying the body in the backyard again. His wife had been wanting a vegetable garden. Why not give the soil extra fertilizer?

～

Sloan finished emptying the cooler, then set it on the back patio—with the lid open—to dry in the late afternoon sun. He owed Becky a bottle of wine for giving him an excuse to leave. The moment Whitney had mentioned Lieutenant Campbell's name, he'd become tense, and hoped the man hadn't called to inform them that Andy or BCI had discovered something that would have them closing up shop on Shady Circle. Not yet. He wasn't ready to stop pretending they were married, or to freely touch her in public without worrying if he'd crossed the line with her and her rules.

Though this morning had started off crappy, the rest of the day had been great. He'd liked Morgan, and hadn't been surprised Whitney's best friend was male. She'd been raised with boys and worked with mostly men. Even during the party, he'd noticed she gravitated toward the guys. He'd also liked the neighbors. The two landscapers and their wives were very-down-to-earth, same with Quint and his fiancée, and he could see them having the three couples over for dinner and drinks. Except, they might be reassigned by the end of the weekend.

With a sigh, he went in search of Whitney. Once upstairs, he followed the sound of running water to his room. When he opened the door, steam drifted into the hallway. He glanced to the closed blinds, then to the bathroom. Whitney stood in front of the mirror, still dressed, and twisting her long hair into a bun. She met his reflection in the mirror.

"Was the call that bad?" he asked, knowing she tended to use soak time as therapy.

"Not at all. Actually, it was good. Campbell wanted to let me know the Stingray will be available tomorrow."

Fantastic. That meant they could begin using the cell-site simulator to track Cameron's calls earlier than planned. Except, if they nailed Cameron and Morales too quickly, he'd have no excuse to be in Cleveland. "That's great," he said, forcing enthusiasm in his voice.

"It is, only Cameron won't be home tomorrow. Irene told me he's spending the day and night at a friend's house to finish up a school project. She'd mentioned it because she was excited the website you're creating for her would be ready in the morning for her to look at and tweak. Plus, with no kids around, her and Dale were going to do something special together."

Rachel had designed a user-friendly site that Irene could make changes to on her own. Per Rachel's instructions, he'd let Irene know that his assistant—meaning Rachel—would be the one to walk her through what she needed to know, and that they would do this Monday morning. According to Rachel—the redheaded firecracker who would continue to keep him in her debt—he and this investigation were not only a pain in the ass, but even God took a day off.

"Then we'll set up the Stingray tomorrow, test it out and have it ready to go when Cameron gets home Monday afternoon." His body went taut as she gripped the hem of her shirt and pulled it over her head. "I…ah, asked Hudson about the range and he thinks we could keep it in this room."

"Our tech guys said the same." She shimmied her jeans over her hips, which brought her panties down slightly, revealing a hint of her rear. "I'm glad for that. I've been trying to figure out how one of us could be in the truck without drawing attention to the neighbors."

She was now down to her bra and panties. Both were pale pink and lacy, and immediately filled his mind with wicked thoughts. Peeling them off as he kissed, licked, nipped and touched her.

"I'm glad we don't have to worry about that anymore," she said, unhooking her bra.

When her breasts showed in the mirror, he suppressed a groan, and tried to figure out what the hell was happening. Not that he was complaining. While he'd already seen her naked—best night ever—he couldn't believe she was…stripping in front of him. Then again, she *had* opened her robe for him last night. Maybe he should stop thinking and go with what he did well— pleasure a woman.

"Today was fun, but I was done with the small talk and tired of drunk Becky." She met his gaze again. "When I was on the phone with Campbell, I looked out the window. I noticed she'd bee-lined for you right after I left," she said, bending at the waist to remove her panties.

When the split of her sex was revealed, he was behind her in a few long strides, but didn't touch her. Instead, he held her gaze in the mirror as she straightened. "Are you an exhibitionist?"

"Not at all."

"Are you doing this because you're jealous of Becky?"

"No, I removed my clothes so I could take a bath."

He took her by the arm and forced her to face him. "Now? It's just after five."

"I was hoping you'd join me." Her breath quickened as she drifted her gaze to his mouth. "If you'd rather not see me naked, leave."

No fucking way. He reached between their bodies and pressed his fingers into her heat, coaxing a gasp from her. Damn, she was warm and already wet, and he was dying to finish what they'd started earlier. "If I had it my way, you'd be naked all the time. I love your body."

As he pumped his fingers, she gripped his shoulders. "After the way you looked at me last night, it's the only reason I had the nerve to do this. I've never…" She released a groan.

He kissed her neck. "Never what?"

"Never…displayed myself like this."

Tension worked through him. He released her bun, then gently grasped her thick hair and tilted her head back. He stared into her eyes, which held desire and trust, and wondered if he deserved to be with a woman like Whitney. She wasn't a wholesome virgin, but he suspected that beneath her confident exterior was an inexperienced woman who longed for love—despite that item not being on her ideal husband list. She was the type of woman who needed a man who would be there for her, help give her the dream house and kids. A man who could give her always and forever. Even if he'd like to be, he wasn't that guy. He was too selfish when it came to his freedom and wouldn't make promises—to her or himself—he wasn't sure he could keep.

"Why me?" he asked, grazing her clit with his thumb. "Is this your way of practicing seduction for when the ideal husband comes along?"

Her mouth curved into a small grin as she pressed her hand against his, forcing his fingers deeper inside her. "If you really thought that, you wouldn't be touching me. You're not desperate enough to have sex that you'd allow yourself to be used."

"How do you know? My job has kept me on the road and I haven't fucked a woman in almost two months. And I've got one ready and willing right here," he said, going for crude and not understanding why. He knew she wasn't using him. If anything, he was using her, hoping to soak up a lifetime of memories—both fake and real—that he could take home to Chicago, where he'd go back to his old life.

She took her hand from his and touched his jaw. "I am ready and willing. Not because I haven't had sex in nearly two years, but because I like you. If you're honestly just looking to get off, then we can stop now. But I don't think that's what you want." She sucked in a breath when he pressed in a third finger. "I think you're so worried that I won't be a quick lay you can simply walk away from, that you're trying to find a way to start a fight so that *I* walk."

"You should." He held her gaze. The sincerity, desire and understanding in her eyes were killing him. Along with her confidence. If she'd been brave and bold enough to be honest with him, he should set aside his fears—because, damn it, he *was* afraid of loving then losing this woman—and tell her the truth. "But I don't want that."

"What do you want?"

He slid his fingers from her, then turned her to face the mirror. After moving her hair to bare her shoulder, he held her gaze in the reflection, kissed her neck, then, hugging her from behind, he rested his cheek against hers. "I want this. To be a real couple. I like you, Whitney. And I'm...afraid of what being with you is going to do to me when the investigation is over."

She turned in his arms. "I am, too. So, what do we do? I can leave and assist with the operation from a distance."

He tightened his hold on her. "I'll miss you," he admitted, and didn't care if it showed weakness. She'd been open, had left herself vulnerable. She deserved the same from him.

"I'd miss you, too." She moved to her tiptoes and kissed him. "I'm not ready for this to be over, yet."

He wasn't sure if he'd ever be ready. "Then we do this. And I'm not talking about sex. I'm talking about no more fighting because we're afraid to let each other know how we feel." Had he just said that? Yeah, he had, and was damned proud of himself for expressing his pussy emotions.

She gripped the hem of his T-shirt and pushed it up his torso. "I want complete honesty between us, too," she said, lightly grazing her nails along his abs. "If something is bothering you, tell me."

"Agreed."

"Good, because it's bothering me that you've seen me naked twice and you're still fully clothed," she said, her tone teasing.

He pulled his shirt over his head. "Anything else?"

"My bath is probably cold, but I'll get over it." She shifted her gaze from his chest, to where his hands were now at the fly of his jeans. "Can I help you with that?" Without waiting for an answer, she pushed his hands aside, then unbuttoned his jeans.

"Do you want to know what's bothering me?" he asked, running his palms over her soft skin.

She slid down the zipper, then slipped her hand inside his jeans and over his erection. "That I was on the verge of an orgasm when you decided to tell me how long it's been since you've had sex."

He grinned, then sucked in a breath when she cupped his balls. "I can't remember now, but that's not it."

After pulling her hand from his jeans, she tugged the denim over his hips. "I think I know what it is," she said, and once his underwear and jeans were around his ankles, she bent at the waist again, then took his length between her lips.

Inhaling deeply, he held her hair up and away from her face. As she pleasured him with her mouth and hands, he shifted his gaze to the giant mirror. Thanks to her long legs and the size of the mirror, he had the perfect view of her ass and sex, and remembered the thing that had bothered him was not being able to go down on her from behind. Which he wouldn't have an opportunity to do. Her wicked tongue, the way she swept it over his arousal as she sucked him, was more than he could handle at the moment. He hadn't been completely honest. It'd been almost six months since he'd been with a woman and, after a week of sexual tension, of nightly baths, having tasted her, kissed her, touched her intimately, he was wound more tightly than he'd thought. If he didn't stop her, there was no way he'd last long enough to give her an orgasm.

She gently grazed her nails along his balls and drew him deeply into her mouth. His knees nearly buckled. "Whitney," he said, before he lost total control of his body.

When she glanced up at him, he had to think of puppies and babies to keep himself from coming. She looked so damned sexy, her gaze on his, her lips dragging up and down his length. "Do you want me to stop?" she asked, then swirled her tongue over the tip of his erection. "I've only done this a couple of times." She pressed his penis against his stomach, then licked him from the base to the tip. "Maybe I'm not doing this right and need more practice."

"I'll gladly let you practice more later." He quickly forced her to stand and hauled her against him. "I need to be inside of you." When he kissed her, she wrapped her arms around his neck, and they moved together toward the bedroom. Needing a taste of her nipples, he stopped them, pressed her against the door and took a taut peak between his lips.

She speared her fingers through his hair, released a soft moan and angled his head back to her mouth. They kissed again, open-mouthed, their tongues twining together as they once again made their way to the bed.

Once there, he broke the kiss to guide her onto the center of the mattress. He spread her legs, bent her knees, then traced his fingers along her inner thighs, causing goose bumps to rise over her skin. "Condoms?"

She propped her upper back and head against the pillows. "Nightstand drawer."

"Don't move," he said. "Stay just the way you are." He slid off the bed. As he took the box from the drawer, he glanced at her. She had her gaze on him, shifted it from his chest and arms, to his erection and looked as if she'd just discovered a secret treasure. At least that was what he'd like to think. Chances were, his adorably sexy, sticky note-loving woman was probably bullet pointing in her head. Fine by him. He'd give her nothing but *pros* to put on her list.

"Let me," she said, when he tore the wrapper. "I'd like to try to put it on you."

She was killing him. "Next time." He placed the condom over the head of his erection. "If you put your hands or mouth on me again, we won't be needing a condom."

Blushing, she grinned. "So, I really don't need to practice the art of giving a blow job."

"Nope, but you're a bit of a perfectionist, so you might want to anyway," he said, moving between her spread legs. He bent, swept his tongue along her sex, then dipped it between her folds.

"I thought you needed to be inside me," she said, her voice breathless as she held his head against her heat.

He did, but was more nervous now than he'd been the night he had lost his virginity. Whitney was special. She'd told him she had only been with three men. He cared about her as a person and a lover, and wanted this to be good for her. For them. "I thought I could use a little practice, too." He flicked his tongue along her clit, then gently drew it between his lips.

With a groan, she tugged his hair. "Later. Come here and kiss me."

Apprehension rolled through his stomach and battled with his eagerness to be with her. He did as she'd asked, while using his arms to keep from crushing her. As they kissed, she pressed her pelvis forward and slid one leg over his. Seconds passed and she pulled back, touched his beard and stared up at him with concern and confusion.

"Second thoughts?" she asked.

"I…no. I don't want this to be a let-down for you."

"How could it be? Are you a virgin?"

He half-laughed. "No."

"Did you make up the stories about your many women?"

"Unfortunately, no."

"Then since I'm going to assume you know what you're doing, what's the problem?"

He loved that she was straightforward, perceptive and could quickly put him at ease. She made it so he wanted to be open and honest, to tell her things he would normally keep to himself. She made him want to take a risk. "I do know what I'm doing. The problem is, I've never done it with you."

Her eyes shimmered with tears. She leaned forward and drew his head down at the same time, then kissed him with so much tenderness something inside of him snapped, while a lightning storm went off in his brain. He should run. Forget the clothes, he should run barefoot and naked back to the safety of his condo before this woman consumed him with emotions he hadn't planned on or thought he'd ever truly possess in this lifetime.

"Thank you," she whispered against his lips, then reached between their bodies and held his erection at the entrance of her sex. "I'm nervous, too."

"Why?"

"Because I care about you, and I don't want you to be disappointed."

"I don't think you could ever disappoint me," he said, then slowly entered her, inched his way deep inside until they both groaned. "You're so tight. Are you doing okay?"

"Never felt better." She wrapped her long legs around his rear. "I'm not a tiny, petite woman. I won't break."

He knew that, but it'd been almost two years for her, and he wanted this to be good for her. "I love how tall you are," he said, pulling out, then pressing in again. "And how perfectly you fit against my body."

She dropped her head onto the pillow and gripped his biceps. "I love how you feel inside me."

He'd never had an actual conversation during sex, unless it was dirty, and he wasn't even sure if that would qualify. But talking to Whitney didn't bother or distract him. He cared whether or not she was enjoying herself, wanted to learn her body and all the buttons he could push to give her ultimate pleasure.

He pumped his hips. "I love being inside of you." He dropped to his forearms and rested his forehead against hers. "You always smell so good. It drives me crazy."

She gripped his ass, encouraged him to drive deeper, harder. "Crazy good?"

"Yeah," he managed, and captured her lips.

As he kissed her, he worked his hips, developed a rhythm. When she lifted her pelvis and matched each of his thrusts, he worried he'd come before her. But as she moaned against his mouth, and her sex clenched his, he knew she was almost there.

He tore his mouth away from hers, placed the crook of her knees against his shoulders and drove deep. Pivoted his hips until she came, then joined her. Exquisite pleasure washed over him, into him, hit every nerve ending. He held himself still and relished the wave, the satisfaction of being with *this* woman.

As he rolled off her and tried to catch his breath, the first thought that came to mind was vanilla. While being with Whitney had been the best sex he'd ever had, it'd been too fast and he worried he'd been too boring. After all, he'd been the one to make it clear he'd been around, and he hadn't delivered.

"I'm sorry. I know that probably wasn't the greatest, but you had me turned on the moment you took off your shirt."

She snuggled against him. "Why would you be sorry? Did you think I was expecting a high wire act or maybe sex swings?"

He chuckled and kissed her forehead. "For the record, none of those things has ever entered my mind. But the sex swing…"

"Not happening," she said, and pinched his bicep. "Seriously, though, why would you apologize? I might not be very experienced, but I thought being with you was fantastic."

And maybe it was as simple as that. He'd thought the same, but had also assumed that by not giving her any kinky or unique sex moves she might think he was boring. "You weren't expecting…a better performance?" he asked without really knowing the answer he was looking for from her.

She draped her body over his and met his gaze. Her eyes still held lingering signs of desire, along with *something more*. Like? Caring? She'd said as much. But there was a deeper emotion there. He wanted to explore what it was, but fear kept him quiet. Apparently, he wasn't the badass he'd always considered himself to be. After one week with Whitney, he'd discovered he was afraid of falling in love, of disappointing her...of losing her.

"You made love to me," she said. "What's better than that?"

His Whitney had boiled it down and simplified what he was complicating. And she was right. That's why being with her had been so good. This hadn't been a quick fuck. This had been the *something more*. "Not a thing," he said, and kissed her.

Afterward, she didn't bother with her soak in the tub, but took a quick shower. He joined her, which led to an abundance of *something more*. Later, they snuggled on the couch and watched TV. As the hour grew late, and they decided to call it a night, they shut down the house and headed upstairs. When they reached the hallway, he took her hand in his before she had the chance to go to her room.

"Sleep with me," he said.

"You don't think we'll get too used to that?"

"Is that a bad thing?"

"Maybe."

And maybe it was, but he didn't care. "I'm not going to be able to sleep knowing you're across the hall. Not after being with you, and not after fighting my attraction to you." There. He'd done it. He had completely opened up and had once again left himself vulnerable to prove he cared about her.

Relief filled her eyes. "I was hoping you'd say that. Let me get my special pillow."

"Special pillow?" he asked, stopping her.

"It's what I use to cuddle with every night."

He drew her close. "Try using me."

After she agreed, and they were in bed, she cuddled against his chest. "You're not as soft as my pillow," she said, then released a sigh. "You're better."

And as he held her and waited for sleep to claim him, all kinds of warning bells told him this was bad because, in the end, distance and careers would keep them from being together. He ignored those bells. He'd spent the majority of his adult life alone and pretending to be someone else. With Whitney, he could be himself, be open, and be honest about his emotions without feeling like he was a lesser man. And he liked it. Loved that, for once, he could be himself. Except...he'd taken so many risks during his career, could he handle this one? Could he find a way to enjoy his time with Whitney and still keep himself distanced enough that losing her wouldn't break him?

As his eyes drifted shut, he loved the way her warm body melted against his. And he knew, deep down, the answer. He was falling for Whitney and would leave Cleveland a broken man.

Chapter Thirteen

The rental house, North Royalhurst, Ohio
Sunday, 10:08 a.m. Daylight Saving Time

WHITNEY TRACED THE flowers surrounding the skull tattoo along Sloan's right arm with her finger. Her naked body was sore in all the right places. Between that and the warmth she was stealing from Sloan, she didn't want to leave the bed. She'd rather lie here with him, cuddle, have sex, maybe take a nap, then do it all over again. But, unfortunately, she was going to have to go pick up the Stingray, and Sloan had to give Irene Easton the information she would need for her website.

She rested her arm on his chest and her head in her hand. "What's the significance behind this tattoo?" she asked, not only curious, but looking for any excuse to stay where she was.

He tucked a lock of her hair behind her ear. "There isn't one."

"What? That's nuts. You purposefully and permanently scarred your body. There has to be some reason behind what you've chosen."

"If you were to get a tat, what would you choose and where would you want it to go?"

"Well, I wouldn't get one. If I did, though, it'd be a swan." She touched her forearm from her wrist to her elbow. "And I'd have it done here."

"Why a swan?"

Very few people understood or knew about the insecurities she still carried from her youth. She trusted and cared for Sloan, and for some reason, she wanted to tell him, share a part of herself. "Let me begin by saying that I don't think I'm beautiful."

Her rubbed her shoulder. "I do."

"Thank you. When I was little, I was a cute kid. Then puberty hit. I had acne, braces, was too skinny, flat chested and all legs."

"Ah." He grinned. "I see where you're heading. The ugly duckling who turned into a beautiful swan."

"Kinda. But the swan represents so much more than that. My grandparents lived on a lake that had swans. When I was a kid, I used to love watching them. They're so graceful. It fascinated me that they could glide across the water leaving little to no ripple in their wake. And when they fly…it's amazing to watch them take off from the water. Their wingspan is huge. Around eight feet, I believe. And as they flap their wings and start to lift, it looks as if they're actually running on top of the water.

"Anyway, for me, the swan represents inner grace and beauty, which are both things I try to maintain in my life." She let out a sigh as she thought back to how she'd considered him a hairy barbarian. "I didn't exactly maintain much of either the day we first met, and I'm sorry for that. As a cop, I've seen people do horrible things, and I struggle to not be judgmental and to hang onto my inner grace, if that makes sense."

He skimmed his fingers along her spine. "I didn't exactly give you much of a reason to be nice. And I'm sorry for that. I'm also sorry I lied about my tattoo. Yeah, it's cool, but that's not the reason I got it. For me, the skull symbolizes the death of an old life, and the butterfly represents the rebirth of a new one."

"How so?" she asked, loving that he, too, was opening up and giving her a part of himself.

He gave her the boyish grin she adored. "I've already told you my real name, and now I'm going to tell you something no one alive knows, and you better not laugh. Because there will be consequences."

"I promise not to laugh at you," she said, though intrigued by what kind of consequences he had in mind.

"I breed butterflies."

"You mean when you were a kid."

He shook his head. "When I first became a cop, we answered a burglary call at an old woman's apartment. Her place was immaculate, didn't look as if anything was out of place and there were no signs that anyone had broken in. When my partner asked what had been stolen, she took us to a little room that contained over a dozen cages. Some were filled with plants, others had caterpillars or chrysalises in them. Apparently, someone had stolen two cages of butterflies that had recently emerged from their chrysalises."

"You investigated a butterfly thief?"

"I did. The woman bred the butterflies, then would go to the children's hospital and let the sick and dying kids free them outside. When I asked her why she did it, she explained that butterflies, like the sick and dying children, lead short but eventful lives. And during their short lives, they undergo major transformations before dying. The thing that struck me the most was when she said, 'The butterfly is on the earth for a small span of time, but during that time, its beauty brings people joy.'"

Tears filled her eyes. "Just like the sick children. Did you find out what happened to the old lady's butterflies?"

"The neighbor did it. She had an extra key to the apartment for emergencies, stole the cages, then gave them to her granddaughter, who, ironically was under hospice care and dying of leukemia." He touched her cheek. "When I left Indiana after my dad passed, I let go of farm life in exchange for the city, hoping to marry my high school girlfriend and make major changes to my life."

"Why didn't it work out with the girl?" she asked, and wondered how it was she knew so much about this man, yet nothing at all. Even more interesting? At one point, Sloan had wanted a wife.

"Because she was smart enough to find someone else. I was eighteen, had no money, no direction and nothing to offer her. She did me a favor. Her rejection forced me to get my act together, to let go of the past and reinvent myself."

Death and rebirth, hence, the skull and butterfly tattoos. "What about the flowers around the skull?"

"Those are gerbera daisies. My mom's favorite. My dad kept a small patch of land filled with them, so she could sit on the porch swing and look at them all summer long."

She'd just fallen three-quarters in love with Sloan. She'd suspected the man was more emotionally complex than she'd first considered, but hadn't realized he was such a deep thinker. Now she wanted to know more, hear the other thoughts moving through his mind, learn more about his past, and the events that had shaped him into the man he was today.

"And the snake tattoo?" she asked. "I'm assuming that's also a symbol of rebirth, since snakes shed their skins."

He half-laughed. "Nope. I just thought it was really cool." His stomach growled.

"How about breakfast?" she suggested.

"How did you know I was starving?"

She kissed him, then rolled off his warm body. "Lucky guess. How do you want your eggs?"

"However you're having them." He stood, then walked toward the dresser and opened a drawer. "T-shirt?" he asked. "Or do you want me to get your bathrobe?"

"T-shirt is good," she said, her gaze still on his powerful, naked body. While she loved the way he looked, knowing his thoughts ran deep, that he was kind to old ladies, raised delicate creatures and loved his parents made him even more attractive to her. Once he'd covered all of his wonderful muscles with a pair of sweats and a T-shirt, and the show was over, she slipped on the shirt he'd tossed her, then went into the bathroom and snagged the underwear she'd left on the floor last night.

He leaned against the bathroom door jamb. "Since I told you something personal about me, I'm curious about something to do with you. How is it that you're OCD-organized and have everything on a tidy bullet point list, yet you're not very...neat?"

"Are you calling me a slob?" she asked, not the least offended, because it was absolutely true.

"Slob never came out of my mouth."

She grinned and put on her panties. "It probably should," she said, heading for the bedroom door. "Here's how I look at it...if I spend all my time cleaning, then I won't have time to check things off my list. And...it might be a control thing."

He followed her into the kitchen. "I would think keeping the house or your room clean would be part of that control."

"Maybe for a normal person." She pulled eggs and bacon from the fridge. "I grew up with six people in the house. My mom would constantly complain about us leaving stuff lying around and was always on us to clean. Since I moved out, I've controlled the cleanliness of my house. I decide if the bathroom counter needs to be cleaned off, or if my clothes need to go into the laundry basket. Does that make sense?"

"Nope." He began making coffee. "And I think that's what you tell yourself. Here's what I think... You make a conscious effort to leave your clothes and things lying around to defy your own inner control freak. I think you control so many aspects of your life that you need some sort of chaos. Maybe it reminds you of living with five other people."

"That's so...perceptive." She ran his words through her mind as she cracked an egg into a bowl. "You might be onto something. When my last brother moved out of the house, it was too clean and quiet. It was about that time that my slobby side started to truly shine through. Nice job, Dr. North. Maybe you should have gone into psychology."

"I'm not smart enough to make it through the first semester of college."

"Stop, I don't believe that for a second. I think you're smart. You know a lot of things."

"I know a lot of useless things." He set two mugs on the counter while the coffee brewed. "I'm not book-smart. I learn as I go."

"My brother, Henry, was like that, and still is. He's what's referred to as a kinesthetic learner, meaning he learns through experience."

He leaned against the counter, his eyes bright with interest. "How do you know if you're that type of learner?"

She scrambled the eggs, and tried to recall some traits of a kinesthetic learner. Gave up, then searched the term on her cell phone. "They're good at sports," she read, "don't have great handwriting and can't spell well. They like adventure books and movies, like to build things and, get this, they like role playing." She set the phone back on the counter, then pulled a pan from the cabinet. "You could be book-smart if you wanted, you'd just have to adjust the way you study."

"Maybe. But it doesn't really matter. I'm not heading off to college anytime soon."

"If you were though, what would you want as a major?" she asked, enjoying talking, cooking, and acting as if they were a *real* couple.

"Business. I'd love to own one, be my own boss."

"What kind of business?"

He filled the mugs. "Based on what I know how to do, I think it'd be cool to own a gun range. I could teach classes on the proper use and certify people for conceal and carry permits." He handed her a mug. "I have a good job with CORE, though. The pay is great, so are the benefits. Plus, I get to travel to exotic places like Cleveland," he said with a smile, just as the doorbell chimed.

"Since you're cooking, I'll answer it."

"Not because I'm only wearing a T-shirt and panties?"

He came up behind her, slipped his hand between her legs, then rubbed her sex through her underwear. "We were having such a meaningful conversation, I almost forgot. Now that I remember, after I get rid of who's at the door, I'm going to—"

The bell chimed again. "Just get rid of them, then come back and show me what you plan to do."

While he went to the door, she took out the toaster. After breakfast, they should shower together before they went their separate ways. Then again, she might be able to talk Sloan into driving downtown with her. She'd love to make one of their pretend dates real, and his motorcycle was sitting in a parking garage collecting dust.

"Whitney," Sloan called from the front door. "Your parents are here."

Her parents? They didn't have the address. "Good to know. Oh, and Santa Claus is on the back patio. Should I let him in, too?"

"Whitney Joan Russell," her mom said on a gasp, while her dad cleared his throat.

She froze. *Oh my God*. Her parents were truly standing in the dining room, and she wasn't wearing a bra or pants. As her face heated, she kept her gaze locked on the eggs in the pan. Maybe if she didn't look at her parents, they would disappear.

"I...I don't know what to say," her mom continued, her voice laced with confusion.

After she took the pan of cooked eggs off the burner and set down the spatula, she drew in a deep breath. She finally faced her parents. "I can explain."

"It's a miracle." Her mom beamed. "Eddie, our daughter not only has a man, but the house is clean."

Her face burned with humiliation so badly, it had to be scarlet by now. She looked past her parents and met Sloan's amused gaze. "Sloan North, these are my parents, Ed and Shirley Russell."

"We met at the door." Her mom came over and hugged her, then whispered, "He's adorable. Now go put on a bra and pants."

"I'm fine, and you can't see anything."

"But your father..."

"That girl ran around in nothing but her underwear until she was seven." Her dad came over and gave her a bear hug. "Nice place." He stepped back, then inspected the kitchen. "We were hoping to meet your partner while we were here."

"Sloan *is* my partner, and how did you know where to find me?"

Her mom's eyes widened. "Oh, I...we...*he's* your partner?" She glanced back to Sloan and raised an eyebrow. "I see we're taking the fake marriage deal to a level of reality that I'm not sure I can approve of."

"Take it easy, Shirley. At least we know our baby doesn't have a pint-sized pussy living with her."

She rubbed her temple. "Really, Dad?"

Mom kept her gaze on Sloan, who was chuckling. "This is true. Well," she began, refocusing on Whitney, "we knew you were going undercover in North Royalhurst, and were concerned about the murders."

"You mother was concerned. I know you can protect yourself. Besides, the killer is taking out men, not women."

"When you didn't call me back last night," Mom continued, "I contacted Morgan. He told me he saw you yesterday and gave me the address." She smiled. "So, we thought we'd stop by on our way home from church."

"Mom, you don't go to church."

"I know, but it sounds good to say on a Sunday."

"The only reason we're not going to burn in Hell for lying is because your mom sends the priest a check every month. Apparently, we're buying our tickets to heaven." Dad looked out the patio door. "Those flowers are going to die. It's too early in the season to plant yet."

Whitney laughed at the same time Sloan did. Why people made a point of commenting about the flowers had become a joke to them. "We were trying to make it look like we're excited about living here," she explained. "Sloan planted them, and bought the patio and porch furniture."

Her mom smiled at Sloan. "You have excellent taste."

"He does," Dad agreed. "Sloan, why don't you show me the hub of the operation?"

"There's not much to see," Sloan said, his posture relaxed, his face and eyes unreadable. "As you know, we shouldn't discuss an open investigation, especially an undercover one."

"Yeah, well, you're sleeping with my daughter, so I think you'll show me whatever the hell I want to see."

Sloan's ear turned red. "Sir, ma'am…"

Her dad rounded the island. "Let's just make us both comfortable and talk cop stuff."

"Yes, sir."

"Christ, call me Eddie," Dad said, then followed Sloan out of the dining room.

Mom looked to the eggs on the stove. "We interrupted your breakfast."

"Why didn't you call before you came over? You never pop by without calling first."

Her mom busied herself by checking out the soft-closing drawers and cabinets. "I want to update our kitchen. These are wonderful. Ooh, and I love these slide-out shelves in the lower cabinets. They're so convenient."

"Mom, please talk to me. What's this about?"

With a sigh, her mom leaned against the kitchen island. "Morgan told us about Sloan."

She was going to make him pay. Dearly. "And what did he tell you?"

"Don't be mad at him. I might've threatened him."

"Threatened him? Wait, you didn't tell him he couldn't come over for Thanksgiving and Christmas, did you?

"Well…"

"His parents live in Phoenix, and that's when his salon is the busiest." She narrowed her eyes. "That's just mean."

Her mom gave her a nonchalant half-shrug, but the guilt in her eyes gave her away. "I wouldn't really ban him from Thanksgiving and Christmas. Morgan is just as much a son to us as our own." She touched her hair. "Plus, who would do my hair?"

She looked to her mother's blond hair, which Morgan had cut into a short, layered bob a few months ago. The cut was stylish, age appropriate and extremely flattering. "Your hair looks nice. Did he add highlights?"

Mom's eyes brightened. "He did. Don't you think it helps cover up the gray along the crown?" she asked, tilting her head forward. "Oh, honey." She went to Whitney and took her hand. "I'm sorry we…no…*I* intruded. But I couldn't help myself. When

I finally got it out of Morgan that you liked your partner, and that he thought you two were a great match, I had to meet him. Your brothers live so far away. You're my only hope of having a grandchild who I can visit regularly."

Because her mom was never intrusive or insinuated herself in her business, she believed her. "My brothers are all within driving distance."

"But then I'd have to deal with their wives."

"You love all of your daughters-in-law, so stop it."

She sighed and looked around. "Is he a neat freak?"

"He's tidy."

"Is he nice?"

"Very."

"Do you like him?"

She grinned. "A lot."

Mom smiled, too, and squeezed her hands. "He's very handsome. I love the beard. Your father can't grow one. It comes in patchy and what does grow is red and gray, which is strange since his hair is still sort of brown."

At sixty-nine, her dad had a full head of hair and hardly any of it was gray. He liked to think that because he was such a huge Ohio State fan that his patchy beard matched the university's signature colors.

"Yes, Sloan is very handsome."

"Tell me about him."

She poured her mom a cup of coffee. As they sat at the kitchen island, she told her where he was from originally, that his parents were gone and he was an only child, that he worked and lived in Chicago, and he was a good man. "I really like him," she said, keeping her tone quiet—in case Sloan and her dad came back downstairs. "I know he likes me, but distance is a factor that can't be avoided."

"You can't move to Chicago."

"The thought never once crossed my mind. I've worked too hard to quit my job, and my friends and family are here."

"But?"

"No buts about it. I'm not leaving," she said, and meant it. She'd become intimate with Sloan knowing she could have her heart broken, had made a rational decision to be with him because she liked and cared about him.

"Would he be willing to move to Cleveland?"

"Mom, we've lived together for a week, and the investigation could be over by this time next Sunday. I wouldn't expect that type of commitment from him, just as I'm sure he wouldn't expect it from me."

Her mom ran her finger around the rim of her mug. "I knew I was going to marry your father after our second date."

"I know the story. But you two also grew up together. You had history. Sloan and I…we have fake history to tell the neighbors."

"Aren't you creating history now?" Before she could protest, her mom rested her hand over hers. "Morgan liked him, and I trust his judgment. And any man who can get you to clean up after yourself must be okay." She grinned. "Is he a good…lover?"

Her cheeks heated again. "Mom, please."

"I already know the answer. I can see it on your face." She touched Whitney's nose. "I'm sorry for intruding or embarrassing you. Your dad wanted nothing to do with it."

"No, I didn't." Dad and Sloan entered the kitchen. "I'll admit that the murders do bother me, but I know my girl is packing and can kick serious ass." He turned to Sloan. "When she was in high school, she used to get into so many fights, that—"

"Dad, Morgan covered the subject."

He tapped Sloan's arm. "I'll tell you about them when she's not around."

Sloan smiled, looked to her, and winked. "Promise."

Dad chuckled, then turned to her mom. "Times have changed. They've got listening devices that I wish we'd had back in the day."

They spent the next half hour talking about the case, then the neighborhood and finally the bodies found at Otter's Field. "Our people at CORE have inside information," Sloan said. "The ME still hasn't been able to come up with a cause of death."

Whitney stared at him, annoyed and slightly betrayed that he would keep this from her. "You didn't tell me CORE was working on this."

"I wasn't supposed to be nosing around the murders. And CORE isn't helping with the investigation. I asked Rachel to see what she could find out because I was curious."

Now she was, too. "What did Rachel learn?"

"Pretty much the same info Vincent gave us yesterday," he said, then explained to her parents that Vincent was a former cop. "CSI found no bullets or casing. The ME couldn't find any signs of strangulation, the toxicology reports on the first few victims have all come back negative, and there were no cut marks to the bones or trauma to the skulls. With nothing but skeletal remains, I can see where the investigators are going to have a hard time with this case."

Dad nodded. "Were there any blood or tear marks found on the victims' clothing?"

"None."

"Yeah, this is a tough one." Dad frowned. "In my experience, most killers have a standard MO. Even if the detectives can't figure that one out, they'll need to try to find a link between the victims."

"I think all they know is that the victims were white males, approximately eighteen to thirty-five years old."

"There's got to be something else," her dad insisted. "A small common thread."

Her dad had been a detective with the Cleveland PD. He hadn't worked homicide, but had assisted in a few murder investigations. Since retiring six years ago, he'd become an armchair investigator, loved watching cop shows and unraveling mysteries.

"I don't envy those investigators," he continued. "I imagine it'll take hundreds of man hours to ID those victims. What's your neighbor's last name? I might know him."

"Dietrich. Vincent's wife's name is Helen."

"Dietrich," Dad repeated. "The name sounds familiar, but I can't picture a face."

"Are we finished with cop talk?" Mom asked. "We've ruined the kids' breakfast and should probably get going."

"It was your idea to come here, so *you* ruined their breakfast."

"Nothing has been ruined," Sloan assured them. "I'm glad you stopped by, and that I had the chance to meet you." He shifted his gaze to her. "Whitney has been a great partner."

Her dad stood. "In more ways than one."

"Eddie," Mom admonished him, while Whitney wanted to crawl into a hole.

Sloan grinned. "Now I know where Whitney gets her bluntness."

Dad shook his hand. "Watch my baby's back."

Her mom also rose, then hugged Sloan. Shock momentarily widened his eyes, then his face relaxed and he gave her mom a squeeze. "Come to dinner before you leave for Chicago."

"Love to," he said as his cell phone rang. After saying good-bye, he excused himself.

She looked at her parents. "He's gone, so say what's on your mind."

"I already did," Mom said.

"I've got nothing to say." Her dad fished his keys from his pocket. "You're a grown woman, who's sleeping with her partner while working an undercover operation. I don't approve of your decision, but I approve of Sloan. He seems like a good guy. Just don't let whatever you two are doing interfere with your job."

Mom wrapped her hand around his arm. "For someone who had nothing to say, you sure said quite a bit."

"It's okay. Dad's opinion matters to me, and so does yours. This is an unconventional situation and my behavior has been atypical. But I can assure you that Sloan and I, along with our team, are doing all that we can to bring this investigation to a successful close."

Dad grinned. "Is that your practice speech for if your lieutenant finds out about you two?"

"That depends…was it any good?"

"Just fine." He gave her a hug. "Be safe."

Mom embraced her. "Call me tomorrow."

After promising she would, her parents left. Whitney closed, then locked the door. She would never live this one down, and was certain Sloan and the operation would end up being the main topic at their next family gathering. God, her brothers would give her so much crap over this. She should tell them what their parents had done to her, so they could have a laugh, then hopefully forget all about it.

She went upstairs to ask Sloan if he was still interested in having breakfast. When she reached the bedroom, he stepped from the steamy bathroom wearing a towel around his waist.

"Did they leave?" he asked, pulling underwear from the drawer.

"I'm sorry. That was…mortifying."

"I admit, I wasn't happy about bringing your dad up here and having him see this." He motioned to the messy bed. "Thank God I put the condoms back in the drawer this morning." He let the towel drop to the floor, then stepped into his boxer briefs. "But don't be mortified about anything. Your parents care about you, and there's nothing wrong with that. Besides, I like them."

"They like you, too." She looked to her feet, and wondered if she should ask him the next question on her mind. Her parents had already embarrassed her enough today, and Sloan's answer might add to the humiliation. "How much of my conversation with my mom did you hear?" She asked the question anyway. If she hadn't, the unknown answer would eat at her.

"Not much." He finished fastening his jeans, then walked over to her and placed his hands on her hips. "Do you think we're making our own history?"

Oh my God, he'd heard. But how much? "I do. And I came up with an idea to make part of our fake history real. Would you like to bring your bike back to the house?"

A big smile filled his face. "Absolutely. We can go for a ride this afternoon." He kissed her. "I'm going to finish getting ready, then head to Irene's. Why don't you shower and we'll go when I get back?"

"Perfect plan," she said, and decided to forget about her parents' visit and focus on the day ahead. She stepped away and into the bathroom, then turned on the shower. As it warmed, she made a mental To Do list, which consisted of little. Since Cameron wouldn't be home, there wasn't anything to watch or listen for on the street. She did want to ready the Stingray for when the kid was around tomorrow, and would also like to review the teams' weekly reports and finish writing her own.

While she stood under the hot spray, Sloan was in front of the mirror combing his hair. It amazed her that they'd easily stepped into a comfortable familiarity, and how quickly that had been achieved. Was it because they'd been living together, or did Sloan's laid-back attitude have something to do with it? Or was it as simple as they were good for each other?

"I'm leaving." He set down the brush, then came over to the shower. His gaze was on her breasts as he opened the glass door. Leaning in for a kiss, he gave her breast a quick caress, then closed the door. "I won't be long. One thing before I go. You never answered your mom."

"What was the question?" she asked, rinsing the shampoo in her hair.

"Am I a good lover?"

She adored him. At this point, she knew him well enough to say he wasn't looking for his ego to be stroked, and believed he wanted to know because she mattered to him, and because he honestly cared about her both physically and emotionally.

She poked her head out the door. "You're the one with more experience than me. I should be asking you that."

"Experience has nothing to do with this." He came closer and touched her wet cheek. "But I don't mind answering you. Last night, this morning…I've never had a better time with anyone."

She smiled into his palm. "I feel the same."

The relief in his eyes confused her. After he finally left, she wondered why, after the number of orgasms he'd given her, after how she'd wanted to have sex again and again, he would even ask, or was worried she hadn't enjoyed being with him. As she toweled off her body, she considered the things they'd discussed: his tattoos, parents, the old lady, raising butterflies… Earlier, she'd discovered Sloan was a deep thinker. Was it possible he was in his head about her? She hoped so, because she wanted to be on his mind…in his heart. She wanted the chance to explore their relationship, not rush through it, and cram everything she could into a few short weeks.

Give him a reason to stay…

If only she knew how.

Chapter Fourteen

Three days later...

The rental house, North Royalhurst, Ohio
Wednesday, 4:06 p.m. Daylight Saving Time

SLOAN SAT AT the card table, bored and anxious for
Whitney to come home. He'd been in front of the Stingray
since Cameron had returned from school nearly ninety minutes
ago. During that time, four cell phones had been in use, but they
were all numbers he recognized. He glanced at the opened notebook he and Whitney had been using to store the International
Mobile Equipment Identifiers or the Electronic Serial Numbers—
either could be used to ID a cell phone's owner, number and
carrier—they'd collected since Monday. Because of privacy laws,
and because their warrant was only good for tapping and tracing
phones owned by the Eastons, data from innocent neighbors
would be tossed later.

Though grateful they had this tool at their disposal, invading
his neighbors' privacy made him uncomfortable. He didn't like
knowing how many times Becky had called her personal trainer
—AKA, her secret lover—or discovering she wasn't just cheating
on her husband, George, she was also cheating on the trainer, as

she was having an affair with her insurance agent. The only reason they'd bothered to ID who'd called her, and whom she'd called, was because of her cryptic conversation with Dale. While they still believed the Easton kids were their connection to Morales, they couldn't discount Dale or Irene until they had all the facts.

The Stingray picked up another number. He glanced to his list. That'd be Vincent, and he was talking to the landscaper, Travis Murphy. After a few moments, the street went silent, leaving him to wait for Cameron to make or receive the call that would change the course of their investigation. Although this part of undercover work was tedious, he'd rather be forced to sit at the card table every evening than have to go back to Chicago. He'd been having too good a time with Whitney to leave yet.

Sunday, after they'd picked up the Stingray and he'd brought his Harley back to the house, they'd gone for a ride, then out to dinner—their first *real* date. It'd been a great time, and he'd loved having Whitney on his bike, her arms wrapped tightly around him. Later, they'd made love, as they had every day since. The weather, as so many had predicted, had taken a cool turn on Monday, and brought rain with it. Fortunately, it hadn't become cold enough to kill the flowers. He'd told Whitney that if meteorologists predicted a frost, he'd put the planters and hanging baskets in the garage.

He didn't know why he cared about the flowers. Or why he'd told her about the butterflies and his tattoo. He also didn't know why he continued to keep telling her other things, memories or thoughts he usually kept to himself.

"Fucking liar," he mumbled, and rubbed his beard. He knew exactly why he shared with her things he'd never told anyone else. He was crazy about her, and wanted her to be crazy about him. Sunday, when they'd talked about college and business ventures, he'd mentioned the gun range, which had been his original plan when he'd been considering leaving the Chicago PD. He'd had the money to start the business, but lacked the confidence to run it. When Ian Scott had contacted him a month before he'd planned to let his superiors know he was leaving the force, he'd immediately jumped at the offer, rather than lose his money to a pipe dream.

But what if Whitney was right and he was smart enough for college? He could get a two-year associates' degree in business, and even do it online. Then he could confidently take that pipe dream and make it real. Except he'd still be where he was today. Alone. That was the hurdle he couldn't jump. He was tired of going through life solo, without a partner, someone he could care about, and who cared about him.

Now that he knew what he was tired of, what should he do about it? Try to find a woman once he was back in Chicago? The thought of kissing and touching a woman other than Whitney made his stomach queasy. She was perfect for him. They were both tall, and both were in law enforcement.

He shook his head. The folding chair groaned its thanks when he stood and relieved it of his weight. "That was lame," he said to himself, heading to the bathroom to splash water on his face. Her height and their careers—while perks—weren't the reasons why she was perfect for him. She had so many great qualities. He couldn't name them all, just knew he loved everything about her. He stared at the toothpaste she hadn't rinsed from the sink. Because it was a reminder she was still here, living with him in this house, even leftover toothpaste didn't bother him.

What bothered him was her mother's question. Not about whether or not he was a good lover, the other one…

Would he be willing to move to Cleveland?

Could he reinvent himself again? Go to school, open a business, take a wife and start a family? He considered Ellie, and what had happened to her because of him and his job. Whitney's dad had said it right. His girl was almost always packing and could kick serious ass. Because she was a detective, he couldn't imagine there'd be an ex-con stupid enough to go after her. But he'd also arrested plenty of dumb people over the years. He'd changed his name, though, and living three hundred and forty-five miles away from Chicago would make it difficult to find him.

"Hey," Whitney said, and he caught her reflection in the mirror as she entered the room. "How are you?"

"Good. Bored." He went to her, loved that he could kiss her and hug her whenever he wanted. "How was your day?"

"Good. Boring." She grinned. "Before we started following the Eastons, I used to think I led a mundane life. I've decided that's just not true." She took off her shoes. "I have exciting news."

"About the investigation?"

She nodded, and took off her jacket. "Remember when Cameron was talking to the woman we assumed was his sister?"

"Did the three a.m. exchange happen?"

She grinned. "Early this morning. BCI has video of both Gage and Blair Easton leaving their apartments. They each met with one individual, and the meetings lasted for only a few minutes."

The thrill of the chase rushed through him. "Did you watch the video?"

"I did. Gage and Blair were given a shoe box sized package, and neither Easton gave anything back in return. Instead of going back to her apartment near Miami University, Blair drove to the University of Cincinnati, met with three college-aged guys, who took the box and gave her what we're assuming is cash—it was hard to see from the video. Gage did the exact same thing, only he stayed in the Columbus area." She removed her shoulder holster. "Irene's birthday is in a few days, and Blair and Gage—if we're right on this—are supposed to come home with money. And if Cameron needs to deliver that money, then we might be able to make a bust as early as this weekend."

The idea was bittersweet. In all honesty, he was done with the investigation. It lacked the oomph and excitement he normally felt during an undercover operation. Yet, the case was what was keeping him and Whitney together.

"Since an exchange was made last night, I think it's a safe bet that one or both siblings will contact Cameron to let him know the deal has been done."

She shimmied out of her pants. "Hold that thought." She left the room, then returned within a minute wearing her comfy clothes. "That's better," she said. "Anyway, I agree with you.

There's a big possibility that they'll call Cameron at some point tonight."

"Did BCI arrest the individuals who bought the drugs?"

"No, they're worried an arrest will spook the Eastons and Morales before we have the chance to ID Morales. But they've put twenty-four-hour surveillance on the college kids who bought the drugs from Blair and Gage." She sat on the edge of the bed. "That didn't settle well with me, because if BCI drops the ball and those drugs end up on the college campuses, we could, once again, have a rash of overdoses. During a conference call with the lead from BCI, I expressed that I disagreed with their decision, and suggested they pull the surveillance, quietly arrest those kids, confiscate the drugs and make sure nothing is leaked to the media about it. I certainly don't want the Eastons or Morales spooked, either." Her brow furrowed and she drew in a deep breath. "That's when the lead investigator—his name is Tom Gilmore—said to Campbell—*not me*—that he should tell me to worry about my own end of the investigation. So, I said, 'You wouldn't know about the deal if it wasn't for our undercover operation.' Then Gilmore turned into a complete, totally condescending and patronizing prick."

Prick was not a word he'd ever heard from her mouth. Now that he thought about it, Whitney rarely swore. Anger festered inside him. "What did he say to you?"

"Oh, you'll love this. He told me to worry about playing house with you, while they take care of the *real* undercover work." She threw her hands in the air. "They wouldn't *have* the proper intel if it wasn't for us. Let's not forget that Gilmore had assigned an agent, days away from retiring, to look into the Eastons' Miami connection. And that lazy jerk almost had Campbell pulling the plug on something that our office and BCI has spent thousands of dollars and man hours working." She let out a frustrated breath. "It pisses me off when what I have to say, or the information I've pulled together, is quickly dismissed."

Because she's a woman working in a male-dominant field. He had the urge to kick someone's ass. Namely, this jackoff, Gilmore. Even if he wasn't having sex with her, he'd take Whitney as a partner any day. She was incredibly organized, knew her shit, and based on her arrest history, was hands down an excellent cop.

He reined in his temper. "Don't let this guy upset you. He's an ass. I read through your files. Not just the one you sent CORE, but everything you have on this case. If it wasn't for BCI, I would've come to the same conclusion about the Eastons' Miami connection as you and your team."

She raised a brow as if surprised. "Everything? Our team tends to skim my reports because they're lengthy."

"They were lengthy, but the information was good. Don't doubt yourself on that." He glanced to the Stingray, then to the computer which was pinging and letting him know the listening devices had been activated. "There's a pot roast in the slow cooker. Go eat. I've got this."

"You worked all day, too."

"I spent the day waiting for something to happen. You actually worked. Go relax."

"I'll bring you dinner."

The pinging made him anxious and eager to hear what was happening at the Eastons'. "It's okay. Really. I'm not hungry."

"If you say so," she said, then left the room.

He was good with her having dinner while he eavesdropped on the Eastons. While he was hungry, he'd eat later. He finally had something to do, a way to contribute to the case, and wanted to take advantage of that. But as he listened in on the family's conversation, he yawned. Once again, they were discussing normal life stuff: *How was your day? How did you do on your test? Did the photo shoot go well? Did your client profit from your idea?* Boring.

"Dinner is served," Whitney said.

He turned as she entered, carrying a tray with two dishes and water bottles.

"I don't know about you," she began, and set the tray on the card table, "but I hate eating alone."

"This isn't necessary."

"Yes, it is. Despite how we acted at the beginning, we've always eaten dinner together." She unfolded a chair and sat next to him. "This might sound corny, but I've liked those times and don't want to break our streak. I'm not sure if you're keeping track, but this is day twelve."

He knew damned well how many days they'd been together, and wanted to keep them coming. "I did know. And...it's not corny. I like sitting at the table with you." He took her hand. "I like everything about you."

Whitney wanted to squeeze his hand and the truth out of him. She'd been thinking the same thing when she'd decided to bring him dinner. Honestly, she'd been thinking more than that. She had been three-quarters in love with him on Sunday, all the way by Monday night, and wanted to burst with the admission. To tell her parents, Morgan, Sloan—no, not him, not yet. They'd met thirteen days ago, had been living together for twelve. How was it possible she could fall in love with him so quickly? Her lists and life goals had said it couldn't happen. That this was too easy. *Why* had it been too easy? What was the catch?

She took herself out of her head and searched for an appropriate response. "And I like everything about you, too," she said, her focus on placing her napkin on her lap.

He half-laughed. "You didn't have to say it back."

"But I meant it."

"Did you?" he asked, then rubbed his beard. "Never mind. I'm not trying to start something."

One thing she'd learned about Sloan was that when he had to deal with any type of emotion that made him uncomfortable, he became combative. "I think you are," she said. "After dealing with Gilmore, I'm looking for a fight, so let's go."

His eyes filled with apology and...hurt. "I don't want to fight with you."

"Then say what's on your mind."

The folding chair creaked when he leaned into it. "You. Us. I met you thirteen days ago, and you have my head so fucked up I don't know what to think." He turned down the volume on the laptop, drowning out the Eastons' dinner conversation. "I need to tell you something important."

Her stomach clenched. The seriousness in his tone and eyes immediately set her on edge. "What is it?"

"I...told you about the girl I moved to Chicago for, but there's another woman you need to know about...someone else I planned to marry."

"For someone who didn't want a wife, it's interesting that you picked out two candidates," she said, and tried to ignore the irritation and jealousy. Both were foolish. She wasn't jealous of the many women he'd had sex with, and shouldn't care about the two women he'd wanted to marry.

"She's the reason I didn't want to get married." He opened the water bottle. "I met Ellie ten years ago. At that time, my career was going well, I had money in the bank and I was..." He rubbed his beard again. "I was lonely. Ellie was sweet and a good person. She helped fill that void, you know? So, I figured I'd ask her to marry me and then I wouldn't have to worry about spending holidays and vacations alone." Regret was banked in his eyes. "That's no reason to marry someone, and she deserved better."

"You didn't love her?"

"I did, at least that's what I'd thought at the time. She was easy to be around, we got along great. Never once argued or bickered about anything."

"Sounds like us," Whitney said with a smile, hoping to lighten the tension now thickening the air.

He returned the smile, but the regret was still in his eyes. "Before I had the chance to ask her to marry me, a drug dealer I'd arrested was released on bail. To get even with me, he broke into Ellie's apartment and beat her to the point where she was in the hospital for weeks."

Whitney's skin crawled and her heart went out to both Sloan and Ellie. "My God. That's horrible."

He nodded. "It was probably one of the worst months of my life. Knowing that she was hurt because of me...I didn't know what to do with that. Ellie did, though, and broke up with me while she was still in the hospital."

"I'm sorry. That had to have been so hard."

"Honestly, I was relieved. The moment she said we were through, I realized she was doing us both a favor. Your ideal husband list was missing passion and love, and that's what was missing between Ellie and me, too. I loved her, but not enough to fight for her love. Everything between us was passive, if that makes sense."

Whitney picked at the roll on her plate. "It does. Before my oldest brother met his wife, he was in a relationship like that. The girl he was dating was beautiful, so I was surprised when he broke up with her. When I asked why, he told me she didn't challenge him emotionally. And without that challenge, there could be no growth in a relationship."

"Deep stuff."

"That's what I thought. I was about thirteen at the time, and didn't quite get it. When I asked my mom about it, she laughed and said, 'I'll be damned. My son actually listened to me.' In other words, he was repeating the advice my mom had given him."

"But it was good advice." He finally picked up his fork. "I think that was part of the problem with me and Ellie. Not that it matters now. She's married and has a couple of kids. I'm happy for her," he said, spearing a piece of meat.

"Why are you telling me this? Don't get me wrong, I love hearing about your past and the things that have shaped you. I... are you comparing us to your relationship with Ellie?"

He shook his head. "Not at all. There is no comparison, and I mean that in a good way." His gaze lit with curiosity. "Someone I arrested nearly killed a woman I was dating. That doesn't bother you?"

The wheels in her head turned, and she finally understood why he wanted nothing to do with marriage, and why he'd prefer to remain a player rather than involve himself in a committed relationship. "What bothers me is that, for ten years, you've allowed what happened to Ellie to keep you from finding happiness with another woman. If you're asking me whether or not I'm worried someone from your past is going to come after me because we're...partners, my answer is no. I know how to protect myself, and I'm always aware of my surroundings. And, obviously, I don't live anywhere near Chicago."

He set down his fork without bothering to take a bite. "I didn't *allow* anything. I was making sure no one else could be hurt again because of me. I wanted to be open about it, so you understood that being involved with me has its risks."

"I appreciate your concern, but I could say the same to you. You're not the only one who has put away bad people." When he went to rub his beard, she grabbed his forearm. "I'm surprised you have any hair on your face. If you want to be open, do it. I want full disclosure."

"Full disclosure? I spent over ten years living a total lie. I pretended to be friends with drug dealers and murderers. Sometimes I didn't have to pretend, and actually liked a few of those men I ended up arresting. They'd made the choice to deal or kill, and knew there was always the possibility of being caught. But what I did was different. I'd become one of them. Hell, I ended up so close to one dealer, he asked me to be at his wedding. I built friendships and established trust—then I betrayed those people. Most times I walked away satisfied we'd taken another bad guy off the street. Other times, there was guilt and...loss."

"Because you liked some of the people you arrested. The man who beat Ellie, was he one of those people?"

He nodded. "I think that's the only reason why he didn't kill her. I'll never know. Before we could bring him in on assault charges, he was killed during a robbery at a convenience store. Ironically, he was there to buy milk for his kid, not to hold up the place." He drank from the water bottle, then shrugged. "He was the one who asked me to be at his wedding."

Now she understood. The arrests she'd made, or had taken part in, weren't people who she knew intimately. They were people she'd researched, watched and investigated. Other than doing her job, she had no personal ties with any suspect. Sloan had, and he'd betrayed people who had believed in him, considered him a confidant and friend. Hatred was an ugly thing. Coupled with revenge, it could be extremely dangerous. Again, why was he telling her any of this? Unless...

"Are you worried something will happen to me?"

"Of course."

Hope and trepidation worked through her. "Do you think an ex-con who has revenge on the brain will find out you're here, think we're actually married and try to harm me?"

"Anything is possible, but I'm doubtful that'd happen while we're here. No one but your team and CORE knows I'm in Cleveland."

She let out a breath. "This is becoming frustrating. You're worried about me, but don't think you should be worried right now. If not now, then when?"

"If we keep seeing each other and make all of this real, then I'll have my concerns."

Her heart rate quickened. She'd fallen for Sloan and wanted him in her life. Not because he covered ninety-six percent of the criteria on her ideal husband list, or because he could help her reach her life goals. She loved *him*, not what he could give her. While they'd met barely two weeks ago, they'd bonded. They'd become friends and lovers, and she hoped that bond would only become stronger, maybe lead to something that would last a lifetime.

Unable to eat, thanks to the nervousness rolling through her stomach, she dug deep and latched onto her courage and confidence. "Do you want this to be real?" she asked. She'd rather know upfront, than keep guessing. Even if the answer might hurt.

"Whitney, I…" He glanced to the Stingray, then quickly pushed the plate aside and grabbed the notebook they'd been using to keep track of the neighborhood cell phones. He handed it to her. "See if this number is on the list," he said, then rattled off the fifteen-digit International Mobile Equipment Identifier or IMEI.

She jotted it down, then compared it to the others. "It's a new one. Hang tight." She called the sheriff's office and spoke with Phil Wallace, one of the officers who handled tracing and tapping phones. After she gave him the number, Phil told her he'd call back once he verified the phone's owner, which took approximately ten minutes. "If this is an unregistered burner phone," she said, after ending the call, "we can't know with certainty that Cameron is using it, unless we put a tap on it and hear his voice."

"There are eleven homes on this street. Outside of the East-ons, we've collected thirteen numbers and confirmed they belong to the neighbors living on Shady Circle. We also have over two dozen numbers from visitors, the landscapers' crew, the people who live in the houses behind us, the mail guy or anyone else who's been on this street. Last I checked, no one but our neigh-bors are on the cul-de-sac, and the people behind us aren't home. This *has* to be the burner phone."

She was hopeful, too. After moving her plate, she slid the laptop closer to her, then brought up the software the department used to listen to wire taps. If they were able to tap the phone, she wanted to be able to listen immediately, and before the call ended.

Her cell rang. She quickly answered, and was told by Phil that the phone was unregistered, but he was able to put a tap on it, and that they should have audio within three to five minutes. After she hung up, she glanced at the Stingray. "If the call is over before the tap begins, we need to pull together the data gathered by the Stingray and find out who was on the other end of the line."

Cameron's voice suddenly exited the laptop's speakers. With a rush of excitement, she drew in a deep breath and listened.

"I bought Mom a fairy garden," Cameron said.

"That's a useless present," the male on the end replied.

"She loves that kinda shit. What'd you get her?"

"Nothing yet. I'll probably get her a gift certificate for a massage or something."

"Like you do every year? At least I was creative," Cameron said.

"You or your girlfriend?"

Cameron chuckled. *"Lexi might've had something to do with it. Did you talk to Blair?"*

"Cameron must be talking to Gage," Sloan said.

"With references to Mom, presents and Blair, it has to be him."

"Yeah, she's picking me up Friday, after my last class. We should be at the house around three or four," Gage said. *"Are you sure this is going to go down okay?"*

"It has before, why would it be different this time?"

"We've never moved that amount. To be honest, I'm freaking the fuck out. I don't like having all this money on me," Gage said, quieting his voice.

"Yeah, well, you're concerned about the cash, and Blair is having second thoughts about what we're selling. Guess what? I don't give a shit. We each have over ten grand coming to us, and don't have another deal until the end of next month. I want that deal, because after that, you guys are home for the summer, so we'll lose two-thirds of the business."

Gage sighed. *"I don't know, dude. I graduate next year. The money is awesome, but the risk? And I kinda agree with Blair. I don't like knowing people could get hurt."*

"Get hurt? Man, they've gotten dead and you know it. But, hey, no one forced them to take it." He paused for a moment. *"Gotta go. He's calling. I'll see you Friday."*

Whitney seethed over Cameron's remark, but let it go for now. She wanted to know who *he* was, and why *he* was calling.

"Hey, how's it going?" Cameron answered.

"Has your assignment been completed?" a man, sounding strangely like Captain Kirk from the television show, *Star Trek*, asked.

She touched Sloan's forearm. "Do you think he's using a voice simulator?"

He nodded. "Or he's a good impersonator. And if he's using a voice simulator app, our he could be a she."

She wanted to remind him that they were trying to connect Cameron to Morales—a Hispanic male—but refrained. Being right wasn't as important as hearing their conversation.

"Yes," Cameron replied. *"Tell me when and where and I'll be there."*

"I'll contact you Friday with the details. Plan on meeting Saturday night."

"My dad is throwing a surprise birthday party for my mom that night. It's at a restaurant, so it'll have to be late."

"I can do late. I'll also have new burner phones, so be sure to bring the three I gave you."

"I was hoping you would. We've had these for almost four months. But…" Cameron sighed.

"Scared someone is watching you?" the man asked, amusement in his voice.

Whitney glanced at Sloan for his reaction. He had his gaze

shifting from the Stingray software to the notebook and was writing down another IMEI.

"No, but we've had a bunch of bodies found in the next development. It's kinda cool, but makes me paranoid."

"Stop smoking dope and keep your head clear. I heard about the bodies. The cops have better things to worry about than a seventeen-year-old pothead."

"I'm not a pothead, and don't you think they might do surveillance, or whatever, of the area? I saw on a TV show that killers like to go back to the scene of the crime."

"You watch too much TV and smoke too much weed. Stop being paranoid. When will my money arrive?"

"Around three or four. Why can't we meet Friday?"

"Because. Expect a call from me at four-thirty on Friday," the man said, then the line went dead.

"We need his IMEI." Sloan used the Stingray's software to pull up the fifteen-digit code. "If we don't get him on Saturday when they make the exchange, there won't be any activity for another month, and we'll lose our access to the burner phones. And...that's odd."

She looked at the screen. "What's odd?"

He slid the notebook to her. "Tell me I'm seeing things," he said, pointing to the IMEI listed under Cameron's phone's data. "This is the number the Stingray just picked up, and it's the same number that called Cameron's phone."

Dread slithered up her spine as she compared the numbers. "Oh my God. They're the same. That...that can't be possible. It would mean the man who called Cameron is *here*, on this street." How could that be? What had she missed during her research of the people who lived on Shady Circle?

"Call Campbell. We need a warrant."

Since their current warrant was strictly for the Eastons, they'd need a new one to tap the cell phone of the man who'd spoken to Cameron. And because he had provided the burner phones for Cameron and his siblings, it was likely he, too, was using an unregistered cell. What they needed was to hear his, or her, voice. Their real voice. She called Lieutenant Campbell and explained what they knew. Campbell said he'd take care of it and call her once the warrant was granted. After she'd ended that call, she'd contacted Officer Phil Wallace again and asked him to trace the IMEI of the man's phone.

"I'm stunned," she said, while waiting for Phil and Campbell to call her back. "I absolutely did not see this coming."

"Same." Frowning, Sloan glanced to the closed blinds. "Let's go for a walk. I want to look around the area."

Minutes later, they left the house, walking hand in hand. The sun had already set, leaving behind a darkening sky filled with shades of grays, purples and oranges. Any other time, she'd enjoy this moment, but not this evening. Although the simulator could have a wide reach, they'd aimed it directly at the Easton house. While it was possible cell phone use from the streets running parallel to theirs could be picked up by the Stingray, and had been a few times, with the way the device worked, and the strength of the signal it sent out, chances were the unknown caller was in an extremely close proximity to their house. Again, that made no sense. She'd researched the people who lived on Shady Circle. There wasn't one person who could be labeled as a person of interest.

They walked out of the cul-de-sac, then took the sidewalk leading to the next street, Willow Lane, which was identical to theirs. No one was out, and there were no unfamiliar cars driving through the development.

"This doesn't click right with me," Sloan said as they made their way to the next street. "This Morales guy...why would he drive over here to make a call to Cameron? What if Morales is a cover? A name one of the neighbors created?"

She shivered and moved closer to him to steal his warmth "Then that would mean someone in our neighborhood, namely our street, has taken the alias of a Hispanic drug lord."

He half shrugged. "It's possible. If I were going to run a drug network, and had underlings doing my bidding, I wouldn't be a thousand miles away. I'd want to make sure no one was screwing up my operation. Especially a seventeen-year-old kid."

"I get that, but let's look at who we live next to. Nell is in her eighties, so she's out. There's the Murphys, who live on a budget and have three kids."

"Just because someone has kids doesn't mean they're not into drugs."

"I understand that, but they're not livin' la vida loca. Same with the Wolffs, who live next door and aren't in town. Skipping over the Eastons, we have the Ainsleys. Again, same scenario as the Murphys—he's part owner of a landscaping business, and not livin' la vida loca."

"Okay, Ricky Martin, what about Becky and George Wagner next door?"

She grinned. "Well, between alimony and child support, financially that's a wash, but they're doing okay. Joe...my research found him to be clean, same with the Zelenkos, which leaves Vincent and Helen, along with Quint."

"Vincent's a former cop. He'd know what precautions to take."

"True. But..."

"You don't want to believe one of our own would do such a thing," he finished for her.

"I don't. I don't want to believe Quint was the man Cameron was talking to, either. I like him. I like *all* of our neighbors. Well, maybe not Becky or Joe."

He chuckled. "Face the facts. One of our neighbors is up to no good." He shook his head. "The day we met, you, Andy and Campbell made it clear that Morales was hard to find. Correct me if I'm wrong, but Campbell referred to him as a ghost."

"And if I recall, you said that if people were talking about him, then he existed."

"Correct, and I stand by that. Morales exists, but as an alias."

Officer Phil Wallace called her as they made their way back to Shady Circle. After he gave her the information they were waiting for, she slipped the cell back into her pocket. "The phone is unregistered. Even if we can't get a warrant, which I doubt will be a problem, at least we know an exchange is happening this Saturday, and around what time Cameron will get a call on Friday. I'll make sure we have plainclothes deputies in place, once we know the details. The GPS device we planted on Cameron's car will ensure we won't lose him."

By the time they'd reached their street, darkness had fallen. As they walked in silence, a light breeze rustled the newly budding tree leaves, while a great horned owl hooted in the distance. All of the homes on Shady Circle had light glowing from a variety of windows. Even the Wolffs' house was illuminated by a few lights, which were on timers to make it look as if someone was home. This meant every person on the street—except the Wolffs—were suspects. Now that she thought about it, why couldn't an eighty-five-year-old woman take part in a major drug operation? Why couldn't an ex-cop, retired electrician, landscaper or car salesman aspire to be a drug lord?

Thirteen days ago, she'd have thought the idea was absurd. But given the evidence they now had, it was logical to assume a criminal was living amongst them.

Campbell called after they'd gotten home, and let her know she had her warrant. She then informed Phil that he had the green light to tap Morales' phone.

Sloan went into the bedroom to continue to monitor the Stingray and listening devices, and to cruise through the files Whitney had for each person on the street. While she should have helped him, she'd decided to clean up the dinner mess instead. As she put the leftover pot roast into a container, betrayal sliced through her. Which was strange and, like everything else about this investigation, made zero sense. These people weren't her friends. She wasn't a permanent resident. Yet, she'd enjoyed the company of most of the neighbors, liked when they waved…liked belonging to the community. Which one of these people had been secretly feeding opioids and fentanyl onto the streets? One question her team had tried to tackle was *where* had Morales gotten the deadly drugs? Had he been manufacturing them himself, or was there someone above him working a dangerous pyramid scheme?

She finished cleaning, then joined Sloan in the bedroom. "Anything new?" she asked, but suspected the answer. If he'd learned anything, he wouldn't have waited until she'd come upstairs to tell her.

"Travis and Nolan are on their phones, talking to each other. Becky and Dale are, too. The listening device in his office picked up his end of the conversation. I don't think they're having an affair. It sounds as if Becky is helping Dale plan something special for Irene's birthday. We can confirm this conversation through the wiretap recordings."

She sat on the bed. "Well, I'm glad to hear Becky is only cheating on her husband with two men, rather than three."

"She's almost a saint," he said with a grin, then carried the laptop over to the bed. "What's up? You look down."

"I don't know." She glanced at him. "This'll sound stupid, but I feel so betrayed."

"I do, too." He propped himself against the pillows, and set the computer on his lap. "I've become friends with Vincent and Helen, the landscapers, too. Monday, when Quint saw my bike, he suggested we go riding next weekend if the weather is nice. I wave to these people all the time, BS with them if I see them when I'm taking out the trash or getting the mail. I don't want any of these people to be bad."

She moved next to him, then rested her head on his shoulder. "This has me rethinking my dream of living in a place like this. No matter how much I'd research the people I lived next to, I would never truly know what went on inside their homes."

"Yeah, but what are the odds you'd move next door to a drug dealer?"

"With my luck, I'd end up living across the street from a serial killer." She sighed and glanced at the laptop screen. "Who do you think we should focus on first?"

"Vincent. As a former cop, he'll know what precautions to take. Except...other than walking his dog, he doesn't leave the house often. If he's not leaving, then how is he meeting with his people? And there have to be others outside of the Easton kids. How else was there a shipment made to Columbus and Cincinnati? And where is he getting the drugs?"

"What does Helen do during the day?"

"Since we've been living here, she's substituted at the local elementary school a few times, she goes to their daughter's house a couple of times a week and, according to Vincent, she's a shopaholic. But can you really picture Helen passing out oxycodone and fentanyl?"

"No, but Quint would be a good candidate. What if he has a connection that hides the drugs in the cars sent to the dealership? He's the general manager, right?"

"He is, so he would have access to any of the cars coming into the parking lot. But…"

"He owns a cool motorcycle and you want to go riding with him." She snuggled closer. "Maybe we're wrong, and Morales was in a car on the street behind us. He could've driven off before we took a walk."

"Maybe. Can you have your team look into all the neighbors' finances?"

Exhausted and disappointed, she closed her eyes. "We don't have enough probable cause for a judge to sign a warrant." She smothered a yawn with her hand. "We can't be sure Cameron was even talking to one of the neighbors."

"I can have Rachel dig into finances."

She cracked open an eye. "Absolutely not. An illegal search could screw up the case." She closed her eye again. "In two days, Cameron will be meeting with Morales. If we can't make an arrest, hopefully we'll at least ID him."

"Are you going to sleep on me?"

She draped an arm over his chest. "Literally. I'm sorry. I'll get up and help you go through the files."

As she forced herself to rise, he closed the laptop. "No," he said, then kissed her temple. "Sleep is good. I can review all this tomorrow, there's nothing more we can do tonight."

When he climbed out of bed, she did the same, then went through her evening bedtime routine. Minutes later, stripped down to her panties, she crawled into bed, then cuddled up next to him. Normally, her mind would bullet point the events of the day. Ever since the first night she'd slept with Sloan, she had easily slipped to sleep instead. Lying next to him, listening to him breathe, feeling the rise and fall of his chest under her palms, his warmth…it all comforted her. She would miss this.

She would miss him.

Not wanting depressing thoughts to ruin her slumber, she pushed them from her mind and thought back to Sunday evening, when they'd gone out on his motorcycle. Rather than relive that night, she imagined them riding along a coast far away from Cleveland, the sun on her back, the waves crashing along the shore.

"Whitney," he whispered, and pulled her closer. "Are you still awake?"

"Hmm," she hummed, her mind foggy and half asleep. She was too tired to talk, too lazy to move or make love.

"I want us to be real."

Now fully awake, she smiled against his chest. "I do, too," she said, sliding her hand down his body until she reached his underwear.

He moved his big palm over her rear, then brought her body on top of his. "I thought you were exhausted."

She wasn't ready to admit she loved him, and wasn't sure if he felt the same. And while distance and careers would make being together difficult, knowing he wanted them to become a real couple gave her hope. "I just got my second wind," she said, and kissed him.

Chapter Fifteen

The rental house, North Royalhurst, Ohio
Friday, 4:38 p.m. Daylight Saving Time

TWO DAYS HAD passed, and he'd done nothing but wait. It was the one thing Sloan hated about some undercover jobs: the waiting. Now he was waiting for Morales to contact Cameron so they had the time and location of the exchange.

Yesterday, BCI finally had done what Whitney originally suggested and arrested the people who had bought the oxycodone and fentanyl off Gage and Blair, as they were about to sell the drugs. He'd agreed with the decision—not that he'd had a say—because the opioids were bad news, and no one from the sheriff's office or BCI wanted another overdose. Thankfully, they'd been able to keep the media in the dark. If Gage or Blair heard about the arrests, their operation could end up in the toilet, Morales could cut his losses, go underground, and find a new underling to sell for him. What bothered him were the five young men who were arrested—three in Cincinnati, two from Columbus, and all were college students. These kids, like the Easton trio, had the world by the balls. Mom and Dad were paying their tuition, for their room and board, had given them cars, and instead of studying to earn a degree, they were out earning money illegally. Had he been given their opportunities, life might've turned out differently for him. He'd never know, and supposed it didn't matter. Still, he thought it was a waste.

At least the drugs were off the streets. Now they needed to ensure no other deals were made.

He glanced at the clock on the computer, to the Easton house, then to the Stingray. His cell rang, breaking the silence in the room. When he saw the call came from Whitney, he picked it up before the second ring.

"Hey, how are you?" Whitney asked.

"Anxious. No call yet."

She did this little growl thing that made him smile. Everything about her made him smile and glad his life had turned out the way it had, otherwise, he would never have met her. "Maybe Morales texted him."

"The Stingray hasn't picked up activity from his or Cameron's phones."

"Damn. Did Gage and Blair come home?"

"About an hour ago. The listening device I planted in the kitchen lost its battery power, so I can't hear anything from that area, and the one in the office hasn't been activated since last night."

"Damn," she repeated. "I'm heading home and feeling lazy. Is pizza okay with you?"

His stomach grumbled. A few slices of pizza and a beer to wash it down sounded good to him. "It's perfect, and—" The Stingray picked up Cameron and Morales's number. "I've got activity. I'll see you in a few."

He ended the call and listened in on Cameron and Morales.

"Do you have my money?" Morales asked, this time his voice was disguised as Oprah Winfrey's.

"I do," Cameron said, his voice hushed. *"I can't talk long. My parents are here and it's not a good time."*

"Understood. Tomorrow night, I want you to go to Mom's Kitchen. Be there at two a.m."

"You want to do the drop at the same place?"

"*Would you rather I sent you downtown? Maybe to Wade Park?*" Morales chuckled. "*I'd love to see a white bread, self-entitled suburban boy find out how well he fits in there.*"

"*No, I'm good with Mom's Kitchen,*" Cameron said, and for the first time, Sloan had heard fear in the kid's voice.

"*Good. Keep thirty grand for you and your entourage. Bring what's left, along with your phones. Go to the dumpster. There will be two boxes. Leave my money in the empty one, and take the other. That package has the new phones and another shipment.*"

"*But I thought we wouldn't be doing another one until next month.*"

"*You thought wrong.*" There was a pause. "*Having second thoughts?*" Morales asked.

"*No, it's just...the stuff I got from you after school last week...I haven't been able to move it around here. I can give that, and whatever else you have for us, to my brother and sister, but I think* they're *the ones having second thoughts.*"

"*Then leave my phones, shipment, and the left-over drugs at the dumpster, then kiss the money good-bye.*"

"*No, I...I'll talk 'em into it. Is there going to be any weed or coke in this shipment? I can move that.*"

"*Absolutely. Just be sure that if you're using it, you're paying for it. Understood?*"

"*Got it.*"

"*Good. And if you're a no-show, remember...I know where you live. I'd hate for your mom to die on the day she was born.*"

The line went dead. Sloan leaned forward and looked out the window at his neighbors' houses. Kids were home from school and playing in various yards. Joe sat in his garage, smoking a cigarette. Becky, wearing one of her exercise outfits, was at the mailbox. Everything was moving along as normal on their street. Except nothing was normal. And that sucked.

At the beginning, he'd hated suburbia. Within days of living here, though, he'd taken pride in a house he didn't own, had come to like his neighbors and had fallen in love with his fake wife.

He leaned into the folding chair and tried to wrap his head around the situation. Not the investigation—they'd bust that wide open on Saturday—but Whitney. From the start, she'd driven him nuts, had his head and stomach in a mess. At first, he'd tried to blame suburbia, and assumed a sickness had been running rampant thought the neighborhood, and that he'd caught it. He'd been kidding himself, denying what he'd known a few days into the operation—he was crazy about a bullet pointing, sticky note loving slob. He wanted to tell her, and, for the first time ever, he'd wanted an undercover job to be a reality. He wanted to be part of her life plan. To help her buy her dream house, marry her and make a couple of babies. The holidays, nights and weekends would no longer be lonely with a house filled with kids running around, Whitney at the helm. He grinned as he pictured her placing sticky notes on baby bottles, or a diaper bag, instructing him what to do.

"Hello?" Whitney called from downstairs.

He left the room. When he entered the hallway, a chill washed over him. Realizing he'd left the near-useless nook open, he went to it, then closed the window. Fritz was out in the yard, chewing on something near the flowerbed along the fence. He looked beyond his and Vincent's fence to the street behind theirs, hoping to see a random car, and prove one of his neighbors wasn't Morales. When he didn't see one, he stepped away and headed down the steps.

He met up with her in the foyer, noticed the box of cookies she carried, and fell in love with her even more. She wasn't just beautiful, smart and sexy, but she brought him sweet stuff. The woman knew her way to his heart and stomach.

After giving her a kiss, he followed her into the kitchen and told her about the conversation between Morales and Cameron. "This is great," she said, her voice filled with disappointment as she picked up her cell phone. "I need to let our team know, and have them on standby."

He stopped her. "If it's so great, why don't you sound excited?"

She set her phone on the island, then twined her arms around his neck. "I'll miss being with you."

Not the house. Not suburbia or the fantasy of living here, but *him*. He gripped her hips. "I told you I want this to be real."

"How? You have your job and life in Chicago. And I…" She stepped away. "I want us to work, but I can't leave Cleveland. Do you have any idea how hard I've busted my butt to get my position? My mom and dad are here. I have friends here and…"

He went to her and touched her cheek. "Stop. I know all of this. I'm the one who would have to make the move, make the career change."

Concern filled her eyes. "But is that what you want to do? You've been living in Chicago for almost twenty years. What if you give that up, and your job with CORE, then discover I'm *not* what you want?" She ran her hand along his jaw. "We met two weeks ago."

He'd thought about all of this, and had his worries. Not about finding a job, or starting over in a new city. He looked at those as exciting challenges. What terrified him was loving her, then having that love rejected if he ended up being a disappointment. "Two weeks isn't a long time. After the operation is over, I could stick around another week."

"I have a ton of vacation," she said, relaxing in his arms. "I can come to Chicago."

"I love that idea. It's a fun town." He kissed her. "We don't have to rush into anything. If I decide to move here, I'll need to give notice to CORE. I also don't want to come to Cleveland without a job or plan, so a move won't happen overnight."

"Then we'll take it slow."

"It'll be hard to do since we're already fake-married, have had sex and lived together, but, yeah. If that's what you want, I'm game."

She grinned. "What I want is you, pizza and a drink. And in that exact order."

"I like that plan, except you need to call the team."

Releasing a breath, she reached around him and grabbed her cell phone. "I can't wait to arrest these people so they can stop interfering with our evenings," she said, then placed the call.

While she did that, and needing fresh air, he stepped onto the patio. Fritz was next door, yapping about something, while Vincent yelled at him to shut it. The rev of Quint's motorcycle drowned out the dog and Vincent. Both men had been home during the time the call to Cameron had been made. The only people who hadn't been around were George Wagner, the two landscapers and the Zelenkos. Which left Vincent, Helen, Quint, Joe and Nell. He could dismiss Joe as a suspect. The man had been sitting just outside his garage smoking a cigarette during the call. He glanced to the privacy fence separating their yard from Vincent and Helen's.

His money was on the retired cop, which sucked. Before they'd realized Morales was likely a neighbor, he'd considered talking Whitney into staying here. Permanently. He loved the house and yard, and could later finish the basement and add value to the home. He'd grown used to the conveniences of the suburbs, liked that the community had good schools, a nice recreation center, and plenty of stores and restaurants. Now, he'd rather they find a place together and make a fresh start away from these people.

They could take their time, just as they would with their relationship, and pick a nice neighborhood far away from dead bodies and drug dealers. Although he didn't want to go back to his Chicago, it was the smart thing to do. He didn't want her to regret being with him, and would do everything possible to find a good job, look into an online school, figure out how he could start his own business...prove to her she was making the right choice, and that *he* was her ideal partner.

The patio door slid open, drawing his attention. "We're all set for tomorrow. Andy is going to call the restaurant's owner and get their permission to set up cameras around the property tonight. The place closes at eleven, so he could have deputies there once the employees leave," she said, unbuttoning her jacket. "I told you what I wanted to do tonight. Are you ready to deliver?"

"Sure, but remind me again...was I at the top of the list?"

She grinned. "Always."

As she walked away, he hoped that would be the case. That she would always care, would come to love him, and keep him at the top of her list.

Somewhere on Shady Circle, North Royalhurst, Ohio
Friday, 5:12 p.m Daylight Saving Time

He entered the empty house through the laundry room. Normally he would strip out of his filthy clothes before traipsing through the house, but he still had work to do. After grabbing a water bottle from the fridge, he exited to the backyard through the sliding doors off the kitchen. Half of the cord of wood that had been dumped in his driveway last Saturday still remained in a heap on the concrete at the apron of his driveway. The other half had been neatly stacked behind the shed and on top of Knot Head's body.

Before last weekend's neighborhood party, he'd moved the logs. As he had pushed the wheelbarrow through the yard, it'd occurred to him that he should save some of the wood for his next victim. He'd originally planned to give his wife a vegetable garden —with natural fertilizer—but the risk of burying a man in an area where she'd dig was too great, leading him to choose a different, more secluded spot. Throughout the week, his wife had complained that the wood pile was an eyesore, and that she worried about the kids playing on it and getting hurt. Fortunately, a couple days of rain had kept the boys inside, and had given him an excuse to leave the wood on the driveway.

Now that he was in the backyard, a shovel in hand, he wasn't sure if there was enough room to bury a body on the other side of the shed, where he planned to stack the remaining firewood. He had a width of about three and a half feet between the shed and fence. There was an eight-foot gap from one fence posthole to the next, though. He could dig a hole between the postholes and make it two feet wide by four feet deep.

Decision made, he slammed the shovel into the ground. The rain they'd had softened the earth. Thanks to the mature trees, the fence and shed, very little sunlight touched this part of the yard, which helped keep the soil very moist. As he easily moved the dirt, he guesstimated he'd have the hole dug in less than two hours. This would give him time to catch a short nap, then ready himself for the hunt.

After working all day, he was already exhausted. By the time he finished the grave, he'd likely be dead on his feet. A cup of coffee should help rejuvenate him. He *had* to hunt tonight. His wife had picked up the boys from school when classes had ended at three-thirty, and they were now driving to Columbus to stay with her parents for the weekend. Although they wouldn't be home until Sunday afternoon, he was concerned the hunt might not go well. He'd learned in the past that it sometimes took a couple of nights to find the perfect victim, and he wanted to give himself two days to hunt down his. If he had no luck tonight, he'd head back out tomorrow. Meanwhile, he'd have the hole ready for killing therapy.

Thirty minutes later, his phone rang. Expecting his wife, he pulled off his gloves, fished the phone from his pocket, then answered. "Hey, honey, are you at your folks'?"

"We just pulled in a few minutes ago. The kids are inside with my parents, and I'm getting our bags, so I thought I'd give you a quick call while it's quiet. How was your day?"

"Great. We were able to catch up on a bunch of jobs we weren't able to do when it was raining. But I'm beat."

"I bet. What are you going to do tonight?"

Hopefully bury a man alive. "The Indians are playing the Mariners tonight. I figured I'd make a pizza, have a couple beers and watch the game. I'll probably fall asleep before the second inning."

They talked for a few more minutes, then she had to go. "I'm going to miss you tonight," she said.

"I'm going to miss you, too. Call me in the morning."

After saying their *I love yous* and *good-byes*, the call ended, and he slipped the phone back in his pocket. Once he had his gloves back on, he went back to digging. Guilt slipped inside him and into his cracked moral compass. He was a bad person. How could he bury people in his own backyard where his kids and their friends played? How could he tell his wife he missed and loved her while he was in the middle of digging a shallow grave for the random man he planned to murder tonight or tomorrow? Why weren't she and the boys enough to make him happy, to help him forget the past and move forward with life?

Or were they enough? He hadn't had a nightmare since killing Saggy Pants. That had been the day when he'd truly realized how toxic he'd become, and how badly he'd wronged his wife. For the past week, life had been as it used to be, only better. His wife had smiled, laughed and talked more. She'd been more affectionate than ever, and they'd had more sex in one week than they'd probably had all year. He'd even noticed a change in the kids. They'd been relaxed, had been cleaning up after themselves, helping their mother before she even asked, and hardly fighting with one another. Had his mood been so poisonous, so infectious, that he'd unknowingly shrouded their house in darkness?

Maybe. Which was why he'd been contemplating this weekend's hunt. Instead of burying a stranger in his backyard, he should take all the wallets he'd collected from his victims, along with his disguises, and put them in the hole. He should entomb the killer he'd become, bury Camp Hope, and the memories of his father and mother deep within the ground, then strive to return to the man he'd been before the first murder. He'd already taken too many risks. Considering he'd murdered two men last weekend, and the police were still excavating Otter's Field, bringing another victim to his own backyard would be reckless.

Sweat dripped down his nose as he looked into the hole. Breathing hard, he glanced to the pile of dirt near it. Yes, he should be a good husband and father, not a murderer.

Except... He didn't know when his wife would visit her parents again. What if he did get rid of his disguises and any evidence linking him to the murders, but ended up still needing them? Right now, everything was great. But wasn't it possible that life seemed to be moving in the right direction because he'd finally had a hunt on the schedule? Maybe he needed just one more session of killing therapy to be sure.

Christ, he truly was just like a junkie. Only murder was his drug of choice.

Satisfied with the hole, he then prepared for his victim's arrival.

He left twine and duct tape inside the shed, next to the shovel, took a spool of each for the truck, then went into the house. The grave had taken longer to dig than he'd figured, and it was nearly eight. He'd have to forego the nap, and take a quick shower if he were to leave within the next forty-five minutes. While most bars and clubs didn't start seeing a crowd until after ten, he didn't want the neighbors to wonder why he was leaving his house at such a late hour, especially when his wife and kids were gone for the weekend.

As he showered, his mind strayed back to his wife again. He would miss seeing her this weekend and having her sleep next to him. She'd been right, and he had needed to remember why they'd married. He loved her. Plain and simple. He'd loved her back then, and loved her even more now. Despite the controlling bastard he'd become, she'd stood by and stuck with him. For that, for the three great kids she'd given him, he was indebted to her. And he swore tonight would be the last night. If he had an unsuccessful hunt, then he'd consider it a sign, deposit the disguises and wallets in the hole and cover it with soil and firewood. If he happened to be successful, he'd still get rid of the evidence and give up killing.

He toweled off, then used the supplies he'd stocked away over the years to change his appearance. Tonight, he chose to go with the clean-shaven head look, and, after slicking back his thick brown hair, he pulled the latex cap over his head, then began using the makeup provided in the kit to blend the latex with his skin. Afterward, he applied a dark beard, and once again used makeup to ensure none of the adhesive showed. The beard had him thinking about Sloan and Whitney, who he now doubted were undercover investigators. A few nights ago, when he had turned off all the lights and was heading to bed, he'd happened to look out of the front window. The Norths needed to invest in better blinds, because even from across the street he had seen the couple fooling around on the living room couch. He understood wanting to do the best you could on the job, and took pride in his own work, but he had a hard time believing Sloan and Whitney wanted so badly for the neighbors to believe they were a married couple that they'd become exhibitionists.

Once satisfied with the beard, he used a pencil to darken his brown eyebrows, then, after washing his hands, he placed colored contacts onto his eyes, changing them from hazel to blue. He smiled at himself to make sure the beard looked natural and stayed in place, then smoothed a hand over his now bald head.

As he left the bathroom to dress, he realized he'd miss this part of the hunt, too. He didn't know why, but he enjoyed playing the role of someone else. Maybe because he could be whomever he wanted, create a history that wouldn't involve psychotic parents and conversion therapy. Whatever the case, he'd hate to part with the disguises.

He dressed in a pair of slim-fitting, tapered jeans—the closest thing he would come to owning skinny jeans because of his large frame—a casual, dark gray shirt that had black trim around the collar and hem, then finished the outfit with a black sports coat and loafers. After he applied a little cologne, he stood in front of the full-length mirror and hardly recognized himself.

Yeah, I've got this.

He glanced at the clock on the nightstand. Eight forty-five. He'd gotten ready on time and, now that it was completely dark outside, he wouldn't have to worry about his neighbors seeing a stranger driving his truck.

On his way out the door, he grabbed the tape and twine, his keys, then exited to the garage through the utility room. Once he was in his truck, and the key fob was in the ignition, he sat there, his guilty conscience warring with the need for one last fix. He shifted his gaze to the boys' bikes, their scooters and sports equipment. He hated his father for what the lying bastard had done to him. If his boys ever found out the truth, would they hate him? Would they be scarred by his legacy and end up needing therapy? More than likely. Which was why tonight's hunt had to be a success.

Minimart & Petro, North Royalhurst, Ohio
Friday, 8:53 p.m. Daylight Saving Time

Butterflies infused my belly as I made my way back to the minivan parked next to a gas pump. I couldn't wait to see my husband's reaction when I surprised him. Especially once I stripped out of my clothes and showed off the sexy bra and panty set I'd picked up on clearance yesterday. He'd sounded so tired when I'd talked to him earlier, but hopefully he was still awake and not too exhausted that we couldn't enjoy each other's bodies. Even if he'd rather go to bed, than make love, I was okay with that. We hadn't had a kid-free night in years, and I looked forward to having the house to ourselves.

I reached the van, then slid inside, setting a cheap bottle of wine and six-pack of beer on the floorboard of the passenger seat. Once my seatbelt was on, and the engine running, I shifted into DRIVE. The Friday night traffic was heavier than usual, and I wondered if the bar and two restaurants that had recently opened down the street might have something to do with it. As I idled at the gas station exit, I watched the intersection, waiting for my chance to make my way home.

The light turned red, giving me my opportunity. As I was about to drive, a couple walking along the sidewalk crossed in front of my van. I swore under my breath. After spending five hours on the road, I just wanted to be home, snuggling with my husband and enjoying a glass of wine. The couple passed. Cars pulled up to the red light and rudely blocked the exit.

I set aside my irritation. In a few minutes, I'd be home.

The light changed to green. While I waited for my chance to go, a black pickup truck drove through the intersection. Oddly, just like my husband's truck, this one had a giant dent along the rear driver's side. When it passed, I recognized the license plate. Disappointed he'd decided to go out after all, I weighed my options. I could go home, wait for him, and hope he wasn't too late, or I could follow him and surprise him at…wherever he was headed.

I had an opportunity to finally drive and quickly made a left turn out of the gas station. A quarter-mile down the road, I stopped at a traffic light. Three cars were between my van and the truck. As I waited, I was tempted to call him and ruin the surprise.

What if he'd been looking forward to having a night without the boys and me around? What if he'd lied about being exhausted and having no plans because he didn't want to hurt my feelings? Worse yet, what if he was seeing someone?

No, he wouldn't do that, would he? Then again, the change in him this past week had been a complete one-eighty. He'd gone from moody, controlling and sometimes verbally and mentally abusive, to a thoughtful, considerate man who'd spent the last seven days showering me with affection, compliments and love. He'd returned to the man I'd married. But where had that man been for so long? Was it possible he'd been having an affair, and the guilt brought on by cheating had been a reflection of his behavior toward me?

Or was I allowing self-doubt and paranoia to get the best of me? Until this past week, we'd hardly kissed or cuddled and had gone weeks, maybe longer without having sex. At first, I'd attributed his lack of interest to exhaustion and sleepless nights, or that maybe the medication he'd been taking to help him sleep had created a nasty side-effect, making it difficult for him to become aroused. Perhaps I'd been fooling myself. If he wasn't getting sex from me, maybe he was getting it from another woman.

Before jealousy took root, I shoved my suspicions from my mind. This was my husband, the father of my children. I trusted and loved him, and wouldn't mentally accuse him of anything until I had the facts. The traffic on I-71 was light, so I kept pace a few cars behind his truck. When he exited, panic gripped me. There was now only one car between us and I worried he'd recognize our van and me. But as he continued on, driving to the outskirts of downtown Cleveland, where the city line bordered the neighboring community of Lakewood, I relaxed and blended in with the heavier traffic.

He turned down a dark side street. I continued on, made a quick left, did a U-turn, then turned right and drove to the next side street. I performed the same maneuver so I could see his truck and the main road. With no cars behind me, I waited. There were several trendy looking bars and restaurants on this stretch of the street, and I sat diagonal from one called Crush.

After a few moments, and worried someone would pull up behind me and I'd be forced to move, he opened the truck's door.

Stunned, I stared at a man I didn't recognize. He had a clean-shaven head, a thick, dark beard and was dressed in clothes my husband wouldn't dare wear. Had he loaned his truck to a friend? I knew all of his friends, and he wasn't acquainted with anyone who looked like this man. But as the bald-headed guy closed the truck door, he spun his key ring around his index finger before dropping them in his pocket—a habit of my husband's since I'd met him. This man was slightly bow-legged, just like the man I'd known for fifteen years, and his gait, his stride, posture and build were also the same as my husband's. Confused, I picked up my cell phone and dialed his number, then watched as the bald man pulled a phone from his back pocket.

Dread twisted my soul, had panic closing my throat. Either this man had done something terrible to my husband, or I'd been married to a stranger.

"Hey, honey," he answered, and hurried back to the side street where he'd parked the truck.

I watched his lips move, heard the voice of the man I'd known for fifteen years. My heart breaking, I called on every ounce of strength I possessed and did my best to remain calm.

"Hi," I managed, and even made my tone chipper. "I was just checking in before calling it a night. What are you up to?"

"After a shower, I got my second wind, so I'm getting ready to walk into Foxy's to have a few beers and watch the game."

"Fun. Well, I won't keep you. What are your plans for tomorrow?"

"I have to work in the morning, but I'll be home by noon. After that, I'm going to finish moving the wood, then do a few things around the yard. What about you guys?"

"My parents are talking about going to the zoo, since it's supposed to be nice."

He chuckled. "I know how much you love that. Too bad you couldn't leave the kids with your folks and spend the weekend with me. I'd rather be with you than a bunch of guys at a bar."

Liar. Seething, I drew in a deep breath to rein in the anger making my body tremble. "We'll have to plan a weekend like that sometime very soon." *That'd be the weekend when I planned to serve him with divorce papers.* "I'll let you go and catch up with you tomorrow after work."

"Sounds good. Hey, I miss you."

"Miss you, too," I said, tasting bitterness on my tongue. When the call ended, I wanted to vomit, then run across the street and let him know I was here, that he was a lying piece of shit and I'd busted him.

Except, other than playing dress up and lying about which bar he was at, what had I busted him doing? He didn't have a woman with him, but was maybe meeting one here. Once he'd entered Crush, I drove the van across the street and passed my husband's truck. I turned into a lot behind the building, then parked illegally. While I waited for him, I opened up my phone browser and typed in *crush lakewood ohio*. The bar came up immediately and I clicked on the website.

The air left my lungs. Gasping, wheezing, convinced I might have a heart attack if I didn't remain calm, I rolled down the window for some fresh air. My vision blurred, my hands shook as I glanced back to my phone and read the headline under the bar's name and logo: *Crush, Lakewood and Cleveland's Premier Gay Nightclub.*

The call from his wife had him hesitating, the guilt returning and left him contemplating whether he should continue with the hunt, or leave. She'd sounded...lonely and tired, and honestly had him wishing she and the kids were home, continuing on with the best week in months. The latex cap made his head itch, the beard was also heavier than he'd remembered and he worried it would come undone. Since he hadn't used the colored contacts in over eight months, they were uncomfortable and making his eyes dry. Maybe this was a sign, a warning that he should nix the hunt. He'd been lucky for ten years. Why chance it? Especially now that his killing field had been discovered.

Deciding to call it a night, he stepped away from the bar, but was shoved back in, causing him to push a guy's barstool forward. The man turned and smiled, then looked over his shoulder. "You shouldn't be allowed out past eight," the man shouted over the music. "You turn into an ass."

He turned and sucked in a deep breath. The man he'd seen leaving Whitney and Sloan North's house last Saturday stood in front of him, smiling.

"Sorry about the hip bump," he said. "But when I saw you, I knew you just had to meet Sebastian." He held out a hand as he moved next to the guy on the barstool. "I'm Morgan, and this is my darling friend, Sebastian. And you are?"

Totally fucked. This was hitting *way* too close to home for his liking. During last weekend's neighborhood party, someone—he couldn't think clearly enough to remember who—had asked the Norths about their first and only visitor since moving to the cul-de-sac. Whitney had said her cousin had stopped by for a visit, and now he stood in front of that man.

"Jim," he answered, in honor of his first kill.

Morgan eyed him and nudged Sebastian with his elbow. "He even has a rugged name. Well, I'll leave you two to get acquaint-ed," he said, then walked into the crowd.

"Morgan sure knows how to make an introduction," Sebastian said. "Sorry about that."

"What can I get for you?" the bartender asked.

He looked to Sebastian, whose eyes were banked with interest. Though Sebastian was still seated, he'd been doing the hunt long enough to gage a man's size. This guy was slight of build, thin, and would fit perfectly in the hole next to his shed.

Think about your wife. Your kids.

"Please don't feel obligated to have a beer with me," Sebastian said. "Morgan is, well, Morgan." He grinned.

"No, it's not that. I…" He nodded to the bartender. "Bottle of Bud." He'd gone through the trouble of doing the disguise, and after running into Whitney's cousin and going unrecognized, the adrenaline was still pumping through his veins. He could use something to help take off the edge.

The stool next to Sebastian's opened up and he took it. He

bullshitted with the guy over a beer, then ordered another. Morgan came by a few times to see if his matchmaking had worked. If only the man knew the truth. He'd tell everyone in the bar to run for their lives. But his getup had been perfect, and he could tell by the longing in Sebastian's eyes that he had a sure thing.

God, he was good. He could snow gay men, his wife and friends, kill and get away with it. Now that he was back in an element, where he didn't belong, role-playing, making the men around him believe he was part of their community, the urge to continue the hunt returned, along with the guilt. Did Sebastian deserve to die tonight? No. Was it this man's fault that Preacher Daddy had been a lying bastard? Again, no. But did he want to watch the dirt fill Sebastian's mouth, see the fear in his eyes?

Fuck, yeah.

The itch to take a life scratched hard at him. Temptation was only a foot away, casually touching his arm, letting him know they could take this to the next level. Only Sebastian hadn't a clue that the level they'd go to would be downward, specifically four feet—according to his estimation of the grave's depth.

"We're going to a party over at Dave's place," Morgan said, as he closed out his tab. "You two should come."

"I took a taxi." Sebastian picked up his gin and tonic—his third since he'd joined the man—and glanced to him. "I don't have a ride."

"I have my truck."

"See, told you he was rugged," Morgan said, then opened his phone. "I'll text you the address." After he finished paying, Morgan hooked his arm through another man's. "Micah and I are out of here. See you soon."

"Are you sure you're cool with this?" Sebastian asked.

He was so torn between doing the right thing and killing this man, he didn't know what to do. "I...I won't know anyone there."

Sebastian smiled. "You know me and Morgan."

He returned the smile. "True. Tell you what...I'll at least drop you off at the party. If I decide to go inside..."

"I'm sure I can talk you into it," Sebastian said, flagging the bartender for their bills.

After they paid, they left Crush. The guilt that had been chasing him followed him from the bar and to his truck. Sebastian was a nice guy. He worked in human resources at a manufacturing company, came from a big family and, based on the people who'd stopped by to talk to him, had plenty of friends. He was likable, in his late twenties, and had his whole life ahead of him. And he was trying to decide whether or not he should end it, or set Sebastian free.

Except the hunt wasn't over, not yet. Knot Head had been the only man he'd killed who hadn't caused him to have one of his 'angry moments', where the past had clouded his mind with memories and voices, to the point where he'd snapped. During those brief periods, he'd had no control over his actions, and no recollection of causing injury to his victims.

Saggy Pants had made the fatal mistake of accusing him of being gay and had ended up having his head smashed in with a shovel. How many times had he hit the kid? How had Saggy Pants reacted? Had he been able to talk after the first blow? Had he begged for his life? To complete the hunt, Sebastian would need to provoke him, just as Saggy Pants had, otherwise he'd be too controlled by his guilt, his morality, to bury the man alive.

Knot Head had been an exception to that rule. The guy had been a threat, had been up to no good and his presence in the neighborhood had been enough to enrage him. Interestingly, he hadn't needed the 'angry moment' to happen when he'd knocked the man unconscious. One part of him was curious to know what he did during the 'angry moments', while the other part of him was too terrified. What if it turned out he liked inflicting pain?

What if he'd been sick and twisted all along, and had been using killing therapy and his father as an excuse? Was that possible?

He knew what a serial killer was, but unlike the killers he'd learned about on true crime shows, he considered himself different, above them. He hadn't been born bad, hadn't tortured or killed animals, didn't possess a warped fascination with death or gain sexual pleasure out of any of his kills. What he'd needed was the high that came after the final shovelful of dirt had been tossed over the grave and how that high lessened the pain, briefly rid him of the demons haunting him, along with a reprieve from the nightmares.

Still... This was wrong.

"Sebastian," he began, "About the party."

"I don't want to go, but I'd still like to get to know you better." The man stood across from him, near the passenger door of his truck. "My roommate is home, and we don't get along. He's actually in the process of moving. Are you comfortable with going back to your place?"

That had been his intent all along. He'd never taken any of his victims home with him, and supposed it was fitting that this final killing session would happen on his own property. Maybe knowing Sebastian was buried in the yard would help with future urges. He could see the backyard from his bedroom window, gaze upon the grave and relive the moment that had brought Sebastian there.

But... That would be wrong.

He would be tainting his yard, blackening it with his demons and allowing Preacher Daddy to rest in peace next to his shed. "You probably don't want to come to my house. I'm all the way in the suburbs. North Royalhurst, to be exact."

"I rent a place in the suburbs." Sebastian grinned. "Independence to be exact, and a short, fifteen-minute drive from where you live."

The man made it hard to be good. "I...Sebastian, I'm married," he admitted, hoping to give Sebastian a reason to bail. Because once Sebastian got into his truck, there would be no turning back. "My wife and kids are away for the weekend. I'm not interested in a *relationship*."

Sebastian opened the door. "Good. I'm not, either."

A strange combination of dread and giddiness surged through him. He'd missed killing therapy, yet wanted to end the sessions before they destroyed him. Taking Sebastian home wasn't smart, but a rash choice that could ruin his life should anyone catch him. Then again, he'd buried over twenty bodies in Otter's Field, and no one had a clue he'd put them there. He'd also killed a man in broad daylight, then another in his backyard later that night. What was wrong with just one more?

He'd promised himself one final high before he gave up killing for good. And he always kept his promises.

He started the truck. "Then it sounds like we're going to my place," he said, and headed for home.

Chapter Sixteen

TEARS BLURRED MY vision as I drove along the interstate. My husband had been living a lie, had deceived our children and me in such a heinous and unfathomable way, that I didn't think I'd ever be able to forgive him. With anger burning me from the inside out, I slammed my hand against the steering wheel.

"I hate you," I sobbed. "I hate you, hate you, hate you!"

Why had he bothered to marry me? Why not own up to his sexuality instead of becoming a prisoner of it? Now I understood why he'd changed during the past ten years of our marriage. When we'd first married, life had been a whirlwind. We'd had a child, had moved north, he'd been busy with school and building the business. Had he lulled himself into thinking he could be happy living the life of a straight man? If so, what had been the turning point for him?

The changes had begun about six months after we'd moved into our home. During that time, my parents had relocated to Columbus. "Oh God," I groaned as fresh tears left a hot path down my cheeks. How many times had he encouraged me to take the kids to visit my folks for the weekend? Now I knew why. He was living a secret life and cheating on me.

Now I understood why he hadn't been showing much

interest in having sex. Until this past week, I'd assumed the problem was me, maybe the gray hair, the weight I'd gained over the years. No, the only thing wrong with me was that I had a vagina.

I wiped my eyes with a napkin from the center console. "Piece of motherfucking shit." Why had he bothered to be sweet and sexy this past week? When we had been making love, who had he thought about? Me, or someone else?"

Cringing, I increased my speed. When he was kissing me, buried deep inside me, had he pretended I was one of his male lovers? With my anxiety and temper high, I wove through the traffic, then drew in a shaky breath. "Okay, okay. Slow down and think."

A sign for the next exit loomed ahead. This wasn't where I usually got off the highway, but it would work today. If I cut through a few developments, then the store parking lots, I could beat him home. Yes, that would work. I wanted to surprise him, catch him in the act and then...

Then what? Divorce him? I made minimum wage. He earned around seventy-five thousand last year. With child and spousal support, I wasn't sure I'd be able to afford to keep our house. Even if I were able to remain in our home, I wasn't sure I'd want to stay. The boys...how would all of this make them feel? They were so young, too young and immature to understand adults made mistakes, and their father had made the motherfucking biggest one. He'd cheated on me, deceived me, our children, family and friends. Oh God, what would the neighbors say? Children could be cruel. How would the kids at school treat the boys? Who was I kidding? Adults could be just as cruel, and I could hear the gossips now...

How could she not know her husband was gay?

I slowed my speed as I entered a development that was a fast cut through to the shopping plaza near our neighborhood. As I drove along, trying desperately to collect my thoughts, I kept seeing the man smiling across from my husband. He'd been cute, in a slim, nerdy sort of way. And he was going back to *my* house, maybe to have sex with *my* husband in *my* bed.

How many had there been? How many men had he had sex with, and had he protected himself?

My skin crawled and a shiver ran through me. I turned up the heat and told myself not to cry, to save that for later. I needed to remain calm and rational, confirm he was indeed having an affair, then find a good divorce lawyer. My parents would help. Thank God the boys were there. Thank God I'd chosen this weekend to come home. If I hadn't, I could've spent another ten, twenty or thirty years living with a lying, cheating son of a bitch.

I pulled out of the development, then into the parking lot. Drove past the grocery store, and a few other shops. When I reached the street that would take me to our neighborhood, I looked left to check the traffic. Saw the minimart I'd been in earlier on the corner, Mom's Kitchen in the lot next to where my van idled, and no oncoming traffic. After making the turn, I drove the short distance to Whispering Pines. Instead of going home, I continued to Maple Drive, the street located directly behind ours, and parked there. I checked my surroundings. Not seeing anyone, I shoved my purse under the front seat, silenced my phone before putting it in my jacket pocket, then dropped my keys in with the cell.

Hurt and betrayal made my nervous stomach churn as I left the van to cut through the yards. Keeping my gaze on Nell's darkened house, I edged around our fence until I reached our porch. Once there, I quickly rushed to the service door on the other side of the garage, then used my key to let myself inside. I relocked the door, then went in through the laundry room.

Now what?

Where to hide? Pantry? Front closet?

The garage door grumbled behind me, squeaking as it rose along the tracks. Panicking, I rushed up the steps, looked around, then hurried into our youngest son's room. Keeping the door open and the lights off, I crouched behind a dresser.

My husband's deep voice rose from the kitchen. "Drink?"

"Sure," the man said. "I'll have what you're having. I also wouldn't mind having a smoke. Do you care?"

"Not at all, but we'll have to head into the backyard."

Since they were going outside, I crept from my hiding spot and into the upstairs hallway, stopping just short of the steps. We had a mirror hanging on the wall at the top of the staircase. I stared at the reflection and, from my position, was able to view the center of the kitchen, the sink and window above it, along with some of the countertop and a small slice of the oven. Glass clinked and cardboard rubbed together as two beer bottles were likely being taken from the refrigerator, which was out of my field of vision.

"Is this a picture of your wife and kids?" the man asked.

I'd recently placed a photo of the boys and me at the corner of our peninsula, which I also couldn't see. My mom had taken the picture the last time we'd been to Columbus. I loved it so much, and how it captured the happiness on our faces, I'd had to frame and display it. And my husband's...*friend* was looking at it.

Outrage momentarily made me lightheaded. I blinked and leaned against the wall for support.

"Yeah." My husband sighed as the fridge closed. "Look, Sebastian, I don't want to talk about them."

Sebastian leaned against the counter near the sink. "It's not easy to come out, so I understand. But it's sad, you know? You have this beautiful family, nice house, live on a cul-de-sac and probably have great neighbors. And...no one knows the *real* you."

"My wife does."

Insulted, I tensed. Who I knew was a liar and a cheat.

"Really?" Sebastian asked, his tone surprised. "She knows you're gay?"

My husband reached over and closed the kitchen blinds. "I'm not gay."

Sebastian laughed, then took a swallow of beer. "I've heard that before. But, hey, if you're one of those people who doesn't want to use labels, I'll go along with it."

"I love my wife and kids, and I've never had sex with a man, or been interested in one. I'm one hundred percent straight."

Confused by the conviction in his tone, I stared at the mirror, at the man who had my husband's voice, but looked nothing like him. Why would he disguise himself, go to a gay bar, then invite

Sebastian back to their house if he wasn't interested in being with the man?

Sebastian grinned. "So, you brought me to your house just to hang out and have a few drinks?" He set his beer on the counter, then moved closer to my husband, stopping when they were only inches apart. "Somehow I doubt that." He fingered the lapel of my husband's jacket. "I think you want this, but are struggling with acting on your needs and urges."

My husband chuckled. "You have no idea."

"See?" Sebastian grew bolder. When he touched my husband's chest, my stomach cramped and twisted, and bile rose in my throat. "You should act on those needs and urges. If you want to stay in the closet, I can keep your secret safe. No one needs to know."

"Know what?" my husband asked, tilting his bald head slightly.

"That you're gay."

"But I'm not."

Sebastian rested his hands on my husband's broad shoulders. "It's okay to admit the truth. I only came out four years ago. It was tough, but the best thing I ever did."

"I'm not gay."

"You were in a gay bar, have brought a gay man home while the wife and kids are away. You're also letting me touch you. So, I'd most definitely say you are. Admit it to me, but most importantly, admit it to yourself. It's freeing. Give it a try and repeat after me: I am gay."

"Ask me again. Push me to confess to being something I'm not," he challenged, his tone dangerous, threatening, and masked with a wry grin that had me worried. Why was he encouraging Sebastian to *push* him into anything?

Sebastian rolled his eyes. "I'm not one for playing games, but I have a nice buzz going, no car and, honestly, I'm horny. You're *so* my type. That being said, Jim, do me a favor and tell me the truth. Tell me you're homosexual. That you love men, and that you'll let me suck your dick."

My husband clenched his jaw. "No." His face and ears turning red, he stared at Sebastian as if the man wasn't there.

Fear slid up my spine. I'd seen this look more times than I could count, and always in the middle of the night when he'd woken me, grunting, groaning, sometimes screaming or crying, flailing his arms and fists and trying desperately to fight his way out of a nightmare. Those nights had been awful, scary and heart wrenching. His hazel eyes would become blank, unreadable. Soulless.

"Come on," Sebastian said with exasperation. "This is crazy. I want what you want, but I'm not comfortable having sex with someone who's having a sexual identity crisis. Been there before, and it turned out very messy." Sebastian gave my husband's shoulders a squeeze. "I *want* to have sex with you. I won't until you admit the truth. Don't play games with me. Just say it. Say it for me. Just one time. Admit you're gay. Admit you want—"

My husband punched Sebastian in the head. The man went down, his skull thudding against the tile floor. Breathing hard, the man that I loved, the father of my children stood over Sebastian. "You're a fucking liar!" He kicked Sebastian in the gut, the ribs, the back. "Those weren't mine, they were yours and you let me, your only son, take the heat. Fuck you!" He dropped to his knees and barreled a fist into Sebastian's face, spraying blood along the tile, the small rug and cabinets below the sink. "I'm not the homosexual, you are. But your *God*, your *parish*, couldn't know, could they? I hate you!" He violently shook Sebastian, then gripped him by the throat.

Convinced he would kill this man, I didn't know what to do. If I stopped him, would he kill me, too? Oh God. Why was this happening? Tears streamed down my face as I kept my hand over my mouth and gaped at the mirror.

Then he stopped. Dragged in a deep breath and shook his head. He looked up at the ceiling, then down to the floor, and quickly scooted away from the groaning man as if just seeing him for the first time in his life.

He rubbed his palm over his head, then quickly glanced at his hand, which trembled. He then plucked at whatever covered his hair, pulled and tugged until it peeled off his head. After tossing it on the counter, he looked to Sebastian. "Why didn't you stay at the bar or go to the party with Morgan?" He kicked at the man's legs. "I tried to talk you out of it, but you wanted this. You wanted to accuse me of being something I'm not."

Baffled, my hand slid from my mouth. Why was he blaming Sebastian? The man had been right to assume my husband was gay. As it was, *I* still assumed he'd been living a lie. And what had he meant by accusing Sebastian of being a liar, and bringing up his God, his parish…?

Your only son…

A chill rushed over me. My father-in-law had been a preacher, a devout Christian who'd taken the Bible literally. His pious and zealous ways had scared me, had made me so uncomfortable I couldn't stand being in the same room with the man. My mother-in-law had been no better. If anything, the woman had been worse. Pushing her God, what her husband preached, on me, and wanting to take control of my baby's life before he'd even been born.

My husband peeled the beard from his face as he slowly rose. Plucked something from his eyes and tossed them into the sink. Then a slow smile curved his mouth. "Time for your punishment, Preacher Daddy."

Preacher Daddy? Immobilized, I stared at the mirror. My husband left my vantage point. I heard the slide of the patio door, then, seconds later, he returned, and lifted Sebastian in his arms. Terrified by what he would do next, yet needing to know, I went to my son's window. Out of fear of being caught, I didn't dare open it. Instead, I stood helpless and watched as he carried Sebastian toward our shed, until the darkness swallowed them both. Seconds later, he walked back to the house, then he returned to the backyard carrying a bag.

When he disappeared into the darkness again, self-preservation had me leaving the bedroom, rushing into the hall and down the stairs. I stopped when I reached the kitchen, gingerly tiptoed my way over the tile to avoid stepping on blood, then exited into the garage through the laundry room. I went out the service door, locked it behind me, then left as I had come. When I was in Nell's yard and close to where our shed was, I stopped and listened.

"You shouldn't have done this to me," my husband said, his voice hushed. "You should have been a real man and owned who you were. But, no. You put the blame on me. Made me suffer."

Sebastian groaned.

My heart racing, I peeked through the cracks in the fence. Nothing but more darkness.

"I…" Sebastian groaned again. "Wh-what are you doing?"

"Burying you. I've killed you so many times and yet you just won't go away," my husband said, frustration lacing his quiet voice.

"Wait!"

Sebastian's shout was muffled, silenced. Then there was nothing but the sound of earth being moved.

Scared he would hear me, I remained still and waited. Let the tears stream down my face and the guilt pierce my heart. I'd spent the night worrying my husband was gay and a cheater. Whether he was any of those things, things I'd eventually accept, it didn't matter. He was a murderer.

That, I couldn't accept.

But was Sebastian dead?

Oh God. I covered my mouth again. Could I save this man? Once my husband was inside, I could go through the gate and uncover Sebastian. But what if he was watching from the bedroom window to ensure his victim hadn't clawed his way out of the dirt?

Indecision made my head ache. I should call the police. Yes. I'd call the police and save Sebastian. But…if my husband went to prison I'd be left with nothing. I could take his share of the landscaping business, but that wouldn't last long.

Think. Think. Think.

The shovel thudded against the ground. The shed doors squeaked as they were opened. Plastic crackled, reminding me of the tarp I'd noticed last week. The clanking of wood was next, and terror struck me immobile once again.

How many times had he done this, and who else was buried in our backyard?

My heart and mind raced as another horrifying thought hit me: the bodies at Otter Field.

No. No way. He couldn't be responsible for those murders.

Why not?

Because he was a good man, an excellent father and, up until a couple of hours ago, had been a decent husband. But he'd buried a man alive, and in our backyard. I should call the police. What then? They would tear my house, yard and life apart. *Oh, God.* My kids. How would they cope with knowing their father was a murderer?

I still didn't dare move. If I pulled my phone from my pocket, I ran the risk of him hearing me, or being alerted to my presence when the phone's bright screen cut through the darkness. Minutes passed. The shed door squeaked shut and the latch clicked. Seconds later, the patio door slid open, then closed.

I ran from my hiding place. When I reached the van, I climbed inside, started it, but kept the headlights off until I reached the corner. I idled there for a moment, trying to decide what to do. He'd put Sebastian in the ground at least ten minutes ago—maybe more—and I doubted the poor man was still alive. Could I have saved him? Gone back into my son's room and called the police?

Tears stung my eyes. Yes. Fear of my husband, of how what he'd done would destroy our family, had kept me paralyzed.

I glanced at the clock on the dash. If I left now, I wouldn't make it to my parents' house in Columbus until after one in the morning. While I desperately wanted to see them, tell them what had happened, I worried how they'd react. Knowing my father, he would hire a team of attorneys and help me file for divorce. With the evidence the police would have against him, my husband would likely go to prison. What if the divorce wasn't finalized before then? Could he still keep his name on the house, get half of his retirement, his business and our savings?

Gripping the steering wheel, I rested my forehead against it. I needed time to think and a few hours of sleep. Where could I go? Who else could I call?

At that moment I realized how badly I'd allowed my husband to alienate people from my life. A few months ago, he'd gotten drunk and had called me a doormat. I'd been incredibly hurt and angry. Hurt he would say such a thing, and angry because he was right. Aggression and confrontation had never been part of my nature. I hated arguing, and liked when everything ran smoothly. I predicted the very near future would not only be rocky, but heart-breaking, devastating—emotionally and financially—and humiliating. I needed to find an aggressive gene somewhere in my body and take control of the situation. My children were the number one priority, and they needed a mother who would fight to ensure they had a bright future, a roof over their head, food on the table and clothes on their back. While I knew my parents would help take care of the kids, I needed to learn how to help myself, too. I'd gone from living under their roof and depending on them, to depending on my husband.

It was time to depend on myself.

Needing a place to stay, I finally turned on my headlights and drove out of the development. Minutes later, I pulled into the parking lot of a hotel located a few miles from my house. After checking into my room, I unscrewed the bottle of wine I'd bought from the minimart and poured some into one of the small tumblers provided by the hotel. I sat on the bed and considered the events of the night.

Clearly, my husband wasn't right in the head, based on what he'd said while in the kitchen, then by the shed. Whatever was wrong with him stemmed from something his father had done.

Preacher Daddy.

What had he meant by *I've killed you so many times and yet you just won't go away?* I knew for a fact he hadn't killed his own father, or his mother, for that matter. Both had been legitimately ill and under a doctor's care.

I drank from the glass and considered what else he'd said…

You shouldn't have done this to me. You should have been a real man and owned who you were. But, no. You put the blame on me. Made me suffer.

"'I'm not the homosexual.'" I repeated his words. "'You are. But your God, your parish couldn't know...'" I rubbed my temple. Was he suggesting his own father had been gay? I had no clue, and frankly didn't care what my father-in-law's sexual proclivity had been.

At this point, I didn't care about my husband's, either. I'd rather tell the world my husband had just burst from out of the closet than admit he was a murderer. I could just imagine what people would say or think, how badly I'd be torn to shreds by the press and social media users. They would question my judgment, my character and my stupidity. How could I *not* know my husband was gay? How could I *not* suspect he was a murderer?

The reality was, how could I? Why would I ever think such a thing? He'd never showed any signs that he was anything but heterosexual. As for being a murderer, if he was responsible for killing others, when had he done it? And what if he had put those bodies in Otter's Field? He wouldn't just be a murderer, but a full-on serial killer. He was hardly ever alone when working a job, always came home on good time. If he wasn't working on the weekends, he was usually doing something around the house or with the kids.

I tapped the heel of my hand against my forehead as it hit me. *Columbus.* Anytime I visited my parents, I'd always taken the kids with me. *Always.* And he'd insisted on it. If he'd killed others, was it possible he'd done so during those weekends when I'd been away?

And what about the exchange between him and Sebastian when they'd been in the kitchen? After blowing out a shaky breath, I drained the tumbler, then refilled the glass. It had been strange, especially at my husband's end. Why bring a gay man home, then deny being homosexual? Even stranger, why had it sounded as if he'd *wanted* Sebastian to keep pushing him? As if he'd needed the man to help make him snap.

I tried to picture the entire evening, everything I'd seen and heard, as a bunch of puzzle pieces. I mentally placed the piece with my father-in-law at the center, added my suspicions that the man had been homosexual, but because he'd been the pastor of a large church, he had denied his sexuality. I considered another piece, and spun it around in my mind, wondering if it would actually fit.

As my husband had beaten Sebastian, he'd said something like, *those weren't mine, they were yours and you let me...take the heat.* What hadn't belonged to my husband, but had been my father-in-law's, and *what* about it was so bad that my husband had to *take the heat?* Unsure, I fit the piece next to my father-in-law's anyway. There was most certainly a connection there. He'd yelled at Sebastian as if the man were his own father, and had become irate when Sebastian had suggested he was gay.

Not quite. I placed another piece next to my father-in-law's. My husband had been calm when Sebastian had first touched him and suggested he was gay. The moment Sebastian had urged him to admit his sexual orientation an immediate change had come over him. A darkness so black and disheartening had taken hold of him, as if he'd suddenly been possessed by an angry demon who'd controlled his actions. I'd seen him angry, but never in a way that had scared me.

A tear slipped down my cheek. I was married to a murderer. Why he'd killed Sebastian didn't matter. My husband's future attorney could say that childhood abuse had caused him to snap, and lapse into a moment of insanity. I knew otherwise. He'd snapped, no doubt there, but he'd made the conscious effort to disguise himself, had purposefully driven thirty minutes to a gay nightclub, then picked up a man and brought him home. And, although I hadn't been able to see Sebastian's grave, I knew enough about yard work to say that his final resting place had been dug out before he and my husband had met, making the murder premeditative. My husband had known exactly what he was doing. Now I needed to figure out what I should do, and how to protect my children.

If he were responsible for the bodies at Otter's Field, the news would make national headlines. Whether I remained in North Royalhurst or moved to Columbus, his choices, the crimes he'd committed would follow my children and me. God, if he'd killed all those men, he could face the death penalty and a long drawn out trial. If convicted, there would probably be appeals, which would put him back in the news again. My family would never be able to rest, to shake the stigma of living with a murderer.

I half-laughed as a morbid thought ran through my mind. If he were to be executed, would I still receive his life insurance?

I sobered and realized it was a valid question, and the answer would likely be no. He'd taken out a twenty-year term policy on himself twelve years ago, right after our first son was born, and had made me the sole beneficiary. Upon his death, I would receive two hundred and fifty thousand dollars. We also had mortgage term life insurance, which would give me one hundred thousand dollars to pay down our mortgage upon his death. We currently owed approximately one hundred and fifteen thousand on our house. If he died tomorrow, I could pay off the house, turn around and sell it for around two hundred and thirty grand, then leave Cleveland with about a half a million in the bank.

My God, I hadn't realized my husband was worth more dead than alive. But what were the chances of him dropping dead and saving the kids and me from having to deal with the aftermath of his murderous choices?

"Slim," I told myself as I stepped in front of the mirror to wash my face. Too bad Sebastian hadn't been carrying a weapon. He could have killed my husband in self-defense. Goose bumps rose over my flesh as I stared at my reflection and blotted the towel along my cheeks.

That was the solution. The answer to my problem. There was no way I could continue to live with a killer, and certainly no way I'd ever let him near our children. I also couldn't live with the guilt if I didn't find a way to let the police know what my husband had done. Except, now the cops might question me. Sebastian was murdered well over an hour ago. Instead of going directly to the police, I secured a hotel room. They might accuse me of covering for my husband, of knowing there were others. And what if I simply left my husband, took handouts from my parents, and kept what I knew about Sebastian to myself. If my husband had killed the men at Otter's Field, he could kill many more. He could kill me. How could I tell my children to always be kind, never lie and do the right thing if I was incapable of setting the right example?

I set the towel on the counter. Too wired for sleep, I poured more wine. I needed to think this through. I'd never spanked my children, so how could I even consider killing my husband?

Because I hated him. His betrayal had sliced through my heart and had carved out the love I'd once carried for him. For over twelve years I'd been faithful, had stood by our wedding vows and had endured many moments of sadness and bliss. Over the past few years, those blissful moments had been few and far between, but they'd been there, and now they meant nothing. *I'd* meant nothing to him. Had he ever once stopped and considered what his actions would do to me, to our children?

I'd probably never know, and I wasn't sure if it was all that important. No apology could erase what I'd witnessed tonight, what I now suspected. So, again, could I kill my husband?

We had a gun safe in the basement. I could easily remove the .38 it contained, then put a bullet in his black heart. But how would I explain my actions to the police? How could I make the shooting look as if it had been done in self-defense?

Ask me again. Push me to confess to being something I'm not...

Yes, that was it. What if I accused him of being homosexual? If he lost control, as he had with Sebastian, and attacked me, I could protect myself with the .38. If my goading wasn't enough, I could tell him the truth, how I'd followed him to Crush, and then all that I had witnessed afterward. At some point, he would likely panic and try to silence me.

The muscles in my shoulders relaxed as the idea grew on me. But as I glanced around the hotel room, I realized there were details that needed to be covered. Why had I gotten a room instead of staying at my own home?

Easy, I'd tell the cops a version of the truth, and how I'd followed my husband and learned he'd been living a lie, and was in fact gay. I'd needed to process the shock, and had decided to get a room for the night rather than confront him.

I looked to the notepad and pen on the desk, and wished I could jot this down, list the pros and cons. But my mom had always said to never write down anything you didn't want someone to know. And what I'd write down was something *no one* could know: my survival plan. Mine, and my children's.

A mixture of worry and anticipation worked through my system as I wondered *when* I should carry out my plan. The obvious answer was tomorrow. The kids would still be in Columbus and wouldn't have to witness something that would haunt them for a lifetime. I could say that I left the hotel to go home to confront my husband about his infidelities, he attacked me, then I shot him.

Why would I arm myself when he'd never threatened me before? I drank more wine and tried to come up with an answer. I'd been to the gun range with him before, so both of our prints would be on the .38. Propping my body against the pillows, I looked to the ceiling. Then it hit me. I could say that after I confronted him, he left the room and returned with the gun. We argued, he…I would need him to hit me or something, but would anyone believe that I'd wrestled the gun from his hand? He stood almost a foot taller than me. If we fought in the kitchen, I could protect myself with a knife, but if I missed…

I set the glass back on the nightstand. Without changing out of my clothes, I crawled under the covers, then turned out the light. Everything I'd come up with was absurdly ridiculous and the delusional thoughts of a woman who'd just discovered her husband was not only homosexual, but a murderer. I'd never been a greedy person, and would rather live off my parents' money than kill my kids' father. A clean conscience wasn't worth the five hundred thousand I stood to gain upon his death.

But as I closed my eyes, I saw blood spray from Sebastian's head, heard the thud of his skull smacking the tile, his groans… the shovel hitting earth. I quickly pushed myself up and turned on the light. Nausea spun around my stomach as acid rose and wove through my chest. Fresh tears soaked my cheeks while a sob tore from my throat.

How could he have done this to me, to our sons? I would have eventually gotten over his homosexuality, but murder?

Raw hatred made my body tremble. I did want to die with a

clean conscience, but I also wanted him to go away. Permanently. The lying, cheating bastard thought I was a doormat, but I could prove him wrong. And why shouldn't my family walk away with five hundred grand? Whether I went to the police, or actually went through with my plan, his secrets would be exposed and I would be scrutinized.

I punched the pillow, then pressed it against my face and screamed, let out the anger, the hatred, outrage and betrayal. Breathing hard, I dropped the pillow, then wiped my tear-soaked face. Fuck my conscience. He'd started this, and I was going to finish it. *He* was the murderer. And if he'd actually killed all those other men, then ending his life would make me a hero. My plan *would* work.

Calmer, I turned off the light again, then rolled on my side.

Yeah, I've got this.

Somewhere on Shady Circle, North Royalhurst, Ohio
Saturday, 1:09 a.m. Daylight Saving Time

He glanced around the kitchen, searching for any blood he might've missed. He'd used bleach to clean up the mess Sebastian had made, but knew from forensic shows that it only took a tiny drop of blood to ruin the perfect crime. And this one *had* been perfect. While he'd been cleaning, he'd burned the latex cap and beard, along with the clothes he'd worn, in the family room fireplace. He'd also busted up Sebastian's cell phone and buried that and the man's wallet, along with all the wallets he'd taken from the men he'd killed before, in the grave at the side of the shed. Tomorrow, after he finished working, he planned to pile the firewood on top of the grave. Then he'd forget about killing. Except...

He looked from the tiled floor to the fireplace where the embers still burned. There were other disguises stowed away in a secret hidey-hole he'd built into the closet during one of the weekends when his wife had been in Columbus. He should probably burn those, too. But...what if the killing itch had hit him hard?

Maybe he should look at those disguises the way his business partner considered the full pack of cigarettes he kept in his freezer. His partner had quit smoking two years ago, but liked keeping the cigarettes there. They comforted him. Let him know that, at any time, should the urge strike, he could have one. His partner hadn't caved, so maybe he could do the same, consider the disguises as his pack of cigarettes in the freezer, then not touch them.

Which shouldn't be too hard. He hadn't enjoyed killing Sebastian. Yes, that sweet moment, where everything had gone fuzzy and the flies had buzzed in his ear, had happened, but something hadn't been right. Even when he'd been burying Sebastian, he'd had a hard time picturing burying Preacher Daddy. Instead, he'd sworn his wife was with him, looking on with disappointment. That had *never* happened, and he figured it was due to bringing his killing therapy to his home, where images and memories of his wife and kids surrounded him.

If he ever killed again, it would never happen here. Now that the rush was over, taking the high with it, he'd never look at his kitchen the same again. His wife had been wanting to replace the tile and cabinets. A remodel wasn't in the budget, but he was handy and could make that happen. Anything to erase what he'd done here.

He glanced to the floor again. Pictured his youngest son moving his little cars or action figures across the area where Sebastian's blood had been. His throat tightened with guilt and the urge to vomit. He rushed from the kitchen to the half bath and threw up the contents of his stomach. After the wave of nausea passed, he ran a shaky hand along his mouth, then flushed the toilet.

Never again.

He left the bathroom, made sure the house was locked up, then went to his bedroom. Once there, he showered. Washed away the dirt, blood and guilt. As he did, he realized there was no such thing as a happy serial killer. He'd been fooling himself into thinking the concept was possible. Instead, he needed to focus on his family, and the happiness *they* brought him.

Once he was toweled off, he pulled on some underwear, then crawled his weary body into bed. As he waited for his mind to shut down, he drew his wife's pillow close and inhaled her scent. He missed her. Missed the kids. Missed being the man he'd been before the first kill, and was determined to change his ways and become that man again.

As his mind slowed, he thought about the date he and his wife had planned for next weekend, along with the last time he'd given her flowers. He should surprise her with a bouquet, then shock her by making a reservation at a nice restaurant. After the way he'd treated her, he had plenty of making up to do. This past week had been a good start, but once she and the kids were home, he'd do even more.

And forget all about the hunt.

Yeah, I've got this.

Chapter Seventeen

The rental house, North Royalhurst, Ohio
Saturday, 2:12 a.m. Daylight Saving Time

"WHITNEY, I NEED you."

Groggy, half asleep, she smiled against the pillow. "So tired…I'll fool around again in the morning."

Sloan chuckled, then nudged her. "I'm not talking about sex, but I'll hold you to that morning thing. We have activity."

She came alert. The sheets fell from her nude body as she sat upright. "Activity?" she asked, smothering a yawn. "What's happening?"

He went to the card table and began tapping at the keyboard. "Not sure. The camera I have on the Eastons was activated. Cameron just backed out of the driveway." More tapping. "The Stingray picked up calls between him and Morales. We need audio."

Her phone rang. She reached over to the nightstand, saw it was Andy, and answered. "Do you have something?" she asked, getting out of bed. She grabbed her panties from the floor, then quickly slid into them. "Because Cameron just left."

"I heard." There was rustling in the background, as if Andy were on the move. "Morales contacted Cameron five minutes ago, and told him the exchange needed to happen now, and to be at Mom's Kitchen by two-thirty. Nothing more."

Cradling the phone to her ear, she hooked her bra. "Damn it, no one is in place."

"Kirchner has a team on the way."

Dennis Kirchner ran their SWAT unit and was excellent at his job. "Good." She pulled on a pair of jeans. "But he and his team are thirty minutes out. We need North Royalhurst PD on this."

"Campbell disagrees," Andy said, breathless. "I'm getting in my car now."

"Why does he disagree?" she asked as she finished dressing in a sweatshirt and tennis shoes, and was pleased to see Sloan had done the same.

"He's worried they'll blow our cover."

She strapped on her shoulder holster. "Sloan and I are going to beat everyone there. But if we need backup, I'm calling the local PD." After pocketing the phone, she finished arming herself, then grabbed two bulletproof vests from the closet. She tossed one to Sloan. "Ready?"

"Let's go."

As they rushed to his truck, she told Sloan what Andy had said. Once inside, she turned to him. "Campbell is wrong on this. North Royalhurst PD needs to know what we're doing. I don't want to be shot at by one of our own."

"Agreed." Keeping the headlights off, he backed out of the driveway. "I'm wondering why the plans changed again."

She took the dash cam from the glove box, then began setting it up on the dashboard. "Morales could be on to us. I can't see how, though."

"Neither can I. I'm just glad Andy took care of things earlier."

Andy and two deputies had gone to Mom's Kitchen around eleven-thirty, and had hidden surveillance cameras throughout the property. They wanted the exchange documented, and to be able to positively ID the suspects, their vehicles…anything that would help make an arrest that would lead to a conviction.

"How do you want to do this?" he asked. "At this hour, we can be to the restaurant in less than five minutes. Unless Cameron made a stop alcng the way, he's probably pulling in the parking lot right now."

Her stomach somersaulted with concern and anticipation This was the moment they'd been waiting for, and it might possibly be a bust. "Morales could be there, too. They could make the exchange before we leave the development." She drew in a calming breath. "Okay, the original plan was to have officers in place on the roof, inside the restaurant and the dumpster. Vehicles were going to be parked behind the shopping center."

"Now we've lost the element of surprise."

"Exactly. The parking lot will be empty, so if we turn into it we might spook whoever is at the restaurant."

He switched on the headlights when they reached the main road, then turned right. The shopping center was on the left about a mile from them. Just before the parking lot entrance was a large plot of land that was currently being developed for commercial use. Not all the trees had been cleared and construction crews had left behind large excavators, bulldozers and dump trucks.

"I have an idea," she said, then suggested they hide the truck behind the equipment, and went on foot to the restaurant. "If there are no cars outside of Mom's, we can run over there, get in place and surprise them once money and drugs are exchanged."

"What if Cameron and Morales are already there? We won't have any cover in the parking lot." He tapped the steering wheel "We could park at the gas station across the street from the restaurant, watch them, then follow Morales."

"If we lose him…"

"Look, I know you want to make an arrest, I do, too. But we'll have surveillance footage of the exchange, hopefully get an ID and if we're able to tail Morales, we can arrest him when he stops." He reached over and held her hand. "There's no reason we should put ourselves in a situation where we need to test the bullet proof vests."

Knowing he was right, she hid her disappointment and nodded. "You're right. Let's go to the gas station. But, you have to admit, my idea was more exciting."

He grinned. "Yes, very cloak-and-dagger." When Sloan

slowed the truck as they approached the shopping center entrance, they both glanced at the restaurant. "Cameron's car is there."

"I see it," she said, then looked toward the intersection, and hoped the light would remain green.

Sloan made it through as the traffic light switched to yellow. He veered into the gas station, drove the truck to the farthest point of the lot near the exit, then angled it so they were able to view a portion of the back of the restaurant. He killed the headlights. "Visibility isn't the greatest, but we don't have many options. Do you see any other cars in the lot?"

"I don't." As she scanned the large parking lot, along with the darkened stores that made up the shopping center, she called Andy. "Hey, have you heard from Kirchner? We have a visual of Cameron's vehicle," she said, then explained where they were.

"They'll be there in about fifteen minutes."

Damn it. She stared across the street. "I want to go for it when Morales shows."

"Whitney, you don't know if Morales will be armed, or how many people he'll have with him."

She knew all this, and that they would need to be patient and wait. After spending months and hundreds of hours on this case, she was struggling to hang onto that patience. She promised Andy they'd hang tight and wait for backup, then continued to watch the parking lot, as well as the entrances and exits.

"Do you see that?" Sloan asked, and pointed to a section of the parking lot veiled in the shadows cast from the lampposts.

Filled with excitement, she pulled a set of binoculars out from where she'd stored them under the passenger seat. Using them, she focused on that part of the lot. "Looks like a small SUV, but it's hard to tell. I can't make out the license plate number, either."

"Cameron's leaving."

She lowered the binoculars. "Interesting. I assumed he and Morales would actually meet."

"Not if Morales is one of the neighbors."

"True. I guess I was still hoping Morales *wasn't* a neighbor." She raised the binoculars and refocused on the SUV, which drove

—with the headlights off—slowly across the parking lot. "The SUV is heading toward the restaurant." When light from the lamppost hit the vehicle, she recognized the make and model. "It's a Ford Escape. Looks like it's royal blue."

"You're sure?" he asked, disbelief in his voice.

"Eighty percent. Why?"

Rubbing his beard, he released a frustrated breath. "Nell's grandson has a 2011 metallic blue Ford Escape."

Unease worked through her.

"His name is Jacob Malinowski and he's Nell's oldest son's kid," Sloan continued. "I think he's around twenty or twenty-one. He, and sometimes his brother, Hayden, come over three or four times a week, take her to run errands and do odd jobs around the house." He shifted the truck into DRIVE, inched it forward, then stopped. "I saw Jacob yesterday when he took out her garbage."

"But I don't remember seeing a blue Escape in Nell's driveway the night we realized Morales was in the neighborhood. Does he ever park in her garage?"

"No, half of it is filled with junk," he said as the Escape neared the dumpster. "The other half has her car, which she rarely drives."

"If Nell's grandson is Morales, and the guy is always on the street, he wouldn't want to actually meet with Cameron. So, what's happening here makes sense."

Sloan lifted his foot off the gas and moved the truck forward again, then stopped. "Can you tell how many people are in the car?" He let out a breath. "I want to drive over there so badly."

"Me, too. But if the car belongs to Nell's grandson, we can easily find him and...he's parked and just got out of the car. He's wearing a hooded sweatshirt, gray, I think. I can't tell his height, but maybe five nine or five ten, slight build."

"Sounds about right."

"I see two silhouettes. One in the passenger seat, one in the second row." The man walked out of range, then returned within seconds carrying a small package. "He's going back to the car."

"Call Andy and tell him what's up, and that we're going to follow him." Once the Escape began to move, Sloan made a left out of the gas station, and cut across lanes to make a right at the intersection. As he waited at the light, the Escape pulled out of the parking lot, and headed toward the direction of their development. "If he goes into Whispering Pines, I'll keep driving, then backtrack," he said, now following the SUV.

She placed the binoculars under the seat, then reached for her cell. Sloan kept a fair amount of distance between the truck and SUV. "We have a turn signal," she said, anxious to bring this case to a close, yet apprehensive about making the arrest at Nell's home. Her grandson and the other two suspects could resist, take Nell as hostage and refuse to leave the house.

When the Escape went into their development, her apprehension escalated. While Sloan looked for a place to turn the truck around, she called Andy and told him what they knew, along with Nell's address. "We don't want to have to bring in a crisis negotiator, or worry about alerting Cameron. Tell Kirchner no sirens or lights. And please make it clear that there is an eighty-five-year-old woman living at the residence."

"Where are you now?" Andy asked.

"Entering Whispering Pines. We're going to park the truck at the rental house, then once SWAT is here, we'll walk over to Nell Malinowski's." She ended the call as Sloan pulled onto Shady Circle. Her earlier unease returned. "There's the Ford. The car wasn't there when we left."

"No, it wasn't. Cameron's home, too," Sloan said, dousing the headlights and parking in their driveway. He shut off the engine. "Why would Jacob go to his grandma's? Seems risky to come here when Cameron is only three doors down."

"That is odd. What worries me are the two people with him. Does Nell know them? Is she aware they're all at the house?"

"Assuming Jacob has a key, he and the others could slip inside while she's sleeping. From the way Nell's garage looks I wouldn't be surprised if she is a hoarder. It could be he wanted to stash the money and burner phones there."

She'd love to run a background check on Jacob, but there was no time. SWAT and several cruisers were turning their darkened vehicles onto the street, blocking anyone from entering or exiting the cul-de-sac or Nell's driveway. She and Sloan left the truck and jogged over to where the task force stood by the SWAT tactical vehicles.

When she immediately spotted Kirchner, she approached him, introduced Sloan, then said, "We believe our suspect is Jacob Malinowski. He has two people with him, and we're assuming the grandmother, Nell, is inside the house. We have no idea if any of them are armed." She pointed to the Easton house. "Our other suspect, Cameron Easton, is in that home. There are four other family members residing there."

Kirchner looked from the Eastons' back to Nell's home. "I'll split the team and have them surround both houses."

"Unless something happens that wakes the neighborhood, I don't want the unit at Cameron's to do anything until we've secured this place."

"Understood. Are we going through the front door?" Kirchner asked, staring at Nell's house, which, with the exception of lights glowing from the basement, was dark.

"We know this woman. Sloan and I will knock on the door. Hopefully she'll be the one to answer. Since we don't know if the suspects are armed, I'd like to get her out of there and avoid a hostage situation."

Kirchner agreed, then ordered his unit to split up and take their positions at both Nell and Cameron's homes. When everyone was in place, she and Sloan both readied their weapons, then walked to the front door.

"I know you're the lead on this," Sloan said, his voice hushed, "but I think we should have waited until we had more information on Jacob. He could have an arsenal stashed here, or a history of mental illness or violence. Don't forget about the missing cop. If Jacob is behind his disappearance, that makes him extremely dangerous."

"If we don't make a move, he could destroy the phones." Adrenaline worked through her, had her alert, on edge. She'd prefer to walk into the home with more knowledge about their suspect, but they couldn't afford to take the time. "The burner phones are the only evidence we have linking him to Cameron."

Knowing those phones had been part of the exchange, and that they were a key component to their investigation was also what allowed them—if need be—to force their way into the house, then carry out a search and seizure without a warrant.

As they neared the front door, the porch light went on, and they both froze. "Motion sensor?" she whispered.

"Maybe." He shifted his gaze to the living room's picture window. "House is still dark."

She drew in a steadying breath, and continued forward. Once at the door, she glanced at him. "Here we go," she said, her stomach tightening with anxiety as she knocked.

When no one answered, she rang the bell. Minutes passed. She didn't want them to have to force open the door and give Nell a heart attack, but at this point, they had no choice. As she turned to signal Kirchner, light footfall came from the other side of the closed door. She tensed. Waited.

"Who's there?" Nell asked.

She nodded to Sloan, who lowered his weapon. Not wanting to scare the older woman, she did the same.

"Nell, it's Sloan from across the street. There's been a break-in at the Wolffs' house, and the police are here. Whitney and I want to make sure you're okay."

The lock clicked, then Nell cracked open the door. Her gaze sharp, wary, she peered at them. "They catch the burglar?" she asked.

Sloan shook his head. "That's why we wanted to stop by your house. Can we come inside?"

"Not necessary. My grandson is here, so I feel safe enough."

"I'm glad to hear that." Anxious to locate Jacob, Whitney flashed the badge dangling from a chain around her neck. "Ma'am, we're looking for your grandson," she said, then pushed her way inside.

"You can't do this," Nell shouted as Kirchner and his unit silently rushed into the house, spreading out and searching rooms. "I know my rights! You need to have a warrant!"

"Ma'am," Whitney began, "this is what we consider exigent circumstances, meaning we not only have probable cause, but reasonable belief that evidence will be destroyed before we're able to secure a warrant. Where is your grandson, Jacob Malinowski?"

Nell backed up and into her living room. "He's a good boy. Leave him alone," the old woman said as she walked backward toward a hutch that stood kitty-corner near the picture window.

Whitney noticed the old woman wore a robe, but beneath it she had on what looked like sweatpants. She also wore a pair of white tennis shoes. Why would an eighty-five-year-old woman be wearing sweatpants and tennis shoes at three in the morning?

Her skin prickling with dread, Whitney aimed her gun at the woman. "Nell, you need to stop where you are and keep your hands out in front of you."

"Don't you tell me what to do in my own house." Nell continued toward the hutch. "And you damned well better believe I'm going to sue you and the county for this. How dare you come into my home and—"

"What are you doing?" Sloan asked as he came into the room

"Nell, stop," Whitney shouted over the sudden commotion floating out from the open basement door.

"We have a body," someone called.

Nell looked toward the basement and blinked several times. The old woman's wrinkly face sagged with defeat. "Time to go," she said, turning her back on them.

"Nell, stop," Whitney repeated, terrified the woman had a gun and would use it on herself, or one of them.

Sloan moved past her, grabbed the woman by the wrist and yanked, forcing her hand from the hutch's center drawer. Holding Nell still, he glanced inside the drawer. "What were you going to do with that .22, Nell? Shoot us or yourself?"

Kirchner entered the foyer and approached the living room. Behind him, deputies escorted two handcuffed young men. Their resemblance was remarkable, and she immediately assumed they were the brothers Sloan had told her about earlier. "Which one is Jacob?" she asked Sloan.

"The one in the gray sweatshirt."

Jacob's gaze was bright with fear as he looked to Nell, who was being handcuffed by another deputy. "Grandma?"

"Hush. Not a word out of either of you. Don't talk until you have a lawyer."

The other young man paled, and his eyes widened with shock. "Mom and Dad are gonna—"

"I said hush!"

"Enough." She turned to the old woman, who glared at her with hatred. "Were you in the car with these two?"

Nell lifted her chin and set her mouth in a grim line.

"We searched the house," Kirchner said. "The only other individual found is dead."

She holstered her weapon. "Hayden Malinowski?" she asked, her gaze on the kid next to Jacob.

"Yes, ma'am," Hayden replied. "We're brothers."

Nell stomped her foot. "Damn it! Shut up!"

Tears filled the kid's eyes, making him look even younger. "Sorry, Grandma. I...I'm scared."

The old woman's eyes softened. "It'll be just fine, dear."

"Hardly. I think Nell is the third suspect who was in the SUV," Whitney said, glancing to the woman's tennis shoes. "I also think she's Rueben Morales. And I'm guessing you two are the ones who delivered the shipments to the Columbus and Cincinnati areas." When the boys looked away, she shifted her gaze to Nell. "Let's get them out of here. We need to make another arrest."

As the old woman was led to the door, she glanced over her shoulder at them. "Don't count on getting any of my homemade fudge this Christmas," she said, glaring at them.

If there hadn't been a body somewhere in the basement, her parting words might almost have been comical. "Don't count on being home for Christmas. Why'd you do it, Nell? Do you know how many people overdosed because of you and your grandsons?"

"Kiss my ass, girlie. I'm not talking."

"Get her out of here," Kirchner ordered.

Andy and a couple of detectives from the Narcotics Unit arrived. Once Whitney had updated them, she had Andy and the detectives go to the Eastons' and arrest Cameron and his siblings.

"I'm glad you did that," Sloan said. "I didn't want to see the look on Dale and Irene's faces when their kids were taken away. Especially, Irene. She's a good lady."

"And it's her birthday." She blew out a breath and looked toward the basement door. "Where's the body?" she asked Kirchner.

"Freezer."

With dread pooling in her belly, she and Sloan made their way into the unfinished basement. The large area was cluttered with boxes and other odds and ends

"Body is in here." The deputy standing by a large chest nodded to it. "Coroner's been notified."

Bracing herself for a grotesque sight, she walked around the deputy, then opened the freezer. Beneath loaves of white bread, she recognized the frozen remains of the missing cop.

Sloan's arm brushed hers as he looked inside. "The cop?"

"I believe so," she said, saddened that the man had been killed, but glad they now had an opportunity to discover what had happened to him. "I don't get why they'd keep him in the freezer."

"Right. Why not bury him in a flowerbed?"

"Exactly."

"Whitney," Kirchner said, "there's something you need to see." She and Sloan walked over to where he stood next to a door. "This is where we found the brothers."

When they stepped into the room, Sloan let out a low whistle. "Well, holy shit."

Stunned and horrified, Whitney took in what could only be a chemistry lab. "Don't touch a thing," she said to the deputies in the room. "Unless you have a Hazmat suit on, everyone needs to get out of here." She looked to Sloan and Kirchner. "That includes us."

The rental house, North Royalhurst, Ohio
Saturday, 8:08 a.m. Daylight Saving Time

Whitney finished toweling off her body, then slipped into a pair of panties. After she brushed her teeth, she made her way into the bedroom. Sloan, who was also freshly showered and also only wearing underwear, stood by the window, peeking through the closed blinds.

"What a mess," he said with a tired sigh.

Crime scene investigators had spent hours processing both homes. They'd just finished with the Eastons when another shift of detectives and deputies had arrived, giving her and Sloan an opportunity to catch a few hours of sleep. Unfortunately, Nell's house would take much longer. Between the body in the freezer and the chemistry lab, investigators would have to sift through an overwhelming amount of evidence and likely work there throughout the day.

She went over to him and looked out of the window. Cruisers belonging to the sheriff's office and the North Royalhurst PD were still parked on the street, along with the BCI's and Cuyahoga County Sheriff's Crime Scene Units. Yellow police tape blocked off both houses. Deputies and police officers patrolled the area, ensuring nosy neighbors wouldn't disturb the crime scenes. On their way back to the rental house, she'd noticed media vans had parked on the streets surrounding Shady Circle, although fortunately, reporters hadn't been allowed on the cul-de-sac.

"There's Vincent walking Fritz," he said. "Joe's sitting in his garage."

She glanced around the circle, just as the two landscapers, Travis and Nolan, drove off together. Becky exited her house with worry lining her pale face. She hugged herself and watched the officers. When her three-year-old came out to join her, Becky quickly scooped Chloe in her arms and rushed back into the house. Whitney hadn't seen the Ukrainians or Quint this morning, but was certain curiosity would have them eventually venturing outdoors.

"I wonder how many of them realize we were part of the drug bust?" She stepped away from the window, then crawled onto the bed. "I don't know why I care, but I do."

"Because you lied about who you are, and lying isn't part of your nature."

"I lie to suspects."

"Using deception during an interrogation isn't the same thing." He got into bed. "I understand how you're feeling. When we went over to the Eastons', and you were with Andy up in Cameron's room, Irene went off on me."

"I'm sorry. That's tough. I didn't hear anything. What did she say?"

"At first, I think she assumed I'd come by to see if they were okay. When she realized I was working with the police, that's when she called me a piece of shit bastard, and wondered how I could live with myself after destroying their lives and their kids' futures." He leaned into the pillows. "I didn't bother responding. She was in hysterics, and rightfully so. It's not every day you find out all of your kids are drug dealers." He glanced at her. "I'm surprised you didn't go with Campbell and Andy. I figured you'd want to interrogate the suspects."

"Normally, I would, but we've both been up for over twenty-four hours, and I'm too tired to think. Besides, I doubt Campbell or Andy are going to get much from any of the Eastons or Malinowskis until they meet with their attorneys."

"I think you're right. The DA doesn't need confessions anyway. The evidence we've already collected is solid."

There wasn't a chance in Hell that Nell or her grandsons could talk their way out of a conviction. A quick background check of Jacob and Hayden Malinowski showed that both boys were brainy and excelled at chemistry, leading to the belief they manufactured the drugs, while Nell ran the other aspects of the operation.

Aside from the lab equipment, investigators had found two kilos of fentanyl, one kilo of heroin, ten pounds of marijuana and one pound of cocaine. Along with those drugs, they'd also discovered a pill press machine and hundreds of pills. They weren't sure what the pills were and would have to wait on test results, but Whitney suspected they would find fentanyl in them.

Fentanyl was a scary and highly dangerous drug. On average, it cost three to four thousand dollars to produce a kilo of the stuff, same went for heroin. But because fentanyl was much more potent than heroin, less of the drug was needed, meaning a dealer could take one kilo of fentanyl, dilute it, then cut and split it to create sixteen or more kilos. Sold on the streets, that amount of the drug could yield Nell and her grandsons over one million dollars. The pills were an even better moneymaker. A kilo of fentanyl could yield well over six hundred thousand pills, which could then be sold for twenty to thirty dollars each, resulting in a giant profit.

It would take days, maybe weeks to sort through everything that had been collected. When they'd left that crime scene, investigators had just discovered where Nell had hidden her drug money. How much was there, she didn't know, and probably wouldn't until later today or tomorrow.

"Except for figuring out which one of the Malinowskis was responsible for killing the cop, I don't think I've worked an investigation with so much evidence pointing directly at the suspects." She lay on her side and rested her head on the pillow next to his. "I don't want to talk about the Malinowskis or Eastons. I'm running out of energy and don't want to waste it on them."

"What time do you have to leave?" he asked, running his palm over her hip.

"I don't. CSI will probably be there late. I'll need to write my report, but I can do that from here."

"And the house? When are we being evicted?"

She half-grinned. "I told Campbell I'll shut it down by Tuesday. I have to arrange for the moving truck and pack up the equipment."

"I need to take the patio and porch furniture to your place before I have to give up the truck. I'm going to miss that truck." Sadness filled his eyes. "I'm going to miss being here with you."

Her throat tightened. "Me, too. This is so bittersweet. We finally put an end to the investigation, and were able to stop millions of dollars' worth of drugs from hitting the street and killing people. I should be thrilled, elated. I mean, this was a huge bust. At the same time, even though I knew the moment would eventually come, I wish we had another week or two."

"We don't need another week or two. We both agreed we

want to make us work." His gaze was probing. "Unless you're having second thoughts."

She scooted closer to him. "Absolutely not."

"Then don't be down. You got the bad guys, you've got me… what more do you need?"

She didn't know. Yes, she was proud of the work they'd done for this investigation and how it had ended. She was also pleased that Sloan was willing to try a long-distance relationship, but she didn't want miles separating them. Not after living together for two weeks.

"I think I just need some sleep," she said, rolling over to curl up on her other side.

He shifted their bodies until he spooned her. "Why do I feel like you're keeping something from me?"

Tears filled her eyes. "I'm not." She loved him, but was afraid to say the words out loud. What if he left for Chicago with the intention of coming back, but then changed his mind? Or, what if he moved here and later decided she wasn't what he wanted in his life? She hated this love thing. Hated how it made her happy, sad and worried all at the same time.

His beard tickled her shoulder just before he kissed the spot. "I have been."

"Keeping something from me? Do you have an ant farm?" she asked, stalling. She wasn't sure she wanted to know. With her luck, he'd confess to having a wife and five kids waiting for him in Chicago.

"That's nasty." He chuckled and kissed her shoulder again. "And not even close to what I was going to tell you. Can you roll over? I don't want to talk to the back of your head."

When she did, concern lit his gaze and he caressed her cheek. "Why are you crying?"

"I'm not. I'm just…I can't lie to you. I'm worried this is it for us."

"I told you—"

"I know you intend to do your part to make our relationship last, but what we've been doing these past two weeks was easy. It was easy to fall into a routine and to become familiar with each other. We didn't have to work at it because we were put in a situation that forced us to be around each other. Now that we'll be living apart, it's going to take a lot of effort to maintain a long-distance relationship."

"You're right." His eyes flashed with irritation. "We should get a fake divorce now and go our separate ways. That would be the easy thing to do." He shifted his big body over hers, rested his forearms on the mattress and brushed his fingers along her cheek. "Except, I'm a hard worker, especially when it comes to something I love. And I love the way we are together. More importantly, I love you."

Fresh tears filled her eyes. "I love you, too. But is that enough?" she asked, so incredibly overjoyed that he'd said the words she'd needed to hear, and terrified at the same time. Could love be all that it took to keep them together?

His gaze softened, became tender and understanding. "I have been on my own for twenty years. Until I met you, I thought I knew what it was to love someone, but I was wrong. Before we both let down our guard, there were days when I was so twisted up inside, my stomach was sick. You did that to me."

Oh my God. What? "I made you sick?"

He grinned. "Not like you think. Whitney, I was falling for you, and I didn't know what to do or how to feel, especially because you didn't seem to like me. I kept comparing what I was feeling for you, to what I'd felt for the other women I thought I loved. And I realized you were different. I don't need to know you for a set amount of time to justify my feelings. I don't need you to take up space during the holidays or the weekends when I'm not working. I need you because you make me happy. I look forward to the mornings because I know you'll be there."

She gripped his biceps. "But I won't, not while we're apart."

"Then let's make it so we're not apart for long. I'm all in on this. I want what you want."

"Are you…talking about my life goals?"

"The house in the burbs, marriage, kids…the kid part scares me, but I've already pictured you leaving me sticky notes to remind me how to handle things."

She didn't just love this man, she was madly, hopelessly *in* love with him. "You have? I didn't think you liked my sticky notes."

He glanced away for a few seconds, before meeting her gaze again. "The little notes you leave me, the desserts you bring home...those things let me know you're thinking about me." He looked away again. "I don't know how this'll sound, but we're supposed to be honest with each other and—"

Anxious for him to spill it, say everything on his mind, she gripped his jaw. "Say it."

"You make me feel special and...important to you. And I hope that I've made you feel the same way. If I haven't, then I—"

She kissed him. "You have and you do. You *are* special to me. You're a good man, and I don't want to lose you."

He kissed her, hard, possessive. "Then don't give up on us because it might not always be easy. You're a good fighter, fight for us to stay together."

Needing to be with him, to have that ultimate physical and emotional connection, she ran her hand over his rear and slid down his boxers. "I will," she said, loving holding him and being held.

Loving Sloan.

She would fight for them. Kick him in the butt when he let his defenses go up, and give him a reason to remember that it was okay to be vulnerable sometimes, to let his guard down and realize that he meant something to her.

After he quickly put on a condom, he entered her. Filled her. Completed *them*. There was no need for foreplay right now. She needed him inside her, loving her body, making that connection that was even more intimate now than any other time they'd been together.

As he rocked his hips and her heart, she clung to his broad back. Relished the moment and cherished him. *He* was her ideal partner, and she didn't need a list to know that. He'd showed her that life wasn't as organized as she'd like, that living by bullet points wasn't always necessary, and that love was scary, yet, with the right person, a beautiful thing.

When her orgasm hit, she held him tightly. "I don't ever want to lose you," she said against his lips.

As he pumped into her, he met her gaze. "You won't." The love and passion in his eyes triggered her climax. Her body and mind let go, and she went to a happy place...saw them together, a baby on Sloan's lap, a dark-haired toddler grinning and running toward them. *Yes.* She'd fight for that, for the future they could have.

While she was still in her happy place, and a second orgasm hit her, he came, too. Peppering her face with kisses as he whispered her name.

"I love you," he said, his voice thick. "That was..." He blew out a breath.

She hugged him. "That was the definition of making love."

He looked at her, satisfied and happy, then smiled. "It most certainly was. Thank you for helping me define that, because until you, I didn't know the definition."

His words warmed her, made her push aside any insecurities about the future. They had a great thing going between them. From here on out, it could only get better.

Chapter Eighteen

Shady Circle, North Royalhurst, Ohio
Saturday, 11:09 a.m. Daylight Saving Time

PANIC GRIPPED MY heart as I drove through Whispering
Pines. News vans were parked along the road, and also on
Willow Lane, the street next to ours. When I turned onto Shady
Circle, my fear escalated. At least six or seven police vehicles were
on our small street, and there were officers standing on the
sidewalks.

Oh God. They know.

A cop held up his hand, stopping me from entering the cul-de-
sac. Trying to keep my composure, I rolled down the window
when he approached. "What's happening?" I asked, darting my
gaze to the yellow police tape at Nell's and the Eastons' houses.

"Do you live here, ma'am?"

I gave the officer my name and pointed to my house. "Right
over there. What's happening?" I repeated.

"I can't give you the details. Please go to your home and stay
inside until we're finished."

Relief washed over me, along with guilt. Something bad had
happened to Nell and the Eastons, yet I was secretly happy the
police weren't here for my husband. Again, he was worth more

dead than alive. And after what he'd done, he deserved to die today. "Are my neighbors okay?" I asked, because I did care. Nell could be...nosy, and I wasn't a fan of the Easton kids, but I did like Irene.

"Just head home, ma'am," the officer said.

Though concerned, I did what the officer requested and pulled into my garage. The wood pile still sat at the apron of the driveway, which irritated the hell out of me. Why I would be angry about that was absurd, considering my real anger was geared toward my husband, and the body he'd buried in our backyard.

"Focus," I said to myself as I parked the van in the garage.

My husband had said he'd be home around noon, and I needed to be ready for him. I left the garage and entered our laundry room, then went straight to the basement. After putting in the digital code to unlock the gun safe, I carefully took out the .38. It trembled in my hands. Guns scared the crap out of me, and were my husband's thing. To spend time with him, I would force myself to go with him to the gun range, so I knew how to shoot and load the weapon. Fortunately, it was already loaded.

I brought the gun upstairs to the kitchen, then set it on the peninsula. What I planned to do was wrong on so many levels. There were cops up and down the street. But if I didn't go through with my plan now, and to avoid having my kids exposed to their mother shooting their father, I'd have to wait until the next time I visited my parents. And how would that look? Not only to my parents, but to the police. They could speculate that I'd planned this, that it was premeditated—which it was—still...

Having a police presence might work in my favor. Who would commit murder when there were a bunch of cops next door?

I should call Helen and find out *why* the police were here, but didn't want to deal with her right now. Besides, being nosy didn't fit into my plan. But if I didn't call her, it would look odd. If I hadn't planned on killing my husband, I would've already been on the phone with her.

Knowing I needed to maintain as much normalcy as possible,

I pulled my phone from my purse and called Helen. "Hey," I said when she answered. "What's going on our street?"

"I thought you and the boys were in Columbus for the weekend."

"I was, but I wanted to surprise my husband with a date night," I replied, since it was the truth, and would still work with my plan. "Are Nell and the Eastons okay?"

"They've all been arrested," Helen said, her tone conspiratorial.

Oh my God. "Arrested for what? Nell's eighty-something. What could she have done wrong?"

"Not sure. But her two grandsons were also taken into custody Irene and Dale weren't, just their kids." I never liked those kids, but I liked Irene and couldn't imagine what she must be going through. If I hadn't planned on killing my husband, I'd have made a casserole to take over to her and Dale. "Jacob and Hayden were arrested?" They were young, late teens or early twenties. I couldn't remember, but they were sweet kids, and were always over helping Nell, especially Jacob.

"Can you believe it?" Helen asked. "Vincent and I keep trying to fathom a reason why, and come up empty. We've had the television on all morning, hoping to get something from the news people, but I think we know more than they do."

"So strange," I said, and meant it. Nell's biggest crime was being nosy. As for the Easton kids, other than a few loud parties, Blair's shouting hysterics and Cameron's driving and pot smoking, I also couldn't come up with a reason why they would *all* be arrested the same night—Nell's family included.

"Extremely. And it gets stranger. You're not going to believe this, but Vincent saw Whitney and Sloan North leaving Nell's, then going to Dale and Irene's."

I leaned against the peninsula. "They were probably concerned."

Helen huffed. "Why would the cops allow them to go into the two houses? They moved in a couple weeks ago. They're not *original* homeowners like us."

"What does Vincent think?"

"That they were working undercover."

"Undercover?" I rolled my eyes, then inspected the floor, where Sebastian's blood had been last night and couldn't find any. Not even on the small rug beneath the sink. "That's a little far-fetched, don't you think?" I didn't care if the Dark Knight and Snow Queen were cops, but I would be disappointed. I loved seeing the two of them together. They made a striking couple and having watched them, I was convinced they were madly in love.

Tears blurred my vision. I wanted what they had. I wanted a man who loved me and put me before all others. Unfortunately, I'd never have that happiness. After what my husband had done to me, to our family, the deception, the utter betrayal, I don't know if I would ever be able to trust another man again.

"Why else would the police allow them in the houses?" Helen asked. "And think about this: Sloan was always home. What if he was watching the Eastons and Nell?"

What if he'd been watching our house? No. If my husband was responsible for the rising body count at Otter's Field, and the police suspected him, Sebastian wouldn't be buried in our back-yard. Plus, the first body was discovered days after the Norths had moved to Shady Circle.

"I don't know, Helen, it all sounds like something you'd see on a TV show."

"I suppose it does." Helen sighed. "I wonder what this will do to our property values."

I didn't want to think about property values, the arrests or whether my neighbors were undercover cops. My husband would be home soon, and I wanted to mentally replay the plan I'd devised last night.

"I'm sure it'll be fine," I said, going into the living room to look out of the front window. Joe sat by his garage, watching the police. Helen also stood by her living room window, the phone to her ear. "Where's Vincent now?"

"Walking Fritz. If that dog doesn't get enough exercise, he digs up the flowerbeds. He's already decimated this year's tulips. The little stinker has been mining for bulbs since the weather broke."

I forced a chuckle. "He's a funny dog."

"Hey, are you doing okay? You sound…down."

"I'm fine. I already had a lot on my mind before I came home to police tape."

"Oh? Anything you want to talk about?"

"No, it's something I need to deal with on my own," I replied, and realized the call to Helen had been a brilliant idea. After the murder, when my neighbor had the chance to gossip about it, she could tell people that she'd spoken to me, and that she had suspected all was not well in my world. Which it wasn't, but would be soon.

"Well, if you ever need to talk, I'm around to listen."

"Thanks, Helen. You're a good neighbor and friend."

We talked for another minute, before I told her I needed to go. After I set the phone on the peninsula, I stared at the .38. Tension worked up my spine, as I glanced from the gun to the picture of the kids and me near it. What right did I have to take their father from them? None. Even if I let my husband live, he wouldn't be much of a father to them from prison. And if he were given the death penalty, our children would have to deal with living through that, not to mention a long trial before it, and the humiliation of having a killer for a dad. They would always have to cope with what their father had done, but if he were dead, at least they wouldn't have to ever face him again, and I wouldn't have to worry about how I would support them.

I looked to the clock on the stove. My stomach balled with apprehension when I realized the time. He would be home any minute. As I stood in the kitchen, I looked around my house, to the family photos hanging on the family room walls, to the toys in the box near the corner of the room, to the kitchen table where we'd shared so many meals and memories. My gaze drifted to the cluttered white refrigerator. Magnets held up drawings the kids had made, pictures, and my husband's work schedule.

Although it could use updating, I loved my house, and I resented, hated, my husband for taking this life from the kids and me. A tear slipped down my cheek. I swiped it away and told myself he wasn't worth the tears. But losing my husband and the life we'd created together saddened me. I still loved the man he'd once been. It was the monster he'd become that I hated.

I carefully slid the .38 near the planter and picture sitting at the corner of the peninsula. Releasing a shaky breath, I wondered if the gun was a mistake. He could easily overpower me. He could easily kill me, then turn around and tell the police *he'd* done it out of self-defense. I couldn't let that happen, or allow a killer to raise my boys, let alone go unpunished for his actions.

No, if anyone was going to get away with murder, it would be me.

He turned onto Shady Circle and waved to the officer he'd seen this morning before he and his partner had left. "I can't believe these guys are still here," he said, happy they weren't there for him. When he'd woken up this morning and seen the officers and police vehicles, he'd freaked the fuck out until he'd noticed which houses had been strung with crime scene tape.

"No shit. I'd like to know *why*. I'm hoping my wife learned something while we were gone."

They'd been too busy finishing a job to have time to bullshit or speculate about why the police were on their street. The only thing he knew for certain was that Knot Head hadn't been lying after all, and Whitney and Sloan were actually working with the police. Before his business partner had come over this morning, he'd seen the two of them leaving Nell's house, and had caught sight of the badge dangling around Whitney's neck.

He wasn't sure how he felt about having had undercover officers living across the street from him, especially since he actually liked Sloan. He supposed it didn't matter. The two would move out of the house, and someone else would eventually buy it. He glanced to the yellow tape. Hell, depending on what had happened at Nell's and the Eastons', two other homes could be going up for sale.

Regardless, he looked at whatever had happened as a sign. He'd managed to fly under the radar for over ten years and had gotten away with killing over two dozen men during that time. Seeing the police on his street this morning had scared him straight. Had made him realize that if he didn't keep his promise to himself and stop killing, his luck might run out one day and his house could end up having the yellow police tape.

He pulled into the driveway. "If you find out anything, let me know."

"Will do. Hey, do you want me to help you move the rest of that wood?"

Normally, he'd welcome the help. But he didn't like the idea of having his best friend helping him cover up his crime. "That's okay. There isn't much there. Go home to your family. I'm sure your kids are upset about the cops being here."

"Are you kidding me? They think it's cool. When your boys come home and hear about it, they're going to be upset they missed the excitement."

"You're probably right," he said, using the remote to open the garage door. "I know I could do without this kind of excitement."

"I guess they didn't miss out after all."

Alarmed, he stared at the back end of his wife's minivan and killed the engine. "They weren't supposed to be home until tomorrow."

"I hope everything is okay," his partner said as he climbed out of the truck.

"I'm sure it's all good." With the intention of grabbing the mail, he walked with him to the sidewalk. "I haven't checked my phone since we left this morning. I probably missed her call." He waved to Vincent, who was across the street with Fritz.

"Mail hasn't come yet," Vincent called.

"I bet Vincent knows something," his partner said. "I'm going to head over and talk to him. I'll catch up with you later."

Anxious to find out why his wife and kids had come home a day early, he hurried toward the garage, entering the house through the laundry room. When he didn't trip over the boys' tennis shoes, he grinned. If he was right, his sexy, sneaky wife had left the kids with her folks so they could have a kid-free night.

Looking forward to whatever she had planned, he took off his dirty boots, then left the laundry room.

"Honey?" he called as he made his way to the kitchen. His wife stood by the patio door, hugging herself and looking out at the backyard. "Hey, what are you doing home? Is everything okay?"

She shook her head and faced him. Her red-rimmed, puffy eyes, the tears soaking her cheeks, had him rushing to her.

"What happened? The kids—"

"Are fine. My parents are, too."

"Then why are you crying? Why are you home?"

"I wanted to surprise you and spend the weekend away from the kids."

Just as he'd hoped, but it'd be tough to have any fun with her if she was upset about something. "What are these for?" he asked, and brushed his thumb along her cheek.

Her head jerked back. "Don't touch me," she said, staring at him with hatred, as if he repulsed her.

She knows. Impossible. The cops, Knot Head and Sebastian's decomposing bodies had him paranoid. There was no way she could...

I wanted to surprise you and spend the weekend away from the kids... The *weekend*, not Saturday, but the *entire* weekend.

His knees weakened and his head grew light. He told himself not to panic, that he could be wrong. "Why can't I touch you?"

She glanced to his hands, which were still dirty from work. "You disgust me. For years I let you make me feel like shit about myself. I let you decide who my friends were, when I went out, what I could buy. Instead of appreciating me for *obeying*, for being the good little wife, you talked down to me, called me a doormat, made me feel as if I were nothing but a maid and a roommate you occasionally liked to fuck."

"Jesus, hon, I—"

"Don't Jesus me! It's true and you know it." She fisted her hands. "You were a bastard, and now I know why."

Dread worked through him. "Yeah, why's that?" he asked,

terrified of the answer, and how it would forever change their lives.

"You've been living a lie, deceiving me, and because I don't have a certain body part you resent me."

She thought he was gay. His hand trembled as he wiped it down his face. Instead of outrage, disappointment ripped him in two. She and the kids were all he had. There was no one else who cared or loved him but them. And he'd ruined everything. Because he couldn't curb the itch to hunt, the demons and nightmares, he had taken a good thing and had destroyed it.

"Body part?" He pushed off the peninsula and took a step toward her. "I don't know what you're talking about."

"*A penis.* Don't insult me. You know what I'm talking about. You're a homosexual pretending to live the life of a heterosexual. *I saw you.*" She narrowed her eyes. "I followed you to Crush and saw you leave with a man." Tears soaked her face, reddened her nose. "Why the disguise? Were you afraid you'd run into someone you know?"

"Honey, I'm not sure what's going on with you, but I did *not* go to a bar called Crush. I went to Foxy's."

"I was there," she cried. "Parked across the street. You stood on the sidewalk, the phone to your ear and talked to me. You disguised yourself with a bald cap and black beard. So, stop lying and admit the truth. Admit you're gay. You owe me the truth, admit it!"

His vision momentarily blackened. That familiar buzz of swarming flies whispered through his head, along with his mother and father's accusations. He quickly tamped them down before the anger became so great he wouldn't be able to control it. She was his wife, the mother of his children. Killing her was not an option, especially when there were over a dozen cops outside his front door.

Sweat coated his skin. His body trembled and he tried desperately to maintain his sanity. "I am not gay," he began, and hated how his voice shook, and the helplessness and vulnerability making his stomach sick. "I have never been with a man, and I have no desire to be with one. I love *you.*"

She released a mocking laugh and shook her head. "God, you're pathetic. I know what I saw. I want to know how many there've been and if you used protection. Should I be worried about my health?"

He gripped her by the upper arms. "I've never had sex with a man. *Ever*," he said with vehemence.

Fear widened her eyes. "Let go! You're hurting me."

He quickly released her and raised his hands. "I'm sorry, I didn't mean to hurt you. You *have* to believe me. I don't know who you saw last night, but it wasn't me." Turning away, he stepped closer to the family room and stared at the fireplace. He hadn't had time to check the ashes this morning, and now wondered if any of the evidence he'd burned there was still left.

"Then that wasn't you standing in my kitchen with a man named Sebastian?"

He froze. Claustrophobia wrapped around him and squeezed the air from his lungs. Lightheaded, he staggered to the wall, pressed his forehead against it and welcomed the shame. For years, he'd been cocky, so sure of himself that no one would ever know or catch him. And the one person in the world who had always been there, who deserved his undying love and respect, knew the truth. For the first time in years, he wept. The last time he'd cried, he had been at Camp Hope, where the 'counselors' had tortured him, tried to drive the Devil from his body. Instead, the so-called counselors and Preacher Daddy had unknowingly implanted demons inside him, demons he couldn't control. Now those demons, his father, his past, would destroy his marriage and future.

"Why?" he whispered. "Why can't I find peace in my life?"

"What are you saying?" she asked on a sob.

He turned to her, leaned against the wall to keep from falling. "I...I didn't mean for it to happen. Any of them." When her face crumpled with misery and fresh tears filled her eyes, his heart broke, and unleashed hatred. For himself, his parents, the counselors and Jim. "I'll never forgive any of them for what they did to me."

"Who? Your dad?"

Confused, he nodded. "How did you know?"

"I heard what you said to Sebastian." She straightened and wiped her nose with her sleeve. "Right before you beat him."

When the swarm of flies came, he always lost a grip on reality and never knew what he'd said or done, just the end result. "What did I say? I always black out during those moments and have no idea."

She stared at him as if he were the headliner of a circus freak show, yet there was pity in her gaze. "Is the cause of those black-outs anger?"

"Yes," he said, and a small sliver of hope pierced his broken heart. Maybe if he'd talked to her from the very beginning, even before ever meeting Jim, he could have cleansed the demons from him and had a shot at happiness. Was there a chance of that now? If he explained everything to her, was it possible she could forgive him?

"You ranted about your father, about him being the homosexual, and said something about *those weren't mine but yours.*" She hugged herself again. "What did he do to you?"

"He…" He'd never told anyone what had happened, not even the other boys at Camp Hope. Worried his legs would give out this time, he slid down the wall and sat on the tile. "My mom found a box containing gay porn, videos, magazine and dildos. She immediately accused me, and my dad joined her. They weren't mine. I'd never seen them in my life. When I denied it…" He looked away as the memories filled his head. "They spent the next few months trying to beat an admission from me. If I wasn't getting the belt, I was being starved or forced to spend weekends in a closet with nothing but the Bible and a coffee can to use as a toilet."

"Oh my God."

"God…He didn't bother to help me then, or any time after. And if my father was preaching on God's behalf, then I wanted nothing to do with Him." He pushed a hand through his hair. "One night, they buried me." He glanced at her, at the shock and horror in her eyes. "My dad dug a grave, put me in it, put dirt all around every part of me except my face. They kept me there for two days, prayed over me, begged God to release me of my sins and *compel* me to admit that the Devil was inside of me, forcing me to have homosexual thoughts. I was *sixteen* and completely straight. Maybe I should've lied and admitted to being something I wasn't, but I couldn't. So I suffered."

She slowly crossed the room. As she did, he noticed the .38 between the planter and the picture frame which held a photo of his wife and kids. His wife, the woman he'd taken for granted, had considered a mousy doormat, was stronger than he'd ever thought. Suspecting she'd planned to take his life made him miserable and proud. Miserable because she'd come to hate him enough to kill him, but proud that she would do whatever it took to protect herself and their children.

"What else did they do to you?" she asked.

"After months of abuse, my father came to my room and told me they were sending me away for the summer. Camp Hope was the place. At first, I was excited. I couldn't wait to get the fuck away from them, but once I was there, I realized I'd traded one Hell for another."

She moved closer, kneeled on the floor and sat her rear on her heels. "What was Camp Hope?" she asked, swiping tears from her face.

"Code for conversion therapy. It was one of those 'pray away the gay' places."

"Pray away..." She covered her mouth and kept her teary gaze on him. "Did they hurt you?"

He nodded, and tried to block the memories but couldn't. "They would tie down my hands, cover them with ice and show me pictures of men. Those were the easy sessions. The other ones...instead of ice, it was copper heating coils or needles in my fingers. The worst was the electric shocks. During all those sessions they made me watch gay porn." He shook his head. "I was a virgin who liked girls. My parents had been so strict. I'd never even seen heterosexual porn. I was a good kid. I always did my chores, never used drugs or drank alcohol. I couldn't understand why they would do this to me."

He rested his head against the wall, fought the painful memories. "It was so fucked up. The torture was bad, listening to my campmates crying themselves to sleep was even worse. But the thing I hated the most was when my father came to the camp to pray with us. *Lord Jesus Christ*," he began, deepening his voice to mimic his father's, "*give me the strength to fight Satan and expel the foul spirit of homosexuality from my body. Satan has deceived me. Lord God, help me repent, forgive me for my sins and wickedness. Cast Satan and homosexuality from me.*"

Her sympathetic gaze held no judgment, and once again had him regretting not telling her any of this. "How did you convince them you weren't gay?" she asked, using her shoulder to wipe her tears.

"I started dating you." When she looked away, he quickly added, "I'll be honest, I dated you to convince them I was straight, but my feelings for you were real. I loved you then, and I love you now. The way I treated you during the years in between, I still loved you, but I was ashamed of myself for the things I was doing. Looking back, you, the kids…you're the only bright points I've had in my life. And I'm so sorry for what I've done to you."

"Did you…" She covered her eyes and dragged in a deep breath. When she looked at him again, he hated himself. Hated the pain he was causing her. "Is Sebastian the only one?"

"No."

"How many have there been?"

"With the exception of my first two kills, I saved the wallets and counted them last night before I buried them with Sebastian. Including Sebastian's, there are twenty-four in his grave. Twenty-three wallets belong to the men they're finding in Otter's Field. But I also killed two young guys last week. One was an accident, the other…I was worried he'd go to the police. He's buried behind the shed. His brother is beneath the pond I just made for the Milsons. When this is over, tell Sloan North he's welcome."

"What?"

"Never mind. It's not important."

She drew her knees to her chest, then rested her head on them and sobbed. He wanted to hold her, ask her what he could do to make this right, but knew it was over. He'd destroyed the trust between them, the love, the years of marriage. And that small sliver of hope he'd clung to earlier faded into nothingness.

After using her shirt to clean her face, she scooted closer to him, then shocked him by taking his hand. Her teary gaze held anguish and love, and it made his own eyes fill with tears. "You've taken twenty-eight lives," she said, her voice strained, raw. "Yet you kiss our kids every night, have been a good dad and husband. Why did you do it?"

"I don't know. The first time was an accident. His name was Jim Montgomery, and he'd gone to Camp Hope. He lived here, recognized me and I got scared. I didn't want anyone to know about the camp, about what my parents had done, or to believe I was something I wasn't. But after I killed him, the nightmares went away for a few months. Then they got worse. Violent, so I thought that maybe if I did it again, they'd go away." He tightened his hold on her hands. "They didn't, they became worse, and so did I. I liked changing my appearance, hunting my next victim, then feeling the rush it gave me."

"Rush?" Her gaze was probing, confused. "I don't understand."

"It allowed me to kill my father over and over. I buried those men alive, just like my father tried to bury me and his secrets."

She kissed one of his filthy hands, then rested her cheek against it. "The box of porn was your father's."

"He confessed that to me just before he died. My mother passed away without knowing she was married to a gay man."

When she hugged him, he clung to her, cried with her, and regretted waiting so long to have this conversation. Finally admitting what had happened to him as a teen had been cleansing. And if he'd done this years ago, the killing therapy might've never happened. He'd never know, and couldn't take back any of what he'd done, justify it or make it right.

As he held her, he glanced to the gun on the peninsula again. He might not be able to right his wrongs, but he could make it so his family wouldn't have to suffer for his sins. "Were you going to kill me?" he asked.

She stiffened, leaned back and met his gaze, guilt clear in her eyes. "Yes."

"I don't blame you. I'm sorry you had to see what I did to Sebastian. He didn't deserve to die. What are you going to do now that you know the truth? The police are right outside. You can go to them and tell them what I did. You can even show them where I buried the bodies in our yard and help them identify the men in Otter's Field." He touched her cheek. "Or you can pretend none of this ever happened."

"I can't pretend that away. I'm sorry for what your parents did to you, but that's no excuse for what you've done."

He'd been so wrong about her. She wasn't a doormat. She was a strong woman who didn't need to be burdened by his atrocities. "Then that leaves only one option: I need you to kill me."

I sat back on my heels and stared at my husband. The pain that had been ripping through me intensified and made my stomach sick. My throat tightened and I tasted bile. I quickly stood and rushed to the half bath, knelt and released what little contents my stomach contained.

As I vomited, my husband pulled my hair from my face and rubbed my back—as he had when I'd dealt with morning sickness during my pregnancies with all three of our boys. I dry heaved as those memories returned and mingled with the ones my husband had just shared. How could a parent treat their child the way they had treated him? How could his *Preacher Daddy* have allowed his own son to take the blame for his sexual preferences? I'd never liked the man or my mother-in-law, but now I hated them, and hoped they rotted in Hell for what they'd done to their son. They'd taken a good kid and had fucked him up to the point he'd needed to kill to rid himself of the abuse he'd suffered.

I couldn't excuse the murders, couldn't justify them. But knowing my husband, I understood that his pride, and how his psychotic upbringing had gotten in the way of rational judgment.

He'd killed twenty-eight men, and two were buried in our backyard.

Tears fell into the toilet as I retched again. I'd planned on ending his life today, planned on making him so angry that he would attack me and give me a reason to protect myself. Instead, he *wanted* me to kill him. *Needed* me to do it. And now I didn't know if I could. Not this way. Not after what he'd told me. He'd suffered greatly as a teen, and that suffering had bled into adulthood. Was it his fault he'd turned to murder? I didn't know, wasn't sure what to do.

My stomach calmer, I unrolled a handful of toilet paper and used it to wipe my mouth. "I...I'm okay now." I flushed the toilet paper and shrugged him off me. "Please, don't."

"Don't what? Touch you?"

I nodded, stared at the contents swirling in the toilet bowl, and swore I saw my life, the goodness inside of me, swirling down the drain. I stood. Our half-bath was small, and he was so big that the space became even smaller. Not claustrophobic, but intimate. I wanted that last bit of intimacy, even if it was wrong. Because deep down, I loved this man. Through the good and bad years, he'd given me three beautiful children and memories I would always cherish. Today, he'd shared his own memories, of his teen years, of what he'd done to those men. I'd wanted to know, and yet I hadn't. And now that I knew the truth, I didn't know what to do with it.

I could turn him over to the police, then deal with dragging my kids and myself through a painful trial. Not an option. I could pretend my husband wasn't a serial killer. Try to go on as if I didn't know he'd murdered twenty-eight men, but I saw a life filled with paranoia. How could I ever leave him alone again? How could I trust that he wouldn't have the urge to punish his father? And, yet, how could I kill him knowing the truth of it all? I'd had a murder plan. With anger as my friend, I'd been ready to go through with it. The anger was still there, but the sadness overpowered it. Anyone watching us might say that he was manipulating me, that he was some sort of sociopath, but I knew better. I *knew* my husband. No, I hadn't known about what he'd done until last night, but I knew when he was being honest and sincere. And he sincerely wanted me to kill him.

"I did plan to kill you," I said, moving around him to rinse out my mouth. "When I saw what you did to Sebastian in our kitchen, then how you buried him, I was so terrified and confused." I started crying again. "I didn't know what to do. I knew I couldn't save him, which was horrible, then I kept thinking that I couldn't let you do it again. After that, I worried how the kids would have to deal with their father going to prison, maybe getting the death penalty, how I'd be able to afford living here and..." A sob wracked my body and I hit him in the chest. "How could you do this to us?"

He pulled me close, held me in his strong arms and I desperately wished I'd never come home to surprise him. I wanted to keep my head in the sand and continue on, keep my family together. When I inhaled the scent of dirt along his shirt, it reminded me that Sebastian was buried in our yard and I shoved him. "I can't do this."

I rushed from the bathroom and into the kitchen. I wasn't a big drinker. Right now, I wanted a shot or two of anything. I needed to numb the pain, my mind.

"I'm sorry," he said as he followed me.

"*Sorry?*" I turned on him and hit him again. "You ruined everything that was good between us. Everything! And now you want me to kill you?"

"You planned to anyway, so what's the difference?"

"What's the difference? The difference is I planned to do it in a way where you came at me."

He raised a brow. "Self-defense. Good choice. How were you going to make sure I'd come after you? I've never once raised a hand to you, or even considered it."

"Then do it now." I smacked him across the face. "Hit me, make me want to kill you."

He swung so fast, I didn't have the chance to block the blow. Blood burst from my nose and immediately oozed to my lips. Stunned, I staggered back until I hit the peninsula. I swiped at my nose, looked at the blood on my hand, then to him.

The sorrow and apology in his eyes broke me. "Are you trying to give me a reason to kill you?"

"I'll give you three."

Our boys.

"Last week," he continued, "I killed a kid. He was about eighteen or so, I can't be sure. Anyway, I didn't intend for him to die. He was watching the neighbor's house and I thought he was up to no good, so I confronted him—he's the one under the Milsons' pond, by the way—when I questioned him, patted him down to make sure he wasn't armed, he started calling me a faggot."

"And you snapped."

He nodded. "What if, when the kids are a little older, and we argue, one of them throws out a term like that to me?"

Oh God. I hadn't thought about that. "But…we're talking about our sons."

"Doesn't matter. I'm fucked in the head." When he laughed, it sounded maniacal, brittle. "What's funny is I thought I could be a happy serial killer. Continue living in the burbs, running my business, making love to my wife and playing at being a good dad. But let's face it, that's not going to happen."

The menacing look on his face didn't match the fear, anxiety and apology in his eyes, and I knew what he was doing. He wanted me to end his life, and was giving me many reasons to do it. But I wasn't like him. I couldn't take a life, then go about my business as if it hadn't happened.

"I'm telling the police," I said, and pushed past him.

He gripped me by the arms, then threw me across the kitchen. My elbows and tailbone took the brunt of the fall as I hit the tile floor.

"No police," he said, walking toward me.

I scooted away, hit my head against the kitchen table and ignored the pain. "I can't kill you!"

"No? Do you plan on sleeping by my side knowing how many lives I've taken? Won't you always wonder if I've done it again? Let's not forget about our boys. Remember, all of my victims have been male."

"You wouldn't hurt them," I said on a sob, and pushed myself off the tile. "They're your sons."

"And look what my father, my almighty *Preacher Daddy* did to his only son." Without warning, he backhanded me, sending me spinning until I righted myself against the peninsula. "What if one of our sons ends up gay?"

I rubbed my aching jaw. "Stop it. That's not the issue. You didn't kill those men because they were homosexual, you killed them because they represented your father."

"Did I? Maybe I liked it. The disguises, the hunt, the chase… watching them swallow a mouthful of dirt."

He rushed toward me, then backhanded me again. My mouth filled with the metallic taste of blood and I gripped the peninsula to keep from falling.

"I burned the disguise I wore last night, but if you go to my side of our closet you'll find others hidden there." He smiled, but it didn't reach his eyes. "I want to be good, but I don't know how."

He came at me again. Before he could make contact, I reached around, grabbed the .38 and aimed it at him. "Is this what you want?" I shouted, the gun shaking in my hands.

"No. But it's the only way. Now you have the bloody face to cry self-defense. Both of our fingerprints are on the gun. You tell the cops that I was the one with the gun, that I got it after you confronted me about seeing me at the gay bar, then tell the truth from there. Tell them what I confessed. I know it'll be bad for the kids, but you're a good mother, you'll help them through the after-math." He looked away for a moment, tears soaking his face. When he faced me again, I saw the seventeen-year-old boy I'd met and fallen in love with, and let my own tears fall. "Can you please, somehow, make sure they know that I loved them? And that I'm sorry. I'm so sorry."

Sobbing, the gun heavy in my hands, I shook my head. "I can't do this."

"What other alternative is there? Please. Do us all a favor and kill me."

Chapter Nineteen

The rental house, North Royalhurst, Ohio
Saturday, 12:22 p.m. Daylight Saving Time

SLOAN JERKED UPRIGHT.

"That sounded like a gunshot," Whitney said, sliding out of bed.

Agreeing, he went to the window and moved the blinds slightly. Officers were rushing from their positions on the cul-de-sac, others were exiting Nell's house.

"Anything?" she asked.

"I'm not sure what's going on, but the deputies and detectives are running over to the Murphys'." He stepped away and searched for his underwear. "They have their weapons drawn."

Whitney's brow furrowed. "Oh my God," she said as her phone rang. "Campbell, what's happening?"

While he dressed, Sloan looked out of the window again. A deputy hurried from the house and toward a cruiser, motioning for the neighbors who'd ventured out to go back inside.

"Oh my God," she repeated, adding, "they have three kids. Are they okay?"

He fastened his jeans and he faced her, just as she told the lieutenant they'd be right there. "Who's been shot?" he asked, dreading the answer. First the two drug busts, and now a shooting? What was with this street and his fucked-up neighbors?

"Travis Murphy," she said, shock in her tone and sadness in her eyes. "His wife, Amy, did it. Campbell doesn't think the kids are there."

Well, there was a small miracle. Once he and Whitney finished dressing, they rushed across the cul-de-sac. When they reached the driveway, they stepped around the pile of wood at the apron and made their way to the porch. A deputy stood just outside the opened door.

"Detective," he greeted Whitney. "The lieutenant is in the living room."

Sloan followed her into the house, and into the living room. Campbell and Dan, the detective he'd met earlier, were at the room's entrance. When they saw Whitney, both approached her.

"Do you know this woman?" Campbell asked.

"I've met her once, waved to her a few times, but that's it." She glanced to Sloan. "Is that about the same for you?"

He nodded. "I was more acquainted with Travis."

"She's claiming self-defense, and the blood and bruises on her face have me wanting to believe her." Campbell looked at him. "She said she would tell us everything, but specifically asked for North to be in the room."

"Me?"

"That's odd," Whitney said. "But let's roll with it."

Confused and curious, he followed them into the living room. A deputy stood next to the picture window, while Amy Murphy sat on a plaid loveseat, rocking her body and wringing her hands.

"Mrs. Murphy," Campbell began, his tone soft, understanding. "Sloan North and Detective Whitney Russell are here."

When she looked up at him, he had the strange urge to hug her and tell her it would be okay. The expression on her swollen, bruised and bloodied face reflected the pain and agony in her teary, bloodshot eyes. "I'm no longer Mrs. Murphy," she said, her voice raw, strained.

"Amy, what happened here?" Whitney asked.

Amy's gaze drifted to the badge Whitney wore. "You're really cops? Helen told me, but I didn't believe it."

"I'm with the Cuyahoga County Sheriff. We were here for Nell and the Easton kids." She sat next to Amy. "We need to get you something for your injuries."

Amy shook her head. "Later." Fresh tears filled her eyes. "I need to do this now. My kids…" She sobbed. "My kids are with my parents in Columbus. How am I going to tell them? Oh, God!" She held her head in her hands and cried.

Whitney glanced up at him and mouthed, "Say something."

"Amy, focus on us, not the kids." Sloan sat on an ottoman near the front window. "Tell us what happened."

She lifted her head. Blood, tears and mucus ran together. The deputy who'd been in the room brought over a box of tissues and set it on the coffee table in front of the loveseat. She released a shaky breath, and plucked a few free. "I was supposed to spend the weekend with my parents. Travis and I, we never get any alone time, so I thought I'd surprise him…leave the boys with my parents, then come home for a kid-free weekend." She winced when she wiped her nose. With the dark circles forming under her eyes, he wondered if Travis had broken it. "When I got back to North Royalhurst yesterday, it was close to nine. Travis said he was going to stay in and watch baseball. I stopped at the minimart across from Mom's Kitchen and bought wine and beer. As I was leaving the parking lot, I saw Travis's truck, then followed him."

As she blotted her eyes with a fresh tissue, she shook her head. "If I hadn't gone, none of this would've happened. I wouldn't know, could've kept living in the dark."

"Know what?" Whitney asked.

"My husband was a murderer."

Hugging herself, she stood and went to the window. Her back to them. Whitney first looked to him, then Campbell and Dan. Everyone in the room stared at Amy in disbelief, him included.

"What did you see?" he asked.

"I…my husband changed over the years. He has…had terrible nightmares. He'd become controlling, sometimes mean, but only to me, never the kids." She glanced over her shoulder.

"He was a good father. I can't take that away from him." Dragging in a breath, she looked out the window again. "I thought the change in him was because of how he felt about me, or because of the medication his doctor prescribed to help him sleep, or his lack of sleep. That wasn't it. What he'd been hiding had altered his personality."

"Why did you follow him?" Campbell asked. "And if your marriage wasn't so great, why come home for the weekend?"

She turned to Campbell. "Because the past week had been wonderful. Travis was acting like he did during our first couple years of marriage, and I wanted to keep the momentum going, you know? When I saw his truck, I don't know, but I had this niggling suspicion that a new woman was in his life, and *that* was why he was suddenly in such a good mood. So, I followed him into Cleveland to a bar called Crush. When he got out of his truck, he was dressed in a disguise. He'd made his head bald and wore a thick, black beard."

Sloan had heard plenty of strange stories over the years, and not a whole lot surprised him, but this one might end up becoming the strangest yet. "You're sure he was Travis?"

Tears ran down her cheeks, and the disappointment and disgust in her eyes gave him his answer. "I called him on his cell, watched his lips move in sync with his words. I'm positive it was him. I'm positive Crush is a gay bar, and I know for a fact he picked up a man that night, because I saw them get in the truck together."

Well, holy shit. He hadn't seen that coming. "What did you do next?"

"I drove around for a while, trying to process what I saw, then got a hotel room."

Campbell pulled out a notepad. "Where?"

"Westchester Inn on Royalhurst Road. I checked out this morning just before eleven."

"Is that when you came home?" Whitney asked.

She nodded. "Last night, I decided I needed to confront him before I brought the kids home. I planned to tell him I wanted a divorce." Her gaze imploring, she stared at Whitney. "He was living a lie and cheating on me. What kind of marriage is that?"

Whitney encouraged her to sit next to her. Once Amy had, Whitney took the other woman's hand. "I understand why you would want to leave him, but how do you know he was a murderer?"

Amy pulled her hand away and covered her mouth. She cried for a moment, then pulled in a deep breath. "When he came home, I told him what I'd seen, and that I knew he was gay. He denied it, but I kept pushing him to tell me the truth. That he needed to admit it to me and himself. I've never ever, in the fifteen years I've known him, seen him so angry. The look in his eyes, on his face…I didn't recognize my own husband. He kept ranting about his Preacher Daddy and saying he wasn't homosexual, that those weren't mine. Then he said something about how his dad had made him bury those men, yelled about it being his fault he had to keep burying the secret over and over. I kept screaming for him to stop and look at me, instead, that was when he hit me the first time. I hit him back, hoping to snap him back to reality."

"Did it?" Whitey asked.

Her eyes took on a faraway look, as if she were reliving what had happened. "He was out of breath and staring at me as if seeing me for the first time. I was so scared." A tear slipped down her cheek. "I didn't know what he'd meant by *those men*. But I *needed* to know." She fisted her hands. "I made the mistake of asking him about it, and about Preacher Daddy and being homosexual. What he told me was cruel and heartbreaking," she said, then explained that Travis's father, who'd been a pastor, had hidden his homosexuality, but that when his mother had found evidence of it, his father had let Travis take the blame. Travis had been tortured, then later sent to a conversion therapy camp, where the torture had continued. "Travis said that ten years ago, he ran into a guy named Jim. And that Jim had been at this place…Camp Hope, I think was the name. Jim assumed Travis was gay, kept pushing him about it, and that was when my husband murdered his first victim." She looked around the room, her gaze, banked with fear and sorrow, touched on each one of them.

"Sounds as if you two had a major heart-to-heart conversation before you shot him," Campbell said, and Sloan didn't miss the accusation in the man's tone. But he also thought it odd that Travis would confess to murder.

She glared at the lieutenant. "*Heart to heart?* Do you think we were sitting at the kitchen table having cookies and coffee, and bullshitting about the weather? I was scared out of my fucking mind! He kept pacing, having these strange ranting moments where he'd be enraged one minute, then crying the next. And all I kept thinking was that I needed to get out of the house and find an officer." Her shoulders slumped in defeat. She rested her forearms on her thighs, her chin in her palm. "At the end of our *heart to heart*, he said, 'I killed two men last week. One is buried behind our shed, the other under the Milsons' pond. If I were a nice guy, I'd tell North he's welcome.'" She met his gaze. "I don't know what that means."

Neither did he.

"Dan," Whitney said to the other detective. "Let's get one of the crime scene investigators to check the backyard." When Dan left the room, she looked to Amy. "What happened next?"

She hugged herself tightly. "I tried to talk my way out of the house. I told him that I didn't believe he was capable of murder, and that I believed him when he said he wasn't gay. But he just laughed at me, and said, 'Of course you would. You're nothing but a stupid doormat.' Then he hit me." She flinched as if she'd been struck again. "He said that because he didn't trust me, he was going to bury me next to Sebastian—I don't know who that is. I promised I wouldn't go the police, but he laughed some more and told me he knew I wouldn't because I'd be dead."

Amy explained that Travis came at her. She'd fallen, hit her head on the table, then had quickly gotten to her feet. That had been when she'd seen the gun on the counter between the planter and picture frame.

Campbell frowned. "Convenient. Do you usually keep guns lying around the house?"

Anger flashed in her eyes. "Of course not. We have three young children. There's a gun safe in the basement. I don't know when Travis brought it to the kitchen, and I don't care. When he came at me again, and I saw the rage in his eyes, I grabbed the gun and aimed it at him. I told him to stay away, but he kept coming." She sobbed and ran a hand through her hair. "He kept coming!"

"You had great aim for someone who I imagine was panicking."

"I've been going to the gun range with Travis for years. Why are you acting as if *I* planned this? I just wanted a kid-free weekend and to spend time with my husband. I didn't ask for any of this."

"Sir, the paramedics are here," a deputy said to Campbell.

"Have them come in here and take care of Mrs. Murph…of Amy." The lieutenant motioned for them to follow him. "What the fuck did we just hear?" he asked when they reached the kitchen.

Whitney locked surprised. "You don't believe her? The attack and the self-defense angle make sense. We can check with her parents, the hotel, the bar and corroborate her story."

"It's not that I don't believe her, but why would her husband tell her about the murders?"

"He didn't plan on letting her live," Whitney suggested, and walked around the peninsula.

An investigator Sloan remembered seeing at Nell's was placing markers around Travis's body. He looked up at them and stood. "Coroner should be here in about an hour. Let's face it, we were here within seconds of hearing the gunshot. The wife admitted to shooting him, and we have a single bullet to the center of the head. My partner was photographing the scene when you had him head outside. Looking around the kitchen…it's clear a struggle took place. I've even found hair and blood on the corner of the kitchen table. The hair color looks as if it could be a match to the wife."

Since he'd already viewed one dead body today, and the one on the floor belonged to a guy he'd actually liked, Sloan focused on the two deputies helping the investigator move wood from behind the shed. He'd like to know what Travis had meant by the *you're welcome* remark. He also wondered if Travis had been the killer who'd buried all those men in Otter's Field. Amy had said a man named Jim was Travis's first victim, and authorities had ID'd one of the skeletal remains they'd found as Jim Montgomery.

Whitney stepped next to him and opened the patio door. "What do you think?"

One of the deputies by the shed lurched back, shock lining his ashen face. "I think we moved across the street from a serial killer," he said, then reminded her about Jim Montgomery.

"Detective," the investigator called. "We've got a body."

"Damn it," she muttered, as they walked to the shed. Once there, they stared down at the face of a young male. Dirt filled his mouth, was packed in his nose. "Travis told Amy his dad made him bury those men, and that he had to keep burying the secret over and over. The ME hasn't been able to determine cause of death for any of the victims from Otter's Field. Do you think he could've buried them alive?"

The horrifying thought made his stomach churn with revulsion.

"We should be able to find out," the investigator said, taking pictures of the area. "I'd have to measure to be sure, but I'm guessing the grave is about three to four feet deep, which is good for us. The soil decreases the rate of decomposition, and I don't see any insect activity."

"How long do you think he's been here?" she asked.

"I can't say with certainty just yet, but he hasn't been here long. Maybe a week or two."

"Amy said Travis killed two men last week." Whitney looked around the yard. "We need to have a look under the Milsons' pond and continue searching this property."

A couple hours later, they'd exhumed the body behind the shed, and had also discovered a second man on the side of the structure, beneath a tarp and two-by-fours. With that body were dozens of wallets, leading them to wonder if the names on the drivers' licenses would match the identities of the remains from Otter's Field.

"I found a wallet on the victim," one of the investigators said as he came out from behind the shed. Wearing gloves, he opened the wallet. "Austin Goldhirsh."

Sloan stiffened. "Goldhirsh? Can I see that?"

The investigator showed him the Illinois driver's license. "He's a long way from home."

"Oh? Where is he from?" Whitney asked.

"Chicago," Sloan said, wondering if the last name was a coincidence, or if Travis had actually done him a favor. "I need a break. I'm heading back to the house."

As the investigator went back to work, she studied him. "Are you okay? You...don't look right."

"Tired. You've got to be, too. I probably need to hydrate and catch a few hours of sleep."

"Sounds good to me. With all that's going on here and at Nell's, I need to stick around for a bit. I'm hoping Campbell gets a warrant to dig up the Milsons' property before I quit for the day. When we questioned Nolan Ainsley, he said Travis had done the majority of the work on the pond. He dug it, lined it, installed the pump and laid most of the rocks. And, last Friday, Travis was at the Milsons' alone."

He didn't want to think about that right now. His focus was on getting back to the rental and calling Rachel. After he excused himself, it took everything in him not to sprint across the cul-de-sac. Goldhirsh had been a name he recognized, and he needed to be certain his suspicions were false. Otherwise, the dead kid had just put a whole new spin on his future with Whitney.

"I need a favor," he said, catching Rachel at home.

Chattering kids filled the background. "I'm off the clock, and it's my son's birthday."

He swore under his breath. "If it wasn't important, I wouldn't ask."

She released an exasperated sigh. "Is this about the body count in your neighborhood?"

"No. It's personal."

"Now I'm intrigued. Hang on a sec." She yelled to her husband, Owen, that she'd be right back, then everything became quiet on her end. "Okay, what do you have for me?"

"I need you to do a search on Antonio Goldhirsh. I arrested him a few years ago."

He heard tapping. After a minute, she said, "He was killed by another inmate about two months ago."

Fuck. "Next of kin?"

"Hang tight." There was more tapping. "Okay...I've got the father, Elam. He died twelve years ago. The mother, Cindy, passed a week after Antonio died. The remaining siblings are Dallas, Austin and Laredo. Good Lord, these people named their kids after Texas cities?"

He didn't care. The dead body of Austin Goldhirsh had been buried directly across the street from the rental house, and his death hit way too close to home.

"Do any of the living siblings have criminal records?"

"Let me look...Dallas and Laredo have juvenile records. Dallas's was for prostitution and Laredo for weed. There's nothing here for Austin. Anything else?" Rachel asked.

"No. Thanks. Go back to your kid's party. I appreciate the help."

"You don't sound like it. What's the deal with the Goldhirsh family?"

He rubbed his tired, burning eyes. "We just found Austin's body buried in my neighbor's backyard, and I have a feeling there's another Goldhirsh buried on the next street over."

"Oh my God. Do you think they were there for you?"

"What other explanation is there? I arrested their brother. Antonio ended up being killed in prison. The mom died a week later...Why else would a Goldhirsh be here, in North Royalhurst, Ohio, at the same time as me?"

"It's extremely coincidental. What are you going to do?"

He looked to the closet where his clothes hung, along with a few of Whitney's things. He didn't want to end their relationship, and had promised he would do whatever it took to make them work. Though it would hurt, he'd rather be alone than put her life at risk.

"I'm going to pack my bags."

Whitney's entire body ached from exhaustion. As the sun set, and a new shift of deputies came on to make sure Nell and Amy's houses remained secured, she forced her tired legs to take her across the cul-de-sac.

"Whitney," Vincent called from his front door, then made his way outside.

Inwardly groaning she reached the middle of her driveway at the same time as Vincent. "Hi, Vincent. I'm sorry about what's happened on your street, but I can't talk about it."

"That's okay," he said, his expression somber. "Irene told Helen what happened with her kids and Nell."

Andy had interviewed the Easton kids that afternoon. Irene and Dale had been there, along with their attorney. Hoping for a lesser sentence, all three had confessed to selling the drugs they thought were being supplied by Rueben Morales. Nell was still refusing to cooperate, but her son had brought in an attorney for Jacob and Hayden. Andy said that they were hopeful the two boys would also confess, shed light on the operation, and who had killed the cop.

"How are Irene and Dale doing?" she asked.

"Best as can be expected. They're disappointed, of course, and praying that the kids don't end up in prison." He glanced to her badge. "But you and I both know that they'll do time."

"Because of what they sold, people died."

He shifted his grief-stricken gaze to the Murphy house. "A lot of people have died around here. I can't believe Travis is gone, or that he was responsible for murder."

They hadn't released anything to the press about Travis Murphy, only the drug bust. But she understood that neighbors gossiped. "Did Nolan tell you we questioned him?"

He nodded. "I got more out of Joe, though. He camped out in

the garage and watched everything. He said he saw three body bags. One came from the house, the other two from the backyard. Nolan told me you were asking about a pond Travis made for the Milsons. Do you think there's a body under there?"

She didn't think so, she *knew* so. The site had been excavated an hour ago, and the body of Laredo Goldhirsh had been discovered. "You know I can't answer that right now. At some point tomorrow, the Sheriff plans to give a press conference. But I can assure you that no one in the neighborhood is in danger."

"Yeah, because Travis is dead."

"Vincent—"

"Whitney, I was a cop for a long time. I can deduce what happened. You've got bodies in Travis's backyard, maybe one in the Milsons' and a bunch over at Otter's Field. Plus, you have a landscaper who owns plenty of digging equipment." His brows drew together and anger took over his grief. "I don't want to believe my neighbor, a man I've known for a decade, was capable of murdering so many people." He shook his head. "I'm just thankful Amy's okay and her boys weren't here for any of this. She is okay, right? Joe said her face was pretty banged up."

"She has a broken nose and a few cuts and bruises, otherwise she's okay...physically." She had no idea how Amy would cope with knowing she'd been married to a serial killer, and she hoped the woman would eventually hire an excellent therapist for herself and her kids. "Her father came in from Columbus. After she was released from the hospital, he took her to a hotel, and is staying with her. The kids are still with her mother."

"I take it she's not going to be charged for Travis's death."

She shook her head. "I can't say anything more."

"I understand." He let out a breath, then looked around Shady Circle, his gaze touching on each home. "This street and the people living here were important to me and Helen. We loved our neighbors and would do anything to help them. To find out what's been going on behind closed doors...it's devastating. Helen is already talking about moving." He grinned, but his eyes still held an overwhelming amount of sadness. "I don't know what she's thinking. Who would ever buy a home on this street?"

"I'm sorry," she said, saddened the events that had occurred during the past twenty-four hours had destroyed the lives and future of the people who lived there. "For what it's worth, Sloan and I have enjoyed living next to you and Helen."

He offered his hand. "Thank you, Detective. I can't say that I'm happy about what went down here, but you, Sloan and your team did a good job."

Without another word, he walked across their adjoining lawns. Now officially emotionally drained, she went into the house. After making sure the door was locked and the garage closed, she went into the kitchen. Though hungry, after viewing five bodies, her stomach was too upset to handle any food. She took a bottle of water from the fridge, made sure the patio door was also locked, then headed upstairs. She couldn't wait to crawl into bed next to Sloan and sleep.

When she reached the master bedroom, she stopped in the doorway. "You've been busy," she said, glancing at the equipment he'd packed. He'd also removed the card table and chairs from the room.

"I couldn't sleep." He used the remote to turn off the television, then sat on the edge of the bed. "Learn anything new?"

"A few things. All the drivers' licenses found in the one grave were checked. Each man was reported missing at some point over the past ten years. Sebastian Farro's roommate reported him missing around the same time we were unearthing his body. The roommate also said that, Friday night, Sebastian planned to meet friends at Crush." She toed off her tennis shoes. "Based on what Amy told us, I have a feeling all the men Travis had killed were homosexual. What's scary? I talked to Morgan Friday morning. Guess what club he was going to that night?"

He rubbed his beard. "Too close to home."

"Way too close. What I find strange about Travis's actions is that none of what he did had anything to do with hating homosexuals."

"No, he hated his father."

"Normal people would talk to a therapist about their daddy issues, not kill nearly thirty people." She pushed her jeans over her hips. "I'm still not seeing a connection with the Goldhirsh brothers."

"Brothers," he repeated, anger and disappointment gathering in his eyes. "You found Laredo's body at the Milsons'."

She walked over and sat next to him. "How did you know?"

"A couple years ago, I arrested their brother, Antonio. He was recently killed in prison, and his mother died a week later."

If I were a nice guy, I'd tell North he's welcome…

Her stomach knotted. She knew exactly where he was going with this. "The brothers were coming for you and Travis stopped them. But how could Travis know?"

"Saturday, when we were at the neighborhood party, Travis asked Vincent if he'd seen a couple of kids driving a Pontiac Grand Am through the neighborhood. You might want to have your people check impound lots. If the car belongs to the brothers, and they died last Friday, it was probably towed."

She rubbed her throbbing temple as she remembered that conversation. "When he asked about the boys, they were already dead. And if he killed Laredo while he was working at the Milsons', he might've been worried someone saw him." She rose, then went to the window. Twilight had fallen over Shady Circle, but from her window, she could see the Milsons' driveway on the next street over. "Why would Travis bury one brother under the pond and the other in his own backyard?"

"Not sure, but I found the garage service door unlocked last weekend. I thought maybe I'd forgotten to lock it, or maybe you had. It could be Laredo was the lookout, while Austin came into our garage and unlocked the door. I usually keep the garage open during the day."

"That makes sense. If Travis killed Laredo while he was at the Milsons', and Austin didn't know, he would've gone looking for his brother."

"And walked directly into Travis's path."

"Right." She stepped away from the window. Her stomach was more upset now than it had been when she'd first come home. "So, is this the point where you tell me it's over between us?"

"Whitney, I…" He stood and pushed a hand through his hair.

"What if Travis hadn't killed them? What if they'd gotten into the house and done something to you? I've already lived through a revenge beating once, and have no intention of putting you at risk."

"What if this, what if that… Unlike you, I'm not going to live my life worrying about something that might or might *not* happen." Tears welled in her eyes as her temper flared. "Are you planning to return to Chicago permanently, or are you going to change your name again and move across the country?"

His gaze held apology. "I'm not sure. I'm going to talk to my boss and find out what he thinks. I recently had an assignment out west. It was a small town. One of those places where people know you. I could move there, buy property away from the town."

"And live in isolation? What kind of life is that?" She fisted her hands. "You are so damned frustrating. You're supposed to be this badass agent and you're letting a possible revenge attack dictate your life."

"How can I not?" he shouted. "Ellie could have died because of me. Those two punks could have hurt you."

"But they didn't," she yelled back. "Why can't you let this go?"

"Because I love you! I love you and it would kill me if something happened to you." He went to her and gripped her by the upper arms. "You are important to so many people. You have family and friends who would miss you, and I couldn't face them if you were hurt or worse because of me."

A tear slipped down her cheek. "You don't think you're important, do you?"

"If I were hit by a bus tomorrow, there aren't too many people who'd agonize over my early departure."

"I would." She rested her palm along his jaw. "I can't lose you, not when I just found you."

He let go, but kept his intense gaze locked on her as he stepped backward. "I'm not ready for us to be over, but I can't control what might happen in the future."

And there was the crux of the problem. *Control.* "I've discovered there are so many things in life that can't be controlled. You helped me with that. You made me realize I can't live my life checking off lists, and that sometimes I need to go with the flow and let my emotions lead me."

"I did?"

She nodded. "You didn't fit into my plans, but you barreled your way into them, and had me rethinking my life goals. I still would love the house, husband and kids, but I want that with you. No one else. I'm sorry, but you're stuck with me."

"Whitney, this isn't a joke."

"Ask anyone who knows me, I can't tell a joke."

"Damn it, I… What are you doing?" he asked as she pulled her sweatshirt over her head.

"I'm going to bed."

"Fine, but we need to finish discussing this tomorrow."

"What's there to discuss?" She climbed onto the mattress, then burrowed under the covers. "I just told you that you're stuck with me. If you think a move across the country is necessary, then I'll go with you."

He swore under his breath and sat next to her on the bed. "I heard you tell your mom you would never leave Cleveland, and I don't want you to do that. You're too close with your family and you worked too hard to quit your job. And what if you do move away with me and decide you hate where we're living, or me, for that matter?"

She reached up and touched his beard again. "Then I move back home. It's as simple as that. I would rather give us a go and fail, than spend the rest of my life wondering what could've happened if we'd just tried."

"You would move for me?"

Her parents wouldn't be happy. She loved her job, loved living in Cleveland and would miss her friends. Moving out of the state had never once made it on any of her lists, but Sloan hadn't been on any of them, either. He made her happy, and she wanted to hang onto that happiness, even if moving away from everything that was familiar scared the crap out of her.

"I go where you go."

His gaze held concern as he leaned in and kissed her. "Get some sleep. We can talk in the morning."

She was prepared to remind him that the discussion was over, but let it go. They were both tired, needed to digest what had happened on Shady Circle, and how it could affect their future. And she was determined that they had a future. She closed her eyes, curled next to his pillow and inhaled his scent. Comforted by it, relaxed, she drifted off to sleep.

The next morning, she was surprised Sloan wasn't lying next to her. She reached over and touched the sheets and pillow. Cold. Had he not come to bed last night? Worried he'd left without telling her, she scooted out of bed and went to the closet. Relieved his clothes still hung there, she then went into the bathroom to fetch her robe. On her way out of the bedroom, she snagged her cell phone from the nightstand, then checked the time. She couldn't remember when she'd slept past eleven and now wished she'd set her alarm. There were reports that needed to be written, and they had plenty of packing to do.

When she reached the lower level, she looked out the picture window. There were a few police cruisers on the street, but the crime scene units were no longer there. Yellow police tape was still strung across the Murphys' porch, but it had been removed from Nell's house. Soon, Shady Circle would once again look as it had before drug dealers and a murderer had destroyed it.

In need of coffee and wondering where Sloan was, she made her way to the kitchen, then froze. Dozens of pink sticky notes were attached to the cabinets, refrigerator, counter, light fixture and patio door. There were some on the island, stove and pantry, too. On the kitchen table was a piece of paper. She picked it up and smiled. The simple headline read, *Sloan and Whitney*, and he'd written *pros* and *cons* under the title. She skimmed through the *pros*:

- In love with each other
- Great sex
- Both tall
- Both own guns
- Great sex
- Would have cute, tall kids
- Understand each other
- Both good cooks

- Both neat (Whitney is getting better)
- Both badass
- Both want a house and kids
- Whitney smells good
- I don't want to live without her
- I can't sleep without her next to me
- Great sex
- I would be miserable without her in my life

She wiped the tears from her eyes and looked under *cons*. When she didn't see anything listed, she flipped over the paper.

"You won't find any cons on that list."

She turned as Sloan made his way to the coffee pot, which also had a sticky note on it. Curious what was on the small papers, she plucked one off the kitchen island. This one read: *Both good cooks*. As she looked at the one near it, she realized he'd emphasized the list he'd made by writing the bullet points on the little notes.

"Why didn't you list any cons?" she asked.

He finished making coffee, then faced her. "I couldn't think of any."

"But last night—"

"I was upset and afraid. I told you, I don't want anything bad to ever happen to you."

She glanced around at all the small pink papers. "If I was the one who wanted to break things off, I could understand why you did all this, but I don't. Was the list for your benefit?"

He nodded and approached her. "After you went to bed, I couldn't sleep. It was still early, so I called my boss, Ian, and told him what happened here, and about you. I even brought up the town I mentioned to you last night."

"And?"

"And, he said that if I want to spend my life running, hiding and being a coward, that he'd call the town's sheriff and get me a job."

Ouch. "You're *not* a coward."

"I know that. He was trying to get a rise out of me, which he did. Before I told him to kiss my ass he said I was a fool if I allowed my past to interfere with the future, then he hung up on me. That's when I started making the list."

"Wow. Ian sounds like a pleasant guy."

He grinned. "He's all right. He called me back a couple of hours later, after he'd had one of our agents question Dallas Goldhirsh. The moment our agent mentioned going to the police about why her brothers had been in Cleveland, and threatened to tell authorities Austin and Laredo's suspected intention, she started talking. Turns out, a cop who knows me gave them my new name. From there, the two found me, then started following me around. That's how they knew about this place. Once Ian explained all this, he said that if I'm worried about being tailed again, he would arrange for CORE agents to pack my things and bring them here, and that I shouldn't bother returning to Chicago."

"How do you feel about that? You've lived there for eighteen years."

"I feel nothing but relief. I know Ian didn't give me permission to move, but having him say what he did, the way he did, allowed me to give *myself* the permission to take back my life. Until yesterday, I don't think I truly grasped how much I've let my fears rule me." He shook his head. "And I kept telling you I wasn't afraid of anything. I should probably remove badass from the list."

"And replace it with another *great sex* bullet point?"

"I couldn't help emphasizing that major detail."

"It's a great detail." She went to him and wrapped her arms around his waist. "When we first met, you reminded me of Wolverine. You were big, hairy and definitely badass. But I don't want a superhero or a man who doesn't know himself well enough to admit his fears. I want a man who loved his parents, helps old ladies, cares about his neighbors and finds joy in butterflies."

He rested his hands on her hips. "That sounds a lot like me."

"I thought so, too," she said with a chuckle. "And all of those things make you badass in my book."

"I love you," he said, then kissed her. "I couldn't have asked for a more understanding fake wife."

She smiled. "I love you, too. And I couldn't have asked for a more loving and wonderful fake husband."

"I'm going to miss calling you my wife." He grew serious and his gaze filled with tenderness and love. "I think we should do something about that and cross one of your life goals off the list."

She stilled and her heart tripped. What he was suggesting was wonderful, scary and what she'd always wanted. But she was an organized planner. The idea of getting married after only knowing each other for a couple of weeks was insane. "I…Sloan, we just met."

"True. Do you have a list dedicated to the timeline it should take before you're allowed to get married?"

"Well, no."

"Good. Because I've waited my whole life to meet you. I love everything about you. I know all your weird habits and love those, too."

"I love everything about you… Wait, what weird habits?"

He laughed, then kissed her again. "I'm just teasing you. Although there is that thing you do when you're eating."

"Stop it," she said, grinning. "So…we're really going to do this?"

"I'm a traditional guy, and will have to talk to your mom and dad first. And this isn't the way I want to propose to you."

She looked around the kitchen and at all the sticky notes detailing why they should be together. "I don't know…I feel like you already have."

He glanced around, too, then met her gaze and smiled. "I suppose I have. It's still not the same as getting down on one knee and slipping a ring on your finger."

"No, it's better," she said, then kissed him. As the kiss deepened, became more passionate, he untied the sash of her robe and pulled a nipple between his lips. "Much better."

Epilogue

Three months later. . .

Sloan and Whitney North's house, Westlake, Ohio
Saturday, 8:02 a.m. Daylight Saving Time

SLOAN LIFTED HIS laughing bride in his arms, then carried her over the threshold. They'd gotten the keys to their house four weeks ago, then had spent time remodeling the 1980s colonial to bring it into the current century. Today was their official move-in day.

"I'm having déjà vu," she said as he set her on her feet.

"Me, too. Except this time, I carried my *real* wife over the threshold."

"I love the sound of that." She wrapped her arms around his waist. "I love you."

"I love you, too," he said, then kissed her. He'd dealt with a whirlwind of changes during the past three months. They'd all been good, especially with Whitney by his side. After they had officially closed the Morales investigation and had left the house on Shady Circle, he'd moved into Whitney's West Park rental.

Ian had kept his word and had CORE agents pack his things and bring them to Cleveland. There hadn't been much. With the exception of his seventy-two-inch TV and new, king-sized bed, he hadn't wanted the furniture from his condo—Rachel had taken what she needed for her and Owen's newly remodeled basement and had donated the rest—just his clothes, butterfly cages and the few things of his parents he'd saved.

Since CORE investigations weren't always Chicago-based, Ian had also kept him on the payroll. He'd wound up traveling more times than he'd liked over the past few months, which had kept him away from Whitney, and had placed the majority of their wedding plans on her shoulders. But his OCD and exceptionally organized woman had pulled it all together. She'd taken a bullet point from their fake history and they'd married at an island resort.

He'd also enrolled at an online college and had started taking business classes. While he loved working for CORE, the travel was killing him. He wanted to be home with his wife, and was working with a real estate agent who was helping him find a location for the gun range he and Whitney planned to open—hopefully by the end of the year.

A woman cleared her throat. "Hello?"

He tore his lips from Whitney's and looked to the opened door. A man and woman, who looked to be in their early sixties, stood there smiling. "Oh, Frank. They're adorable."

Frank rolled his eyes. "They were making out and we just interrupted them. I told you we should've waited."

Whitney offered her hand. "It's okay. I'm Whitney North, and this is my husband, Sloan."

The couple introduced themselves as Barbara and Frank Valcone, and they reminded him of Vincent and Helen. Because it was illegal for her to use her badge to research any of the people on their new street—and his bullet-pointing wife was by the book—they knew nothing about their neighbors' backgrounds. And that was fine by him. Whitney had dug into the backgrounds of the residents of Shady Circle and they'd still been surprised by what their neighbors had been doing. Besides, what were the odds they'd move across the street from drug dealers or a serial killer again?

"I love your porch furniture," Barbara said, then added, "And your flowers are beautiful."

Yesterday, he'd loaded his truck with the patio furniture he'd bought for the home on Shady Circle, along with the planters everyone had been convinced would die. Remembering how their North Royalhurst neighbors had commented on the flowers had him thinking, as he'd done often since leaving the rental house, about those people, and wondering how they'd coped with what had occurred on their street. The only neighbors they knew about were Nell, the Eastons and Amy Murphy.

Nell's grandsons had confessed to creating the fentanyl and to supplying the drugs to the Easton kids. Jacob also claimed their grandma had poisoned the cop, and that he'd put the body in the freezer. Once Nell had learned what the boys had told the district attorney, she, too, had confessed. All three had pleaded guilty, and were currently waiting on a sentencing hearing. The Easton kids were in the same position, and their attorneys were working hard to ensure they wouldn't serve much, if any, time. Due to the number of deaths and overdoses caused by the drugs they'd distributed, he didn't predict a good outcome for any of them.

As for Amy, no charges had been brought against her. The evidence had pointed to self-defense, and the information she'd been able to give detectives had led them to discovering Travis Murphy had murdered twenty-eight men. Within a few weeks of Travis's death, all of his victims had been exhumed and identified, and Amy had moved her children to Columbus.

"Thank you," Whitney said. "Sloan is the one with the green thumb."

As they talked with the couple, other neighbors came outside and headed over to their house. They were all friendly and welcoming, and he looked forward to getting to know them. When the moving truck arrived, with the exception of Barbara and Frank, the neighbors went back to their own homes.

"We're so thrilled to finally have neighbors next door again," Barbara said. "The house sat vacant for almost six months while the previous owners were going through a divorce."

Frank placed a hand on Barbara's arm. "Don't be a gossip. Let's go home, and let them get to work."

"I think they should know what went on in that house. There might still be some…*toys* hidden in closets."

"Toys?" Whitney asked. "What are you talking about?"

Barbara glanced at the neighboring houses, as if making sure no one else was around to hear her. "Well, you're not going to believe this, but the previous owners were *swingers*."

"Swingers?" Whitney echoed, and wrinkled her nose.

Frank chuckled. "Not our thing either."

Barbara gasped. "I should say not."

They gossiped with the Valcones for a few more minutes, then he and Whitney went to work on unpacking their things. Later that night, exhausted and ready to spend their first night in the home they'd purchased together, he crawled into bed with her.

"It was a great first day," she said, holding his left hand and running her fingertip along the Celtic swan engraved on his wedding band. They'd opted to design each other's wedding rings. She'd gone with the swan, while he'd had the jeweler give her a platinum band with a butterfly pattern, and at the center, a one-carat diamond.

"We got a lot done."

She rolled on her side and faced him. "I think we should leave the rest of the unpacking for during the week. Tomorrow is supposed to be another beautiful day. Let's invite my parents and Morgan and Micah over. I'd like to christen our new grill."

"Great idea." He moved her under him, then nudged her legs apart. "First, I'd like to christen our new bedroom."

"Great idea," she repeated with a grin and wrapped her legs around him. "How do feel about knowing swingers used to live here? Kinda kinky, huh?"

"Don't get any ideas. I've never been good at sharing."

She chuckled. "I'm being serious."

"As long as there are no bodies buried in the backyard, I don't care who lived here. This house is *ours* now."

She touched his beard. "And together we're going to make it a home."

Somewhere on Shady Circle, North Royalhurst, Ohio
Sunday, 11:12 a.m. Daylight Saving Time

Real estate agent, Diana Davidson, used the sole of her shoe to secure the *Open House* sign into the grass at the entrance of the cul-de-sac. She retrieved the balloons she'd picked up from the party supply store from her car, then tied them to the sign. Satisfied the knot wouldn't come undone, she made her way back to the car. Before climbing in, she glanced around Shady Circle. Eight out of the eleven homes had a *For Sale* sign in the front yard, and she was trying to sell five of them.

"Diana," a man called.

"Hi, Vincent " She met him at the sidewalk, then crouched to pet his dog, Fritz. "Are you and the neighbors feeling lucky today?"

"We all bought St. Joseph statues and have them in the yards. I even put one in Nell and the Murphys' yards."

There were a few superstitions she'd share with her clients if they were having trouble selling their homes. One was burying a statue of St. Joseph.

Diana looked to her clients' yards. She was representing Vincent and his wife, the Malinowski estate, the Murphy property, the Ainsley family and the Wagners. Her competitor was trying to sell the empty house next to Vincent's—rumor had it that the sheriff's office had undercover cops recently living there—along with Quint Oliver's and the Wolffs, who, unfortunately, had lived between drug dealers and a murderer.

"The statues look great, but you're supposed to bury them. That's why we refer to St. Joseph as the *underground real estate agent.*"

"Fritz will dig up whatever I bury in my yard, and there's not a chance in hell that I'll take a shovel to the Murphy property."

Diana watched Vincent and Fritz ·walk off, then once again looked at all the *For Sale* signs. She shook her head. "This has to be the most fucked-up street in suburbia," she mumbled, then smiled when a car turned onto Shady Circle and the passenger rolled down her window.

"Hi," the woman said. "Are you the realtor?"

"I am. Which house are you interested in seeing?"

"Looks like we have our pick."

"I can arrange for you to look at all of them. Are you first time home buyers?"

She nodded. "We live in the city, and are anxious to move to the burbs, where it's quiet, boring and nothing bad happens."

Diana grinned. "Yes, nothing exciting ever happens in the suburbs."

****

Kristine will raffle off one $50 gift card among all subscribers of her newsletter each month. To sign up for Kristine's email newsletter please go to www.kristinemason.net.

Whose story is next? VLAD!
For those of you who love Vlad, his story will be released winter of 2018! Don't know who Vlad is? Meet the former Russian mob assassin in Ultimate Kill (Book 1 Ultimate C.O.R.E.).

C.O.R.E. Series

C.O.R.E. Shadow Trilogy
Shadow of Danger (Book 1)
Shadow of Perception (Book 2)
Shadow of Vengeance (Book 3)
Ultimate C.O.R.E. Trilogy
Ultimate Kill (Book 1)
Ultimate Fear (Book 2)
Ultimate Prey (Book 3)
C.O.R.E. Above the Law
Perfectly Twisted (Book 1)
Perfectly Toxic (Book 2)
Perfectly Tortured (Book 3)
Sinful C.O.R.E.
Sinful Deeds (Book 1)
Sinful Sacrifices (Book 2)
Sinful Vows (Book 3)

Psychic C.O.R.E. Series

Celeste Risinski, the heroine of Shadow of Danger (Book 1 C.O.R.E. Shadow Trilogy), is back with her own series. Join her as she learns how to deal with being a wife, mom, baker and...psychic investigator.

Reality T.V. Romance Series

Pick Me

Love Me

Unmask Me

Contemporary Romance

Kiss Me

About the Author

Kristine Mason is the bestselling author of the popular romantic suspense trilogies, C.O.R.E. Shadow, Ultimate C.O.R.E., C.O.R.E. Above the Law and Sinful C.O.R.E. She is also known for her Psychic C.O.R.E. series, Celeste Files. She is currently working on her next series, along with more contemporary romance novels.

Although Kristine enjoys writing contemporary romance novels, she focuses most of her energy on her romantic suspense stories, which she loves for their blend of dark mystery/suspense and sexy romance. She is fascinated with what makes people afraid, and is famous for her depraved villains whose crimes present massive obstacles for her heroes and heroines to overcome.

Kristine has a degree in journalism from The Ohio State University and lives in Northeast Ohio with her husband, four kids, and adorable mutt. If she's not writing, she's chauffeuring kids, gardening, or collecting gnomes. Oh, and she makes a mean chocolate chip cookie, too.

Stay connected with Kristine:

www.kristinemason.net
authorkristinemason@gmail.com